Rita reached the car aning white in the freezin
series of sobs that seer
soul, making her fear sh
that came from her wer
they were savage and painful to her, making her gasp for
every new breath until, finally, her body shook and tears
flooded down her cheeks as she bowed her head against
her folded arms on the steering wheel. Eventually the
power of her grief subsided and Nathan's name came to
her lips . . .

JO HARRIS

Close Relations

GRAFTON BOOKS

A Division of the Collins Publishing Group

LONDON GLASGOW
TORONTO SYDNEY AUCKLAND

Grafton Books
A Division of the Collins Publishing Group
8 Grafton Street, London W1X 3LA

A Grafton Paperback Original 1990

ISBN 0-586-20610-8

Printed and bound in Great Britain by
Collins, Glasgow

Set in Times

To my parents

Chapter 1

When Nathan died, when he killed himself, the family started to disintegrate right in front of Rita's eyes. Paul broke up into little pieces. He loved Steve and William, of course, but Nathan was the eldest child, their first-born, and had always been special to Paul. Rita watched helplessly as Paul grew older; shrunken somehow, with greying hair now, he had the look of an old man about him. He was forty-two years old but some days he could easily pass for a man of fifty or even older.

She reached forward, picking up her coffee cup, but the drink was tepid now, lukewarm under the hot Californian sun.

'All right, Mum?' Steve asked, crossing the grass towards her.

'Fine,' Rita smiled at him, sitting back in her comfortable chair under the swaying palms. 'Where's William?'

'He'll be out in a minute,' Steve said, dumping his school bag on to the circular redwood table and sitting opposite his mother. 'Busy day?'

Rita laughed, looked at the array of textbooks and notes in front of her. 'All the time I was teaching English at London University I thought how marvellous to sit down and have a space of time in which to write my book about Virginia Woolf . . .' She smiled at Steve. 'Since coming to California I've been more inclined to swim in the pool and lounge in the sun.'

'That's okay,' Steve nodded. 'You should be enjoying it.'

'Should I?' she asked, sounding a bit doubtful.

'Of course,' Steve insisted.

Rita considered that for a moment. They'd moved from London two autumns ago, just a few months after the funeral. Paul had been offered a teaching post at UCLA Medical School and the move was planned for over a half a year. Paul's career as a consultant in paediatric medicine was extremely successful but the lure of America, the huge salary, the unlimited resources for his research, plus the prestige, were too tempting for him to ignore. And so they uprooted the boys, William thirteen and Steve fifteen, leaving their collective past behind. It seemed a cruel joke now. In reality the past had been transported with the rest of their luggage to this new life in California.

'Don't you like it here any more?' Steve asked.

She looked at him and grinned. 'Of course I do, it's wonderful. How was school today?' Rita asked, quickly changing the subject.

'Okay,' Steve shrugged.

'What did you do?'

'English, Math, French and Art.'

'Good,' she nodded, as William wandered over to them. They chatted for a while before deciding to take a swim in their huge pool. Rita watched them go. The boys were fully assimilated into their Californian life, what Paul's mother called 'Disneyland'. Paul was immersed in his new role. Only she, it seemed, had been left high and dry. Everything was done for her and Rita felt that she was just sitting, waiting around for something to happen.

The boys returned from the house after a little while. She watched as they chased one another down to the swimming pool, then dived into the blue water. Rita stood up and, collecting her things together, walked from the tall palms towards the big white house.

They had exchanged Chalcot Square for this classy

suburb of Los Angeles, high above the smog with a view over the sprawling city mass below. They were, after all, affluent, even by West Coast standards, and their house was typical, five bedrooms and six bathrooms, pool and tennis court, a maid to help in the house, a Mexican gardener, a pool man to ensure the purity of their water. There were roses in front of the long terrace which were all in bloom, giving off a glorious scent in the warm afternoon as she approached them. Honeysuckle tumbled over a pergola which ran from the bottom of the terrace steps to the poolside. Everything still seemed brighter to Rita, colours more enhanced, flowers, buildings, even people brought out in sharp relief against the cutting edge of the Californian sky. Everything was perfect, her surroundings, the way they lived, everything that was a possession, purchased by Paul's two hundred and fifty thousand dollars a year, was wonderful. She was in the land of plenty and yet it didn't matter very much. Thoughts of Nathan seemed to wipe clear away any pleasure or enjoyment she might have felt. It was all that she could have dreamed and now it was meaningless.

Once in her swimming costume, Rita joined the boys, sitting under the shade of a blue and white candy-striped umbrella, watching them in the water; always watching.

'Come on in, Mum,' William called from the side.

Rita smiled. 'In a minute.'

'I'll race you,' he encouraged.

'I just want to read through this,' Rita replied, holding up her notebook. 'I've hardly done anything today so it won't take me long.'

William ducked down into the water and swam after his brother.

Rita's work was interrupted when Max arrived to take care of the pool.

'Hi,' Max said, grinning down at her.

She shut the notebook and turned to him. 'Hello, Max, how are you?'

'Busy,' he replied. 'My dad works us hard. I finish school and then start work.'

Rita laughed. 'You love it, all the pretty girls by their Canyon pools . . .'

Max laughed too, waving at Steve and William before attending to his tasks.

She watched him from behind the safety of her dark glasses. Max looked after Sharon's pool next door. Sharon was Rita's first friend in Los Angeles, her first and best friend. Sharon was always telling her how beautiful he was and how innocent he looked. Max was square-jawed and blue-eyed with cropped blond hair. 'He looks like a Nazi!' Rita told Sharon.

'Nonsense, he looks great,' Sharon insisted.

Max was wearing white shorts today and a light blue T-shirt with 'Len's Pool Services' across the front of it. Len was his father, a heavier, older version of his youngest son. Max was a tall youth with an attractive physique: strong legs, powerful shoulders and a wonderful tan. Rita was admiring the curves of his backside as he bent forward, looking into the clear water. There was a gap of skin showing between the shorts and the bottom of his T-shirt and she could see the strong ridge of muscle jutting out on either side of his spine. Lascivious thoughts filled her mind until, finally, Rita diverted her attention from Max and, opening her notebook, completed reading her afternoon's work.

The shadows had grown long by the time Rita entered the house again, to shower and change after her quick dip in the pool. Her bedroom was huge, with walk-in cupboards, she could never remember to call them closets, which had mirrored doors. The fitted carpet was pure white, the walls were cream and the ceiling black. It was all quite daunting after the Laura Ashley prints of her bedroom at Chalcot Square. She looked down at their vast American bed. Her marriage was falling, had fallen, apart. Rita knew that. Paul had barely touched her in eighteen months. At first, after Nathan's suicide, he came to her in his grief, using sex as a form of escape route from his own pain. Now there was nothing. The man she'd loved seemed to have disappeared. Rita could still recognize this man as Paul but it was as though only a shell existed and, if she were to poke him hard, there would be nothing inside. Paul would simply crumble away into dust.

After drying herself, Rita slipped on a pair of blue panties, pretty silky things her mother had sent at Christmas. They were from Marks and Spencer, and the old woman had included the price ticket and till receipt in case Rita wanted to exchange them. She smiled at the memory. Her mother couldn't imagine a country which didn't have a Marks and Sparks in every high street.

She looked at her reflection in the wall-to-wall mirrors. Rita was still in good shape, her tummy was flat, her breasts firm, nothing sagged horribly. Since she'd been in Los Angeles Sharon had dragged her into various exercise classes. The Jane Fonda work-out routine had played a large part in their lives over the past year and Rita was in better condition now than she had been for years. Sharon played tennis, swam and attended yoga class, she jogged and lifted weights, and now Rita did all of this too. Sometimes Rita wondered just what it was they were keeping in shape for, but Sharon insisted that it was for 'themselves', and Sharon looked a good ten years younger than her forty-five years. Rita wasn't sure what Paul thought about it all. As he paid her such scant attention she assumed he hadn't noticed. She put on a fresh pair of

11

baggy khaki shorts, pulled on a white T-shirt and, running a hand through her still damp hair, went down into the kitchen to make a start on dinner. Rita had drawn the line at actually having a cook. That, she decided, was something she could still handle herself.

Paul arrived home a little after seven. She walked into the lounge just as he was easing himself into a chair, resting his head back, eyes tightly shut. Rita was wiping her hands on a clean tea-towel which she'd tucked into the waistband of her shorts for protection against splashes. The tea-towel was very bright and lurid and had 'Hooray For Hollywood' printed in bright orange lettering. Taking one look at Paul, she went back into the kitchen, where she reached up into a cabinet for a bottle of aspirin, and took it back to him with a glass of water. Rita handed him the water and, opening the child-proof top, shook out two tablets, which she dropped into his other hand, waiting until he'd swallowed them before speaking.

'Okay?' she enquired.

'I've got a thumping headache,' he complained. 'Been nursing it all afternoon.'

'Don't they have pain-killers in your hospital, then?'

He looked up at her but didn't respond.

'Were you operating today?' Rita asked, taking the glass from his outstretched hand.

Paul shook his head. 'Lecturing to a group of European chest experts . . . I told you.' His voice took on a slight edge, as though she never listened to anything he said.

Rita shrugged. 'Dinner will be ready in half an hour.' She looked at him and then out of the tinted lounge windows. 'The kids are still in the pool. I'd better tell them.'

'I think I'll have a lie-down on the bed for a while, then,' Paul told her. 'Might take a bath.'

She nodded and left the room. Paul never made any effort. The one time in the day when they could sit down as a family and he'd probably miss it. 'I'll save you something if you don't make it for dinner,' Rita said over her shoulder as an afterthought.

Later, Rita was sitting in the lounge reading a current best-seller when Steve came in to join her. He'd left immediately after dinner to play tennis and was now damp and sweaty.

'Okay?' he asked, sitting on the arm of the sofa next to Rita. 'Where is everyone?'

'Your father's head is still thumping away and your brother, I sincerely hope, is in his room cleaning out that damned hamster cage.'

Steve nodded.

'I suppose you want feeding again now.' Rita closed her book, looking up at Steve, noticing just how much he looked like his father, the same curly black hair, the straight nose with its slightly flared nostrils, the dark brown eyes, the strong jaw with the slight dimple in the middle . . . the same thick neck which gave the impression of power. Steve was clean-cut and handsome, only the Californian accent and the bright clothes still served to surprise her.

'We had a pizza at Jem's,' he replied, answering her question.

Jem was Sharon's second son, almost exactly the same age as Steve. They had become firm friends, were in the same class at school and wanted to go on and read Law at the same law school. Rita looked out through the dark windows. 'It's past ten o'clock,' she said, looking down at her watch.

'Is Dad all right?' Steve asked.

'He was asleep when I looked in a while ago.'

'We never see him, he works all of the time, just like when we were in London . . .'

'He's an important man with an important job to do.'

'He's a doctor,' Steve replied almost scornfully. 'Lots of kids at school have fathers who are doctors, but *their* dads don't work all of the time!'

'Well, I think your father's situation is a little different.' She knew that Steve was fishing and she didn't feel like discussing Paul with him tonight. 'He has a very busy schedule . . . he has an international reputation, you know that,' she said as though that were enough to explain what was really happening in this house.

'Is everything all right, Mum?' he asked suddenly.

Rita smiled. It was an instinctive thing she had taught herself to do, a smile to cover her tracks. 'Everything is absolutely fine,' she replied without hesitation. 'Your dad is overworked, that's all.'

'Really?' He sounded as though he wanted to believe it but there was still an element of doubt in his voice.

'Absolutely,' Rita assured him, snapping shut the large tome on her lap, looking at the picture of the author, a woman of indeterminate years with red hair and a wide smile. Rita had read somewhere that she had been paid over a million dollars for the film rights. No wonder she was smiling!

Steve got up, stretching and yawning, pushing his hands high above his head. 'A shower and bed, that's for me . . . I'll look in on William.'

Rita nodded. 'Will you see if he's cleaned that animal out? It smelt disgusting in there today. Rosa was most upset when she went in to clean.'

Steve grinned. 'I'll tell him, Mum. Don't worry.'

'And don't you do it for him,' she warned. 'He has to learn.'

'Okay, okay,' Steve said, leaving her.

14

Rita put her book to one side and put her head back, closing her eyes, reluctant to make a move, reluctant to go up to her room and face Paul.

'What's the matter with you?' she asked Paul as she undressed that evening.

He had been sitting up in bed, reading through a thick file of case-history notes. 'There's nothing the matter,' he replied, without moving his eyes away from the notes. 'Don't start.'

'There's everything the matter.'

'Rita, now don't start,' he said again, still reading.

'Nathan wouldn't have wanted us to be like this . . .'

'I don't want to talk about this now,' he interrupted.

'You've never talked about it . . . not really.'

'I can't, don't you understand?' He put the sheaf of papers down at last.

'It's unfair on Steve and William and on me . . .'

'Steve and William are fine,' he said coldly.

Rita laughed bitterly. 'I don't know how you can say that, you hardly ever even see them . . .'

'That's rubbish. Why do you always have to over-dramatize everything?'

'Steve knows there's something wrong, he's concerned about never seeing you. They're not children any more, Paul. They notice things, they *feel* things.'

Paul got up from their bed and moved to the window, opening the door and stepping out on to the balcony, looking down at the lights blazing in the seething basin of Los Angeles.

Rita stood at the open door, staring at the back of his head. 'Paul, everyone eventually overcomes their grief. They have to, in order to continue their own life.'

'I moved here, I continue, I work, I function,' he said, without turning around.

A sultry breeze brushed at the bedroom curtains, the atmosphere was heavy and uncomfortable. For once, Rita could see the necessity of air-conditioning. She sighed and walked out to him. 'Is it me?' she asked quietly. 'I suppose that it must be.'

Paul didn't reply. He was gripping the balcony rail so tightly that his knuckles were white.

'You've never talked about Nathan, you've never once even said his name.'

'I can't . . . not at the moment . . . Jesus.' He pushed a hand back through his hair in a gesture of exasperation. 'You want everyone to throw themselves down on to the ground and prove their grief. Well, I can't do that, but the fact that I don't yell and scream doesn't mean that I hurt any less.'

'I never suggested that, but it's been two years, Paul, and life has to return to normal at some point . . . if we are to continue,' she added.

He turned to her then. 'You're absolutely bloody impossible sometimes, Rita. You have everything here that anyone could possibly want, the boys love it, you have time for your writing . . .'

'I don't have you,' she said, 'I don't have you. How the hell can you pretend that everything is so fine? What about us?'

He stared right at her then, his eyes sparkling, as though he was going to cry, but from frustration and anger rather than grief. He didn't say anything and, leaving her standing there, picked up his papers from the bed and left the room. He had to complete his work.

Rita walked back inside, closing the door and feeling the room growing cooler around her. She felt completely rejected. Nathan had been her son too and Paul made no allowance for her grief. He had wrapped himself up in his

16

own like armour plating and excluded her, shutting her out until there was no going back. Nathan had become something other than a dead son, he had almost come to resemble the death of their marriage. Instead of bringing them together for consolation and release, Nathan's suicide had driven them apart. She sat down in the dimly lit bedroom. Nathan's death had not been a cry for help, he had planned it in a meticulous businesslike way. Rita closed her eyes . . .

It had been one of the few really hot days of high summer, when London was at its worst. Packed with tourists and looking dirty and faded, hot and smelly and uncomfortable, the streets baking and shimmering in the heat. It had seemed unnatural from the start. Steve took William off to London Zoo for the day. They were both going through a reptile and creepy-crawly stage, begging her to let them have a Red-Kneed Mexican Tarantula. Rita had, so far, resisted and, instead, paid a fortune that summer in trips to Regent's Park. She was teaching a summer school, an Open University foundation course in English Literature which she was enjoying immensely. Nathan was working through the summer to raise some extra cash for his impending holiday in Greece with a bunch of his school friends. He was due to go to university that October and his future, both immediate and longer term, seemed bright.

That morning saw the normal chaos, the usual fights for the bathroom, the general mayhem over the breakfast table. Paul left for a breakfast meeting with a group of American surgeons at seven-thirty. She left before the younger boys, pinning a note to the kitchen notice board for Dolly, who would be in just after nine to clear away the mess. Nathan left the house before she did, rushing past her in the hallway as she gathered her things together on the hall table. He paused for a moment at the front

17

door to exchange some banter with her before slamming the door behind him and racing away. She remembered that he'd laughed at something she said. She could always recall his smiling face. It was the last time she had seen him alive.

Rita examined that morning carefully over the subsequent months and years but she couldn't pinpoint anything untoward. It was just a normal morning at Chalcot Square, boys thundering up and down the stairs, doors slamming, squabbles and play fights and silly jokes. She had gone for her bus a little later, walking out into the hot sunshine and noticing the dark green leaves of summer on the trees in the square looked slightly dusty and drab in the unexpected heat. Rita could remember everything very clearly. She had tied her hair back in a little ponytail and wore a short denim skirt, a green cotton blouse with a deep V at the neck, and sandals. Her legs were bare, freshly shaved that morning in order to catch, perhaps, just the hint of a tan. It all seemed remarkably clear and ordinary to her, even now.

The time of Nathan's death was put at between two and two-thirty in the afternoon. He had not arrived at work and no one could trace his movements. No one could remember seeing him return to the house. Dolly left Chalcot Square around ten o'clock to do the shopping and she was away for over an hour. Nathan could have slipped back then but no one knew for sure. Dolly wouldn't have gone near the bedrooms on that day anyway as it was her morning for the kitchen and breakfast room. There was no note, no odd behaviour beforehand, no explanation. Nathan, who had appeared to have absolutely everything, who had appeared to be a normal, healthy, intelligent eighteen-year-old, had come back into the house, gone upstairs to his room and swallowed the contents of a bottle of sleeping pills – she'd had no idea he had been to see his doctor, she'd known nothing about this prescription.

Rita had arrived home to find Chalcot Square full of blue flashing lights and curious bystanders. She remembered seeing this scene from a long way off, the odd blue lights flashing through the evening air and between the trees. She had been curious for a moment and then found herself running hard, running faster than she ever had in the past, sprinting the last few yards and charging up the front steps, through the open door and into the dark hallway.

Paul came up again at last, walking in front of her and entering the bathroom. Rita lay on top of the bed, watching an old Joan Crawford movie. She heard the drumming water against the tiles. Paul had already been to bed once, now he was showering again. He had been doing this a lot just recently, she noticed. It seemed to be a ritual he went through, it relaxed him, he said. He emerged in a while with a white bath towel wrapped around his waist, his hair slicked back and his body slightly damp. She glanced at him as he fumbled in a cupboard for some fresh pyjamas. He was a big man, slightly paunchy now, but still in good shape for a man in his forties. Paul had always taken care of himself. He turned in her direction, dropping the towel and stepping quickly into a pair of plum-coloured pyjama trousers that his mother had sent.

'What's the film?' he asked, stepping over the towel and walking in front of her again to reach his side of the bed.

'God knows,' she shrugged, continuing to stare at the screen.

'I'm sorry,' he said contritely.

19

'Paul, we have to resolve this,' she replied. 'This is tearing us all apart.'

He sighed deeply but made no response.

Joan Crawford was crying, great rolling tears pouring down from her immense wide eyes, which were now held in close-up. Rita turned to him. He was very hirsute, thick black hair across his chest and on his forearms and running from his navel in a heavy line underneath the waistband of his awful plum-coloured pyjamas. It had once been a joke between them, Rita accusing him of turning into a werewolf. Now she regarded in a dispassionate way the body she had once craved. She had noticed at the pool that afternoon how Steve was taking after his father in the hairy stakes as well.

'Are you listening to me, Paul?' she asked.

'It'll be all right in a while . . . you'll see.'

'I wish I could believe that.' Rita looked right into his dark eyes.

'Give it a few months,' Paul said quietly.

'I wonder where we will all be in a few months,' she said, turning to the screen again.

Paul did not respond to that.

'Steve and William need you now, not in a few months. You're wasting so much precious time, they'll be grown up and gone before you realize it.'

Paul rolled over on to his side, turning his back to her. He closed his eyes and feigned sleep.

'Nathan is gone,' she continued. 'He killed himself, Paul. Accept it, for God's sake.'

'Be quiet, Rita,' he replied, angry at last.

'Why won't you talk about it? We never even discussed it, never . . .'

'I can't . . . I can't talk about him.'

'Why ever not?' Rita sounded amazed.

'Because I can't.'

20

'That's no answer, Jesus Christ!'

'I can't talk about it, can't you understand English?' He sat up, furious with her now.

'He was my son too, don't be so damn selfish.'

Paul got up from the bed and walked towards the door. 'Stop it,' he instructed her, his voice very hard. 'You're tearing us apart with this, your eyes so full of accusations . . . Well, who knows why Nathan did it? All I know is that talking about it incessantly won't change a damn thing . . . It won't bring him back.' He stared at her for a long moment before closing the bedroom door behind him and padding along the corridor to the guest room.

'And where does that leave me?' she asked herself, hunching up and resting her head on her knees. Joan was smiling now, something wonderful must have happened. Rita picked up the remote control and flicked the television off. 'Where does that leave me?' she said again.

Paul had left for work when she got up the next morning. It was seven-thirty. Rosa was already clattering around with bucket and mop washing over the tiled floor of the utility room. William had followed her down the stairs with his usual bundle of damp sheets and, whilst he attended to these, taking them down to the laundry room in the basement, Rita began to sort out the breakfast things.

'And how are you this morning, Rosa?' she enquired, reaching up for a packet of cereal.

'Okay,' Rosa replied, appearing at the doorway, leaning on the mop. 'But you look tired.'

Rita smiled. She hadn't slept but she supposed Paul had dropped off like a log. 'I'm fine, Rosa.'

The Mexican girl grinned and returned to her task. She worked so hard and rarely stopped to chat. Rita felt quite guilty sometimes but her attempts at conversation with

Rosa about something other than floor wax or washing powder had fallen flat, failing dismally. Rosa arrived at seven, worked, had a break at eleven, worked, had lunch, worked, had an afternoon break, worked and left at four. No wonder the house shone.

Rita had no idea where she lived, what she did after work, if she had a boyfriend, a lover. Rosa didn't wear a gold ring and so she didn't think there was a husband. Rosa had come to them through an agency, with impeccable references, and had worked like a Trojan ever since. Two years of unstinting service. She was quite small, but sturdy with flawless olive skin, black eyes and jet black hair that she always wore up in a neat bun. She was probably in her early twenties, pretty and really quite engaging, with a lovely smile and always humming or singing to herself. The one bit of information Rita had discovered, quite by accident, was that she liked Madonna. Rita had found her one morning cleaning around Steve's room and admiring some of Madonna's record covers.

'You like her?' she asked.

'Oh yes,' Rosa smiled, 'I admire her very much.'

Rita shrugged. 'Admire', eh? She had gleaned this piece of information and added it to her sparse picture of the girl in her smartly pressed grey uniform and starched white apron.

Steve came down in his towelling robe as William returned from the basement laundry room.

'Did you clean that animal out last night?' she asked William as he passed by on his way to shower and dress for school. She noticed that Steve was watching the scene as he stood by the refrigerator, pouring himself out a glass of orange juice.

William looked at her and then down at his bare feet. 'No.'

'Why not?' Rita demanded. 'You promised to look after it . . .'

'Wendy,' William interrupted, 'she's not an it!'

Rita found herself becoming very annoyed. 'Clean it out,' she snapped, 'or get rid of it. I don't care which but I'm not having that rodent stinking out the house.'

'She's not in your room, she's not bothering you.'

'Don't cheek me, William, just do it. It's bad enough you drenching your sheets every night without that animal sitting up there in its own filth.' She was immediately horrified at what she had said and William just stood there, his eyes welling with tears and his face burning with embarrassment.

'Now?' he stared at her.

'Now.' She stared back.

'I'll be late for school.'

'So, I'll send a note.'

He gave her an evil look and then stormed upstairs.

'That was a bit harsh, wasn't it?'

She turned to Steve, who was sitting at the table sipping his orange. 'It's none of your business, just stay out of it.'

'He would have done it, you know how sensitive he is about wetting the bed.'

Rita nodded. 'He has to learn,' she insisted, looking at Steve and seeing Paul.

William stormed by them carrying the round cage, multi-levels of clear plastic hamster luxury. He took it outside and round the house, to the huge garage, where the food and bedding materials were kept.

'You'll make him worse if you say things like that to him, Mum,' Steve continued, draining his orange.

'I asked him to do it last night.'

Steve shrugged.

'And don't look at me like that, I can't allow him to get away with everything. It's bad enough with . . .' But she did not finish her sentence.

'With what?' Steve pressed her.

'Oh nothing,' she replied sharply, turning to finish laying the table.

'It's Dad, isn't it?' he persisted. 'You and Dad?'

'Just leave it, Steve,' Rita said, banging cereal dishes on to the table.

'Things have been really weird around here for quite a time now . . .'

'Steve,' she warned, to shut him up.

'It's obvious that things are not right between you . . .'

'I don't want to discuss this now,' she said, her voice becoming lower. Her meaning was clear, she didn't want Rosa to hear.

'Well, when are you going to discuss it? When you're divorced?'

Rita was going to say something but then noticed William standing in the doorway. 'I came in for some cleaning stuff – for Wendy's home.' He remained there looking at Rita and Steve.

'Find Rosa,' she replied more gently, 'she'll get you what you want.' She watched him leave. 'Well, that's just great,' Rita said angrily, 'that's all I bloody need.'

'William will have to know soon,' Steve continued, as if his parents' divorce was now a reality.

'Your father and I are not getting a divorce,' Rita said adamantly. 'Where do you get this incredible imagination from?'

Steve was pouring milk from a large carton on to his cereal. 'You must think that I'm deaf, or stupid.'

Rita stared at the carton. Americans love nutritional information, and there was a list of all the vitamins the milk contained and why each one was good for you. She

24

poured herself a coffee. 'We had an argument last night
. . . okay?' She met Steve's eyes at last. 'Mother and Dad
argued. Parents do, you know.'

'And some parents more than others . . .'

'Don't you be so smart. You don't know what you're
talking about. Don't be so *bloody* smart. You're seventeen years old!'

'What has that got to do with anything?'

'It has to do with you showing us a little bit of respect
sometimes.'

'Well, don't you think that works both ways?' Steve
said without hesitation. 'Reminding William that he wets
the bed isn't exactly showing him respect.'

'Don't you have to get ready for school?' she asked
coldly.

Steve watched her for a moment before scraping his
chair back over the dark tiles of the kitchen floor and
leaving Rita to her own devices.

William came back with the hamster home now sparkling
and clean and smelling sweet. He refused breakfast,
which, Rita assumed, was meant to make her feel bad.
'Don't be such a martyr,' she called after him but he did
not reply. They were both late. Steve, who usually left
early in his new car to impress as many females as
possible, waited behind for his brother, who had already
missed the school bus. She saw Steve put his arm around
William's shoulder as they walked to the car. She watched
as they drove away, as the red VW. Rabbit zipped out of
the long driveway, trailing a cloud of wispy exhaust
smoke. Rita felt awful. She took out her anger by
throwing the breakfast dishes into the dishwasher. Banging about like a mad woman. She heard the high whine of
the washing machine spinning the sheets and felt horrible.
Was she really such a dreadful mother? How could she

25

have said such a thing to William? He was fifteen years old, life was difficult enough without his own mother trying to humiliate him.

Rita sat in William's room for a long time looking at the hamster as it sat cleaning itself on the top storey of its tower. She watched as it clambered about its domain. It seemed such a sad creature and Rita wondered if hamsters experienced loneliness and missed other hamsters. Was it cruel to keep it caged up in such sanitized comfort away from its natural habitat (she wasn't sure where exactly that was), free from predators? The red plastic and chromium home was magnificent of its kind, every luxury, but was it kind? Was it humane?

'Hello, Wendy,' she said as the little creature fixed its beady eyes on her. 'My God,' she said out loud to herself, 'I must be cracking up . . . sitting here talking to a hamster!'

'Pardon, did you say something?'

Rita turned to find Rosa in the room, dragging a vacuum cleaner in one hand and carrying a plastic box full of cleaning things in the other.

'No,' Rita smiled, 'I was just making sure that Wendy was all right.'

Rosa nodded and then proceeded to get on with her chores.

Rita went into her room and got out her freshly laundered tennis kit. Her coach would be arriving at any minute and she wasn't exactly in the right frame of mind for her regular tennis lesson. In fact she had never felt less like it than today. After a moment's hesitation she replaced the neatly pressed tennis skirt and blouse and, instead, put on her khaki shorts and a baggy white T-shirt. She was

26

leaving the room when she realized that she hadn't put her bra on and ran back in to find one.

By the time she reached the court Kirk, her tennis coach, was already there, hitting balls on to the practice wall at the back of the court. The tennis court was hidden from the main house behind high trees and bushes built at a point where the garden began to dip into the canyon. The walkway down to the court had just been watered on either side and there was a sultry, steamy feel to the air where the huge ferns swept over from the crevices of the dark rock, shaded by the overhanging cedar and laurel.

Kirk was very young, early twenties Rita supposed, and a professional coach. Like everything else, Sharon had recommended him and, consequently, Rita had been taking regular lessons for the past two years. Kirk was very tall, six feet four at least, extremely athletic, extremely good-looking in an almost clone-like Californian way. His hair was blond, a natural blond which was bleached even lighter to a fine ash colour under the sun, and he had a preppy kind of face with wonderful teeth and sparkling blue eyes but he was so tall that Rita often had to laugh at the size of him. He always looked immaculate and he always wore a sun oil which added to his natural sheen and carried with it an attractive, musky scent. If it wasn't for the fact that he always worked her so hard, she felt sure that she would have gone weak at the knees anyway just at the sight of him.

'Shirking today are we, Rita?' he asked, turning from the practice wall as she clanged the gate shut and stepped on to the red court surface.

Rita grinned. 'Two minutes, that's all.'

'Okay.' He picked up his basket contraption, which was full of tennis balls, and walked to the opposite service line. 'We'll knock up for a start . . . ready?' he grinned at her as she trotted into position.

27

Rita poised her racket and began to return the balls he fired at her, sometimes to her forehand, sometimes to her backhand, sometimes down the line, sometimes high, sometimes skidding and low. He made her chase and scamper and charge, moving her around the court at whim, goading her to hit harder and harder. Rita was good, she returned almost everything and his basket of balls remained full as they kept the yellow ball in play. After fifteen minutes, longer than usual, he came to the net and had a quick discussion about her backhand, which they were about to practise. A brief pause and they were off again, Rita returning beautifully crafted shots.

As the lesson progressed, the events of the morning faded away and her concentration became more and more intense. She began to strike the ball harder and harder until with one ferocious return she passed Kirk and watched him sprawling headlong on to the hard surface, his racket clattering away into the deep pools of shade at the side of the playing area. He rolled over and was sitting down looking up at her as she came up to the net.

'Trying to kill me now, eh?' he asked, laughing.

Rita looked down at him. 'Are you all right?'

'Where did that one come from?'

'God knows.' She looked at him. 'You've cut your knee.'

Kirk looked down at a graze over his kneecap where blood was oozing. He picked himself up and walked over to retrieve his lost racket, coming back to the net. 'Did I teach you that?'

Rita smiled. 'I suppose you must have.'

Kirk jogged back to the base line and began feeding her balls again. 'Gently now,' he called to her, 'I'm injured!'

Rita laughed and consequently missed the next shot.

* * *

She sat Kirk down on a kitchen stool and brought out the first-aid box. He seemed even taller indoors. After she had cleaned up his wound and put a plaster over it, she poured them both a long glass of orange juice. She asked Kirk where he was going to next and he chatted to her in his amiable way, but she wasn't really paying attention to him. She was wondering what he would be like in bed and she found herself becoming excited at the idea. Although she had known Kirk for two years, she didn't really know him well. They had a professional relationship and, anyway, he was young enough to be her son. This last fact quite shocked her. She was investigating, in her imagination, having a sexual liaison with a boy of Nathan's age. Kirk was smiling at her now. Having finished his drink, it was time for him to go. She walked him out to the shiny black sports car. It was English, an MGB with its top down. Kirk threw his tennis things on to the back seat and eased himself in behind the wheel.

'Thanks for the plaster and the drink,' he said, still smiling.

'My pleasure,' Rita grinned back like an idiot.

'Same time next week, then.' He started the engine and pulled away, waving as he went.

Rita waved back, thinking, as she walked back to the house, that he must be aware of his physical presence. Or perhaps it was just that she was beginning to lose control over her emotions. She closed the heavy front door behind her, leaning up against it for a moment. Yesterday it had been Max the pool boy and today it was her tennis coach. Her life was turning into a sordid cliché. She would be hitting the bottle next and waking up in trashy motels next to dead bodies she hardly knew.

Rita stepped forward, playing an imaginary shot through the air-conditioned atmosphere, the one that had sent Kirk flying. She grinned to herself as she climbed the stairs, remembering the power in that return and how it had felt so good, relieving her pent-up aggression and frustration. She looked in on Wendy on the way to her room. The hamster had buried itself under its bedding. Rita paused for a moment before going on to take her shower. Rosa had been through her bedroom and everything was neat and tidy. The bathroom shone and smelt of pine disinfectant.

Just as Rita was about to switch the shower on, her telephone rang in the bedroom. It was Sharon, who wanted a long chat about nothing in particular. Rita suggested they meet up later but Sharon was having her hair done and then driving out to Santa Barbara to visit her sister-in-law. They arranged to have lunch the following day, and when Rita finally hung up, after thirty minutes, her ear was burning where the receiver had pressed against it. In London she would have popped next door for a chat and it had taken her a long time to get used to Sharon ringing from so short a distance. However, now she rather enjoyed it.

She walked to the window and stepped out on to the balcony. Looking across the garden and out to the valley beyond she could see a veil of smog hanging over the city, purple-grey, between the rushing freeways far below and the blue Californian sky. In the distance there were lots of white houses, just like hers, and green patches, a golf course and a park and, beyond, the urban sprawl of Los Angeles with the Hollywood Hills, further still, looking purple through the smog. It was almost magical in its awfulness and in a funny kind of way Rita had come to enjoy it. After two years it all still seemed new and strange to her. She focused her attention on the swaying palms at the far edge of the garden with the redwood table underneath. She looked at them and smiled to herself. She would never get used to it.

Chapter 2

Sharon and Bill were coming round that week-end for a barbecue. Bill was an orthopaedic surgeon working at the same university hospital as Paul. Sharon and Bill had become their close friends almost from the start. They had similar backgrounds and were leading similar lives. They had five well-built Californian children; four boys, Thomas, Jack, Jeremy (Jem) and Bill, who was the eldest, and one daughter, Judy. Their children were all blond and blue-eyed and extremely athletic and Sharon referred to them as 'the Reich'.

Rita saw more of Jem than the others because he was Steve's best friend. In two years Jem had become closer to Steve than anyone and it was as though he could sense Steve's moods and read his thoughts. They were at the same school, played in the same teams and were studying similar subjects. Rita liked Jem. He had an open face, was sensitive and amusing. A stocky, muscular youth, five feet eight or nine as opposed to Steve's more rangy six feet.

All Sharon and Bill's children were very self-confident without being smart-alecky or overbearing. They were a very close family, they sat down and talked together and obviously enjoyed one another's company. They were fiercely protective of each other and, being such a tight grouping, so independent, it took a lot to gain their acceptance. The children treated Sharon and Bill like older members of some exclusive gang.

Sharon and Bill were physically at odds with each other. It was one of their favourite jokes. She was taller than him. He was older than her. Bill was a thickset man in his middle fifties with brawny shoulders and arms. He was balding and a little overweight. Sharon complained that he looked more like a trucker than an eminent surgeon, and Bill laughed a lot and told excruciating jokes to anyone who would listen. He was gregarious and full of fun. Rita was always surprised how well Paul got on with him, they were very different. However, she supposed their professional association brought them closer together. She often wondered if Bill cracked jokes during operations – she assumed that he probably did.

Sharon she loved. She was, as far as Rita was concerned, the personification of Californian Woman. Lithe and tanned, carefully groomed and stunning to look at. She was forty-five years old, she still wore her blonde hair long, and was a natural athlete. Rita liked to watch her when they played tennis together, Sharon was so graceful, her actions so precise and economic. Sharon was tall and leggy, healthy and wealthy and very wise. She had a Master's degree from Stanford University in Educational Psychology and had been pursuing her PhD in Early Childhood Education when she had met Bill and, as she described it, 'dropped everything for motherhood'. Rita had never quite understood that but Sharon insisted she had never missed academia or a career in education. They had married in 1966.

Sharon was the first person Rita had met as she unpacked and attempted to make some sense out of her new life.

'You're Rita, Paul's wife,' Sharon had said as she walked in through the lounge windows. 'I'm Sharon, from next door,' she introduced herself, smiling into Rita's somewhat confused face. 'Paul's wife. Our husbands work at the same hospital.'

After that it was as if she had always known Sharon,

gradually being drawn into Sharon's world. Rita felt like a pigmy next to her and as though she had been dragged through a bush backwards. Even after an arduous exercise class, Sharon somehow contrived to look cool and collected. A casual hand swept through her long hair and everything fell back into position – perfection. Rita was a frizzy brunette with dark brown eyes, rather pretty eyes, she always thought, one of her best points, and one of those difficult skins that never tanned easily.

After six months of Sharon, her hair was a sleek bob, shorter than she would ever have dreamed of wearing it in London. 'Get rid of that goddamn perm!' Sharon had commanded. Her make-up was changed too. Sharon's beautician had shown her how to emphasize her eyes, and her skin had an all-over tan. Rita could barely walk for the first few months after enrolling in the numerous classes that Sharon invited her along to 'try'. She had been taught more about her own body in the first six months of her stay in California than in all the previous thirty-nine years. When their aerobics teacher yelled at them to 'keep those buttocks tighter', Rita no longer had a desire to burst into hysterical fits of laughter, instead she did it because she now believed.

Sharon was looking at her now across the redwood table under the swaying palm trees. Rita had just finished telling her about the events of the past twenty-four hours. She fixed Rita with her incredible blue eyes and took her hand, squeezing it tightly.

'You need therapy, all of you, family therapy.' Sharon looked deadly serious about this.

Rita smiled slightly. 'Can you imagine Paul going in for that?'

'Sure, why shouldn't he want to sort this mess out?'

'I wouldn't even suggest it,' Rita said bitterly.

'Are things that bad?'

Rita nodded, looking directly into the eyes of her friend as tears sprang to her own.

'Has he always been so anal-retentive?' Sharon asked.

Rita grinned at that, even though tears were spilling down her face. 'Nathan's suicide was like a door shutting between us . . . At first I thought it was his work but that's just an excuse . . .'

Sharon nodded. 'The boys always seem okay to me. I mean, they cope with our way of life out here.'

'There are still problems,' Rita admitted.

'Sure, but they're lovely kids, Rita, and the young tend to cope better than we often give them credit for.'

'It's just . . .' Rita began and then paused, almost afraid to articulate what she felt. 'I don't want history repeating itself. You know, I watch them like a hawk sometimes but I can't protect them for ever, I can't wrap them up in cottonwool and hide them away.'

'They're more resilient than you think. Kids always, *always* bounce back,' Sharon insisted.

'God knows what would happen if Paul and I were to split up.' She looked terrified for a moment.

'Is that likely to happen?'

Rita looked out towards the purple Hollywood Hills. 'I told you, Steve already thinks that it's on the cards . . . I can't keep glossing over the very obvious fact that something is seriously wrong with my marriage. God, Paul's mother would have a field day if we divorced. She never thought I was good enough for him!'

'Now wait up just a minute,' Sharon warned. 'We've gone from a problem to a divorce here. Let's just take one small step at a time, honey!'

Rita laughed. 'Jesus, what to do, eh?'

'You should go into psychoanalysis,' Sharon said.

'Me? Why, do you think I'm insane?'

Sharon ignored her comment. 'I know a really good doctor, here . . .' She reached for her bag and fumbled about inside it until she had found what she was looking for. 'His card.' She pushed it across the redwood table into Sharon's hand. 'He's excellent.'

'Have you used him, then?'

'Sure, I mean, of course.'

Rita looked at her. 'Really?'

'Really – you don't have to be *insane* to see one, you know. At least, I hope you don't!'

'I'll see,' Rita sighed.

'Call him,' Sharon instructed. 'Just go and talk to him. No one will force you to go back if you don't think it's going to help.'

'Paul would have a fit.'

'Screw that!'

'Really? You think I should?'

'No one's talking to you, honey, and you can't carry the burden of this loss for ever . . . you have to release your guilt somewhere . . . Jesus, you worry about the others when you're the one who's cracking up!'

'I'm not "cracking up",' Rita said in surprise. 'Do you think I am?'

'You're obviously stressed, Rita,' Sharon replied matter-of-factly.

Rita twisted the small grey card around in her hand, looking down at the dark red printing, 'Dr Martin Allan', was all it said, with his telephone number and office address in the bottom right-hand corner. 'I'll think about it,' Rita said at last.

'Do it,' Sharon told her and then changed the subject, talking about the plans for the barbecue the following evening.

Rita sat back and listened to her friend, laughing at some joke concerning Bill and the boys, beginning slowly

35

to relax. There was a warm breeze which caused the palms to sway and the sunlight to dapple them as they decided who was going to prepare what. She reached over to pour them both a glass of the ubiquitous orange, handing one to Sharon, who was busy making a list. There was no smog today, a clear blue sky and an uninterrupted view over towards Los Angeles. The white houses in the valley reflected the sun and their pools splintered and sparkled in its reflection, and the hills rose up in the far distance, purple and brown.

'Are you concentrating?' Sharon asked.

Rita turned back to her smiling friend. 'Sure, salad things . . . I'll do the salad and get some of those jumbo-size crisp things.'

'Chips,' Sharon corrected her. 'We call them chips. When are you going to speak our language?'

They both laughed. 'That's one class you failed to enrol me in.'

'I know,' Sharon said without looking up from her planning, 'I'm just an interfering broad.'

Rita smiled and thanked God for that.

Paul was sitting at the poolside dangling his legs into the water. The daylight was fading and the sky was turning darker. At the horizon were the beautiful bands of shading colour caused by the smog and the dirty atmosphere, a gorgeous pink fading into a delicate shade of blue and a shimmering white-hot band as the sun sank behind the hills, cutting their outline sharp and clear.

The lights from the house were brighter now and Paul could hear the sounds of the two families combining with the music from a ghetto-blaster. The smell of steaks cooking on the open griddle wafted over, and there were other aromas too. The warm evening air carried them on its gentle breezes – the scent of the roses and honeysuckle, the smell of the newly cut grass which took him back to his childhood in Hampshire and the summer evenings of his youth.

Paul had been swimming with Sharon but now he sat and watched her cutting effortlessly through the water, which was suddenly illuminated as the underwater lights snapped themselves on. Bill was supervising the barbecue while the kids were helping out. Rita was preparing a vast Californian salad.

Sharon pulled herself out of the water at last. She was wearing a rainbow-coloured costume, cut high at the bottom and low at the top, fitting her skin exactly. It looked black in the half-light. She came and sat down on the warm concrete next to him, putting an arm around his shoulders. The warmth from her body entered him and he shivered. She smelt of chlorine and wet hair and of a perfume, a fragrance that he couldn't place, and she smelt sweet and musky and warm.

'How are you?' she asked. 'How are you, you great English hunk?'

Paul smiled, feeling slightly uncomfortable at her close proximity, a little aroused, his senses very acute. He felt an impulse to kiss her, to taste her, but his hands were still gripping the poolside tightly. 'I'm okay,' he replied.

'Only okay?' Sharon laughed.

'I'm tired, Sharon. This is the first moment I've had to relax all week.'

'You should find time for relaxation . . . there are other things to life than work.' She said it as a joke but there was an underlying seriousness to her statement.

Paul nodded in agreement, 'I've been promising Bill a round of golf for months. I pay a fortune to join that prestigious club and never use the bloody place.'

'Bill says that you work too hard.'

Paul laughed. It sounded flat and humourless. 'Well,

they expect you to earn your money here and we have a lot on at the moment.'

'This is California, Paul, you're supposed to be having fun!'

He turned to her then, facing her as the darkness seemed to envelop them, looking into her eyes. 'I'm leaving Rita,' he said.

Sharon stared at him for a moment and then pulled away. 'Are you serious?'

He nodded and then he began to cry. The tears welled up in his eyes and fell silently.

She took his hand and squeezed it. It shocked her to see him like this, Paul had always appeared to have such monumental self-control. They used to joke about it. The typical British stiff upper lip. She had often accused him of being so terribly 'English' about everything and now, here he was, quite out of control.

'Does Rita know this?' she asked at last.

Paul shook his head. He felt completely ridiculous but he trusted Sharon. He had never been that close to her, she was Rita's friend, but he trusted her, probably more than anyone else. 'I'll tell her tonight.'

'But how can you go through with this charade tonight? We're supposed to be having a happy get-together . . .'

'It'll be all right, I promise,' he replied, his voice becoming firmer, more assertive.

'But Rita . . .' She sounded appalled.

'Don't say anything to her, Sharon.' Paul exclaimed, beginning to panic.

'I won't say anything.' She was horrified at the very idea.

'I'll be all right, everything will be all right,' he said quietly.

They were silent then for a long moment. The music had changed and it was quite dark now. He could just make out the dark outline of the hills, and the lights of Los Angeles looked brighter and brighter. He could see the red tail lights and the bobbing headlights of the cars on the freeways. There was laughter and a great amount of activity on the terrace and he felt completely removed from it all, completely isolated and distant.

'We'll have to go back up,' Sharon said at last.

'You go,' he replied. 'I'll be with you in a moment.'

She stood up and walked round the floodlit pool to pick up her robe from a chair on the opposite side. 'Are you going to be all right?' she asked, slipping her arms into the voluminous towelling wrapper. Her voice echoed slightly across the water.

Paul took a deep breath. 'Tell them I'll be up directly.'

'Right.' Sharon slipped on some moccasins and made her way back across the garden, moving from the light of the poolside into the blackness of the lawn, following the lights from the house through the pergola, then climbing the wide stone steps on to the terrace.

Paul watched her disappearing into the darkness, swallowed up by it and disengorged a little while later. 'We thought you had drowned,' he heard Bill's voice drifting across through the night air, which was suddenly still. 'Is Paul in the pool?' he heard Rita ask.

He pulled himself up. His towel was at his side. He picked it up and, wrapping it over his shoulders, walked slowly back to the house. He could feel the grass damp under his bare feet. It felt comforting, reminding him of childhood. Freedom.

Rita had noticed how uncomfortable Paul seemed all evening. He usually made an effort to be sociable, even though it was only Sharon and Bill and family. However, he had spent most of the evening talking shop with Bill, leaving her to chat with Sharon and the kids to look after themselves. Now he was sitting out on the terrace with the last bottle of wine. Steve and William had gone to bed and she had just finished clearing up. Sharon had offered to stay behind and help but Rita thought she looked tired – a bit on edge – and she'd told her to go home. The house was very still after the clatter and noise of the barbecue. She stepped out on to the terrace and took a deep breath. The fragrance of the roses was very strong and she stood there for a moment enjoying it. Paul looked up. He had been staring into his wine glass as though deep in thought.

'I'm going to bed,' Rita said and turned to go.

'Rita,' he called her back, putting the half-empty glass down and standing up to face her. He had changed after his swim and was wearing a white shirt and a pair of Levi's which were new and hardly broken in.

Rita hesitated, watching him carefully. There was an air of expectation between them, a certain tension.

Paul took a few steps towards her before stopping. 'I have something that I want to say . . . I should have told you earlier but the party . . .' He allowed his words to trail away.

'What is it?' she asked bluntly, preparing herself for something awful.

He took a nervous step forward, which meant they were approximately an arm's length apart. 'I've thought about this a great deal . . .'

'Are you walking out on me, Paul?' she asked, suddenly understanding. When he didn't immediately answer she knew that he was.

'There isn't anyone else,' he began quickly, 'I just have to leave . . .' He looked at her briefly. 'Things are just going from bad to worse . . . I think it's for the best, all things considered.'

'All things considered,' she repeated to herself. 'I see.'

40

Her voice was strong, bright even, as though a great weight had just been lifted from her shoulders. 'When will you be leaving?' she asked, sounding incredibly nonchalant. She was amazed at how cool she seemed when her heart was beating so quickly, rat-a-tat, rat-a-tat, rat-a-tat.

'I've taken a house.' He looked away for a moment. 'At the beach . . . Malibu . . .'

'Isn't that where all the film stars have their beach homes?' It was turning into a general chat. Rita couldn't understand why she wasn't screaming or throwing things at him. The bastard, he was wrecking her life.

'It isn't very grand.'

'Oh.' As if she were in the slightest bit interested, but then she had begun this particular conversation. 'When are you leaving?'

'Tomorrow. I thought I'd leave early so as not to disturb anybody.'

Rita considered that. Was he being kind or was he being a coward? 'What do I tell the boys, then? Dad's gone away on an extended trip?'

'No, of course not.' He pushed his hand back through his thick hair, usually a sign of irritation or embarrassment with Paul. 'Tell them the truth.'

'The truth,' she said blankly. 'What is the truth? Nathan committed suicide and now Dad's left us too?' Rita was becoming irritated.

'For God's sake.'

'Look, do what you want but don't implicate me in your little plans.'

'You don't seem very concerned about what I do,' he replied.

'I'm not about to beg you to stay, if that's what you mean.' Rita turned suddenly and went inside.

'I didn't mean that,' he replied harshly, following her.

41

'Look,' she said angrily, 'you haven't so much as touched me in eighteen months. I've just about worked out that something isn't quite right . . .' Rita tapped at her temple. 'Something in here tells me that my husband has lost interest in me and that, I can assure you, is not a very pleasant thing to admit.'

'There hasn't been anyone else, if that's what you think.'

'Then what?' she asked. 'I've known you for twenty-three years, nearly twenty-four. Don't you think that is long enough, don't I know you well enough for you to tell me the sodding truth?' Her voice broke with anger and frustration.

'I'm impotent with you,' he said softly.

Rita felt sick. It was what she had always known, their savage couplings after Nathan's death and then nothing, no physical contact whatsoever. They were standing in the middle of the lounge. She could hear a motorcycle roaring away in one of the canyons, its sound amplified, making it seem closer. It suddenly occurred to Rita how foul the lounge curtains looked. How could she have chosen them? How could she have made such a mistake?

'I see,' she said finally. The whole scene had a night-marish quality about it. She suddenly felt tired and wanted to sleep so very badly. Paul was still standing there looking concerned.

'Are you going to be all right?' he asked.

Rita didn't reply. Instead she walked away from him and up to her room, where she lay down on the bed and stared up at the black ceiling.

She got up early the next morning and watched him driving away, the red flash of his brake lights startling in the early dawn air. He accelerated the big Mercedes and she continued to follow the silver car until it had disap-peared down the canyon road. Paul had left a hurried note on the breakfast table with his address and telephone number. He would be in touch soon. Rita couldn't decide whether he was just being kind or terribly cruel but she was sure that it was over.

'Paul moved out of the house the following day and he didn't return that evening.' Rita smiled a little, thinking how predictable it was that she should even consider he might. His note had said that he 'had to think things over' but Rita knew it was past the thinking stage. She looked at the doctor, Dr Martin Allan, sitting there behind his impressive desk with all of his impressive credentials. He was youthful and was wearing a blue striped shirt, open at the collar, and grey trousers. A dark jacket was hanging from the top drawer of a filing cabinet.

The office was large, its white walls covered in contemporary oil paintings of what she supposed were representational views of Los Angeles. They were uniformly bright, yellows and reds, lurid greens, orange and many shades of blue. She could identify things like the Hollywood sign and the palm trees. There was a pink Chevrolet driving out of one painting, a smudged blonde who looked like Marilyn Monroe on another. She wasn't sure if they were hanging there to aid the doctor's therapy or whether he simply had bad taste. Either way Rita found them distracting, even slightly irritating. Behind him was a wall of tinted brown glass through which she could see flat white houses built amongst the trees climbing up the canyon sides.

'And your husband is now living at Malibu?'

Rita nodded. 'And six weeks later I'm the one sitting here opposite you.'

'But you've seen him since he left the marital home?'

'Sure.' She checked her recent inclination to slide into

43

an American accent. 'He sees the boys at week-ends . . . I drive them down . . .'

'And is that okay with you?'

'Of course, he's their father, it's fine with me . . . he's spending more time with them now than ever before.'

Dr Allan nodded. 'I see . . . Were there strains in the marriage before your eldest son died?' He flicked back through some notes. 'Before Nathan died?'

'It was suicide,' she reminded him, 'and, yes, there were tensions, of course there were, as in all marriages . . . We were busy people . . . Paul is an exceptionally bright man, he was always very involved in his work.'

'What kind of things would you say caused tension between you?' he asked.

'The usual things,' she fenced his question away.

The doctor smiled. 'Yes, but no two marriages are exactly the same. What sort of things do you think caused tensions between your husband and you?'

'You mean before Nathan's suicide?'

'We can start with before,' he grinned encouragingly.

Rita thought for a moment. 'Well, as I said, Paul's work was immensely demanding . . .'

'He was a consultant?'

Rita nodded. 'In paediatric medicine. He specialized in chest and respiratory disease – obviously, that isn't a nine-to-five job.'

'You were working too?'

'I taught at London University, English Literature,' Rita explained.

'Was that demanding, would you say?'

'I was conscientious, I would say I worked hard, that I did a good job, yes.' She was suddenly defensive about her work.

'So, you had a full-time post, your husband was very

involved in his profession and you also had the house to run and the child-care.'

Rita nodded. He made it sound such a lot, but then she realized her time had been pretty full. 'They were teenagers by the time Paul's reputation was really taking off,' she added.

The doctor ignored that. 'Did it ever make you feel resentful, the fact that you were taking the brunt of the domestic duties and, meanwhile, your husband was forging ahead in his career?' He put his head to one side, watching her carefully whilst holding the end of a pencil at his lips.

'It was just something that we did, it was never actually agreed. Paul's job always seemed, somehow, more . . .' She searched for an appropriate word.

'Important?' he suggested.

'He was dealing with matters of life and death. I suppose if you quantify it like that, then it must be more important.'

'So, you saw your job as being less important?'

'Not exactly.' Rita felt confused. She had never considered the relative values of their careers. 'I suppose what I've just said must mean that I did!'

'Did you ever feel resentful?'

'About Paul's career?'

The doctor nodded, putting the pencil down on the desk top and staring at it for a moment.

'No, I felt that I was helping him.'

'By keeping the kids off his back?'

'By dealing with the day-to-day issues.'

'Making life easy.'

'He would leave our house at seven-thirty and wouldn't be back, sometimes, until ten o'clock in the evening . . . Naturally he didn't feel like coping with domestic trivia . . . he was normally too exhausted anyway.'

45

'But you coped with it,' he stated, as if he had been there.

'As I said, I wasn't dealing with life-and-death issues. I could understand how Paul couldn't simply run his life to a strict time-table . . .'

'Okay.' He looked at her and then down at his notes. 'Tell me about Nathan.'

Rita blinked and attempted to gather her thoughts. 'Nathan was an intelligent child, he had a good mind I always thought. He had an attractive personality, I think, everyone liked him . . .' She paused, finding it very difficult to answer the doctor's question. 'I don't know what else to say.' She felt very pathetic. 'He was good at sports but then he was also very good academically . . . I always thought that Nathan had it all . . . he was also very good-looking . . . I suppose all mothers think that about their children,' and she smiled at the memory of him. For a fleeting moment she could see him quite distinctly.

'How did the other boys get on with him?'

'Steve and William adored him – Steve was very close to him.'

'So, you would say that you were a close family?'

'We argued and fought and loved . . .'

'A regular family, then.'

Rita laughed. 'We were just an ordinary, normal, British family.'

'The first-born often gets to feel a degree of responsibility for the younger siblings. Was there any indication of that with Nathan?'

'You mean, did we pressure Nathan into being some kind of child-minder?'

The doctor opened his hands in a non-committal gesture. 'It can often happen without either parent or child being altogether conscious of it. Parents will tell the eldest child to be grown-up and help. Mothers will tell quite

46

small children that they are, in the case of boys, of course, the man of the house in Dad's absence.'

'I never pressured Nathan into that kind of role.'

'Nevertheless,' the doctor insisted, 'children are often cast into that role despite what people want.'

Rita listened but made no response.

'What happened when Nathan died?' he asked after a longer than usual pause.

She did not reply.

'What did you feel?' he encouraged.

'I thought that I had failed and,' she sighed, 'I kept on searching for all the reasons that might have made him do such a thing . . .'

'And were there any answers?'

'I've never understood why he took his own life.' She shook her head. 'It has always been quite inexplicable to me.'

'What about your husband?'

'Paul has never spoken about it.'

'Never?' His voice registered a mild surprise.

'He obviously sought his own answers.' She sounded almost dismissive.

'His own answers?' he repeated quietly.

Rita nodded. 'Well, he must have . . . he has consistently refused to unburden himself to me.'

'And that bothers you?'

'It makes me bloody angry. Paul has behaved through all of this as though he were the only one affected by Nathan's suicide.'

'Why do you think that is?'

'God knows.' She was silent for a while, staring down at the edge of his desk top.

'You've been married for a long time?'

'We've been together for over twenty years.'

'Happy?'

'Yes.' She looked up at him almost defiantly.

'No problems, then?'

'Of course there have been problems. No one can go through twenty years without problems unless they're both catatonic!'

A faint smile played across the doctor's mouth at her reply. 'What would you outline as your main problem?'

'Our lack of communication . . . his selfishness . . . my duplicity . . .'

'Duplicity?'

'The fact that I was always covering for him with the boys . . . Don't bother Dad because he's tired, Dad is interested but he's really busy now . . . I attended everything, the open evenings, the school plays, the sports days, the football games on freezing Saturday mornings . . . I was the attender, you could say.'

'But he had a good relationship with Nathan and the younger ones?'

'Oh, God, yes, Paul loves his kids and Nathan was always in such awe of his father. He had got a place at medical school, he was very proud of what Paul had achieved.'

'And was Paul proud of what Nathan had achieved?'

'Yes, of course, he was pleased that Nathan had a career mapped out and was going to do something useful with his life.'

'So Nathan worked hard to emulate his father?'

'I suppose so. There was never really any discussion about it, it just seemed that Nathan was always going to be a doctor.'

'And the other boys?'

'I don't know. Steve is talking about reading Law at university, William is still too young for a career choice.'

'And yet, with Nathan, you always knew.' The doctor slipped his observation in.

'Yes, Nathan always knew.' She looked at him, feeling that she had made a mistake.

'Was he as good as Paul?'

'As good?' Rita was confused again.

'At school.'

'I don't think he had exactly the same academic ability as his father but he worked harder probably.'

'You mean Paul had it easy?'

'I mean that Paul was very bright, he would have been brilliant at whatever he turned his hand to . . . some people are just like that.'

The doctor blinked. 'Do you think that Nathan felt under pressure to follow in his father's footsteps?'

'Well, no one ever said, "You must be a doctor."'

'People don't necessarily have to articulate those kind of things.'

Rita shrugged.

When she didn't respond the doctor added, 'Did anyone ever tell him that he didn't have to follow in his father's footsteps?'

She felt lost then. 'No one ever told him that he had to be like his father.'

'I see,' he replied, nodding, reaching for a desk diary and turning over some pages. 'Same time next Tuesday morning okay with you?' he asked.

Rita was surprised. The time seemed to have flown by and she certainly didn't feel that anything had been resolved, she only felt more confused. 'What? I mean yes, I think so . . . is that it?'

He smiled and was already coming from behind the desk, ready to escort her to the door. 'For the time being. Until next Tuesday, then,' he said, holding the door open for her.

'Next Tuesday,' she repeated like an idiot, finding herself in the outer office with the pretty secretary, who was filling in an appointment card for Rita. 'Next Tuesday,' she said to herself. She felt absolutely shattered, a great wave of tiredness rolling over her. The sunshine outside made her eyes hurt and she found the heat oppressive and overwhelming for a moment.

Rita quickly found her car and was soon heading back to the house, the cool, air-conditioned atmosphere inside the big Ford making her feel better. She accelerated out of the feeder lane on to the Hollywood freeway and moved swiftly away.

The house was deserted when she arrived back. She had stopped on the way and her arms were loaded with brown bags full of groceries which she dumped down on to the gleaming kitchen surfaces. It was almost one o'clock and Rosa had already left for her afternoon off. She packed the groceries away and was just sitting down on a shady part of the terrace with a sandwich and a cup of tea when Sharon came over.

'Old habits die hard,' Sharon said, sitting down opposite her in one of the comfortable chairs. 'How did you get on?'

'I'm not sure,' Rita replied.

'Did you like him?' Sharon smiled.

'I'm not sure, he seemed very pleasant.'

'I see.'

'Tea?' Rita asked her.

Sharon looked doubtful. 'Is it strong?'

She handed her cup across and Sharon took a sip, pulling a face which made Rita laugh. 'I'll get you a coffee.'

'No.' Sharon got up and disappeared into the house, emerging a little while later with a glass full of rum and Coke. Ice cubes were clinking about. 'That stuff,' Sharon said, pointing at the tea, 'is too strong for me.'

'Well, cheers, anyway,' Rita said, sipping from the fine bone-china cup.

'Will you go again?' Sharon asked her.

Rita shrugged. 'I expect so.'

'You don't sound too sure.'

'I feel exhausted,' Rita explained.

'It will make you feel better, honestly.'

Rita raised a smile from somewhere. 'I feel so disloyal . . . I think I spent the session slagging Paul off!'

'If that's what you feel . . .'

'I don't know exactly what I feel. I feel confused and I feel angry with Paul.' She looked at Sharon. 'I feel disloyal too.'

'Don't be ridiculous.' Sharon sounded amazed. 'You'll begin to feel more positive after a few more sessions.'

'But what if I don't?'

'You will,' Sharon insisted.

Rita poured herself another cup of tea, sipping and finding some comfort from it. The boys would be home in a while and she would have to prepare their evening meal and attend to their problems and answer their questions and be interested, when all she wanted to do was lie down with a pillow over her head!

'Are you and Dad going to divorce?' Steve asked her later when William had already left the dinner table to go up to his room and attend to Wendy. He had made a big point of telling her, reminding her, that he was going to clean his pet's home out. So, Rita understood that he was still smarting over their argument of a few weeks before.

'We haven't spoken about it,' Rita said reasonably, wishing that she didn't have to deal with this now. She hadn't told them yet that she had been to see a psychiatrist. She didn't want to upset them any further. Steve would immediately assume that she had cracked up and he would tell Paul, who would think the worst . . . The implications were too much to contemplate. She had visions of Paul snatching the kids and custody hearings . . .

'I thought this was supposed to be a temporary arrangement. He's been at Malibu for six weeks.'

'Look, Steve, your father was the one who decided upon this course of action, right?' She glared at him across the cluttered dinner table, pouring herself a glass of iced water.

Steve brushed his hand back through his hair and messed around with the food on his plate. 'Was it us?' he asked.

'Certainly not, don't be ridiculous. Your dad needed a rest. You see him almost every week-end, don't you think he looks calmer?'

Steve thought about that. 'You mean Dad is sick?'

'No.'

'Well, he looks okay, sure, but he seems lonely as well.' He looked serious. 'Don't you miss him?'

'Of course I miss him,' she assured Steve, hoping it sounded genuine enough. In truth Paul's absence was something of a relief. Rita no longer felt as though she were walking around him on broken glass. It was, in fact, a massive relief not to have to pretend that everything was fine for the benefit of Steve and William.

'School breaks up in a week,' Steve said.

Rita nodded. 'That's good.'

'I don't suppose Dad would let me use the beach house?'

She looked at him. 'Why would you want to do that?' she asked, knowing damn well.

'Oh, it would be nice to stay down at the beach during the week.'

'I see.' Rita quickly carried out some mental calculations. 'The fact that your dad will be away in Houston for the first few days of your vacation wouldn't have anything to do with this urge for the coast, would it?'

Steve blushed a little but held his ground. 'I didn't know that. Could I go if he says yes?'

'We're not stupid, Steve,' she assured him. 'Your dad doesn't want to come back to a wrecked house . . . and God knows what else you'll be up to.'

'Mum!' Steve sounded shocked at her suggestion.

Rita reached forward and began to collect the dishes together. 'Listen,' she said, standing and taking things over to the sink, 'have you thought about majoring in Drama rather than Law? I'd imagine that you'd be very good.'

Steve grinned. 'Come on, Mum, you were young once . . .'

'And you're only young once . . . I know, I know, but you'll just have to learn to control your adolescent urges.' She fixed him then with a sterner gaze. 'And I'm not having you using your father's beach house as a bordello.'

'I was planning to swim,' he insisted, getting up to leave.

'Yes, and pigs can fly.' She smiled, returning to the task in hand.

'Jem's coming over for tennis, I'm going to get changed.'

'Right,' she said, watching him go.

Steve called in on William, who was busy in the large three-car garage cleaning out Wendy's home. He put the golden hamster into a cardboard box whilst he carried out this task. Rita had driven her car into the garage and Steve's Rabbit was parked on the driveway which sloped down to entrance gates.

'Okay?' Steve asked his brother, picking up the hamster and allowing it to run up his arm. The little rodent paused for a moment on Steve's shoulder before moving across, hesitating again for a second, and then running down his other arm. He picked up a chunk of carrot and fed it to Wendy.

'Did you find anything out?' William asked.

Steve shrugged, picking Wendy up and dropping her carefully back into the box. 'Mum said they're not divorcing.'

'So, what's happening?' William paused for a moment to wring out his cleaning rag into the bucket of hot water.

'Beats me . . . She won't let me use the beach house either.'

William took a fresh cloth and began to dry out the clean hamster house. 'Is Dad moving back, then?'

'She didn't say. What do you think?'

'I don't know.' William fitted the two pieces of the house together again, putting fresh bedding in the top section. He picked Wendy up and put her back. She immediately ran down the plastic tube into the bottom half and began to run inside the wheel, which spun faster and faster. 'Nothing has gone right since Nathan died. They've just argued and been miserable.'

'So, what are you saying, that you'd prefer them to live apart like this for ever?' Steve asked.

'I've seen more of Dad in the last six weeks than in the last two years. He seems a lot happier.'

Steve nodded in agreement. Jem was walking up the driveway towards them. 'I'm playing tennis now. Are you coming to watch?'

William picked up the hamster. 'I've got a report to write for the morning.'

Steve followed his brother out of the warm garage and met Jem, who was carrying a bundle of rackets.

'Have you got some balls?' Jem asked.

Steve laughed. 'I've got new balls, got them today.' He put a hand on Jem's shoulder and they walked across the garden towards the court. Steve cracked a joke and their raucous laughter carried through the still evening air.

Rita found William in his room. He was lying on his bed staring up at the ceiling. His television was turned on but the sound was off. The floor around his bed was scattered with family photographs. A picture of Nathan, grinning madly after just winning a tennis match, faced her. William had been crying, it was quite obvious, but Rita said nothing. She walked to the window, which was open wide, and listened to the sounds drifting up from the tennis court. Steve and Jem were whacking at the ball. It seemed to go on and on, a long rally. The hypnotic, metronomic sound suddenly stopped and, following a brief pause, she heard Jem's anguished voice, obviously angry with himself for losing the point. She imagined Steve turning away from the net and grinning to himself. He was a good player and it would take a lot to beat him when he was on form.

'So,' she said, looking down at William, 'what have you got to tell me?'

He moved his head towards her. 'Nothing much.'

'Nothing much?' She sounded surprised.

William sat up, leaning his head back against the wall. 'No.'

Rita sat down on the edge of his bed and looked into his eyes. She reached down for a handful of the snaps he had been inspecting. Glancing at them, she found herself looking at the last photograph she had taken of all three boys. It was on the steps at Chalcot Square, a week or so before Nathan died. They had all been going to a dinner in Paul's honour. One of the many farewell events they had attended over the course of the last months in London. The boys all looked very smart in suit and ties. She remembered thinking at the time how grown-up they suddenly looked, handsome and obviously very happy.

She put the photographs down. 'Confusing times, eh, William?' And reaching forward instinctively, she felt his forehead and brushed the hair away from it. He was fairer than Steve, a reddish blond, and he was a well-built lad who, she supposed, would be bigger than either of his brothers. Rita assumed that he took after her side of the family, her father.

'Are you and Dad getting back together soon?' he asked, looking directly at her.

Rita's mind spun. How much more could these kids take? She immediately felt guilty for Paul's absence. 'Your dad and I . . .' She noticed how he was hanging upon her every word. She cleared her throat. 'We have a lot of things to work out, things that really have nothing to do with what is happening here or our life in California . . . When people have been married for a long time, problems just sometimes arise.' It sounded ridiculous, she wasn't making any sense, so she tried again. 'It has nothing to do with Steve or you . . .'

'Has it to do with Nathan?'

'Well, it has something to do with Nathan's death . . . At least, that has obviously been a terrible, terrible blow to the whole family.' Rita's voice grew husky and broke for a moment. She cleared her throat. 'Your dad just needs some time, maybe a lot of time, to think about things . . .' Rita looked into William's searching eyes. She didn't feel that her comments were making things any clearer.

'I miss him, Mom. I miss Nathan a lot,' he said simply.

Rita took his hand. 'Well, I know you do, darling, of course you do . . . We all miss Nathan.' She felt tears

56

stinging in her eyes but she attempted to smile and, putting her arms around William, hugged him to her. 'But we have to go on . . . we have to do that.' She broke apart and held him by the shoulders. 'You must talk things out, William, it's really, really important to talk, to me or Steve or Dad . . .'

William sniffed, wiping his hand over his mouth, determined not to cry in front of his mother, but he nodded in agreement when she spoke.

Rita took an unsteady breath. 'Listen, I'm going to take some drinks down to Steve and Jem – I could do with some help, okay?'

'Sure, I'll be down in a minute.'

Rita grinned, running downstairs to the kitchen and sorting out some refreshment. She did not feel in control. She could not take the grief of a whole family on to her shoulders, it simply wasn't fair. Turning on the cold tap, she splashed her face with the icy water, cupping it in her hands and lowering her head into it. Rita did this many times and slowly the sickness and the panic went away. She could hear William on the stairs and, quickly drying herself with a length of kitchen paper, she faced him, smiling as he walked into the room.

Rita explained how she felt to Sharon the next morning after their aerobics class. Rita had seemed filled with a new energy and whilst all around her were exhausted towards the end of the hour, and even Sharon was showing signs of fatigue, she felt that she could go on and on. They had lunch at a new vegetarian restaurant in an exclusive shopping mall in Los Angeles.

'Look at that,' Sharon said, nudging Rita. A Fila edition Ford Thunderbird had pulled up outside the restaurant and a couple climbed out wearing co-ordinated

Fila sportswear. 'Designer-label people and designer-label car!'

Rita laughed.

'You were full of energy today,' Sharon said, sounding impressed.

'I'll suffer for it later on, I expect.' She watched as a beautiful youth sat down at a nearby table. He was with an older woman, an agent perhaps. He was looking down at the menu and she could see his long eyelashes. His hair was jet black and his skin was tanned. He looked Italian, she thought. She kept looking, she couldn't take her eyes off him, and then he raised his eyes from the menu and, looking directly at her, grinned. Rita grinned back. She was sixteen again. The whole thing lasted a matter of seconds but it made her feel incredibly alive.

'Who is it?' Sharon hissed from the corner of her mouth.

Rita shrugged. 'Isn't he gorgeous!'

Sharon turned nonchalantly, as though searching around for their waitress. 'He's a child,' she said, spinning back to her friend. 'What's come over you? First it was Max, and then Kirk, and now this. He's a *baby*,' Sharon leaned across the table and spoke in a stage whisper.

Their waitress appeared and took their order. Rita wasn't the slightest bit hungry but she ordered a salad with cottage cheese. 'I think I'm going mad,' she admitted to Sharon.

'You're just a bit frustrated, honey.'

'Well, I can't have an affair, that would really upset the apple cart . . . The kids keep asking me when Paul is coming back!' She related her discussions with Steve and William.

'Can't you try explaining it to them?'

'I have tried. Steve keeps asking me if we're going to

divorce and William is going through enough without this as well. I could kill Paul.'

'I wouldn't do that,' Sharon advised gravely.

Rita laughed despite herself. 'Maybe Dr Allan will have some answers to all this crap!'

'What do you want to happen?' Sharon asked bluntly.

'I'm not really sure . . .' She glanced over at the beautiful youth, who was engaged in deep conversation with the older woman. 'Maybe I should proposition Max or Kirk!'

'Well, sex with an eighteen-year-old might solve your immediate problem but I wouldn't recommend it as a long-term answer.'

The waitress came back with their orders, smiling and wishing them an enjoyable meal. Rita looked at her salad, picking up a sliver of carrot, and nibbled at it feeling like William's hamster. 'I just want a bit of human contact, that's all. I don't even mean sex.' The boy looked across at her, a fleeting glance.

'Well, you know what I think?' Sharon began. 'I think you should start to consider your own needs for a while. The boys have their own lives to lead, they'll be off your hands soon and then what? Paul has obviously made his decision but what is Rita going to do?'

'I'm forty-one years old, what can I do?'

'What has age got to do with it?' Sharon asked, picking up her glass of white wine. 'This is LA. You never have to grow old!'

'My feelings for Paul are totally confused. We haven't really had a marriage for the past two years but I obviously must still feel something for him.'

'Must?' Sharon looked at her. 'Why must you?'

'After twenty-three years it can't just end in this mess.'

'But how do you know that this wouldn't have happened anyway?'

59

Rita shrugged. She didn't know. 'Perhaps he blames me for Nathan's suicide.'

'Oh no, come on, Rita, not the guilt trip again, *please*.'

'It's either that or he is using Nathan as an excuse for the fact that he has just gone off me.'

Sharon looked thoughtful. 'You're going to have to sort this out with him.'

'Don't you think I haven't tried?'

'Apart from anything else, you have to protect your future.'

'What future?' Rita asked, suddenly feeling very sorry for herself.

Sharon raised her eyes skyward. 'Stop being so English . . . Let's have a bit of Californian optimism!'

'Maybe I should go back to London.'

'To what?' Sharon demanded to know.

'I could get a job . . .'

'You have your work to finish on the Woolf book, isn't that a job?'

'I've hardly started it.'

'There you go, then.'

'It's an academic text,' Rita said, sounding disillusioned. 'It'll end up on undergraduate reading lists and will never be looked at!'

'Well, you'd better write it first,' Sharon replied.

Rita grinned. 'You're right, of course. I'd better stop moaning and get on with something.'

'Sure, it's a beautiful day, we're young, in our prime, let's enjoy ourselves.'

'What do you suggest?' Rita asked, laughing.

'We could cruise Hollywood Boulevard and pick up some young guys!'

Rita choked on her wine. 'Sure, and contract some awful disease!'

'You're such a pessimist,' Sharon complained, smiling at her idea, 'such a killjoy.'

They looked at one another and burst into fits of convulsive laughter, which caused heads to turn in the exclusive restaurant. The beautiful youth looked over with an expression of confusion and handsome disdain. They left soon afterwards, driving back to Sharon's neo-colonial style house, where they sat out on her breezy veranda and drank mint tea.

Sharon's house was up the winding canyon road from Rita's. From the veranda, Rita could just make out the red tiles of her roof amongst the trees.

'What does love mean to you?' Sharon asked.

'Never having to say, "What about the bloody over-draft?"' Rita suggested fatuously.

'No, really, how does it affect you?'

'God knows, I was always falling in love when I was young, but then I met Paul and I *really* fell for him . . . I was completely out of control with him.'

'Really?' Sharon laughed.

Rita nodded. 'Well, it was the sixties. I don't think I'd considered liberation then.'

'And you knew straight away?'

'Yes,' Rita nodded. 'Looking back, I'm sure that it must have been something to do with his fabulous good looks . . . and he was going to be a doctor, which was also something for a girl from my background.'

'Calculating young broad, eh?' Sharon joked.

Rita laughed. 'Actually, I think it must have been pheromonal, you know, instant attraction. We must have been secreting symbiotic secretions!'

'My God!' Sharon put a hand to her head. 'Did you have sex straight after meeting him?'

'Not straight away,' Rita replied. 'We waited until after the dance.'

'My God!' Sharon repeated, laughing. 'It wasn't that way with Bill and me at all.'

'No?' Rita put down her mint tea and poured herself a glass of the wine Sharon had brought out.

'No, we didn't even like each other very much when we met. He thought he was great, you know, a qualified doctor, and he more or less told me that my PhD research was for shit!'

Rita chuckled. 'A great beginning.'

'And I was taller than him, wobbling about on those ridiculous stilettos with my hair like this . . .' She held her hands about six inches from either side of her head. 'You know, swept up and sprayed into position with a can of lacquer like a helmet!' Sharon laughed at the memory. 'So I looked down on to this shorter person and thought, "Screw you, buster."'

'And then you married him,' Rita said, sipping at her wine.

'No, our first meeting was at a dinner party at Stanford with mutual friends . . . some friends, I remember thinking afterwards!'

'But you couldn't forget about him afterwards?'

'Oh, sure, I did forget about him until he called me a few weeks later . . . Can you imagine that, not the next day, or the end of the week, but a *few* weeks later, and invited me out to some concert or other.'

'And then you fell in love,' Rita insisted.

Sharon shook her head, dispensing with her tea and reaching for the wine bottle. 'No, we argued over something ridiculous and I broke my heel on a grating and spent the evening walking about like the Hunchback of Notre Dame . . .'

'Sounds super.'

62

'I can't really remember how we eventually got it together. I guess I found out that he had a sense of humour. He certainly wasn't the most handsome specimen I had dated but there was something about him. Of course, he had some hair in those days and he had a powerful build . . . a good tennis player and swimmer . . . I guess we must have reconciled our differences and played tennis or something . . .'

'Don't you remember?'

'No, he was just *there*, part of the fixtures and fittings, and when he wasn't there I started to miss him, and so we got married. Much against my mother's wishes, I might add.'

'Oh, really, why?'

'She didn't care for him then, said he was too brash . . . She told me on the eve of my wedding day that it wouldn't last and I said, "What the hell, at least if I need surgery it will be at cost price!" and that was, what, twenty-one years ago?'

'And did she change her mind?'

'Not really, until she died – and we had been married fifteen years by that time – she always told me it would never work . . .' Sharon smiled at the memory.

'And you gave up your PhD for him,' Rita added.

'There wasn't much to give up. I'd been working my tail off for years and I guess Bill was just there at the right time . . . I really wanted kids. It seems almost a blasphemy to say that nowadays, doesn't it?'

Rita reached for the wine and poured herself another glass. She was feeling relaxed and just a bit intoxicated, listening to Sharon's pleasant voice and smiling at the reflections of her life with Bill. Rita had been leaning back, closing her eyes from time to time. She finished her wine and replaced the glass on the table in front of her.

When she woke up it was almost four o'clock and Sharon was still sitting opposite her, reading a book.

'Welcome back,' Sharon said, looking up as Rita yawned and stretched.

'I'm sorry,' Rita apologized.

'Don't be silly, I like my guests to feel relaxed!'

'It was all that wine,' Rita said, her head aching a little. 'I really shouldn't drink at lunch times, it's absolutely fatal and I was planning to do so much this afternoon.'

'Well, honey, the best-laid plans, etcetera . . . Just relax. It'll do you good, more good than all your worrying.'

Rita stood up, smoothing down her white cotton sundress. 'I shall have to make a move,' she told Sharon.

'I'll come and give you a game of tennis later this evening, when it's cooler. Are your floodlights working?'

Rita nodded. She felt stiff from her exertions in the aerobics class earlier in the day. 'Thanks,' she said as she began to leave.

'For what, getting you drunk?'

Rita laughed, waving as she turned the corner of the large house and walking the short distance down the rutted canyon road to her own front gates.

The boys were swimming and she walked across the grass towards the pool, sitting down and watching them for a while. Steve was practising his crawl, moving swiftly through the water with clean, well-coached efficiency. He was in the school swimming team and took his responsibility to it very seriously. Length after length after length he swam, without pausing. Meanwhile William had climbed on to a bright green airbed floating gently on the opposite side of the pool, wearing his mirrored sunglasses and reading a copy of *Rolling Stone*.

Rita waited until Steve had come up for air and was

clinging to the poolside, puffing out his cheeks and gasping, before she made a move. Her heels clicked on the concrete as she walked round to him. Squatting down, she tapped him on the head. His black hair was slicked down. William had tossed his magazine to the side and, turning on to his stomach, was paddling the airbed over to them.

She chatted with them about their day for a few minutes before walking back into the house, where she changed out of her crumpled dress into shorts and baggy matching khaki T-shirt. She felt comfortable and at ease in what had become her 'uniform' since living here.

Rita sat down on the edge of her bed. She looked at herself in the wall-to-wall mirrors and thought about the boy in the restaurant. She could still see his beautiful face, suntanned, olive-brown skin, the sheen of youthful perfection. He had had raven-black hair and startlingly blue eyes framed by long black lashes. He had intrigued her, just as beautiful things always did, just as Paul had once done all those centuries ago! The boy had worn blue jeans and a Fred Perry sports shirt underneath a tweedy Armani jacket. She remembered the three buttons at the cuff of the expensive jacket and the shadowy stubble, the perfect features and those dangerous blue eyes. Sharon had said there were thousands of men just like him in Los Angeles, as they drove back after lunch.

'What do you think he was?' Rita had asked her.

'God knows. An actor.' She'd paused as they made a left turn. 'Or a model . . .' She'd checked her rear-view mirror before pulling into the outside lane. 'A gigolo maybe, she was certainly old enough to be his grandmother . . .' As they overtook a row of speeding trucks, Sharon had glanced across at Rita, 'She was probably paying for the scamp!'

Rita had looked shocked. 'Do you really think so?'

'Listen, if you're that interested I'll turn the car around and we can go back to ask them.'

'Don't be ridiculous,' Rita had answered.

Sharon had dismissed her friend's reaction with a laugh. 'LA is no different than anywhere else. My God, you lived in London all of your life, every big city has the same people crawling through them. Stop behaving like Rebecca of Sunnybrook Farm!'

Rita had laughed then and turned the conversation to other things.

She knew that she was being ridiculous and, giving herself a stern look, she got up from the bed and went down to prepare a meal for her gannet progeny. Whatever her feelings, the reality of her life was the children, and Rita knew that their security was paramount.

For all his bluff and role-play, she was aware that, at seventeen, Steve's maturity and world-weariness were a façade. Steve might ask her about divorce in a nonchalant manner but Rita knew how terrified he really was. The family was breaking up. It would probably never be the same again and both William and Steve were painfully aware of that fact, and the longer Paul stayed at the beach the more obvious it became.

So, Rita watched them carefully and held her own needs, her own desires, in check. She was neither being noble nor masochistic. In truth it was all she could do, because anything else happening within the family, she was sure, would drive her over the edge. She could not protect them twenty-four hours a day but she was determined to do whatever she could until they had left her and found their own way. She resisted her own feelings of guilt as much as possible but they were abundant and, often, overwhelming.

The boys were coming up from the pool and Rita

watched from the kitchen windows. They were, physically, strong and healthy, they were both intelligent and loving. Rita was proud of them, for the way they had endured and come through the last two years . . . the last six weeks since their father moved out. As they walked together over the Mexican gardener's flawless grass, she knew that they were her reality now and she hung on to that fact with all of her strength.

Chapter 3

After the second or third or fourth visit to her analyst, Rita found herself becoming more at ease with the situation. More confident both with Dr Allan and with her own responses. She felt herself more able to deal with Paul and, increasingly, was forcing the issues with him, determined that he should not hide behind a wall of aggressive silence any longer. She dressed more carefully for her Tuesday morning visit to the doctor. She dug out some of her smarter dresses, had some of her more stylish suits altered to fit her new slim-line figure. Sharon asked Rita if she had a crush on her analyst! Rita was positive she hadn't but, whatever the reason, she felt the need to look her best.

'And how are you today, Rita?' Dr Allan asked, smiling as she entered his inner sanctum.

She took her usual seat in front of his desk and smoothed down her dove-grey skirt with the knife-edge pleats. She had on her smart white silk blouse and carried the fitted suit jacket over her arm. 'I'm fine,' she said, placing the jacket carefully on the empty leather chair next to her own. She put the small matching bag at her side.

He settled back, placing his hands behind his head, smiling encouragingly. 'So, Rita, what would you like to talk about today?'

This was a little disconcerting for he normally instigated the proceedings, asking her questions and listening with care to her replies. Now she felt as though she were walking into a maze. Rita thought for a moment before beginning.

'I don't know what's going to happen to me after all of this . . .' She paused. 'Through all of this traumatic period in our lives I sometimes just feel that there isn't much room left for me, for my feelings, my desires . . .' She stopped, looking into the doctor's face.

He was nodding, encouraging Rita to continue. She noticed that he was simply listening today and not taking any notes. He was sitting forward now, his hands held together in relaxed fashion on the desk top in front of him.

'Well, I suppose,' she continued, 'the fact is that my life seems to have been in suspended animation for the last two years. I haven't had relations . . . I've been celibate for the last eighteen months. Sex was always an important part of our marriage . . .' There, she had said it but she was also feeling somewhat disloyal to Paul and guilty, as though he would know what she was saying about him in these expensive sessions which he, indirectly, was paying for.

'Is part of the anger you feel in respect of Paul because of his lack of interest or inability to have a sexual relationship?' He leant back again. 'In one of our previous sessions you spoke of the way he came to you after Nathan's suicide, you said more in anger and grief than in love.'

Rita nodded, a slight feeling of nausea passing over her. 'There was a tremendous amount of pleasureless sex in the first few months after Nathan died. I mean, I'm not really sure if Paul actually got much enjoyment from it . . . It could not be described as love-making, I suppose that's what I mean.'

'Did you ever speak to him about it?'

'I tried to initially but I told you he has refused to

discuss anything with me . . . Any attempt to talk about our sex life used to result in contemptuous silences or angry scenes which upset us both . . . It seemed best to live through it and hope we could, somehow, salvage the marriage. Before he left he told me that he found it impossible to have sex with me anyway.' She turned away and stared at one of the garish oil paintings for a moment.

'You use a lot of phrases like "salvaging the marriage", is it a lost cause as far as you are concerned, Rita?'

'I knew, almost as soon as Nathan died, that Paul had fallen out of love with me.' Tears suddenly sprang to her eyes. She took a paper tissue out of her bag and dabbed at them as she continued speaking. 'I was never aware of feeling that before Nathan killed himself, but it was *very* clear to me afterwards.'

'And who would you blame for that?'

'Blame?' It seemed a peculiar question.

'Yes, was there any blame involved, do you think?'

Rita shook her head as though finding the question, the idea, incomprehensible. She blew her nose hard and took a deep breath. 'I don't know how to answer that,' she replied at last.

'Do you have an answer?' he asked her.

Rita shrugged, feeling tearful and confused. 'I don't have an answer, no.'

'You said that you knew Paul had fallen out of love with you?'

Rita nodded.

'But did you fall out of love with him?'

'My feelings changed towards him. At first I assumed that his behaviour was due to the terrible way Nathan died . . .'

'But your attitude changed?'

'I wasn't allowed to express my grief, I was catering to Paul and to the demands of William and Steve – especially

70

Steve, who was completely inconsolable. He would spend days, weeks, it seemed like weeks, locked into his own grief . . . Steve idolized Nathan. Sometimes I would be up for the whole night with him. I would be dealing with the brute force of Paul on the one hand and the absolute grief of Steve on the other . . . In a way it was grotesque.'

'What about William?'

'He seemed to cope better. He was distressed, of course, but, somehow, he was more self-contained. Since then he has experienced periods of withdrawal when he has to be alone and he's wet the bed consistently . . .'

'You've had a lot to put up with, you'd say?'

'I'm not Mother Teresa! I don't mean to suggest that it has been unremitting, for most of the time we're pretty normal, you know.'

'Most of the time?'

'Most of the time.' Rita looked straight at him.

'What happens during the times when you're not all being "pretty normal"?' he smiled.

'Well, one of the boys might be feeling the strain. Paul might have just left for Malibu. I might be missing sex and taking it out on the boys . . . God knows.'

'What are you going to do about this enforced celibacy?'

'Actually, it's only seemed important over the last few weeks, the last month or so. I feel suddenly as though a great chunk of my life is missing . . . I've been feeling rather libidinous just recently, I look at young men and think of only one thing!' She smiled at how foolish this must sound.

The doctor grinned too. 'So, what are you going to *do* about it?'

Rita sighed. 'Nothing. I don't suppose I will do anything . . . You know, I sometimes feel guilty about these sessions with you. My problems must be minute compared

71

to some people's. I live in a luxurious house in a fashionable residential area, not quite Beverly Hills but on the borderline, and most of the time life is really great. I play tennis and swim and have laughs with my friend Sharon . . .' She laughed nervously. 'Is this making any sense?'

The doctor gave her a bright smile. 'Why did you come and see me, Rita?' he asked.

'Because I want more control over my life.' She wasn't absolutely sure if that was the reason.

'But from what you've just said you have control.'

'I mean greater control . . .'

'And what will you do with this "control" when you get it?' He posed this question as though he could hand it out across the desk to her, like the Wizard of Oz dispensing Courage and Brains and a Heart!

Rita shrugged. She felt as though the maze had swallowed her up and now she was stuck in the middle not knowing which way to turn. 'If I had control, if I didn't keep getting upset, if I knew the right things to say when my kids get upset about their brother, if Paul hadn't just left . . .'

'That's a lot of "if I's",' he commented, grinning his slightly lop-sided grin.

'I don't want anything else to happen,' she admitted.

'And could you have prevented things from happening, Rita? Could you have stopped Nathan from swallowing all of those sleeping tablets?'

She bit hard into her lip, shaking her head slowly from side to side. 'I *feel* that I could have done something . . . should have done something,' she finished quietly.

'So, we're back to it all being Rita's fault,' he said.

Rita looked at him but did not reply. She stared through the tinted brown windows and viewed the flat white houses on the hills. She imagined women in those houses with their families, complete and around them. She began to feel very sorry for herself indeed. She thought of Paul in his house down at Malibu and felt angry with him. He didn't have to bother himself with the day-to-day events, he didn't have to comfort his children when they were upset. All he did was have them at week-ends and point them in the direction of the Pacific Ocean! She was unconsciously twisting her wedding ring round and round on her finger.

'I thought,' the doctor continued, 'that we had decided to forget this guilt trip.' He nodded. 'Yes, I thought that was our agreement.' His eyes pierced her own.

'It would be easier to do that if it weren't all so inexplicable, if Nathan had shown some cause, some reason . . .'

'There may never be a reason. Are you proposing to spend the remainder of your life searching for one? He may have just woken up one day and decided that he wanted to die. You may just have to face that possibility.'

Rita shook her head. 'I can't believe that, he had everything to live for.'

'Obviously not.'

She looked at him and hated him for a moment but she could not answer. They sat it out, enduring another long silence. Rita could hear the *tick*, *tick*, *tick* of the small carriage clock on his desk.

'I can't absolve you from your guilt, Rita,' he began. 'You have to do that yourself by accepting there may be other answers, other ways of looking at Nathan's suicide.'

She still didn't respond.

'There will come a time in your life when you want to move on and that will be very hard with all this luggage you carry around with you, full of guilt and anger and grief.' He suggested this very gently.

'I lost my *son*, doctor . . . The pain does not get any better, it's just that some days are easier than others.'

He nodded. 'I understand.'

'You can't possibly understand,' she replied, almost to herself. She took out a fresh tissue and blew her nose again.

'Rita, do you know what I feel?' he asked, sitting way back in his big leather chair. 'I feel that we ought to talk about Nathan next time.'

'I thought that's what we had been doing,' she answered, feeling tired and annoyed. She was on the verge of crying and her throat ached with the effort of preventing another flood of tears.

He smiled his encouraging smile. 'Let's think about that for next time,' he softly insisted.

Rita drove the few blocks to the same vegetarian restaurant where she sat, still smarting from her session with Dr Allan. She had begun the morning feeling really good about herself for a change but now she was full of doubt and uncertainty. She wasn't sure what she expected from this man but she certainly didn't expect to feel worse! She had no idea what he was getting at. Did she blame anybody? The waitress came over for her order. Rita gave the menu card a cursory look and ordered a peach and peanut salad and a glass of Perrier.

'Ice and lemon?' the girl asked.

Rita nodded. She felt overdressed, as though she were going to a wedding, or a funeral. Her shoes were uncomfortable, she wasn't used to wearing such high heels, and the silk blouse, so carefully chosen, was too fussy with the silly, floppy bow at its neck.

It was early and there weren't many people at lunch yet. She had chosen a seat in the courtyard, where there were hanging ferns and shaded tables under pastel-coloured umbrellas, blues and pinks and greens, mauves and greys. The restaurant was supposed to be the height of sophistication and she felt completely out of step, dull and frumpish.

She was deep in thought, mulling over the events of the last hour, when her meal arrived. The girl wished her an enjoyable lunch. Rita attempted to smile, still feeling disillusioned and annoyed. Wasn't psychoanalysis supposed to make her feel better? Maybe she would ask Dr Martin bloody Allan just what he was driving at next week.

The boy spoke first and Rita looked up, surprised and completely taken off guard. He was sitting at the next table and, as she looked up, she found herself staring into his wonderful blue eyes. She hesitated before speaking.

'I'm sorry?'

He smiled. 'I was saying that I saw you in here the other day.'

'The other day?' she replied like an idiot.

'Yes, you were in the main room with a blonde woman.'

Rita nodded. He was even more gorgeous close up, with a dazzling smile and carefully tousled black hair cut very short at the sides, almost shaved. If, at that moment, he'd invited her to leave with him, she was certain she would have done so. Despite Sharon's cynical comments, she couldn't believe there were many like him in LA . . . or anywhere else, for that matter. He had a deep voice but was softly spoken, with a discernible New York accent.

'You like it here?' he asked.

'I was in the area,' she explained. 'It was handy.'

'You're English, right?' He smiled as though he found that pleasing.

Rita nodded. Her throat felt dry. She reached for her drink.

'You living in LA or just visiting?' he continued.

'Oh, I'm living . . .'

75

'. . . if you can call it living!'

She laughed. He was wearing a dark Yves St Laurent suit jacket, black Levi 501s, a white shirt, unbuttoned at the collar, and a thin black tie.

'How long have you lived here?' he asked.

'Two years.'

'Two years?' he repeated.

'You're not from Los Angeles,' she said.

'No, that's for sure,' he laughed, showing off perfect, brilliantly white teeth, 'East Coast, that's definitely more my style . . . Greenwich Village, New York, although I was born and brought up in Hoboken, New Jersey . . . the same town as Frank.'

'Frank?'

'Sinatra,' he responded.

Rita nodded, not really seeing the point of the connection. 'You're a fan of his?'

He nodded enthusiastically.

'I take it that you don't like Los Angeles.'

The boy shrugged. 'I'm working out here. I've hardly seen any of it . . . I'm a singer.'

'I see, and you're making a record?'

He laughed. 'No, an agent, that was her you saw me with last week, has me up for a part.'

'In a film?'

'TV, a soap. The dollars are big but I'm not sure if it's for me.' He shrugged again. 'They haven't made up their minds either.'

She grinned. 'Fingers crossed then.'

'They paid for the trip and the hotel. What the hell, I get two weeks at someone else's expense!'

They chatted on in an amiable fashion until Rita had finished her lunch. 'I hope that everything goes well,' she told him as she signed the credit-card voucher, 'and that you get to eat some lunch!'

He grinned. 'I'm supposed to be meeting a guy I know from New York. He's passing through here and I thought it would be nice to see a friendly face. My hotel is fine and the pool is great but you can only swim and watch so much TV.'

She stood up to leave. 'I hope you enjoy the rest of your stay.'

'Thanks for talking, it was good . . . I hope I didn't disturb your lunch too much.'

'Not at all.' She was about to walk away but turned back to him. 'By the way, what is your name?'

'Marco.' He stood up, making a belated and formal introduction. 'Marco Salvatori.' He grinned, which was extremely appealing. 'My friends call me Marc, which is also my stage name, Marc Salvatori, a bit of a mouthful . . .'

Rita introduced herself, still holding his hand.

'It doesn't seem a very English name,' he suggested.

'My mother named me after Rita Hayworth, who was her second favourite film star. I'm afraid the resemblance ends with the name!'

He shook his head. 'Not at all . . . who was her favourite film star?'

Rita laughed. 'Marlene Dietrich. I was lucky, my younger sister got landed with that.'

'And does she look like Dietrich?'

'No, but she was blonde as a child and I was more of a redhead, I suppose . . . anyway,' she said, removing her hand from his, 'it was nice to have met you. I'll look out for your name on the credits in the future.'

'You'll probably have to look long and hard.'

She was about to leave again but a thought struck her. 'If you get sick of your hotel food, why not give me a call?' She was already scribbling her phone number on a

77

clean serviette, which she handed to him. 'I'll leave it up to you.'

He seemed genuinely surprised and pleased. 'I may just take you up on this.' He looked at the number and slipped the serviette into his immaculate jacket pocket. 'Thanks, thanks a lot.'

'And now, I *really* have to fly.' And Rita left him rather reluctantly, amazed at herself for being so brazen but, at the same time, feeling pleased. Marco Salvatori would never call her. She was old enough to be his mother. She wasn't even sure if she believed his story . . . she imagined him throwing the number away and laughing at her for being so ridiculous, such a ridiculous old broad! Rita climbed into the big Ford and drove away. What did she care?

Rita spent the afternoon working at the redwood table under the palms. She read through her notes and began to organize the chapters for the book. Academic text or not, read or not, she would finish the damn thing and send it packing, back to England, where the head of her old faculty was still keen to see it. She had kept in contact and in a recent note he had asked her for a completion date.

It was a hot afternoon, the valley shimmering in the heat beneath her. She had dumped her suit and, having pulled on her 'uniform' was feeling much more relaxed and comfortable. Rita worked on through the sultry afternoon until four-thirty, when the boys, who had been swimming in the pool with Jem and some other friends, decided to come up under the palms to bother her. She was, anyway, coming to a logical end and was ready to stop for a while.

'When are we going to get to read this?' Steve asked.

'Since when have you been interested in Virginia Woolf?' she asked bluntly.

'Miss Silver was talking about her in class today,' he replied.

'Oh, and did you tell her that your mother was a world-famous authority on Virginia?'

Steve pulled a face. 'No, you're not, are you?'

'Not yet!'

'What's there to eat, Mum, I'm starved,' William said.

'Nothing, I thought we could eat out.'

'McDonald's?' William asked, becoming interested.

'Whatever, although I'm sure all the monosodium glutamate and E numbers make you go a bit nutty!'

'McDonald's don't have all that stuff in them,' William insisted.

'Are you coming along, Jem?' Rita asked.

'I'll have to see Mom first.'

'Okay,' Rita nodded. 'We'll leave here about seven. Perhaps she would like to come as well, and what about Tom and Jack and Judy?'

'I'll ask,' Jem replied, stretching out on the grass underneath the palms.

Rita looked at them all in their swimming suits. Steve and Jem were really young men now. Steve had filled out so much in the last two years, she wondered, vaguely, if it was due to all the vitamins the Americans packed into their food. William was fifteen going on twenty, not as hirsute as his brother but gathering muscles where there had once been puppy fat. She watched them racing back to the pool.

'Last one in's a dildo!' Steve shouted and, turning back to her as he ran, called, 'Come on, Mum, don't be so geriatric . . .'

Rita laughed. Jem was the first to dive in, William next, Steve, of course, had to show off and take the diving board entrance, cutting into the water with a feathery splash, the droplets catching the bright sunlight. Steve was a great swimmer, he could beat the others hands down. She considered that he was really a better athlete than Nathan, even though, in the family, Nathan's reputation was always held up as a shining example. In fact, Nathan's reputation for everything was regarded with an almost holy reverence, as though he could do no wrong. If he were here now he would never beat Steve across the pool, or on the tennis court, or even scholastically, and yet if she were ever to suggest this Steve would reject it out of hand. Maybe it was just the way they had all come to cope with Nathan's suicide, putting him up there on the highest pedestal.

Rita stood up and wandered across the grass. Once out of the shade, the afternoon heat almost seemed to weigh down upon her shoulders. As usual her bathing costume was on under her shorts and T-shirt. She stripped these off at the poolside, diving in as the hot concrete surround baked the soles of her feet.

'Race you?' Steve suggested.

Rita declined, swimming slowly towards the shallow end, where Jem was resting, sitting on the bottom, his arms outstretched on the glazed blue tile ledge where the water slopped in and was taken, through a series of ducts, to the purification unit, which hummed continuously in the background behind the pool house. She sat next to Jem and they both watched Steve swimming up and down the pool until it became almost hypnotic. William had taken to the airbed and was floating, eyes closed, in the corner of the deep end.

'Steve's a great swimmer, isn't he?' Jem said.

Rita nodded. 'I don't know where he gets it from. Neither Paul nor I excel at it.' She looked at Jem. 'Anyway, don't put yourself down, you're not such a bad sportsman yourself . . . What is it you're up for? School Sports Hero?'

Jem laughed, moving his arms off the ledge and sloshing water over his upper body to cool himself down. 'It's Sportsman of the Year and Steve has it won.' He nodded to himself, watching across the splintering blue water as Steve cut smoothly through another length of the pool. He had a look of pleasure on his face at Steve's technique.

'I think you underestimate your ability, Jem,' she chastised him gently.

'No, ma'am,' he smiled back to her. 'You saw him at our last swim meet . . . He was up that pool before the opposition were even off the starting blocks.'

Rita took his hand and dragged him away from the side. 'Come on, we'll show that son of mine a thing or two,' and with that they both proceeded to swim across the pool.

'Jem has been such a good influence on Steve,' Rita said later as they sat out in the evening sun waiting for the kids to finish playing on the computerized game machines. In the end they had taken two cars and driven to a McDonald's, where Rita, halving her cheeseburger between Steve and William, had crunched through a few french fries and a bit of lettuce. 'I sometimes wonder what we would have done without him around to steady Steve.' She remembered how, that afternoon, when Steve had been swimming up and down, up and down, in almost maniacal fervour, it had only taken a quiet word from Jem for him to quit. As it was, he was so exhausted that they almost had to drag him out of the water.

'Well, honey, I've always thought that Jem was a bit like a dog, you know . . . old faithful.'

Rita roared with laughter. 'Oh, but that's so cruel!'

'No, Jem's your faithful friend . . . he's always been

that way. He doesn't make friends that easily but once he does, boy, that's it. You've got a pal for life.' She smiled at Rita, taking her hand and squeezing it. 'And what about you? How are things?'

Rita told her about the morning session with Dr Allan and of meeting the beautiful youth in the restaurant.

'You did?' Sharon asked in surprise.

Rita nodded, feeling foolish now.

'What will you do if he should call?'

'Come on, Sharon, you know as well as I do that it's highly unlikely.'

'Why is it unlikely? You're a *very* attractive woman and some young men prefer their women more mature.'

'You said he was a hustler.'

'I suggested that he might be.'

Rita suddenly began to panic. 'God, what shall I do if he calls?'

Sharon laughed, throwing her head back so that the evening sunlight caught her hair and turned it golden. 'Well, now, then you have a problem . . . or not, as the case may be.'

'What would you do?'

'Me?'

'Help me, Sharon,' Rita insisted.

'Cross the bridge when you come to it . . . What do you want to do?'

'God knows.'

'And he's not about to tell you, honey. I'd look closer to home for the answers. If this kid calls you . . .' She shrugged. 'Then you can decide. After all, you don't have to see him.'

'Do you think it was stupid?'

'I'm amazed at your bravery . . . Now, think to yourself, would you have *dared* to do such a thing pre Dr Martin Allan?'

'I was angry with Dr Allan. By the time I got to lunch I could probably have done anything, I wasn't really thinking straight.'

'Or maybe you were,' Sharon replied.

'Oh, God, Sharon, that boy is so gorgeous . . . I'm forty-one years old and I have a crush on someone!'

'So, that's good, isn't it?'

Rita didn't know. She held on to Sharon's hand, appalled at her own lack of decorum. 'But I'm not sixteen.'

'What was it Mae West used to say, and she was even older than us? Ah yes. "A man in the house is worth two in the street!" Well, Rita, your logistics are a bit out on this one but you're getting there. Maybe we could change it to a man in the restaurant?'

'A *boy* in the restaurant,' Rita insisted.

'Whatever . . . Just relax. If he calls, arrange to meet him, invite him to the house for dinner. I'll chaperon you if you like . . .'

'You told me that this town was crawling with his like.'

'Yes, that may be true, but they're not all crawling up your driveway and, in any case, he did look a bit different from the rest . . . I mean, his clothes, for one thing, they were obviously expensive, don't you think?'

Rita nodded, clinging to straws.

'So, he probably is what he says he is,' Sharon concluded.

'Or a high-class male prostitute!'

'Rita,' Sharon warned.

Rita smiled and changed the subject. In a while their children began to drift away from the noisy machines. Piling into the cars, they drove back in convoy formation as the sun fell lower in the clear sky, casting its long, dark shadows.

* * *

83

The boys broke up from their school that Friday and Rita drove them to Malibu the next morning for a long weekend with Paul. He would bring them back on Monday afternoon, giving her an uninterrupted period for work on the book. Paul had to fly to Houston late on Monday afternoon and would have to come into LA in any case.

Paul looked terribly relaxed. He came out to meet them as Rita pulled up beside the silver Mercedes. Steve and William made straight for the beach, and Rita let them go as she considered the Pacific could work wonders on Steve's condition. She followed Paul through the cool beach house, on to the balcony which ran the length of the house and gave a fine view over the ocean. Wooden steps at one end led down to the beach.

The house had two large bedrooms, a kitchen/diner, a huge living area, two bathrooms and a small study. It had pine-clad ceilings and beautiful wooden floors which were varnished and gleamed. The house came with maid service, which meant Paul still had someone to pick up after him. It was, Rita had to concede, extremely attractive and comfortable.

Paul had been working out on the balcony. He had lost weight and was as attractive and healthy-looking as she had seen him in years. She commented upon this fact.

'I'm still jogging on the sands every morning,' he replied.

'That's good,' she nodded. They sat down and were silent for a while. Rita was watching Steve's progress as he ran into the water.

'I have an option to buy this place,' Paul said suddenly.

She looked at him, considering that he now had a boyish appearance. Perhaps she had been driving him into an early old age. 'Are you going to?'

'I'm very tempted,' he replied. '*Very* tempted.'

'Why don't you, then?' She realized, in saying this in such an offhand way, without really thinking, just how far they had drifted apart.

'I might,' he told her, still grinning.

Like the cat that's got the cream, Rita thought. Her mind was a mass of confused thoughts. He looked really well and really handsome, like an overgrown college freshman, in his running shorts and red sweat shirt. Rita felt that she was looking at Steve in about twenty years' time. They were so much alike.

'So, how are you, Rita?' he asked.

'All right. My work is going well, I'm getting quite a bit done . . .'

'Are you still seeing that doctor?'

She nodded.

'Is he helping you?'

'I think so, yes.'

'He has a good reputation,' Paul added.

'Have you been checking up on me?'

Paul shook his head and laughed. 'No, I was just finding out a little bit about him.'

'Protecting your investment, then.' She was deliberately trying to rile him and she didn't know why.

'Come on, Rita,' he said good-humouredly. 'I'll get us a drink.'

She followed him into the cool house, into the kitchen, where he took out some good Californian white wine and poured them each a glassful. Rita sat on one of the high kitchen stools at the teak breakfast bar, sipping her wine.

'Dr Allan says that we should talk about Nathan.' She stared into her wine. 'About Nathan's suicide.' Rita could feel Paul growing tense beside her and that, somehow, made her feel better. She looked into his face. '*I* have to talk about it,' she told him. It was almost a challenge.

'Keep your bleeding heart to your psychiatrist, Rita,

don't inflict it upon me . . . There's nothing more I want to say on that subject.'

'But you've never said anything.' She laughed in her utter amazement at his statement. 'You've never said a fucking word.'

'Don't start, Rita.'

'There has to be some reason for his death. If we take it step by step, we can find that reason.'

'I won't rake over the bones of our son like this.' Paul got up and walked out of the kitchen.

Rita followed him into the lounge, where he was standing at the wall-length windows, staring out towards the ocean and the boys. 'You have got to help me, Paul,' she pleaded now. 'I have to go over and over and over it in my head until I know, for sure, that it wasn't my fault . . .'

'Your fault?' He turned to her. 'What the hell are you talking about, how could it be your fault?'

'Because I was his mother.' She pointed at her chest. 'Because I should have known that something was wrong . . .'

'You couldn't possibly know a thing like that. For Jesus Christ's sake, Rita, we're just people, we're just not capable of knowing all the reasons why things happen . . .'

'We were his parents,' she replied. 'We damn well should have been aware, we should have known what was going on with our own son.'

Paul stared at her. 'I won't be drawn into this, you'll drive us both insane with it . . .' He went out through the windows and along the balcony, and ran down the steps on to the sand.

Rita followed, catching up with him just a few yards away from the bottom step. 'You can't keep running away

86

from it,' she told him, grabbing at the sleeve of his sweat shirt, attempting to stop his progress.

Paul suddenly wheeled round, turning to her. For a moment it seemed as though he would strike her but, instead, he placed his large hands on her shoulders, squeezing tightly. His voice was gruff and broke from time to time but his eyes remained dry and wild with his anger. 'Do you know what I thought when I found Nathan? Do you?' He shook her. Rita didn't answer him. 'I thought, God, boy, you look so beautifully peaceful, so absolutely perfect. When people die they're talked about as being at rest, and here was my son, and he was at rest . . . It suddenly occurred to me that here was someone who really just wanted to die, who had had enough and, perhaps, Nathan's decision to kill himself didn't have any other reason than that . . . he just wanted to be released.'

Rita had covered her mouth with her hands and was moaning in a low, grief-stricken voice, 'No, no, no,' repeating it over and over again.

'So, what is there to say, that we were lousy parents, that we pushed him too hard? Well, maybe that's right . . . Who knows? Why do you always want there to be a reason?' he demanded angrily.

'Because children don't kill themselves without there being one. There has to be something fundamentally wrong somewhere . . .'

'Why, because Rita says so? Because you're so laden down with your own guilt that you can't see there doesn't have to be a cause?'

'He was eighteen years old!' she yelled at him, making it sound for all the world like an accusation. 'I have to discover what went wrong.'

Paul broke away from her. 'That's enough,' he warned her, holding his hands spread out in front of him, symbolically pushing her away. 'Just go,' he said, his voice suddenly very calm.

87

'Paul, please talk to me about that day. I just want to go through everything . . .'

'You just want to destroy it all, Rita . . . Nathan's memory, your life . . . what about Steve and William?'

'Don't you think that they ask themselves the same questions?'

Paul stared at her. 'Steve and William are fine.'

'They're not "fine". . . none of us are bloody fine. Steve is grinding himself into the ground, trying to live up to Nathan's reputation, and William is still upset, still mourning . . .'

'You talk as though I've forgotten. I was the one who discovered Nathan.'

'Then why won't you help me?'

'Because it doesn't do any good to keep going over it time and time again.'

'But you never allow me to talk about him . . .'

'Rita, I can't spend the rest of my life thinking about Nathan's death. Every time you bring it up again, all you're doing is opening old wounds. We don't have to forget about him in order to move on.' He sighed. 'There are other things in life.'

'Don't you feel any guilt?' she asked, her voice a whisper.

'Of course I feel guilt. The difference between us is that I don't allow myself to wallow in it. I get on with my life.'

Rita felt as though she had been slapped in the face. 'You don't understand. You didn't at the time and you never will.' She started to walk towards the beach-house steps.

Paul stood for a while, staring blindly out to the ocean.

Steve and William had unpacked the Ford. They seemed to have brought enough with them for the entire holiday . . . two giant holdalls, a football, a beach-tennis kit, a portable television. It was all dumped in the sandy drive-way, then Rita reversed the car out and drove away. Paul went back to his work, leaving the boys to store their things away.

'Do you think Mum looked upset?' William asked as they carried their holdalls into the house and through to their bedroom.

Steve sat down on his bed. The room was cool and dim, with the curtains drawn against the heat of the sun. 'I expect they had words.' He winked at his brother. 'Nothing to worry about. Dad seems calm enough.'

'You can never tell with Dad.'

Steve grinned. 'Come on, let's have another swim before lunch.'

'I thought you were hung over.'

'Feeling better by the minute,' he said, standing and taking a deep breath. 'Better by the minute.'

'Are you coming swimming?' William asked his father as they walked out on to the balcony.

Paul declined. 'Later, perhaps. I'll finish this and then sort out something for lunch. I suppose you're both ravenous?'

William nodded, following Steve down the steps and on to the sands. They chased each other across the beach, diving headlong into the surf and swimming far out until they could tread water and view the beach house as just a speck in the distance. They swam for about twenty minutes before returning to the beach and sitting on the sand at the water's edge.

William was digging his hands into the wet sand, lifting his fingers out and watching the gooey mess drip off. 'Do you ever miss London?' he asked Steve.

'No, not really,' Steve replied. He had been lying on his back, allowing the water to roll up over him, but now he sat up. 'Why, do you?'

'Sometimes.'

'What do you miss?' Steve laughed. 'We never had anything like this in London.'

'Oh, I know,' William agreed. 'It's just that I miss it sometimes, the old house and Chalcot Square . . .' He smiled almost wistfully. 'We had some great times there, though, didn't we?'

'We have great times here,' Steve replied.

'But London was . . .'

'London was the past,' Steve insisted. 'This is where the future lies.'

'Don't you ever want to live there again?' William sounded a little shocked.

'No, why should I?'

'Oh.'

'Why, do you?'

William thought for a moment. 'I wouldn't mind.'

Steve lay back again, resting his head in his hands, closing his eyes against the sun, allowing the ocean to roll up over him. 'This is the place for me,' he said dreamily. 'I don't ever want to go back and live in London.'

'Do you think Dad will stay here for ever?' William asked.

'I don't know,' Steve yawned. 'Why would he move, unless someone offered him a better post, more money and prestige?'

'What about Mum?'

'I don't know,' Steve replied. 'Why would she want to go back? Isn't her life here as well?'

'I guess so.' But he didn't sound too sure. 'What if they should divorce?'

'They won't divorce,' Steve said reassuringly. 'Why should they?'

'Well, they don't seem to be getting back together.'

Steve got up suddenly. 'Come on, Dad will be getting

lunch . . . I'll race you back.' He sprinted off across the sand.

William watched his brother and, getting up slowly, wandered towards the beach house across the hot sands.

In the evening Paul took the boys out for a meal, finding a restaurant a little way down the coast where they all tucked into thick steaks.

The boys talked about school and their various sporting activities. Paul had been unable to come to Steve's last 'swim meet' and was anxious to know the results and timings. He told them about work and a little of his latest project. Paul was extremely busy and had what he referred to as an 'asthma symposium' in Houston the following week. Eventually, however, the conversation gradually ceased, Paul running out of suitable ideas, and they lapsed into silence.

Paul was still feeling annoyed with Rita for her outburst that morning. He was concerned that her attitude towards him was almost entirely hostile and negative, although he was aware that his own behaviour since Nathan's death had not done much to help matters between them. Paul was a firm believer in the old maxim about time being its own healer, and he had hoped that Rita might have become less affected by Nathan's suicide as time went on. She was still searching for the same answers and solutions as she had been two years ago. As far as he was concerned, there was no ready answer and there never had been. He didn't think there necessarily *had* to be but Rita's outburst had, as usual, made him feel unsettled.

He knew that his feelings towards her had changed irreversibly. In truth, he felt very little. Nathan's death had opened up a yawning gap between them. They had been together for over twenty years by that time and their lives had become very separate. They shared the same bed, the children bound them together and, as far as most marriages went, theirs had been a good one, he supposed. He had never felt the need for anyone other than her, he had been sure that he loved her and that Rita loved him. There still wasn't anyone.

Paul hated to admit it even to himself but Nathan's death had reduced him to a man who knew nothing other than work. Of course, he had always found his job very demanding and also very stimulating but now it was everything. Through work he was able to push everything else to the back of his mind. Moving to the beach had made things easier too. The tension between him and Rita was much reduced and the boys were only there at week-ends, which made the pain seem less.

Paul suddenly saw Nathan. He remembered picking up the wrist and feeling for a pulse, but knowing by the cold skin that his son was dead. Nathan had been lying on his side, one arm draped over the edge of the bed. It was his usual sleeping position and for a second Paul had thought that everything was all right, but he was used to death, he could smell it and sense it. He had pushed Nathan over on to his back and checked for any signs of life . . . It had been a sweltering afternoon and the room was uncomfortably warm, a bluebottle buzzing and batting itself against the closed window. He had picked up the pill bottle from the floor and, almost in a detached, professional manner, taken note of the name and dosage before sitting for a moment, looking at Nathan. There had been absolute peace on his face, even the hint of a smile. The minutes had ticked by. He'd known he would have to make the statutory telephone calls. Rita and the boys would be home soon. But still he had sat. He'd had no sense of time, it could have been minutes or hours, but eventually he had moved and gone into his bedroom, where he'd phoned for an ambulance and, soon afterwards, all hell had broken loose.

'Dad,' William said, attracting Paul's attention. 'Dad.'

Paul looked up to find the waitress standing at their table, pencil poised.

'I'll have a banana split,' Steve announced, smiling across the table at the pretty woman.

'Just coffee,' Paul said. 'What about you, son?' he asked William.

'Apple pie.'

The waitress nodded and gathered up the plates. Paul asked them what they wanted to do in the morning but they seemed undecided, even a little fed-up. They finished the meal in silence and were back at the beach house a little after ten.

William went straight to bed, planning to watch a film on the portable television he had brought. Steve sat with Paul in the lounge. The glass doors to the balcony were open and they could hear the Pacific breakers rolling in across the dark beach.

'So,' Paul began, putting down a paper he had been reading, 'what are you planning to do over the summer?'

Steve shrugged. 'I hadn't really thought.'

'What's Jem doing?'

'He doesn't know yet . . . His folks are going to Hawaii.'

'Yes,' Paul nodded, 'Bill told me.'

'I don't suppose that you and Mum have planned to go anywhere?'

Paul was a bit taken aback by Steve's question. It was the furthest thing from their minds, he hadn't even given it a thought. 'No.' Paul shook his head slowly. There was another long silence. 'Perhaps you and Jem could do something together,' he suggested. 'You could always use this place,' he said brightly.

'I don't think Mum would like that idea very much,' Steve said, remembering his discussion with Rita about that very possibility.

'No?'

'No.'

'Oh.' Paul didn't ask why. He could imagine all the reasons but, all the same, he felt that Rita could give the boys a bit more leeway.

'Dad?' Steve began.

'Yes, what?'

'Why did you move down here?'

Paul thought about that for a moment. 'I'm sure your mother explained that to you.'

'She said that you needed time to think. She didn't say what about, though.' He looked down at the floor. 'She said you needed a rest too.'

Paul didn't reply. He felt uneasy and didn't particularly want to discuss this topic now, or ever.

When he realized that his father wasn't going to answer him, Steve pressed on regardless. 'At first we thought you'd left because of us, William and me, but you see us every week-end, so maybe it's something else . . .' He paused. 'Nothing has been the same since Nathan died, has it?' Steve added.

Paul shifted uncomfortably in his seat. 'It has obviously changed us all,' he said.

'You never talk about him, do you?' Steve said.

Paul made no response.

'I don't even remember you using his name . . .'

'Is this leading somewhere?' Paul asked defensively.

'We've been walking on eggshells around you for the last two years . . . not mentioning Nathan, not talking

94

about him . . . Can't you see that it only makes things worse?'

'Your brother is dead, Steve. Why can't we just leave it alone? Why does everyone think it necessary to keep dragging up the past?'

'Because talking about things can help.'

'It won't help me,' Paul insisted. 'How can it help? Will it bring Nathan back to us?' he asked bluntly.

'Do you know *why* he did it, Dad?'

Paul started to get annoyed. He sat and watched and listened to Steve and realized that he was no longer a child but physically big now, and mature. He heard Steve's Californian accent and understood how much of a stranger to him Steve had become. It made him feel anxious and terribly discouraged. At last he stood up and walked to the window, stepping out on to the balcony, 'I'm sorry, Steve, but I don't want to talk about this right now.'

'Why can't you be more open and honest with us?' Steve asked, following his father out. 'If we knew what was happening it wouldn't be so bad.'

'Nothing is happening,' Paul insisted.

Steve gave an incredulous laugh. 'So, why are you and Mum not living in the same house any more?'

'There are reasons why people no longer go on living together,' Paul replied quietly.

'Yes?'

'And I'm not about to discuss them with you now, is that clear?'

Steve shrugged and dug his hands into the back pockets of his jeans. 'Well, someone had better discuss something with somebody around this family soon, that's all I can say.'

'You can't possibly understand. Jesus, you're seventeen

95

years old, you don't know what goes on inside relationships.'

'I've heard you and Mum shouting at one another enough times to know that something is wrong . . . That never happened before Nathan died.'

Steve felt disgusted and went back inside. He wanted to leave then and there but knew they were stuck until Monday. He heard his father clattering down the wooden steps to the beach, and he walked across the shining floors to his room, where William was fast asleep. The television was still on, a noisy war film was at the height of a bloody battle as Steve turned it off.

Steve felt rejected. He was confused by his father's attitude, his lack of understanding, his inability to communicate at a basic level. Undressing quickly, he lay back in the darkness, listening to the ebb and flow of the tide. William murmured something unintelligible as he turned over in his sleep. Steve suddenly felt angry with Nathan for causing so much grief and unhappiness, so much confusion inside the family.

Rita had a late lunch with Sharon. She had driven back from the beach like a lunatic, furious with Paul and annoyed at becoming upset. Sharon listened sympathetically as Rita unburdened herself.

'He's an absolute bastard,' Rita said through a mouthful of tomato.

'He was probably upset,' Sharon said.

'Don't make excuses for him, he's behaving like a stupid child . . . Can I wonder that the boys act the way they do with him as a father?'

'Your kids are fine,' Sharon insisted firmly.

'He won't *talk* to me . . . It's as if there's a wall between us, or we're not talking the same language . . . It's absolutely pathetic.'

'Have you tried seeing it from Paul's perspective?'

'He behaves as though none of us were touched by Nathan's death but him,' Rita carried on without listening, 'and he has no intention of coming back.' She stared at Sharon.

'You don't exactly sound as though you would want him to at the moment!'

'He's planning to buy that bloody beach house . . . Well, let him. What do I care!'

'Honey, if you know it's going to begin a row, why do you always insist upon talking to Paul about Nathan?'

Rita looked surprised. 'Because unless we can deal with this together and finally sort it out, I might as well kiss twenty . . .' She paused. 'Twenty-three years together goodbye!'

'Are you serious?' Sharon took a drink of wine. 'Are you sure it's that bad?'

'It's that bloody awful,' Rita nodded. 'Why can't he act like a reasonable human being?'

'You're opening up old wounds.'

'These wounds are still raw and bleeding,' Rita sighed. 'I can't ever see an end to it. We're like headless chickens running around the farmyard . . . directionless and out of control.'

'Maybe he just needs a *lot* of time,' Sharon replied. 'Even two years may not be enough.'

'He just wants to wallow about in his own bitterness and grief . . .' She looked at Sharon. 'Do you know, I think it's become a way of life with him. Perhaps he even enjoys it!'

'That's a bit unfair,' Sharon said.

'Is it? God knows, I've given him the benefit of the doubt enough times but I think he just needs to feel horrible all of the time . . . Maybe it's the only way he can justify his present life.'

97

Sharon looked unconvinced. 'Discovering a dead child must be one of the worst things imaginable . . .'

'I know, I know, I know,' Rita replied wearily. 'But Paul isn't doing a thing to help himself . . . He thinks that working twenty-four hours a day is enough.'

'It seems to me that you can't help any more.'

'I've given up,' Rita announced. 'I mean, what's the bloody point? It could take another lifetime to unravel everything that's happened to us since Nathan's suicide . . . You go along beautifully for twenty years, I'm not saying our marriage was always blissful exactly but it was solid enough, strong enough, anyway, to cope with most things . . .' She stopped and looked away. 'I suppose that's it, really, you just never expect your children to die, it's just not an assumption that one makes . . . You expect them to bury you!'

Sharon nodded but said nothing.

'Well,' Rita said, smiling suddenly, a little too forced, a bit too brightly, 'I'd better take a piece of my own advice and, pressing on regardless, spend this week-end working on the book.'

'Does that mean you're putting out the "Do Not Disturb" signs?' Sharon asked her.

'Good God no.' She sat back for a moment. 'I'll call you later, if that's all right.'

'Sure.'

Rita got up to leave. 'Thanks for lunch.' She reached across the table and squeezed Sharon's hand. 'See you later,' she said.

'Don't overdo it,' Sharon called after her.

Rita smiled. 'I'll probably spend the afternoon sun-bathing . . . you know me!'

Sharon laughed, watching her go.

* * *

Rita was sitting by the pool, her books and papers spread out in front of her. Now she was engrossed in the project, suddenly it all seemed so much clearer, the research notes she had made in London, the photo-copies of the articles, the pile of Woolf's books . . . everything seemed to be coming together. She closed her eyes and considered some words she had just read and then scribbled some more notes into the margin of her typescript. She had written the introduction several times but was still not entirely happy about it. She was in the middle of another attempt to find an opening paragraph she was satisfied with when she looked up and saw him walking down across the grass from the house.

'I tried at the house . . . several times . . . there wasn't any reply,' he began, standing facing Rita on the opposite side of the pool.

Rita put down her pen and, bending from under the large sunshade, emerged into the hot sunshine. 'Hello,' she grinned. 'Come and sit down.'

'Okay,' he smiled.

She noticed that he was wearing the black 501s, the same sports shirt, and was carrying the Armani jacket, which was slung over his shoulder. 'You look hot,' she said as he approached.

'Hi,' he laughed, sitting down on a sun lounger. 'I hope you don't mind . . . I just decided to come on the off chance.'

Rita shook her head and sat down opposite him on the other lounger so that their knees were almost touching.

'Am I disturbing you?' he asked, looking beyond her to the cluttered table.

'No,' she replied without explanation. 'I was about to finish for the day.'

He turned his attention to her. Because they were sitting so low, his knees were raised high and he rested his elbows on them. His hands, made into loose fists, were placed on either side of his temple. 'Well, I didn't get the soap and . . .' He looked serious. 'I leave on Monday morning.'

'I'm sorry about the show,' Rita said.

Marc grinned. 'That's show business and, as you know, there's no business quite like it!'

She laughed. 'You're taking it very well, anyway.'

He turned his head towards the pool. 'I'm up for a part in New York on Thursday . . . What the hell, eh?'

'Did they say why you didn't get it?'

'No screen credits . . .' He shrugged. 'No experience, too young . . . too old, too pretty, too ugly . . . You can take your choice!'

'You tried,' Rita encouraged. 'That's the main thing.'

He nodded. 'This is a beautiful place.'

'Yes, it is,' she agreed. 'Would you like to swim?'

'Sure, but I'm not exactly dressed for it.'

Rita pointed behind her in the direction of the pool house. 'You'll find something in there to fit, if you like.'

Marc smiled.

She was already in the water when he emerged wearing a pair of Steve's Speedo trunks. They were navy blue with red and white stripes slashed across one side. He was bigger than Steve, with strong, broad shoulders, slim waist and sturdy legs. He had black hair on his breast bone and on his legs but the remainder of his body was brown and smooth. He dived into the pool, surfacing close to Rita.

'Okay?' she asked.

He spluttered and laughed. 'This is a great pool.'

Rita laughed too. 'Well, be my guest. I'll do a couple of lengths and then get us something to drink.'

Marc swam away from her, breaking into a crawl and

moving swiftly and expertly through the water. She watched the twisting shadows and reflections underneath her and then the sheen of Marc's skin as he cut through the blueness, the parts of his body broken up in the splash and roll and wave as he turned and headed back towards her.

'I've left you a towel,' she called from the side.

He swam to her, looking up, squinting through the sunlight. 'You didn't stay in for very long.'

'That's okay . . . I never do.' She pulled a baggy T-shirt over her damp costume.

Rita left him floating on top of William's airbed and walked over the grass to the house, where she made herself tea, taking a bottle of Coke and a bottle of beer out of the refrigerator and carting it all back to the pool.

Marc was standing under the fresh-water shower when she arrived, the fine spray catching the sunlight like diamonds. He was reaching up, eyes tightly shut, hands slicking back wet hair.

Rita threw him the fresh towel as he tracked across to her. He chose the Coke and lay out in the hot afternoon sun whilst she remained under the shade at the table. They chatted amiably for a while about nothing in particular.

'You live here alone?' he asked at last.

'Yes,' Rita nodded. She knew that it was part of the game.

'It's just that I couldn't help noticing your wedding ring.'

'Oh, that.' She looked at it for a moment. 'I'm separated.' It seemed ridiculous to lie. What difference could it possibly make to him whether she was married, divorced, widowed?

Marc stretched and, turning his head, grinned at her. It was an exceptionally appealing little grin. The shadows grew longer as the sun moved round, and the afternoon

101

became still and sultry. In a while they swam again and afterwards sat on the edge of the pool, continuing their discourse, a flow of conversation that moved easily between them. He was laughing at something Rita had told him about her childhood, and then she asked if he would like to stay for dinner. Marc reached down and splashed water over his legs. 'You don't have to go to all that trouble, really.'

'It's no trouble,' she assured him. 'I'd like it if you would.'

He nodded. 'Okay, I'd like that, thanks.'

She had a sudden, desperate desire to touch him. She still had a distinct feeling of unreality about the whole afternoon and he was almost too good to be true. He was perfectly affable and easy to get along with, even courteous.

The phone in the pool house rang and Rita got up and went in to answer it. A girl was calling for Steve and Rita quickly explained that he wouldn't be back until Monday afternoon. She replaced the receiver and turned to find Marc standing at the doorway. The light seemed almost white behind him, the glare from the water was almost painful and his outline was crisply defined and framed where he stood.

'Who's Steve?' he asked, laughter in his voice.

'You're wearing his costume,' Rita replied. The pool house felt stifling and oppressive. The louvred window shutters cast irregular shadows across the floor and walls. It was quite dim inside but as her eyes became more used to the light she could see where his clothes were draped casually over a chair.

Marc closed the door behind him and stepped towards her. She could sense the heat from his body just before he kissed her, sliding his arms around her and drawing her gently towards him.

Marc pushed her swimming costume slowly down,

peeling it from her smooth, brown skin. She leant into him, feeling the touch of his fingers against her naked body. Marc took her into his arms and they kissed for the first time, Rita experiencing a mixture of emotions before finally being swept along on a torrent of pent-up desires which made her feel as though she were burning up. Looking up into Marc's eyes she smiled, touching a hand to his face before leading him across to the springy, creaking little day bed which sat in the corner of the pool house.

Rita sat down on the faded floral cover, waiting as he fiddled with the drawstring of his borrowed trunks which had caught into a tight knot. There was silence between them, just their breathing and the background hum of the pool's filter plant. She was impatient for him now, wet with desire and anticipation. Her heart thumped hard in her chest. Eventually Marc undid the knot and released himself from the tight, constraining material, dropping the trunks and kicking them away into the half-light as he approached the bed, smiling at Rita as he climbed on to it.

For a brief moment Rita could hear Sharon's voice whispering inside her head, 'Cradle-snatcher, cradle-snatcher.' She no longer cared, though, turning into him, kissing him, reaching down and cupping his tightening balls in her hand, feeling the length of his hard penis. His hands caressed her body as she continued to explore him. Rita breathed in the musky, damp scent and tasted him, warm and salty.

In a little while Marc moved down on her, arousing her to new heights, his tongue lapping against her clitoris as she pressed her thighs tightly around him, feeling the sharp prickles of his beard. She wanted him now with a greater urgency, moaning as she writhed up in ecstasy, overwhelmed and excited beyond belief. Nothing else mattered to her; everything, her whole existence, was concentrated upon this one act, and she was lost to this young man.

Finally Marc rose up, sliding himself into Rita, the tigering shadows from the louvred window moving over their writhing bodies, forming a pattern of primitive desire. The tiny, hot room was full of their smell and their sound. Rita suddenly climaxed and Marc, calling out, thrusting into her with greater urgency, achieved his own orgasm and soon they were apart once more, lying side by side for a moment before holding one another in a sleepy embrace.

'Okay?' he asked after a long silence.

Rita smiled, running her hand over his chest, kissing his soft lips gently. 'This is so strange,' she admitted.

'I'm strange?' he asked with mock surprise.

Rita shook her head. 'No, this, the situation.'

'For me as well,' Marc admitted.

'Oh, no, you're young.'

He laughed at that. 'I don't make a habit of this kind of thing.'

'I didn't mean that . . . But youth is a time full of opportunities and experiences.'

'Screwing around, I think is what you mean.'

Rita looked into his eyes and then broke apart from him, lying on her back and staring up at the dirty white ceiling. 'Having different relationships, that's what I mean.'

'I thought you had to either be married these days or, at least, into monogamy or celibacy.'

Rita grinned but didn't reply.

'Anyhow,' he continued, 'I don't have the time for relationships.'

'So, what does that mean?' she asked him.

'It means that I don't screw around.' He turned to her. 'You don't believe me?' There was laughter in his voice.

'Listen, you're absolutely gorgeous . . . Of course I don't believe you.'

He raised himself up on one elbow, looking at her, 'You're not so bad yourself.' He bent to kiss her. 'What about you?'

Rita shook her head. 'You've just broken my duck.'

Marc looked totally confused. 'Pardon me?'

She laughed. 'You're the first in a long, long time.'

'Then,' he said, smiling, 'maybe we'd better make up for lost time.'

Rita woke up with a start. At first she thought the arm around her was Paul's but, understanding that it couldn't possibly be, she searched through the fog of her sleepy memory and then remembered. She looked up at her bedside clock. It was just past nine-thirty and, very gingerly, she eased out from underneath Marc's arm and crept into the bathroom, where she examined her morning face. Turning away quickly, she switched on the water in the shower stall and waited for the steam to rise, sitting on the edge of the bath. She wasn't sure whether she had the stamina for this kind of excitement.

They'd never eaten the dinner she'd promised, she hadn't even reached the kitchen. Instead Rita sent out for pizzas, aware that the delivery boy was seeing a rather dishevelled-looking woman who had obviously thrown her clothes on with express speed. He gave her a knowing look, smiled broadly, and wished her a pleasant evening. He might just as well have added, 'If you know what I mean!'

They ate the pizza out of boxes in her bed. Rita grabbed some milk and a packet of cookies on her way up. The junk food giving them the energy to continue, she was able to mount him in a fashion that Paul would never have approved. It was a great success, as Rita controlled events, lowering herself on to Marc's erection and climaxing very quickly afterwards. She remembered hearing someone almost scream out loud and realized that it was her. Marc juddered to yet another orgasm, shaking his head from side to side on the pillow as he came inside her.

Later, they showered together, and she had taken great pleasure in soaping down his body and, as the steam billowed, Marc had grabbed her and, in danger of crashing through the glass cubicle, fucked her again, both of them collapsing in a tangled heap under the powerful shower jet . . .

Now she stepped under the shower again, washing carefully, and afterwards, when her skin was pink and glowing and her wet hair combed back, she took stock of herself and thanked God for this kind interlude.

Marc met her in the kitchen. He was wet from the shower and had a bath sheet wrapped around him like a Roman senator. He paused for a moment at the door and, with a dramatic flourish, entered quoting Shakespeare, '"Friends, Romans, countrymen, lend me your ears; / I come to bury Caesar, not to praise him. / The evil that men do lives after them; / The good is oft interred with their bones; / So let it be with Caesar."' He had performed this in a very passable English accent.

Rita beamed across the large kitchen at him. 'Have you done any Shakespeare?' she enquired.

'Sure.' He walked across to her and kissed her, putting his arms around her.

'Where?'

'LA.'

'Where in LA?' She sounded sceptical.

'In your kitchen!'

'Idiot,' she said, hugging him. 'You sounded pretty good.'

'Only pretty good?'

Rita shrugged, breaking away from him. 'Have you ever done any?'

Marc nodded. 'But only in acting class . . . No one would ever take me seriously enough for those kind of roles.'

'Why?' Rita asked, genuinely surprised.

'For the same reasons as you had when you first met me.'

'And what are those?' She had stopped preparing breakfast and was standing holding a spatula in her hand.

'Don't point that thing at me,' he warned. 'It might go off!'

'Tell me,' Rita said more sharply, 'what are the reasons?'

'Oh, 'cause I'm too pretty – pretty . . . I know it sounds like I'm an egomaniac or something but, in my world, your face can be your fortune and it can also be your downfall . . . If the face fits . . .' he smiled, dismissing the conversation. 'Nuts, eh?'

She grinned. 'I wouldn't get depressed about having a beautiful face!'

Marc blushed. 'Jesus, Rita . . . come on.'

'No, I'm serious. How can you regard your looks as a misfortune? You're bloody lucky.'

'Okay, okay.' He raised his hands. 'I know.' He sat down at the table, playing with a coffee cup. 'I know.'

They ate breakfast on the terrace. He was ravenous, devouring a large cooked breakfast and a pile of toast. Rita sat nibbling a slice whilst she watched him. Marc had borrowed a pair of Steve's shorts and she was admiring the play of muscles in his shoulders as he attacked the food.

'Are you looking forward to going home?' Rita asked.

He nodded. 'Sure. I mean, this is great . . . blue sky, sunshine, swimming pools, but don't you ever get bored with it?'

Rita smiled. 'I think you get used to it.'

'I like contrast. You get plenty of that in New York, boiling summers and sub-zero winters. Maybe it's nice for you because you're English.'

'What's that supposed to mean?' Rita laughed.

'I thought the weather in England was supposed to be unpredictable.'

Only she, Rita considered, could end up talking about the weather with the most fabulously attractive man she had met in years!

Marc left around midday. It was a rather formal parting, in the circumstances, just a chaste kiss on the cheek and she was watching him leave. Rita cleaned up her room, finding Steve's wet swimming trunks under the bed. Marc had folded the borrowed shorts carefully and left them on a chair. An hour later she was sitting working under the palm trees at the redwood table and his visit seemed almost like a dream. In a few hours he would be on a flight to New York. In a day he would have settled into his apartment in Greenwich Village. She would already be a distant memory and, within a short while, forgotten about completely. Perhaps she should have asked him for a photograph but what would she have done with it?

Rita paused for a moment, looking out across the valley. There was a layer of smog which obscured the foothills in the far distance and she looked beneath it at the white valley houses and imagined the families around their Sunday barbecues and in their pools. She worked all through the afternoon and went over to Sharon's house in the evening for dinner.

'Where is everyone?' Rita asked.

'They're all out,' Bill replied, handing her a very strong gin and tonic, 'except Jem, who is working this vacation in order to buy himself a car and is pooped out.'

'What's he doing?' Rita asked, sipping her lethal drink.

'He's working on the check-out at Ryan's Groceteria and Delicatessen,' Bill replied.

'Jem's a good lad.'

'It was his idea too.' Bill sounded pleased. 'We offered to buy him a car but he wanted to do something for himself, I guess.'

'My kids have everything handed to them on a plate.'

Bill sat down beside her on their comfortable sofa. 'They're all the same, Rita,' he assured her. 'Gimme, gimme, gimme!'

'Except Jem.'

Bill laughed. 'And how are you? Lonely in that big house with your boys away?'

She shook her head, feeling slightly embarrassed. 'No, not really . . . I'm fully occupied with the book, as you can imagine.'

'I saw Paul over lunch in the week,' Bill said.

'Oh yes, how did he seem to you?' Rita enquired.

'Okay. I was trying to pin him down to a date for golf but we were unable to arrange anything.'

'I think he's very busy. Paul has the boys for week-ends but, by all accounts, he works for most of the time.'

Bill nodded. 'A real high-flyer.'

Sharon came into the lounge. 'Who is?' she asked, pouring herself a drink.

'My husband,' Rita replied.

'Oh.' Sharon sat down opposite them. 'Manage to get a lot done this week-end?' she asked Rita.

Rita frowned. 'Quite a bit.'

'Good.' Sharon smiled brightly. 'You're certainly looking very well on it, isn't she, Bill?'

'Do we get a copy when it's published?' he asked.

'I'm not sure you'll want one. It's not exactly for mainstream consumption . . .'

'Don't listen to her, Bill, she's just being coy. It'll probably become a best-seller!'

Rita laughed. 'The life and works of Virginia Woolf?'

'Dinner will be five minutes,' Sharon announced. 'Bill, be an absolute darling and find out if Jem wants feeding.'

'I bet he's fast asleep,' Bill said, getting up and wandering out of the room.

Rita turned to Sharon and quickly told her about the events of her week-end. Sharon found it all highly amusing and by the time Bill returned with Jem the two women were giggling and cackling together on the sofa.

'Your mother and Rita have been hitting the booze again, son,' he said to Jem.

After the meal Rita stood by as Sharon loaded the dishwasher and made coffee.

'Will you see him again?' Sharon asked.

'What do you think?' Rita said.

'I think it sounds rather romantic.'

'Hardly that,' Rita assured her friend.

'Oh, well, as long as you enjoyed your divertissement,' Sharon said, sitting down as she waited for the coffee to percolate.

Rita had taken the cups and saucers from their cupboard and was placing them on a large tray. 'I can't help thinking that it was all a little bit unbecoming.'

Sharon laughed at that. 'Unbecoming? You sound like a Victorian matron.'

'Debauched and dissolute, that's me . . . It's the last time I indulge myself in that way.'

'Are you to take holy orders?'

'I might as well.'

'For God's sake,' Sharon complained, 'why feel guilty over a tiny little fling? It doesn't make any sense.'

'*I* don't make any sense,' she insisted.

'You make lots of sense, I just think you're afraid to let go, to enjoy yourself.'

Rita concentrated on that idea for a moment. 'You're probably right, but what am I supposed to do now? Take a succession of young men to bed with me?'

'If that's what you want to do, why not?' Sharon replied forcibly.

'I don't want,' Rita told her. 'It's the last thing I desire.'

'Okay, so what are you planning to do?'

Rita shrugged. 'I have my book, the kids and the summer holidays to get through before I think about anything else.'

'In another year Steve will probably be away at university, unless he stays in Westwood and joins his father at UCLA.'

'So, William still has high school to complete.' She knew what Sharon was about to say and was feeling defensive.

'Rita, come on now, don't be so obtuse. What's going to happen when the kids have gone? You really do have to plan ahead.'

'You mean, like divorcing Paul?'

'Not necessarily.'

'Then what?' Rita asked pointedly.

'You and Paul have to sort things out,' Sharon replied simply.

Rita sighed. 'What do you think I've been trying to do?'

'Have you discussed what is going to happen about your marriage?'

'Paul refuses to "discuss" anything, it's like trying to squeeze blood out of the proverbial stone getting him to be rational about anything . . . You know that.'

'What if he finds someone else?'

'Has he then?' Rita asked, feeling suddenly very interested.

'I don't know,' Sharon insisted.

'Have you heard something?'

'No.' She stood up to pour the coffee. 'Don't look at me like that, I haven't heard a thing.' She picked up the tray. 'Really.'

'Why should I care?' Rita asked, holding the kitchen door open.

'Why indeed?' Sharon grinned, passing by and clattering along the hallway.

'We're going to the beach in the morning. Why not come along for the ride?' Sharon asked at the door as she left. Jem had been instructed to walk Rita down the canyon road. She had protested that she would be quite safe but they had insisted.

Rita laughed. 'Which beach? There are about forty miles of them!'

'Listen, we're Angelenos and to us they're all "the beach",' Bill remarked, laughing.

'It will be Santa Monica or Venice . . . Those who condescend to accompany us will make the final choice,' Sharon told them.

'I can't . . . Paul's bringing the boys back in the afternoon.'

'You could call them,' Sharon suggested, encouraging Rita to come.

'But they've just spent the week-end at Malibu.'

112

'What's Malibu compared to Santa Monica or Venice?' Sharon coaxed.

'What time?' she asked, looking towards Jem, who was waiting patiently at the bottom of the steps for her.

'I'll call you first thing,' Sharon told her.

'Okay.'

'They like Venice. I remember when we took them a year ago,' Bill said.

'Yes, but they were not so blasé about their new home in those days.' She left it at that, putting her arm over Jem's shoulder, waving good-night to them, and walking down their illuminated driveway with its modern, knee-high lamps every few yards. The canyon road, she had to admit, was very dark and unfriendly.

'Are you all right, Jem? You've been quiet all evening.'

'I'm exhausted from my labours,' he replied, laughing as they walked along.

'It'll be worth it,' she encouraged.

'Did you work in vacations when you were a student?' Jem asked.

Rita smiled to herself. 'Yes, I did. Every summer holiday I worked in the kitchens of a local hospital.'

'You were a cook?'

'Good God, no, I was a washer-up.' She almost shuddered at the memory. 'Deep metal sinks, like baths, full of greasy water . . . It was revolting and I can honestly say that I hated every minute.'

'Why did you do it, then?' Jem asked in all innocence.

'Because we were poverty-stricken.'

'Really?'

'Really.'

'Oh.' Jem was silent for a while until they turned into Rita's drive. 'I never knew that.' He sounded serious.

'It was a long time ago,' Rita said brightly, 'and times

113

change.' They had reached the house, where the hall lights were blazing.

'Do you want me to come in . . . just to make sure?'

'No,' she assured him, 'that's fine, Jem. Thank you very much, you're a gentleman.' She kissed him on the cheek.

Jem blushed. 'That's okay . . . Will you tell Steve I'll probably call round tomorrow after work?'

Rita said that she would. 'Thanks again,' she smiled, watching him saunter away and, turning, went inside. She was careful to check the locks before going upstairs to bed. The house was silent and echoed as she walked its hallways and corridors.

She lay in bed, picking up the best-selling tome she had started weeks ago, flicking over the pages until she reached the part where she had last left it. The heroine was about to be ravished in a suite at the Beverly Hills Hotel after picking up a handsome youth in the Polo Lounge. It always seemed much better when you read about it than when you actually did it, Rita decided, as the lurid, descriptive passages of sexual encounter passed before her eyes. Was her life now imitating this particular 'art' form, she wondered, putting the book down after a while and switching off the bedside light. She was considering whether or not to spend the next day at the beach when sleep finally caught up with her.

Rita rang Paul's number early the following morning. He had just come up from the sands after an extra-long jog and was out of breath as he grabbed the receiver. She explained she planned to go with Sharon and Bill to the beach and would leave instructions for the boys, should they wish to follow on. The conversation was short and to the point but she sounded terribly bright and seemed to have forgotten about their argument.

Paul put down the phone and roused the boys. They

had to clear away their things and pack up. As usual, the beach house looked as though a bomb had hit it. The lounge was strewn with papers and magazines, there were cassette tapes and articles of clothing all over the place. A Walkman was hung over the back of a chair, an expensive camera was lying carelessly on the floor. There were Coca-Cola cans and sandy training shoes left where they had been dropped.

The week-end had deteriorated into empty, sullen moments, silences and confusion. Paul had lost himself in work and the boys had surfed and watched the surfers, fooled around on the beach, plugged themselves into the isolation of personal stereos, eaten vast quantities of junk food whilst watching TV or reading pop magazines. He had offered to take them to Malibu pier for a spot of fishing on Sunday morning but they'd been disinclined to do that, and so the hours had dragged on.

Now Paul was relieved that they would soon be back in the capable hands of their mother. He loved them intensely but, at times, couldn't stand having them around. William appeared to be withdrawn and in a big sulk, whilst Steve was icily polite.

He had listened to them on the beach below as he'd sat out on the balcony, preparing for the Houston trip. At times he could hardly believe they were the same boys, their accents and whole bearing having altered so radically in the past two years. This change had been metamorphic, from London public-school boys to typical middle-class Californian adolescents. Paul was never entirely sure if this was a good thing or not, but it was, obviously, too late to do anything about it now.

Steve was first out of bed and slopped through into the kitchen, where he poured himself a glass of orange juice, taking it out to the balcony and sitting at the table in the bright morning sunshine. A cooling sea breeze moved the large beach towels they had hung out to dry on the balcony rail.

'Your mother just rang,' Paul told him, stepping out, still in his jogging shorts. He explained what Rita had told him.

Steve shrugged. 'I don't know . . . I might.'

Paul looked at his son for a long moment. 'I want to leave here by mid-morning,' he warned. 'Will you get yourselves organized after breakfast?'

Steve nodded.

Paul went to his room. William was taking a shower, the TV was on in his room and the radio was blaring in the kitchen. Paul sat down heavily on his bed, cradling his head in his hands for a moment.

Rita and Sharon were watching the weightlifters in the warm morning sunshine at Venice beach. Bill had been called away at the last minute, an emergency at the hospital, and only Thomas, Sharon's youngest, had wanted to come along. He was thirteen and, like the rest of his siblings, blond and tanned. He came up to them with a jumbo-sized carton of Coke full of crushed ice, which he was slurping through a plastic bendy straw.

'Don't you ever stop seeking oral satisfaction?' Sharon said, turning away from the pumping muscles.

Thomas grinned in mid-slurp, sitting down beside them on the bench. 'Can I rent some roller skates?' he asked his mother.

'We've only been here an hour and you've already virtually cleaned me out!' Sharon complained.

'Come on, Ma,' he complained. 'Don't be so pinchfisted.'

'Me?' Sharon asked with false shock and horror. 'Listen, why can't you go and play on the beach like all the other kids?'

'All the other kids are on roller skates 'cause their moms aren't mean to them!'

Sharon seemed to be thinking about that for a moment. 'Okay, where do you hire these things from?'

Thomas pointed along the beach-front to a row of shops. 'Come on, Ma,' he encouraged, making horrible sucking noises with his straw as the Coke ran out.

'Right,' Sharon decided with determination, 'we'll all go for it.'

'What?' Rita asked, suddenly realizing what was in prospect for her. 'You're joking.'

'Come on,' Sharon said, taking her hand and pulling her up. 'He's thirteen years old, what does he know about roller skates? I was brought up on them.'

Rita went along with this plan, much against her own better judgement, and felt ridiculous as she emerged on all eight wheels, grabbing Sharon's hand for extra support.

'They won't go in a straight line,' she complained as she careered into her friend and they locked skates. Sharon began to giggle as they headed towards the sand, tipping off the walkway and stumbling down on to the beach in an ungainly heap.

Thomas, meanwhile, had skated serenely on and was a mere dot in the distance. 'I thought you said you could skate,' Rita said.

Sharon was laughing so much she could barely draw breath to talk. 'You are the one who can't control your movements!'

Rita looked down at their legs, which were tangled together, and lay back on the warm sand, her body heaving with hysterical laughter.

'The way you were waving your arms about, I thought you were attempting to take off!' Sharon said, tears streaming down her face as she convulsed into another fit of laughter.

'I think my skates need a ten-thousand-mile service . . . or a pit stop!' Rita chortled.

'Listen, have you ever been on roller skates before?' Sharon asked, wiping at her eyes.

Rita shook her head. 'No, my mother always said they were silly and dangerous . . . How right she was!' She was still laughing when a shadow fell over her and she was aware of a rather disgruntled son staring down at her.

'Mum,' Steve said in a disapproving tone.

'Oh, Steve,' Rita said, attempting to regain some control, watching William coming up to them from the car. 'You found us.'

He looked at her with a stern and serious expression. 'What are you doing?'

'Your mom and I . . . we had a sort of crash on the home straight.' Sharon caught Rita's eye and burst into another peal of laughter.

Rita, who had pulled herself up into a sitting position, fell back on to the sand again. 'Oh, Steve,' was all she could say, snorting and convulsing as she tried to suppress more hilarity.

By the time they had disentangled themselves, with the help of William and Steve, and were standing up, without their skates, they felt rather like two naughty school girls. Sharon had grazed her knee and was dabbing at it with a tissue whilst Rita was rubbing at a damaged elbow. Steve had taken William for a swim.

Eventually they all ate a packed lunch on a car blanket spread out under a beach umbrella. They swam and lazed about in the sun for the next hour or so, planning to leave in mid-afternoon before the freeways became too congested. Sharon had gone into the water for a final dip and

Rita was reading the *Los Angeles Times* when Steve, dripping with water, sat down close by.

'Mum,' he said after a while.

'What is it?' Rita asked, turning from her paper.

'Do we have to keep going to Malibu *every* week-end?'

'You don't have to do anything, Steve.' She sat up. 'Why, has something happened?'

He shook his head, pushing at the wet sand between his toes. 'No, but do we have to?'

'I think your dad would be a bit upset if you didn't,' she replied firmly.

'Do you?' He sounded surprised.

'Steve, don't play games with me. Have you had an argument with your father?'

He was silent for a while. 'Not exactly . . . I just get sick of having to go there. I mean, how long is it for?'

'I don't know, Steve,' she replied honestly.

'You must know . . . is Dad coming back to the house, then?'

'Not at the moment.'

'So, who's playing games now?'

'You've argued, haven't you?'

'We had words,' Steve replied.

'What about?'

'Oh, you know, things . . . nothing very much . . .'

'Did you tell him that you didn't want to go every week-end?'

'Not in so many words.'

'Well,' she sighed, 'what did you tell him?'

'Nothing,' he admitted.

'Do you want me to talk to him?'

He shrugged.

She reached across for a towel and handed it to him. 'If I tell him, he'll probably think it's my idea, so if you don't

119

want to go on a regular basis you'd better tell him yourself . . .'

'Well, how long is he going to stay there?'

'For as long as it takes.'

'Look, I think we have a right to know what is happening.'

'If I knew for sure I'd tell you.' Rita felt herself becoming tense.

'Do you know if Dad is ever coming back to the house?'

Rita shook her head. 'He's thinking about buying the house at Malibu.'

'You mean, for ever?'

'For the foreseeable future,' she replied calmly.

'So, that's it, then. You're as good as divorced!'

'We're nothing of the sort,' Rita protested. 'I'm afraid everything isn't as black or white as you would like it to be, and I don't propose to discuss the state of my marriage with you on a beach!'

'When, then?' he asked, annoyed with her. 'When will you talk about it?'

'When, young man, there is something to say. Now let's drop it.' She glared at him. 'Okay?'

Steve got up and dried himself.

The week progressed. Rita saw Dr Allan and didn't feel they were getting anywhere. Kirk told her her backhand was much improved, and she devoted afternoons, where at all possible, to completing the book. The Californian summer continued with temperatures in the eighties. Steve's humour seemed to improve and William was out and about with friends, disappearing for most of the day.

'Who do you know in New York?' Steve asked one morning. He handed her a post-card with a night-time view of the illuminated Chrysler Building.

She looked at the picture and turned it over to find that

Marc had sent his telephone number and the comment, 'If you are ever in New York!' She grinned to herself.

'Who is it from?' Steve persisted with his questioning.

'Oh, a friend of ours is visiting the States from London . . . Alex Castle. Do you remember him? A real bore.'

'Why's he sending you a card from New York?' Steve sounded mystified.

'Why? Showing off, I suppose . . . How do I know?' Rita asked, standing up and stuffing the card into the back pocket of her baggy shorts. 'Come on, you can help me with the clearing-up.'

William walked by with Wendy's multi-storey home in his arms. 'You'll wash that hamster away,' Rita told him.

'I thought you didn't want her stinking up the house.'

'I don't.'

William stared at Rita. 'So?'

They were both looking at her as though she were mad. 'What is this? First I get the third-degree from your brother and now you're quibbling over a damn hamster house . . . Go on, get away with you!'

The boys looked at one another and burst out laughing. 'Mum's had a card from old man Castle. It's sent her into a stroppy decline,' Steve said.

'Why is he sending you cards?' William asked, mystified.

Rita, finally seeing the funny side to all of this, impaled upon her own lie, laughed too. 'Go!' she instructed both of them.

'What about the clearing-up?' Steve asked.

'Haven't you got a tennis lesson this morning?' she countered.

'Yes, ma'am.'

'Right then,' she nodded, and became engrossed in her work. Steve was already leaving and William had left with Wendy. Rosa was singing in the utility room, clattering

121

about with a floor mop and pail. Rita took the card out and looked at it again, 'If you are ever in New York!' He was the last person she had expected to hear from again. Rita turned the card over and stared at the dramatic outline of the Chrysler Building illuminated in all its glory. New York. She wondered if it could ever be a possibility.

Chapter 4

Paul's parents arrived in late September when the temperature was still in the eighties and the skies stayed blue and clear. The trip had been planned for many months and, as Paul hadn't seen fit to tell his mother and father what was happening between him and Rita, he suggested that he move back into the family house for the duration of their stay.

'You have to be joking,' Rita told him, frankly horrified at the suggestion. 'You really intend to move in for three weeks and act out a ridiculous charade?'

He glared at her. 'They're my parents and it would hurt them terribly to find out the real situation. My father is an old man. It could kill him.'

'Rubbish. He's survived your mother all these years. The little matter of our separation won't do him any harm.'

'Rita, for God's sake, it's only for three weeks.'

She thought for a moment. 'And what do I tell the boys? That Dad's finally coming back to live with us?' She was standing on his balcony, looking out to the Pacific surf. 'Or do I let them in on the plan?'

'We don't have to tell them anything, do we?' He sounded a little more uncertain.

'No, Paul, *we* don't but *I* do, as it's generally me who has to do all the dirty work . . .'

'Nonsense,' he complained.

'Is it?' she asked, turning to him. 'When was the last time you answered any of their questions about us, whether we are going to divorce or not, whether Dad is coming home or not . . . Jesus, it's the recurring theme in our household.'

'Rita,' he said in desperation, 'will you *please* go along with this?'

She shrugged. 'It's absolutely bloody ridiculous. God knows what it'll do to the boys.'

'It won't do anything to the boys,' he replied angrily. 'You can't mollycoddle them for ever, you know.'

Rita fumed but decided against arguing any further. They were arriving in a few days and she didn't propose to entertain them by herself. At least if Paul was around during the evenings it would make things less fraught.

'It's not his fault he has that woman for his mother I suppose,' she told Sharon as they prepared the salad for a barbecue to celebrate Thomas's fourteenth birthday.

'What do you feel about having Paul back home?' Sharon asked.

'I'm not very happy about it, as you can imagine.'

'And the boys?'

'Steve just said, Did this mean we were officially getting back together?' She tossed some lettuce into the enormous wooden salad bowl.

'What about William?'

'He has remained officially silent on the whole issue . . . I expect he's told Steve what he thinks about it, though.'

Sharon smiled. 'Well, honey, maybe it will be okay.'

'I doubt it,' Rita replied.

'Is this their first trip to LA?'

'It's their first trip outside England. God knows why they're even bothering to come. She'll only moan for the whole time . . . His mother hates the heat and she really resents the fact that we came out here in the first place.'

'You don't get along?' Sharon asked innocently.

Rita took a deep breath. 'I think that's rather under-stating it.'

'I see,' Sharon replied, sounding like a doctor who had just diagnosed a terminal illness.

'Paul is an only child. They had him late and I don't think she ever got over the shock. At any rate, she never ceases referring to it as a "mistake" and gives graphic accounts of her labour . . . Mary is a rather domineering type, keeps his father very much under control, calls him "Daddy". I can't bear it!'

Sharon roared with laughter. 'She sounds interesting.'

'Oh, she's interesting, all right,' Rita replied, attacking a stick of celery with her sharp knife.

'What does his father do?'

'He's been retired for years, he must be eighty-three, poor henpecked old thing . . . used to be a doctor in general practice. I suppose Paul followed in his footsteps, although he rather left them both behind a long time ago now.'

'Does Paul get along with them?'

'He's always been quite close to his father, which was a source of irritation to his mother, but, generally, there seems to be rather a gulf between them. They're all clearly non-tactile. She used to tell me, when I hugged and kissed the boys as children, that they would grow up into milksops!'

Sharon looked appalled. 'You're kidding!'

Rita shook her head. 'You'll see for yourself in a few days . . . Mary likes to organize everyone and she can't stand disorder of any kind. You know, she'll go absolutely spare when she sees the way we live out here.' A wicked gleam came into Rita's eyes. 'She considers things like barbecues as heralding the fall of civilization as she knows it!'

'What *are* you going to do with her, Rita?'

'I have a list of places where I'm going to take them, the Norton Simon Museum, the Huntington Library, the Botanical Garden . . . and Paul can take them to the beach house and on to the J. Paul Getty Museum . . . I intend to swamp them with "culture" tours because she's convinced that we all walk around wearing those Mickey Mouse hats and live in a kind of Disneyland extension.'

'You'll kill them. You can't drag them out all of the time!'

'Listen,' Rita began, pointing a stick of celery at her friend, 'I've got them for three weeks. I think we may run out of things to say to one another after the first few hours!'

'They can't be that horrendous,' Sharon said in disbelief.

'Oh no?' Rita looked hard. 'Wait until you meet them, her especially, before you say that . . . Paul's dad isn't that awful, he just needs a constant supply of hot tea and a readily available bathroom. I've often thought of asking Paul to fit up some kind of drip feed, teapot to arm in one simple tube!'

Sharon laughed at that. 'What about William and Steve, how do they get on with them?'

'They don't mind the old man, she's just too fussy for their liking.' Rita smiled. 'When she sees what they wear to school she'll have a fit!'

'Well, honey,' Sharon said, tipping the last of the tomatoes into the salad bowl, 'it sounds to me as though you've got your work cut out.' She looked into Rita's sour face and laughed. 'It's only three weeks.'

'Only!' Rita sounded appalled. 'Time will stand still . . . It could be a year . . .'

Sharon picked up the heavy bowl and carried it over to the refrigerator. 'Come on, Rita, help me do the balloons. . .'

Rita stood up and stretched, following Sharon out on to the veranda, where some of the kids were already hanging up decorations and lights. It was her last day of freedom for a while and she intended to enjoy it.

When Paul arrived early the following morning the house was silent. Not wishing to disturb anyone, he went into the kitchen, where he made himself some coffee. There were a couple of empty wine bottles on the table and some used glasses but, apart from them, the kitchen looked unused and spotless. He was pouring himself a mug of coffee when Rita emerged, looking dishevelled and bleary-eyed. She was wearing his white terry-towelling robe, which gave her the look of a child dressing up in adult clothes. She was drowning inside it.

'What time do you call this?' she asked, taking the mug from his hands and sipping the hot black liquid. She sat down heavily at the table.

'I call it eight forty-five,' he replied, amused at her state and pouring himself another mug of coffee.

Rita pushed a hand back through her messy hair. 'What time are they arriving?'

'Around five o'clock.'

'Oh.' She looked up at him. He was still in his red jogging shorts and wearing a blue sweat shirt with 'I Jog At Malibu' across the chest. She couldn't quite come to terms with that, it seemed so out of character. He had on white socks with black and red stripes at the top and blue Nike jogging shoes. Even in her present, slightly morning-after state, she thought he looked okay, even rather attractive. The eminent surgeon cum Malibu beach bum, she decided, except she wasn't really sure if they had such things as beach bums in the million-dollar real estate down at Malibu.

'I thought I'd come this morning and spend some time with you all.'

Rita lowered her head over the steaming mug and saw her eye reflected in the black coffee. 'I see.'

'I hope that's all right.'

She nodded, closing her eyes and yawning. 'The boys are swimming this morning, maybe you could join them . . . Kirk's coming to give me an extra lesson later.' Rita yawned as she pushed back her chair and pulled herself to her feet. 'What time are they coming?' she asked again.

He laughed. 'About five o'clock.'

She was about to go up for a shower but paused and turned back to him for a moment. 'You seem awfully chipper this morning,' she said, sounding suspicious.

'Jogging,' he replied. 'It makes you feel good, you should know that.'

'It never makes me feel that good,' Rita replied, walking away.

'What's the matter with you this morning?' Kirk asked, trotting up to the net. 'You're glued to the base line.'

Rita approached him. 'I had too much to drink last night,' she explained, looking at Kirk. No one, she decided, ever looked as good as Kirk in his tennis shorts. It was eleven o'clock in the morning and he looked great, bronzed and clean-cut and bubbling with fitness and health. 'Do you ever drink too much, Kirk?' she asked.

He grinned. 'Sure, but never when I'm working.'

Rita didn't think that he would. 'You're a good boy, Kirk, I bet your mother's proud of you.'

Kirk laughed. 'Okay, Rita, let's take a look at your forehand.'

Rita groaned. Her legs felt leaden and she wasn't concentrating properly. She could kill Sharon for entering them for the round-robin tournament at the country club.

She had until the first of December to perfect a game that had been languishing perfectly comfortably for the previous twenty years' hacking about on public courts.

'What kind of shape do you think my game will be in for the tournament?' she asked him as she reached the middle of the court.

'What kind of shape do you want it to be in?' Kirk asked her.

'God, I want it to be bloody good . . . Those women at the country club have all played Wimbledon in their youths!'

'That's kind of an exaggeration, Rita,' Kirk replied, laughing out loud.

Rita smiled. He had a very attractive laugh too. 'They take it all very seriously.'

'So do you.' He pointed to his knee, where a slight scar still remained from a previous tussle with her. 'Remember this?'

'Okay, okay, let's hit forehands.'

Kirk started to feed her the ball and she began to return, hitting it harder and harder, making him stretch and run around for his returns. Kirk would encourage her every return and Rita would respond, remembering all the things he had taught her and all the hours they had spent together on this court. He allowed the lesson to overrun by fifteen minutes because, he explained afterwards, she was 'hot'.

Rita was drenched with sweat and Kirk threw a towel over her shoulders as she bent down, hands on her knees, breathing heavily. He sat on a green bench at the courtside and rubbed at his short blond hair with a dark green towel. Kirk was also drenched.

'Okay,' he said, looking up at her, 'how do you feel now?'

'Wrecked,' she replied. 'Maybe I'm a bit too long in the

tooth for this,' she suggested, feeling dreadful, her heart banging away fit to burst.

'Nonsense.' He got to his feet. 'Work,' he told her, clenching his fist, 'that's the secret.'

Rita smiled. She had always rejected the idea of the healthy, sporting life until they moved here, and now, despite her previous misgivings, she did feel a sense of achievement in her endeavours on the court or jogging with Sharon or at aerobics class or just swimming a few lengths every day. 'Where do you go now?' she asked him as they walked up from the court.

'Beverly Hills.'

'Westwood's slumming it for you, then,' she joked.

Kirk ignored her comment. 'Can I beg a drink from you?'

'Sure,' she said, waving to the boys as they walked by the pool. Paul was sitting on the side, giving instructions to Steve, moving his arms in a crawling motion through the air above his head. The house felt wonderfully cool after the heat of the court and the exercise. 'Coke do you?' she asked.

Kirk nodded, sitting down at the table, pulling the metal tab on the can and putting it to his lips. 'Boy, that was a hot one,' he said, wiping his mouth.

Rita was taking her tennis shoes off, expecting to find blisters on her feet but there was no sign as she examined them. She watched as Kirk finished off the can, Coke dribbling down his chin.

'Next week, then,' he said, standing up.

Rita nodded, seeing him out through the kitchen door and round the house by the garage to the drive, where Kirk's little black sports car was parked next to Paul's huge silver Mercedes.

'Maybe you might consider a couple of evening lessons

130

before the tournament,' he suggested. 'It would be more comfortable and we could do some real work.'

'Okay,' Rita agreed, the gritty driveway hot and uncomfortable under her bare feet. She waved Kirk away and speculated what Paul's mother would say if she could see her now in the baggy khaki shorts and matching T-shirt. 'Real work,' she repeated Kirk's words to herself, wondering quite what, exactly, he had meant by that.

They drove to the airport in Paul's Mercedes; Steve followed in the Ford, accompanied by William. Everyone had showered and changed, the boys into fresh jeans and sweat shirts, Rita into a plain white cotton sundress and Paul into a light-weight tan-coloured suit, white shirt and tie. They managed to find adjacent parking spaces and all trooped into the international arrivals terminal building. The London flight was in but there would be a delay before the flight was processed. Paul seemed a little on edge, the boys hung back looking bored. Eventually Paul wandered off to discover how long the wait would be. Rita found some seats and sat between William and Steve, an arm around each of their shoulders.

'Do Gran and Grandad know what's going on?' Steve asked as soon as his father was out of earshot.

'Your father doesn't want to upset them,' Rita replied, trying to make it sound reasonable and logical, an explanation they would accept. 'He's worried about Grandad's health . . . You know, he's a very old man.'

'So, Dad's going back to the beach house as soon as they return?' William asked.

Rita squeezed the boys to her. 'Look, it will be okay, really.' She marvelled at her own ability to act, or was it to lie? Rita wondered if there was really any difference between the two. At any rate, she almost believed this piece of fiction herself although she knew that it wouldn't be okay. All she really wished was that she could have been stronger with Paul, resisted the moral blackmail and refused to go through with this hare-brained scheme.

Paul came up to them and told Rita that the passengers were starting to come through, and they all went off to meet the old couple.

His parents looked, somehow, shrunken. His mother, ramrod straight and pencil thin, her hair a steely grey cut into a neat, precise, rather smart style, came first. She was wearing an expensive tailored suit, a sort of mannish pin-stripe in Prussian blue. Her black patent leather shoes, again, were incredibly smart but seemed a little too high, making the old woman totter slightly so that her head nodded from side to side almost imperceptibly. She looked, Rita thought, a bit as if she were on invisible strings being held by a puppeteer whose mind wasn't quite on the job in hand.

Paul's father shambled on behind, pushing a luggage trolley which the boys soon took control of. He was a stout man and he had bad feet and tended to shuffle, as though his shoes were too big for him. His suit was also very smart, a light grey wool fabric, but, because the old man was somewhat stooped, it seemed oddly misshapen.

His mother shook everyone's hand, complained about the terrible flight and hoped they didn't have very far to drive because 'Daddy isn't feeling too good.'

The old woman looked at Rita through her clear, green eyes and then at the boys. 'So, this is how they dress in Los Angeles,' and turning to her husband, 'You see, Daddy, I told you . . . Disneyland!' and she laughed a humourless, fluttering laugh. 'You look terribly thin, Paul,' she grumbled. 'Too thin.'

'I've been jogging, Mother,' he replied.

Again the humourless laugh. 'Jogging?' She turned to her husband. 'Did you hear that, Daddy? Paul's jogging.'

132

'What in?' the old man asked, squinting in order to concentrate on what she was saying.

'And you, Rita, how are you? I must say you're looking well . . . You were always such a pasty-faced thing and now look . . .'

Rita smiled but she was far from amused. Inside her head she could hear a voice, 'I can't stand it, I can't stand it, I can't stand it,' repeated over and over again. When they reached the cars, Steve and William loaded up the cases into the Ford whilst Rita and Paul helped the old couple into the Mercedes. The men sat in the front, the women in the back. Paul's mother craned her neck to watch the boys. 'Can he drive that car?' she demanded to know. 'Can he drive that?'

'Of course, Mary,' Rita assured her. 'Steve's a very competent driver, isn't he, Paul?'

Paul mumbled something, glancing nervously at his father, who, slumped into the passenger seat and securely strapped in, looked as though he wasn't going to make the drive back to the house.

His mother stared out at the passing scenes with growing horror. 'Look, look, Daddy,' she said excitedly, tapping the back of his seat, 'all those perfectly horrible stucco houses with red tiles on the roof.' She turned to Rita. 'I hope you don't live in a place like that.' It was meant as a joke because it was followed by the humourless laugh.

Rita gritted her teeth and caught Paul's worried expression in the driving mirror.

'. . . and palm trees,' the old woman continued, 'and the traffic . . . and that snack bar shaped like a cowboy hat . . .' And on she went, keeping up her never-ending commentary as though Rita and Paul had never noticed any of it before.

* * *

133

'Is it me, or do you find it cold in here?' Paul's mother asked when they were, finally, seated in the lounge, having a cup of tea.

'It's the air-conditioning, Mary,' Rita explained.

'I'm surprised you don't all have terrible colds, coming in out of that dreadful heat into this ice-box.'

'You get used to it after a while,' Rita assured her.

'I hope so,' she said, making a shivering noise and pulling her suit jacket around her. 'Do you never just open the windows?'

'Later in the day perhaps.' Rita stood up. As she went into the kitchen to top up the teapot, she gave Paul a hard stare. When she returned, his father was snoring in an armchair whilst his mother, seemingly oblivious to the exhausted condition of her husband, was holding forth about the roses along the terrace. She would, she announced, have a look at them later on.

'We have a gardener,' Rita informed her.

'Is he an expert on roses?'

'I don't know . . . He's a gardener, he's an expert on gardening,' Rita replied.

'Believe me, Rita, after a lifetime of caring for roses I can tell when bushes need attention.' She gave her a pitying look. 'Don't worry, dear, I'll give you the benefit of my advice later, but now I think we really ought to get Daddy upstairs and I must admit to feeling rather tired myself.'

Rita thanked God and showed the old woman to their room, Paul helping his father up the stairs and many paces behind. His mother seemed to approve of the bedroom. Rita had chosen the guest room at the opposite end of the house to her own bedroom. She made sure that the old folks knew where everything was and left them to rest and, hopefully, sleep off the jet-lag.

* * *

134

'My God,' Rita said, flopping into a chair.

'They're exhausted and old,' Paul explained.

'No,' she replied, 'your mother has always been like that.'

Paul sat on the sofa unbuttoning the collar of his shirt and loosening the knot of his tie, slipping it down. 'They'll sleep for a while now, anyway.'

'You're going to have to spend a lot more time with them,' Rita warned Paul. 'I can't deal with Mary by myself and Dad needs a lot of looking after.'

'Mother takes care of him,' Paul said wearily.

'I wonder if we ought to get a male nurse in to help out,' Rita mused.

'There's no need for that . . . You know they are late risers, you can virtually forget about them during the morning.'

'Great, so that just leaves me the afternoons . . .'

'I'll get some time off,' Paul encouraged.

'Famous last words. How will you manage that?'

'I'm the boss,' he smiled.

Rita looked unconvinced. 'Three weeks,' was all she said, almost in disbelief.

Steve and Jem were sitting on the side of the pool in the late evening sunshine. They had just climbed out and water ran off them in rivulets, forming little pools where they sat. William was practising a racing breast stroke and they were encouraging him.

'Are you glad your dad's back?' Jem asked.

'He's not back,' Steve replied. 'They're just play-acting for the sake of his folks.' He turned to Jem and grinned. 'Pathetic, eh?'

Jem kicked a foot through the water. 'What are your grandparents like?'

'Old, my grandmother is a pain in the butt! My grandfather is okay, he's just incredibly geriatric now . . . You should have seen my mum's face when they first arrived,' Steve laughed. 'He didn't look as though he'd survive the walk from airport to car.'

'Is he okay?'

Steve nodded. 'Sure.' He stood up and walked the length of the pool, following William's progress through the water. 'Kick,' he shouted to his brother, 'kick harder.'

William held on to the side at the opposite end, breathing hard and looking up at Steve. 'Was it all right?'

Steve grinned, standing with his feet apart, hands on hips. 'You have to go for it, William, really put some effort in it . . . You know, attack, attack, attack.'

William sucked in a deep breath of air before pushing himself off from the side and swimming hard across the length of the pool again.

Steve went back to Jem, who was standing up and towelling himself dry. 'Finished?' he asked.

'I've got work in the morning,' Jem explained.

Steve flopped down on to a lounger, staring up at the fading sky, which had turned from deep blue to almost white above the pinkish band at the horizon. 'Have you thought about university?'

Jem went into the pool house, where he stripped off his wet trunks and, drying himself, was framed in stark silhouette at the open doorway. 'Have you?' he asked, pulling on a pair of navy shorts.

'I was thinking of trying the East Coast.'

Jem came out, held the wet trunks under the freshwater shower and wrung them dry. 'I haven't really thought . . . It seems such a long time away yet.'

'It'll go quickly . . . I know one thing for sure. I'm not doing pre-med.'

'No? What will your dad have to say about that?' Jem

sat down on a white chair and looked at William, who was still swimming.

Steve turned his head to look at Jem. 'I doubt if he will say very much . . . He always expected Nathan to become the doctor. I've never really wanted that. Now Law, that's the thing to get into.'

'You'll break with family tradition, then.'

Steve shrugged. 'Nathan broke with family tradition . . .' He sat up. 'I mean, he killed himself, didn't he!' He watched as William hauled himself out of the water. 'Well done,' he said, throwing his brother a towel.

'What do you think?' William asked.

'Great,' Jem told him.

'Listen, with two great coaches like us around, how can you go wrong?' Steve asked, laughing.

William rubbed at his hair. 'I'll see you later,' he said, walking away from them. 'I've got some calls to make.'

'I'd better be going as well,' Jem told him.

'You don't have to go yet,' Steve insisted. 'I never see you these days.'

Jem laughed. 'I see you all the time.'

'Listen, when are you going to choose your car?'

'When I have enough money saved, I guess.'

'What are you going to have?'

Jem rolled up his wet trunks in his towel. 'My dad's paying some towards the price. He'll want to have a say, I think.'

'You mean, you don't get to choose what you want?'

'Listen,' Jem said, standing and bouncing the rolled towel off Steve's head, 'I *want* a Porsche but do you think I'll get one?'

'I had to make do with a Rabbit but it's okay,' he conceded, if a bit grudgingly, pulling himself off the sun bed and walking towards the house, his arm on Jem's shoulder. 'Do you want to play tennis tomorrow?'

137

Jem nodded. 'Listen, about what you said, did you mean it? Are you really planning on an Eastern university?'

'I was thinking about the possibilities open to me but, the way things are around here, I shall have to choose somewhere closer to home . . . I mean, if Mum and Dad decide to make their separation official . . .'

'Divorce?' Jem asked.

Steve nodded. 'And there's William to consider,' he added.

'Do you think they will?'

Steve sighed. 'I don't know . . . Maybe being together for these three weeks will do something, but I doubt it. Since Nathan died everything has just fallen to pieces, my dad's so uptight about everything, my mum attempts to make life as normal as possible, and we are caught in between . . . It's difficult not to be disloyal at times, it's hard not to just want to get away from it.' They had reached the drive by now and Steve was leaning against his father's Mercedes. 'Don't get me wrong, Jem, my parents are great, but Nathan's death has just altered everything so much . . .'

Jem nodded but felt at a loss as to what he could say to his friend. He felt Steve needed some encouragement, someone to tell him that everything would be fine. 'Well, maybe they will get back together . . . You never know.'

Steve grinned. 'Well, anyway, I'd better go in and see the old folks.' He waited until Jem had reached the driveway gates, waving to him before going inside, where his grandparents were sitting in the lounge drinking tea and watching the news on TV. He sat and talked to them for a while, smiling and being polite, but he found them hard work. She was so full of bile and criticism, a body brimming with hate and resentment with a frosty exterior, a cold smile and terrified eyes. His grandfather was sitting at the opposite end of the room, in front of the large television set, with a hearing-aid device plugged in, attaching him to it like an umbilical cord.

'You've changed so much, Steve, and you've lost your beautiful accent.' She bemoaned this fate as she might the death of a child. 'Do you like living out here?' she asked, her face looking pained.

'Sure,' he replied, getting up and wandering across to his grandfather. 'I like it very much.' He sat on the arm of the chair and took his grandfather's hand, looking at the almost translucent skin, spotted with age, and the blue veins twisting underneath.

'Hello, son,' the old man said loudly.

Steve laughed with pleasure or nerves, he wasn't entirely sure which. 'Hi.'

'Have you been swimming?'

Steve had slipped on a tracksuit for the sake of decorum, but he realized that the damp was showing through from his swimming trunks. 'Sure have,' he nodded. 'Are you going to swim tomorrow?'

'I might have done a few years ago . . . but not now.'

'Why not?' Steve asked, carrying on with the jest.

'Because your grandfather is not well. Don't put ideas into his head.'

'I was only joking, Gran,' Steve explained.

'You're the eldest son now, Steve, and that is a responsibility for you.'

'Gran, I *know* that Grandpa can't really swim any longer.' He felt exasperated with her. 'We were joking.'

'Nathan would never have been so silly,' she told him.

'Nathan killed himself,' Steve answered her angrily. 'Or maybe you had forgotten that.'

She put a hand up to her shocked face. 'If these are the manners they teach you in California . . .'

'I have some things to do,' he said, interrupting and

139

leaving her at the same time, excusing himself and brushing by his father as he left. He heard Paul asking what
was going on.

Paul was at the house when Rita returned home the
following afternoon after a lunch date with Sharon. She'd
left her parents-in-law in the capable hands of Rosa, who
was taking great care of them.

'Where have you been?' he asked angrily, following her
into the lounge.

'Out with Sharon,' Rita explained, looking at the old
folks, who were fast asleep on the shaded terrace. 'Why
aren't you at work?' she asked, turning to Paul.

'I've been waiting for you to return,' he fumed. 'Rosa
said you wouldn't be long.'

'We did some shopping . . . Why are you waiting?'

'Why?'

Rita nodded.

'Someone has to be in the house.'

'Why?' Rita asked with some amazement. 'Your
mother spends half the day cleaning with Rosa, hours
telling the gardener how to prune the bloody roses . . .
You're not seriously suggesting that she needs me to
baby-sit her, are you?'

'You know, Rita,' he began, just before storming out
to his car, 'you have a very mulish streak. I've never
noticed it before.'

'I developed it when you walked out on me, Paul,' she
replied ever-so-sweetly. She heard the front door slam
and the powerful Mercedes screeching away and, making
sure his parents were still snoring, crept upstairs to
change.

Later in the week Rita and Sharon accompanied Paul's
mother on a shopping trip. Rita had decided that Rodeo

Drive and Wilshire Boulevard would give the old lady a treat. She prepared carefully, she had her hair cut and wore a smart summer dress, cream and calf-length, sleeveless, with a square neckline. She wore shoes which matched the dress, with high heels and open toes, and she had painted her finger and toe nails in a flame-red varnish. Sharon, coming in through the lounge windows, whistled when she saw her.

'You look fabulous,' she told Rita, as they waited for Rita's mother-in-law to emerge from her bedroom.

Rita grinned with pleasure. 'We both do.' Sharon was wearing a businesslike suit, black material with fine silver threads running through it, a white blouse, dark tights and black court shoes. She wore her hair up, showing off her long neck.

'It's like waiting for Mom to show and take us on a shopping spree,' Sharon said.

Rita noticed that they were talking quietly, almost in whispers. She began to giggle.

'What have you done with the old guy?' Sharon muttered as they heard a door bang upstairs.

'Paul's taken him back to the hospital . . .'

'Nothing serious, I hope,' Sharon replied, smiling.

Rita burst into laughter, putting a hand over her mouth and taking a deep breath in order to control her growing hysteria. 'No, he's spending the day with Paul, seeing patients, I think.'

Sharon nudged her as Mary descended the stairs, taking each step very gingerly. She was dressed in a peacock-blue fitted suit with matching accessories. Her hat was wide-brimmed with a high crown and a tiny veil. The suit jacket had half-sleeves but she was pulling on elbow-length peacock-blue gloves as she walked into the lounge. 'Jesus, it's the Queen Mother,' Sharon said out of the corner of her mouth.

Rita, resisting the impulse to burst into laughter, coughed instead. 'Mary, you do look nice.'

The old woman smiled. 'And so do you and Karen.'

'Sharon,' Rita corrected her.

'Quite.' She looked at them for a few seconds, her clear green eyes scrutinizing their outfits from beneath the veil. 'Are we all set?'

Rita nodded and picked up her bag and keys from the table. 'Right, then,' she said, leading the way out to the car.

They had lunch along Wilshire Boulevard. Her mother-in-law hadn't enjoyed Rodeo Drive, finding it rather ostentatious for her liking, but the department stores on the boulevard had appealed to her and they had spent the morning in the likes of Bullock's, Saks, Joseph Magnin and Lord and Taylor. 'The shop assistants here are terribly obliging, aren't they,' she had said. 'A bit like in England before the war . . . nothing too much trouble. At home you'd think they were doing you a favour by bothering to serve you at all.'

'Really, is it that bad?' Sharon asked.

'Absolutely, it's a fright . . . isn't it, Rita?'

Rita, whose feet were hurting from the high heels, was ready for a long rest but Mary seemed full of energy, even of bonhomie. She found it a bit unnerving. 'Yes,' she agreed, for the sake of continued good relations, if nothing else, 'they can be rather stroppy at times.'

'Have you ever been to London, Karen?' Mary asked.

'Sharon,' Rita corrected.

Her mother-in-law smiled, a little painfully, as though it were Rita who kept on making this mistake. 'Have you, my dear?' she continued.

'Oh, sure, several times.'

The old woman nodded in satisfaction. 'A bit different to this Disneyland, isn't it?'

'I liked it,' Sharon replied, stealing a glimpse at Rita, who was cringing in her seat.

'It has the history, you see, the continuity over hundreds and hundreds of years . . . I expect that you miss those sort of things here.'

Sharon took a sip of her wine. 'We have the climate, though . . . As I recall it, England was always cold and it was *always* raining.'

'That's for sure,' Rita agreed.

'Don't you miss England, Rita?' Mary sounded surprised.

'No, not really . . . I miss my family, of course.'

The old woman nodded. 'I was very shocked at how much the boys had changed, how different they were.'

'Oh, Mary,' Rita smiled, feeling herself growing tense, 'they haven't really changed that much, they're just growing up now.'

'They have those accents and they *look* different. But then, everyone looks different here, everyone seems giant size!' She laughed the mirthless laugh. 'And everything seems so terribly casual.'

'It's a free and easy way of life,' Rita said.

'I can't think why Paul decided to come here. He never struck me as being particularly "free and easy", quite the opposite in fact. But then even he is different . . . so thin!'

'Paul isn't thin, Mary,' Rita objected, 'he's fitter than ever.'

The old woman didn't look very convinced. 'Well, you're all here now . . . we have to accept it. I'm just pleased that Daddy was able to see you all once more. He's getting very ropy.'

'We're coming over at Christmas, Mary,' Rita reminded her. 'Don't get morbid now.'

'We've still got a few department stores left to do after lunch,' Sharon said brightly.

'Yes,' Mary said, smiling suddenly. 'I thought I might go back to Bullock's and try on those shoes.'

Rita winked across at Sharon. She concentrated upon her lunch whilst Sharon talked about England, asking Mary questions about her home and life in Hampshire. Mary, disarmed and the centre of attention, turned on the charm and bored poor Sharon almost under the table with the history of her life.

'I never want to go near a department store again,' Rita said, sitting down heavily after kicking off her uncomfortable shoes. She put her feet up on the coffee table, pushing away the heap of parcels and plastic store bags in front of her. Mary had gone up to her room to rest and Sharon was putting the kettle on.

'Well, it wasn't too bad,' she encouraged.

'It's just a complete blur to me,' Rita said. 'If I see one more clever dress display I'll be sick!'

Sharon laughed. 'Well, Mary seemed to enjoy herself . . . She certainly bought enough.'

'That's the main thing, I suppose.'

'She seems to have had a rather exciting life. Was her family really so wealthy?'

Rita nodded, closing her eyes. 'Apparently her grandfather owned lots of things, mines and shipping lines and industrial concerns . . . I don't know what she did with her share.'

'Maybe it will all come down to the boys,' Sharon suggested.

'There were a load of children, I think that she was one of ten . . .'

'Twelve,' Sharon interrupted.

'Anyway, whatever cash there was is probably long gone. She always maintains that she married Paul's father because the family were desperate to get all the girls married off, due to financial embarrassment.'

'She told me at lunch that her family hadn't wanted her to marry a doctor, it was a step down the social scale, don't you remember?'

'I'd probably fallen unconscious by that time, with boredom!'

'Coffee?' Sharon asked.

'Tea . . . I bet you're really looking forward to Universal Studios on Sunday!'

'My dear, I wouldn't miss it for the world,' Sharon replied in her best English accent.

Rita eased herself out of the chair and followed Sharon into the kitchen, her mind still full of the glittering shine and colours of LA shop display.

She had been sleeping beside Paul again for almost two weeks. Rita had looked upon it as a dreadful imposition but felt that it would have been absurd to relegate him to a guest room. In any case, it wasn't as if they were having a relationship. By the Friday of the second week he had forgiven her for arriving home late on Tuesday afternoon and was unusually talkative as they got ready for bed. She cleaned her teeth whilst he took a bath and they chatted about the events of the previous two weeks. There were moments when it was as if they hadn't decided to live apart, moments, reflections of their past together, before Nathan's suicide.

'Do you really think Mary hates California as much as she says?' Rita asked him, sitting on the edge of the bath.

Paul grinned. 'My mother has made an art out of

145

complaining. I doubt if she even knows when she's enjoying herself.'

'What about Dad?'

'He's okay . . . You know, Rita, he's not half as deaf as he makes out. When I was with him at the hospital the other day he heard everything!'

Rita laughed. 'If you were married to your mother, maybe you would feign a bit of deafness too!'

'Pardon?'

She flicked some of the soapy water into his face. 'I'm not as bad as Mary,' she replied, defending herself.

Paul looked at her for a long moment, shaking his head. 'No, you're not.'

She smiled as she stood up and walked through to the bedroom. Climbing into bed, she began to read the book she had started at the beginning of the summer.

Paul followed her through in a short while, a bath towel wrapped around his waist. He sorted out some clean pyjama bottoms and wandered back into the bathroom, then she heard him cleaning his teeth. When he returned he was naked and she couldn't help noticing that he was in pretty good shape. He must have shed over a stone in the last few months and he looked so much better, less careworn. She had noticed before that something about him had changed. Maybe being away from her had served to rejuvenate him! Or, perhaps, it was simply the ocean breezes at Malibu. He climbed in beside her and lay down, his head cradled in his hands. Rita continued to read, flicking over the pages of the thick book. The heroine was being ravished in the toilet of a New York-bound jumbo jet by an incredibly handsome Italian prince she had just met in the first-class lounge. Rita closed the book and, putting it on her bedside table, switched the lamp off. Her leg brushed against Paul as she settled down to sleep.

'Good book?' he asked her.

'It's not bad.'

'What's it about?' He seemed interested.

'Sex in high places,' she replied, not really wishing to divulge the plot in case he thought her completely asinine.

Rita didn't particularly want to make small talk in bed with him, it seemed a little ridiculous to her. They appeared either to be screaming at one another or being extra polite. Her feelings were confused. Did she still love Paul? It was a rather odd question to ask herself when he was lying in bed beside her.

She turned over, her back towards him. She supposed they could salvage their marriage but didn't think that was good enough. Her own emotional state was too precarious, she didn't feel strong enough to cope with the threat of Paul's rejection. Rita also resented what had already transpired between them and, when he was in a frame of mind to be kind and considerate, it only confused her more.

Rita joked about sex, she laughed at the rampant copulation of the heroine in her book, she pretended that it wasn't important but, since her brief fling with Marc, she had felt the loss of her sex life even more keenly. Maybe it had been a mistake to open up that particular Pandora's box.

She listened to Paul's breathing as it became regular and deep and was soon fast asleep herself.

Rita was woken up by people talking. Light was streaming into the bedroom from the hall and Paul was sitting up in bed rubbing the sleep out of his eyes. Steve was saying something about William.

'What is it?' Rita said, suddenly quite awake.

'It's all right,' Paul said calmly, slipping out of the bed. 'William has been sick, that's all. Go back to sleep.'

She looked at Steve as though for verification. 'What's the matter with him?'

'He keeps being sick.'

Rita climbed out of bed and, dragging on the old towelling robe, followed Paul into William's bedroom. She could see Paul holding a hand to William's forehead as his son began to vomit into the toilet again. She went downstairs to fetch some cleaning cloths and disinfectant and by the time she returned William was back in bed. Paul was taking his temperature as she went into the bathroom to clean up the mess. It took her a couple of minutes to swab around the white tiled floor and Paul was sitting on the edge of William's bed when she emerged. William was lying with his eyes closed, looking ghastly and very white.

'He's okay, just a simple tummy upset,' Paul told her.

'What did he eat?' She sounded concerned. 'I hope we don't all come down with it.'

'I had a taco from a taco stand at the beach this evening,' William groaned.

'He'll be fine, Rita,' Paul assured her. 'He has a slight temperature and he'll feel pretty rotten for the next few hours, but you know what they say, better out than in!' He grinned. 'Why don't you go back to bed?'

She supposed that these were the honeyed tones he employed to next of kin. 'Do you want anything, William?' she asked.

He shook his head.

'Go to bed,' Paul insisted. 'There's no point in us all losing sleep . . . and that goes for you too,' he said, looking at Steve, who was still leaning up against the door jamb.

'He's fine,' Rita yawned, touching Steve on the shoulder as she crept back to her room. However, she was unable to sleep for a long time. It was typical that

148

one of them should be ill when Paul was in the house. Rita felt it reflected badly upon her, that Paul would think she never warned them against anything. 'Don't eat food from suspect vendors', the words were clear in her mind. She had guilty visions of salmonella poisoning, and people died from that, didn't they?

She woke up suddenly, already halfway out of bed, her heart pounding, terrified by a nightmare she could no longer recall. Rita flicked on the bedside lamp, wondering if it had all been a dream, but when she turned, Paul was not there. She walked to the window and pulled back the heavy curtains. The room felt uncomfortably warm. She had turned the air-conditioning unit down because it clattered and kept them awake. Pushing open the doors, she stepped on to the balcony. There was a red glow at the horizon, beneath the arc of black sky where the stars still shone. Lights blazed on the freeways but where she stood it was quite still. A dog barked in the distance. The red band at the horizon grew thicker and lighter. Rita went back inside and fell asleep for another hour or so, waking when it was daylight although still early. At six-thirty she went back to William's room, where she found them both fast asleep, Paul curled up on the cramped window seat. She went down into the kitchen and made herself some tea, carrying her cup and saucer out on to the terrace, sitting on the damp morning steps, looking through the sweet-smelling pergola to the still waters of the pool. She bowed her head and cried silently for a long time.

William spent Saturday in bed on a diet of water and some preparation that Paul had in the car, which had to be mixed up in the water and consumed in vast quantities.

'It contains sodium chloride, dextrose and bicarbonate,' Paul explained.

149

William had turned up his nose at it but drank it when he was informed, in no uncertain terms by his father, that the trip to Universal would be off if he didn't.

They spent the afternoon by the pool, Paul's father propped up under a shady umbrella whilst his mother made tentative forays into the sunlight, smothering her exposed parts, forearms, face and neck, with a number fifteen sunblock lotion. 'Do you use a blocking cream?' she asked Rita.

'I do when I remember,' Rita said, pulling herself out of the pool.

'You should use it constantly,' his mother warned. 'You all should,' she said, addressing Paul and Steve too. 'Isn't that right, Paul?'

He grinned at his mother. 'Don't fuss, dear. We do.'

'Have you got any on now?' she demanded.

'Not at the moment but there's a good reason for that.' He stood up and made a running dive and a great splash into the water.

'I'd better go and check on William,' Rita said, excusing herself and moving swiftly away from the hectoring of Paul's mother. 'I'll bring some tea down,' she called back. His father moved instinctively at the mention of 'tea', thus proving Paul's theory that his hearing was still reasonably intact. Rita smiled to herself at such fraudulent behaviour.

'What's Gran up to, then?' William asked as Rita handed him a glassful of Paul's medicine mix.

'Don't ask,' Rita replied, tugging his pillow out and banging it back into shape before placing it behind him again.

'Can I get up, Mum?' William asked.

'What did your father say?'

'He said that I couldn't get up today . . . but I feel okay now.'

'You look pale.' She put the jug of water on his side table and felt his forehead. 'And hot.'

'I'm starving,' William complained.

Rita looked down at him. 'Maybe you could have a piece of dry toast and a boiled egg a bit later on.'

'Oh, Mum.' He screwed up his face. 'What are you having?'

'At the risk of incurring the wrath of your grandmother, we are having a barbecue out by the pool . . . Maybe Dad will let you come down and watch us eat it!'

'Oh, Mum,' William said again in dismay.

'Sharon and Bill are coming too, with their kids, so you'll have a constant supply of visitors.'

'Ask Dad,' he pleaded, like a prisoner begging for release from a dungeon.

Rita began to leave him, pausing for a moment at the door. 'Do you promise never to eat tacos again?'

'Yes,' he agreed readily. Too readily, she thought.

'Well, we'll see.' And she left. William used his remote control to turn up the volume of his television set so that the sounds of gunfire and whooping Red Indians could be heard all the way down the stairs. She took a loaded tray to the pool, dispensed the cups of tea and then sat out in the sun next to Paul, who was lying face down on a lounger.

'How's the lad?' he asked.

'He's beginning to revolt,' she told him.

'That's good . . . Does he want to get up?'

Rita nodded.

'What do you think?'

'You're the doctor.'

'You're the mother!'

Rita smiled. 'Leave him a bit longer. He could probably

come to the barbecue this evening and have a bit of salad or something.'

Paul turned over, reaching down for his tea. 'That sounds fair enough.' He looked at Rita. 'This is the life, isn't it?'

Rita didn't respond to his question. She was beginning to feel a little tired with acting out the role of happy housewife. She was becoming sick of pretence. The only way, she knew, for Paul to really come back was if their relationship was whole again and, in all honesty, even in her wilder moments, she could never see that as a realistic proposition. She couldn't see the point of a celibate marriage either, even though she'd read about them working well for others. People who had argued constantly over their sex lives suddenly becoming dear friends and living in perfect harmony. No, she concluded, Paul was just not interested in her. Even his stay at the beach hadn't kindled any amorous feelings. Perhaps this was simply the state some marriages reached and, if that was the case, then she was relieved they had not just drifted along any further. Rita did think he was still attractive and, perhaps, she might have seriously considered a genuine reconciliation. Dr Allan had asked if love was existent between them. She still wasn't sure.

She lay back and closed her eyes. Paul was talking across her to his mother about the relative price of property in Los Angeles and London. She remembered hearing them discussing the house in Chalcot Square before drifting off to sleep.

The two families came together that evening for one of their regular barbecues. Rita felt even more distanced from Paul, who was behaving just as perfectly as ever, the perfect host, the perfect father, the perfect doctor, the perfect husband . . . Sharon's sister-in-law had joined the gathering with her children and so the place was full of strapping Californians who all seemed to be terribly gregarious and bursting with good health. Rita could tell that Mary was finding it all a little too much to cope with. Paul's father, on the other hand, seemed very content and relaxed as he swigged innumerable glasses of malt beer.

'Okay, Dad?' Rita asked as she came out of the house with enormous bags of rolls.

He smiled happily, raising his glass to her. 'Don't tell Mary,' he said in a stage whisper. He was engaged in conversation with Bill, who had taken the old man under his wing and wanted to know all about English medicine before the Second World War.

Rita passed on, dumping the bread on the preparation table close by the barbecue where Paul, wearing a chef's hat and white apron, was busy cooking steaks. Sharon handed her a drink and told her to sit down. The kids were all in the pool, which was suddenly illuminated as the daylight faded away into darkness. Kathy, her sister-in-law, was sitting at the table with them. Rita had met her on several occasions in the past and liked her a lot. She had three teenage girls and had just got divorced. Sharon had invited her along to celebrate. Mary was sitting further along the terrace, deep in conversation with Jem. Poor Jem, Rita thought as she sat down, he was far too polite to excuse himself and find more entertaining company. Steve was swimming and William, finally allowed out of his room, was sitting by the pool house, watching the others enjoying themselves.

'Do I offer congratulations or what?' Rita asked Kathy.

'Good riddance,' Kathy replied, holding up her glass. 'I'm free of the saphead, thank God!'

Sharon laughed. 'She was married to a doctor as well, all of Bill's family became doctors!' She shook her head in disbelief.

'Hal is a geriatrician,' Kathy said. 'He has adverts on TV, "The Hal Western Retirement Villages". He caters to California's middle-income-bracket senior citizen.'

'Oh, yes.' Rita suddenly remembered seeing him standing in front of a group of happy oldsters. He had a Liberace smile and a rather obvious wig, which looked bright orange on colour TV. 'That's Bill's brother?'

Sharon nodded. 'Listen, don't knock it, Hal's Happy Homes have made him a millionaire!'

'What a sap,' Kathy said, downing her wine and reaching for the bottle to begin again. She poured another glassful and proposed a toast. 'Here's to California's community-property laws.'

'That means Kathy is pleased with her settlement,' Sharon explained.

'Too right,' Kathy said. 'I get to keep the house in Beverly Hills, the kids and the animals . . . He gets to keep his old folks . . .'

'. . . and she gets half the profits,' Sharon said. 'Not bad, Kathy, not bad.'

'The only drawback is that I had to live with the jerk for eighteen years!' Kathy replied with a degree of venom.

As Kathy carried on with the verbal abuse of her ex-husband, Rita sat back and took a good look. Kathy was probably about her age. She was pretty, although, for all the merriment, her face was showing the strain. Kathy's hair was coloured a chestnut-brown which appeared a little too harsh for her fair complexion and blue eyes. She wore it long, perhaps a little too long, a bit too flowing, a might too tressy. Her make-up was immaculate, her nails were perfectly burnished and shaped. Kathy was wearing a short denim skirt and a low-cut blouse and high white shoes which showed off her fabulous legs. She was obviously someone who worked hard at her appearance, she hadn't an ounce of extra fat on her body and was

154

clearly proud of that fact as the tight clothes she wore hugged every curve.

'How long have you been married, Rita?' Kathy was asking.

'Me? Oh, God, years, twenty years.'

'Happy?' she asked, lighting up a cigarette.

Rita stole a glance at Sharon. 'Well, we're still married.'

Kathy shrugged, looking over towards Paul, who was standing with his back to their table. 'Your husband's quite dishy, isn't he?'

Rita turned her head to look at him. In fact he looked rather ridiculous in his floppy hat, long white apron and dark shorts. She didn't say anything.

Sharon poured them all more wine. 'No one ever says that about Bill!'

Kathy laughed. It sounded slightly hysterical and loud. 'Bill is just great,' she said, her words slurred.

'I'd better go and help sort out the food,' Rita said, excusing herself, glad to get away. She wondered if she was going to end up like Kathy, not quite mutton dressed up as lamb but in danger of heading that way, slightly blowzy and dreading the future.

Paul smiled at her as she began to unpack the paper plates and plastic cutlery.

'The kids seem to be enjoying themselves,' he said, watching the activity around the pool.

'All except William.'

Paul chuckled. 'That'll teach him to eat suspect food.'

Rita looked around her. Sharon and Kathy were having a good laugh, probably at Hal's expense. Bill and Paul's father were in deep conversation, even Mary was smiling. Only she, it seemed, was out of step with the jolly atmosphere. Rita had drunk several glasses of wine and yet still felt stone-cold sober. Kathy approached them, armed with a camera, telling them to smile. Paul, holding

155

a spatula up to the camera and grinning foolishly, put his arm around Rita, holding her tightly to him.

'Say cheese,' Kathy shrieked.

Rita tried hard to raise a smile but she felt uncomfortable, Paul's arm wrapped around her waist felt alien and unwanted. Kathy seemed to take an age to take the picture and Rita became more and more annoyed. Paul was being the life and soul of the party, he had stepped back into her life and taken it over, and she was furious with him. The camera flashed into their faces, leaving Rita with tiny silver globes floating in front of her eyes. She quickly extricated herself from Paul's grip and set about finishing the preparations for serving the food. Sharon came up to give her a hand.

'Are you okay, Rita?' she asked.

'I don't know,' Rita replied, 'I honestly don't know.' For a moment she thought she would burst into tears but managed to control herself. 'I just wish . . .' She paused. 'I wish that Paul hadn't thought up this stupid plan. The sooner we get back to normal around here the better.'

'Is he going back to Malibu?' Sharon asked.

Rita stared at her, wide-eyed. 'Jesus, you don't think that he proposes to stay on, do you?'

Sharon laughed nervously. 'I don't know what he's planning.'

'He's being so nice, that's what makes it hard . . . Anyone would think that we were the happiest married couple in town, good old Paul and Rita!'

'Well, honey, isn't that the general idea behind all of this?'

Rita nodded. 'It's my fault, of course, I really should have put my foot down . . .'

'So, why didn't you? You could have, you know.'

'Oh, I don't know . . . I suppose part of me wanted to see if my marriage was really over . . . God knows!'

156

'Maybe you've found something out, then,' Sharon suggested.

'Yes, what an absolute bloody fool *I* am!'

'Nonsense.'

'It's like sleeping with the winner of "Mr Frigidair", I'm reduced to absolutely nothing . . . It's humiliating and cruel.'

'Have you told this to Paul?'

'You must be joking.'

'Maybe you should.'

'Sharon, he doesn't talk about anything, we're in there playing at being Mummy and Daddy . . .'

'I don't know how he can behave like that,' Sharon admitted.

'What, because I'm so gorgeous?' she asked, sounding embittered.

'Well, you are. Don't be so negative . . . Do you know what I'd do?' Sharon asked.

Rita was dumping salad on to the paper plates in a haphazard fashion. 'No, what would you do, shoot him?'

Sharon smiled. 'I'd go for it, honey!' She winked at her friend.

'Go for it?' Rita asked, feigning ignorance.

'Sure, I'd seduce my own husband.'

'Oh, come on, Sharon,' Rita grinned at last, 'he'd create merry hell!'

'He can't create anything, dummy. What about the aged parents?' Sharon nudged her friend gently in the side. 'He wouldn't like them to hear anything untoward, now would he?' she asked reasonably.

'And what happens when he rejects my advances?'

'At least you'll have tried. If he rejects your advances, then so what?'

'What if he doesn't?' Rita asked, beginning to get concerned.

Sharon raised her eyes. 'Just try and see what transpires.'

'He left me because he doesn't fancy me.'

'He's in situ now, honey. Give yourself another crack at him before giving up completely.'

'I turn him off . . .'

'Listen, what's the worst thing that could happen?' Sharon asked her.

Rita thought for a moment. 'He could say something beastly and then I'd feel rotten for another six months.'

'At least you won't spend the rest of your life wondering what might have been.'

'You mean that I'll know my marriage is really finished.'

'You'll know where you stand,' Sharon replied.

'I'm beginning to hate myself . . . He's in the wrong and I'm prostituting myself to save a marriage which is already over.'

'If you thought that you'd never have allowed Paul back, not even for three weeks . . .'

'What are you two whispering about?' Paul asked, joining them with a tray of cooked barbecue steaks. 'Come on, the natives are getting restless.' He smiled and looked very handsome. 'Are you going to help dish out?'

Rita looked at him and no longer knew what she felt.

The barbecue came to an end just before midnight, although Paul's mother and father went to their room an hour before that. Mary had been on her best behaviour and hadn't been too objectionable, whilst Paul's father seemed to have enjoyed himself immensely, going to bed in a very jovial frame of mind. Paul was also happy. He had consumed a great deal of Bill's wine and was now lying on the bed in his underpants. He seemed relaxed and talked to Rita as she got undressed.

158

Rita went into the bathroom, where she cleaned her teeth, rinsing out her mouth and smiling at herself in the mirror. She dabbed at her lips before returning to Paul, who was lying, spreadeagle, on his back, fast asleep. She stood by the bed for a moment. He looked incredibly peaceful, almost childlike. How could she seduce a child? Perhaps that was the problem. Despite his reputation, his renowned brilliance, his expertise, he was just a child, or, she thought, maybe all men were children hiding behind the façade they so carefully constructed in order to face their world. Rita pulled the sheet up, her hand touching his chest. She rested it there for a moment, feeling his regular breathing. He had once been her world but what was there left now? She flopped back on to her pillow, angry at her own stupidity. How could she rekindle a love affair that had been dead for years?

After a while she put on his old white terry-towelling robe and went down through the silent house into the lounge. She switched on a table lamp and sat with her legs curled up under her on the sofa. She could see her reflection in the dark windows, waiflike and shrunken inside the oversized bathrobe. Rita thought back to the time before Nathan's suicide and soon realized their sex life even then had long since failed to excite her. She could remember how her mind was often on other things and how she would wish that Paul would get it over with so that she could get some sleep. But at least Rita had still felt a part of something then. They may not have been voracious lovers by that time but a certain comfort in being together had remained, and she had considered that their marriage was working.

She altered her position, lying down now and resting her head on a large cushion, pushing her hands up into the baggy sleeves to keep warm from the chill of the air-conditioning. Her pride had been hurt from Paul's rejection but, more than that, she had to face the probability that their past now lay in ruinous disarray, all their history, their time together cast aside in the space of a few months. And Rita knew then that there was no future, a fact she now had to confront and deal with as best she could. Whether they made it official or not didn't really seem especially important to her at that moment. The marriage was over and, instead of tears, she felt an overwhelming sense of exhaustion, as she fell asleep on the sofa.

Paul didn't mention anything about Rita's alternative sleeping arrangement of the previous night but there was a certain tension between them over breakfast.

Everyone was ready to leave by eleven o'clock. Rita travelled with Paul and his parents in the Mercedes, Steve took the Ford with Jem and William, whilst Bill and Sharon drove their Jaguar with Thomas and Jack on board. Once at Universal Studios they all piled into the open trolleys, towed in trains behind a tractor unit, with candy-striped awnings and jolly-jolly tour guides who grinned all the time and were incredibly enthusiastic.

The tour was highly amusing, they saw sound stages, star dressing rooms and property warehouses. They were driven through the back lots, where, in the space of a few minutes, they passed various sets including a New England fishing village, and a Bavarian square with a little French and Italian architecture thrown in for good measure. They were bombarded with a papier-mâché rockfall, driven through the Red Sea as it parted, and confronted with 'Jaws'. There were cowboy stuntmen being shot and falling off saloon rooftops, the boys became extras in a video representation of a space epic. The trolley tour showed them a street in a flash-flood, a building bursting into flames, and an old-fashioned train with a cow-catcher on the front bearing down on them, stopping just in the nick of time. Mary was horrified at it all and clutched 'Daddy's' hand at each new amusement.

'I thought that fish thing was perfectly horrid,' Mary said as they all sat having a cooling drink later on.

'It was "Jaws", Gran,' William explained.

'No wonder the world is in such a state!' she complained.

Rita laughed. They were sitting at a café high above the back-lot sets they had just driven through. She could see another trolley train jerking its way around, she saw the water gushing down the main street and could imagine the cameras clicking madly as the tourists' reflexes jerked into snapping action. She looked away to where Sharon and Bill were still sorting out the drink and snacks for their offspring. 'It was only a rubber shark, Mary,' she replied.

'It could have been nasty for someone with a dicky heart,' Paul said.

'Rubbish,' Rita snapped back. 'You would have to be a complete idiot to take it seriously . . . Who hasn't heard of "Jaws", for God's sake.'

'Yes, well, that's just typical of you to disregard other people's feelings,' Paul responded angrily.

Rita turned to him. 'What the hell is that supposed to mean?' she asked, her voice becoming louder.

'Whatever you think,' Paul said, 'you say, no matter how hurtful.'

'Oh yes, and what have I done to hurt you?' she challenged.

'Me?' He gave a sardonic laugh. 'I don't know how you can even ask that.'

'Well, I am asking it, Paul, because I don't know what you're bloody well talking about.' Rita was aware that the tables around them had become very quiet. Sharon had turned to look across from the drinks stand and stopped

161

Jack walking across to where Steve and William were sitting.

'Okay, I'll tell you, I'll spell it out, shall I?'

'Please do,' Rita replied, her voice flat and emotionless.

Paul's face contorted into an anger she had never witnessed before. 'I was forced to leave my home because of you . . . I was driven out by your incessant demands concerning the past. All you ever want to do is rake over the dead bones of Nathan.'

Rita pulled back from him. She felt sick, as though she had been hit violently in the stomach. 'It isn't true, it isn't true,' she moaned, almost to herself. 'You were the one who never wanted to face up to the truth of his death.'

'I've had Nathan's death up to here,' he shouted, hitting at his chest, standing up and pushing his metal chair back with a vicious swipe. 'It was never enough for you that he died . . .' He leant across the table, his whole body tense and shaking with rage. 'No, you had to destroy everything else, searching for reasons that don't exist.'

'They *do* exist,' Rita almost screamed back, her voice breaking into sobs.

'Stop it!' Steve yelled, racing across to their table.

Paul hesitated for a moment before storming away, leaving a vacuum of horrified silence behind him.

Rita looked at Steve's face, which clearly showed his mangled emotional state. William was sitting very still, his face deathly white. His grandparents looked completely lost and confused. Mary had dropped her tea cup on to the floor, splashing her dress with the hot liquid, but she didn't appear to have noticed it. The old man was slowly shaking his head from side to side. Sharon and Paul came across and began to organize the children, who went off towards the car park. Bill took the old folks away, which left the two women facing one another across the café table.

162

Rita wiped at her red eyes and smiled defiantly. 'Well,' she said at last, 'I suppose this is the right place for dramatics!'

Sharon looked concerned. 'What the hell happened?'

Rita shrugged, blowing her nose and feeling that all eyes were on her. 'Can we just leave?'

Sharon helped her gather the accumulated baggage of a day out, a camera, William's sweater, a peaked cap with 'Universal Studios' on the front . . . 'Come on,' she said, handing Rita her bag, 'let's get you home.'

Paul was not there when they arrived at the house. He must have driven straight from the studios to Malibu, Rita realized. Bill had taken Paul's parents back in the Jaguar with Jack and Thomas. Sharon had driven the Ford with Rita, Steve, William and Jem. No one said very much on the return journey. Rita stared out at the traffic, Steve looked as though he would burst into tears at any moment. Only William appeared to be calm, even Jem seemed more ruffled. When they pulled into the driveway Bill was already helping the old man out of the front seat. Mary went inside and straight to her room, Jack and Thomas stood aimlessly beside their father's car.

'Okay,' Sharon said, pulling on the hand brake, 'I think that we could all do with a drink.'

Steve went to his room, followed by Jem. William said he was going to swim for a while. Rita, regaining her composure somewhat, asked him if he felt all right. 'Sure.' William looked back. 'I just feel like a swim, that's all.'

The rest of the day went by in a blur and by the late evening things had settled back into a kind of normalcy. Most of the children were around the pool, Steve and Jem had gone out to a film, leaving Sharon and Bill sitting out on the terrace with Rita. After a few bitter words, confused and upset, Mary had retired for the night. Paul's father was plugged into the TV set in the lounge, watching a baseball game. He also seemed a bit happier.

'Well,' Rita said, sipping brandy which was warm and comforting, 'I suppose that's it!'

'I've never seen Paul so angry,' Bill admitted.

'Join the club,' Rita replied, feeling tired, not really wanting to talk about it any more but reluctant to brush aside her friend's concern. 'I think this ridiculous pretence has been too much for both of us . . .'

'Do you want me to talk to him?' Bill asked.

'No,' Rita replied. 'Thank you for asking, though. Paul will come round in his own time and we can then discuss the next step, perhaps . . . How do you seek a divorce in this state, for example?' She smiled as though it were only a joke.

'Rita, don't worry about that now,' Sharon replied. 'What you need to do is get a good night's rest.'

It was the sort of thing her mother might say. Rita smiled and took another sip of brandy. 'Another few measures of this and I'll have no trouble sleeping, I can assure you.'

'Would you like me to stay over?' Sharon asked.

'No.' Rita took her hand. 'I'll be absolutely fine, really I will,' she assured her.

Her mother-in-law joined Rita on the terrace late the following morning. 'I'm afraid Daddy's very upset,' she informed her.

Rita looked up from her work. She had been trying to focus her mind on something practical and avoid thoughts of Paul and everything that meant. However, it had proved a pretty useless exercise and she had read the same paragraph over and over without it making any sense. 'I'm sorry to hear that,' she said. 'Is there anything I can do?'

Mary sat down at the table, taking a cursory look at Rita's work. 'I've given him a tablet, he'll be all right in a little while.'

Rita looked at the old woman. There were deep circles underneath her eyes, she obviously hadn't slept too well either. 'I'm sorry about yesterday, too, it must have been rather a shock for you both.' Rita sounded extremely contrite.

'I'm absolutely astounded,' Mary began. 'How long have you been living separately?'

Rita thought for a moment. 'A few months, since the start of the summer.' She paused. 'Late spring, early summer . . .'

'Can you tell me why?'

Rita didn't feel much like it but she launched into a potted history, outlining some of the events, the reasons as to why she was no longer living with Mary's son.

Mary listened carefully. 'And, no doubt, the boys plague Paul for the answers too . . .'

'They're confused, Mary.'

'I think you've given them too much rope. Whatever has happened? They used to be such polite children!'

'Since Nathan died they've had to grow up very fast . . .'

The old woman shook her head. 'No, that's not it, they're completely changed, those accents and their behaviour, William skulking about the place, Steve rushing from pillar to post with hardly the time to say hello. Well, I'm sorry, Rita, but I feel it's partially your responsibility . . . It's at times like these boys need a father.'

Rita checked her initial response, which was to scream abuse at her mother-in-law, and instead, fists clenched under the table, turned to her. 'I wasn't the one to leave, Mary. It was Paul who walked out!'

'But why? That's the question.'

Rita attempted a further explanation. She spoke of Paul's intransigence, his refusal to discuss Nathan. 'I have to know the reasons behind Nathan's death,' she said.

'Is that why you're seeing a psychiatrist?' Mary asked, as though Rita had already been pronounced mad.

'It's a way of coping with it, yes,' Rita nodded.

Mary tut-tutted. 'You have to be strong, Rita. Instead of that you've become very hard. Why can't you resolve your differences with Paul, forgive him?'

'It's not as easy as that. Besides, I refuse to live a lie . . . Children don't just kill themselves, there has to be some logical explanation.'

'But, my dear, in the process of searching for your answer you're pulling your family in all number of different directions. They don't know where they are!'

'Steve and William are fine,' she responded angrily. 'Of course they've changed, they're becoming young men . . .'

'I never understood why you didn't allow them to continue their education in England . . . This Disneyland can't be helping matters very much.'

'It was Paul's decision to move here, I was attempting to keep the family together.'

'Well, you haven't succeeded very well, have you?' Mary asked bluntly.

'I expected you to take Paul's side,' Rita began. 'He was the one who walked away from us, living alone at Malibu.'

'The problem is, Rita, that you think there has to be some romantic explanation for Nathan's death. Has it never occurred to you that suicide can simply show a lack of moral fibre, the easy way out?'

Rita stared in disbelief. 'What absolute twaddle,' she said heatedly.

'The truth is often the most difficult thing to accept.'

'The truth? What the hell do you know about truth? What do you know about me or Paul or Nathan? It's all very well sitting there handing out all of this sanctimonious bullshit . . .'

'Rita!' The old woman looked horrified.

Rita stood up to leave. 'That's right, you're offended that I use bad language . . . Why weren't you as offended at Nathan's death? You're just like your bloody son, your emotions have been hidden away for so long you're incapable of showing compassion . . .'

'You're talking nonsense, Rita. Have you taken complete leave of your senses?'

Rita almost burst into laughter, it sounded so ludicrous. 'Let's just forget it,' she said, walking away along the terrace. 'Forget it!'

They spent the remainder of the week skirting around one another and being awfully polite each time they did meet. Rita didn't see Paul again until it was time for him to pick the old folks up and take them to the airport. He had seen them a few times in the week but she had been out when he called. Steve and William agreed to go to the airport with their father after a lot of coaxing from Rita.

'We'll see you at Christmas then,' Mary said, shaking Rita's hand.

Rita nodded, forcing a smile across her face. She kissed the old man on his cheek and wished them a good flight. Paul asked her if they had all their bags and she replied in the affirmative. She waited until the big car had turned into the canyon road at the bottom of the driveway before wandering across the grass to the redwood table, where she sat for a long time.

It was late afternoon and the garden sprinklers were on, spraying fine jets of water into the air. As the sunlight caught at the water droplets, she could see rainbow colours appear. Rita sat back, her head tilted upwards, looking through the fanned leaf formation of the palm leaves above as they moved in the gentle breeze. She wondered what her next step should be and considered returning to London, but the thought of uprooting the boys again was too much to contemplate, making her head spin. Rita had nothing in particular to return for and no one in particular to keep her in California. She looked down at the white houses in the valley and the cloud of smog hovering above them in the distance. She smiled, despite the disasters of the previous three weeks, and felt a strange sense of relief now it was all over. Whatever she might have considered previously about salvaging her marriage, it was all too late now and there was no going back.

Chapter 5

'So, Rita,' Dr Allan began, 'what are your feelings about Paul now?'

'Now?' She thought hard. 'I was thinking about my life with him . . . I mean before, before Nathan's suicide.' She paused. 'I think I was probably bored with our relationship.'

'And yet you took him back.'

'I didn't exactly "take him back".' She smiled at the idea, it sounded so old-fashioned.

'You allowed him back inside the house,' he suggested.

'It's still Paul's house.'

'Into your bed?'

'It's still his bed,' she waved the idea away.

'What were you thinking when he did come back?'

'Thinking? I wasn't thinking anything . . . he'd asked me to go through with it for the sake of his parents.'

'Were you quite at ease with the new situation?'

'No, certainly not, I was confused,' she admitted. 'Part of me thought I should try again, forget what he had said to me, and see what happened.'

'What about the other part?'

'I didn't want anything to do with him . . . he'd told me that I made him impotent,' she reminded the doctor.

'So, you were contemplating sexual relations?'

'I wasn't contemplating anything . . . Paul seemed quite relaxed about everything for most of the time and he certainly behaved as though we were still married . . . I mean, of course, we *are* still married . . .' her voice tailed away.

'Did you think he wanted a reconciliation?'

'He was back in the house, we were sleeping together, he seemed perfectly at ease with the situation . . . I had to keep pinching myself to believe that it was happening.'

Dr Allan smiled. 'But, when you didn't have sexual intercourse, when Paul didn't show any signs of wanting to make love, how did you feel?'

'I felt ambivalent.'

He nodded and made a brief note. 'And then you argued at the studio and everything just came to pieces again?'

'Yes, he was obviously as unhappy with me as I was with him . . . I hated the play-acting, anyway. If we weren't going to come back together as a proper married couple, then I was never going to be interested.'

'So, what has happened now, would you say? I mean, in terms of your relationship with Paul.'

Rita shook her head. 'My respect for him is somewhere beneath zero and I would imagine he reciprocates that feeling.'

'I see, yes.' He flicked back a few pages in his notebook. 'What would you like to happen now?'

'I would like us to be able to sit down like two grown-ups and discuss everything in a sensible way.'

'Do you see that as a possibility?'

'No.'

'Never?'

'Not for a *long* time.'

'But you are two sensible grown-up people,' he argued.

'Paul won't discuss any of the issues . . . You know, I sometimes think he should be the one sitting here facing you!'

'Would he do that?'

'Not in a million years.'

'What can you do, if he'll never talk about the issues you see as being important?'

She shrugged. 'I suppose I have to wait until he does feel able to talk.'

'Is that a probability?'

'Maybe . . . He's angry with me, he thinks that I deliberately wrecked his parents' holiday . . .'

'Did you?' the doctor interrupted.

Rita paused before replying. 'I'm sure that I didn't do as much as I could to make it a fabulous holiday.'

'And?'

'And it makes me feel guilty, so that's another weight to hang around my neck, I know, I know.'

'You know, Rita, you collect guilt the way some people collect stamps!'

She laughed at that. 'I know it's dreadful but I can't really stand his mother . . . nor can Paul, if the truth be told, and she doesn't exactly brim over with the milk of human kindness where I am involved. I never really understood why they wanted to come out for three weeks. His father sleeps for most of the time. I'm sure they were both really unhappy . . .'

'So, you were dealing with his parents and trying to cope with your emotions where Paul was concerned. That's a tall order, Rita, a very tall order.'

'I think I might have behaved a little better all the same . . . I could have been nicer.'

'This is the self-sacrificing Rita emerging again,' he said, tapping the side of his nose with the end of his pencil. 'Why do you have to be perfect?'

She felt quite shocked at that and took a while to answer him. 'I feel I'm far from that, doctor.'

'Have you ever considered being a little easier on yourself?'

Rita didn't know how to answer him.

'It seems an easy lesson to learn, doesn't it? But sometimes it's one of the hardest.'

'You mean I'm too hard on myself?' There was an element of disbelief in her voice.

'On yourself and, maybe, on your kids, even on Paul . . .'

'I have never expected anything of my children, or even of Paul, come to that,' she insisted.

'No, and why is that? I'll tell you why. It's because Rita will take it all on board, Rita will do it all . . . Maybe you expect too much.'

'I don't expect perfection.' She laughed at the idea.

'Not perfection necessarily, but people rarely live up to what we would like them to be. This is harder to cope with when it's people we love.' He was looking at her intently, as though focusing his ideas into her brain.

Rita began to feel nervous, that uncomfortable feeling in the pit of her stomach, the rising guilt of a life-time beginning to surface. She was unhappy with the way his discussion was moving. 'I'm not perfect,' she repeated, 'and I've never expected anyone else to be.'

'You told me a while ago that you thought Nathan had it all,' he was making reference to some notes as he spoke, 'I was never sure what you meant by that. Could you expand it for me?'

Rita felt as though she were being cornered. 'Nathan was bright and intelligent, he had a comfortable life, we were relatively affluent . . .' She ran out of things to say. 'I suppose that's what I meant, he had brains, looks and a bright future.'

Dr Allan had been listening carefully. 'How does that compare with your own experience? When you were Nathan's age, after all, you studied hard and won a place at university.'

Rita grinned. 'When I was young I had to do my school

work in a crowded, noisy living room. It was that or a freezing bedroom.' She laughed at herself. 'I know, it sounds awfully Dickensian, doesn't it?'

The doctor smiled. 'So, when you say he had everything, you mean he had it easy?'

'Not easy.'

'No? But easier than you.'

'Different from me.'

'Not easier?'

'Less difficult, certainly, but he still had to work hard.'

'You also talked about having failed when he died.'

'Yes,' Rita agreed. She had clasped her hands together and was turning her wedding ring round and round on her finger. 'I still feel that.'

'But you couldn't possibly have known what he was going to do, there weren't any signs. So, how can you have failed?'

'It doesn't have to make sense . . . perhaps it doesn't, but, nevertheless, it's how I still feel.'

'Did you give any thought to my question?'

'Which question?' She laughed nervously. 'There have been so many.' Rita knew which question.

'Last time we were speaking about your feelings for Paul.'

'You asked me when I stopped loving him,' she nodded.

Dr Allan sat back in his chair waiting for her to answer.

'I'm not sure if I can answer that.'

'Well, try, give it a shot. You're amongst friends, shall we say!' He turned on one of his most charming smiles, which made his whole face light up.

'I sometimes speak of having fallen in love with Paul but . . .' She was hesitant, as though trying to find the appropriate words. 'I was always so out of control with him, I found him extremely desirable, a certain, how can I say, symbiosis?'

'You mean you had great sex?' The doctor smiled broadly.

Rita laughed. 'Yes.' She flushed a little, feeling embarrassed. 'We were very compatible when we were young.'

'Then say it! Don't be ashamed of admitting to something like that . . . You know, people have actually consulted me because they have many problems in that particular area of their lives!' He laughed.

'I can imagine,' she replied.

'So, what are you telling me?' he asked softly.

'I've thought more just recently about my marriage and, it frightens me to say this, but,' she turned her head away for a moment, 'I don't know if I was ever actually in love with Paul.'

'You don't know or you know?'

'It seems obvious to me now,' she replied.

'So, how does that make you feel?'

'It feels a little sad.'

'And what else?' he wanted to know.

'What else?'

'Yes, and don't say it makes you feel guilty!'

Rita laughed, despite her confused reactions at having admitted this in public, as it were, for the first time. 'I feel that it releases me from some sort of obligation that was my marriage.'

'And so, where does that leave you?'

'That I have more control over my destiny?' she asked tentatively.

The doctor nodded. 'Maybe so, maybe so.'

Rita grinned with pleasure, her hands clenched tightly together, her wedding ring digging into her fingers.

Rita felt elated for a while after leaving the doctor's office. At last it seemed they were really getting somewhere. However, when she examined this thought there

174

didn't appear to be any tangible change in her feelings. She was still in the same situation as she had been before entering the doctor's room. She clung to that sense of elation for a while, and it gave her a certain comfort to feel it so strongly.

She called in on Sharon, who was having some work done in her house, a new kitchen. She found her in the old kitchen with a tall man who was introduced to her as Gary.

'This hunk is going to make my kitchen into absolute paradise,' she said, her voice full of laughter.

Rita smiled and said hello to him. Gary was well-built, with the usual tan and blond hair. He was wearing Levi's and trainers with a black sports shirt, looking more like an athletics coach than a builder. Gary also possessed an extremely attractive and winning smile. He discussed a few more details with Sharon, pointing to various areas on the plan he was holding, and then left, promising to be back bright and early the following morning to begin work.

'Why are you having this kitchen out?' Rita enquired. 'It's always seemed fine to me.'

'It's years old and Gary will do an absolutely fabulous job . . . It's going to look superb.' Sharon beamed at the thought. 'Why don't you get him to build you a kitchen?'

'I don't need a kitchen,' Rita replied firmly.

'You know, don't you, that Gary is the man who built your redwood table and chairs?'

Rita hadn't realized and she looked surprised. 'I always imagined a little old man working in a saw mill had made them.'

'He's stunning, isn't he?' Sharon winked at her.

'You're incorrigible,' Rita complained, laughing.

'Listen, honey, he's handsome, straight and useful

around the house . . . What more could you possibly want?'

Rita raised her eyes to the ceiling. 'Your imagination is working overtime, but he is very good-looking, I'll give you that!'

'It wouldn't hurt you just having him around to measure up the place and quote you a price.'

'I don't need a new kitchen . . . Besides, Paul would have a fit.'

'What's it got to do with Paul?'

'He'd have to pay for it.'

'Stop quibbling, let him quote you a price. Gary has a fine reputation and he's between jobs at the present time.'

'Between jobs?' Rita was confused.

Sharon nodded. 'Yes, didn't I tell you? He's an actor, you know, bit parts in films and on TV.'

'Oh.' Rita didn't sound terribly impressed.

'Let him look at your place, Rita, you know what good-quality work he does,' Sharon almost pleaded.

'What are you, his agent or something?'

'Boy, wouldn't I like to be!' Sharon replied.

Rita laughed. 'Okay, if he wants to come and quote for a new kitchen, he can. But I'm not having one built . . . I don't care how fabulous he is!'

Sharon made them a late lunch, which they ate on their laps in the lounge, falling back into the comfortable seats and talking about Rita's session with Dr Allan. Rita didn't stay too long as she had to get back and work for a couple of hours.

'I'm taking the completed book to London with me in December,' she told Sharon as she was about to leave.

'I wasn't sure if you were still taking that trip,' Sharon said.

'Sure am,' Rita smiled, 'although I think it will be just *moi* and the boys!'

Sharon nodded. 'I'll send Gary round sometime tomorrow then,' she said as Rita left.

'Okay.' Rita looked at her friend. 'Is there anything else that I should know about him . . . You know, just in case I decide to have him come and work in my house?'

'He's not married,' Sharon replied, 'and I don't think he's with anyone at the moment.'

Rita gave a disbelieving laugh. 'Oh no?'

Sharon shook her head. 'I don't think so.'

Rita grinned. 'Well, a new kitchen is the one thing I don't need at the moment.'

'Honey, everyone needs a new kitchen built by Gary. Just seeing him every morning is enough to get the old heart pumping!'

'Is Bill aware you've got the hots for this man?'

'Rita!' Sharon feigned shock at her question. 'I have no such thing . . . Besides, fantasy is supposed to be entirely healthy . . . hasn't Dr Allan told you that yet?'

Rita pulled a face. 'Maybe Dr Allan should build my new kitchen. I'm paying him enough, and at least I'd get something tangible for my money!'

'Just you wait and see,' Sharon encouraged. 'It will be the best investment you could possibly have made.'

'Dr Allan or the new kitchen?' Rita asked.

'Both, honey, both.'

Rita walked back to her house and, taking everything to the redwood table, began the final section of Virginia Woolf.

Gary began work on Rita's new kitchen in the second week of November. Paul had complained bitterly at the unnecessary expense but she had gone ahead with it anyway. She needed something, a project to involve herself in, something practical, even if it was only a kitchen.

At first she had eyed him from a distance. He was, of course, very good-looking but, unlike so many other good-looking men, Gary didn't really seem to trade upon this fact. Once she had chosen the tiles, flooring, type of wood for the units, what oven and hob she would have, what kind of lighting and what colour paintwork, he was left to work.

The temperature in Los Angeles in November was still in the low to mid-seventies, a fact Rita still found novel, and she worked away happily on the terrace. Gary had taken to eating lunch nearby, and they began to learn the introductory facts about one another. He was interested in her writing, having graduated in English Literature and Drama at Berkeley.

'You're an actor, an English major and a carpenter?' she said, laughing.

'My acting is incidental,' he replied, smiling.

'Oh, really, and why is that?' Rita asked, looking at his broad shoulders. Gary always worked in Levi's and trainers and wore athletic-type running vests. The one he had on today was a shiny blue material with the Nike logo in white across the chest. His skin was coated with a fine layer of sawdust and there was a ringlet of wood-shaving in his blond hair which she had leant forward to pick out.

'I've never been offered anything of substance to do.'

'But you still take parts in films.'

Gary nodded. 'Sure, bits that help pay the rent.'

'You could teach acting,' she suggested.

He smiled. 'I don't have enough patience.'

'I see.'

'I'm thirty-eight years old. It doesn't seem to me that I'm going to break into the big time now, but then I guess life doesn't have to work out as you would have liked it.'

'It almost certainly never does,' she answered, with more feeling than she had meant to.

178

'Sharon tells me that you are separated?'

Rita nodded but didn't feel like making any comment.

'I've been down that particular road . . . twice!'

'Any children?'

'Sure, one, a boy . . . a young man now,' he corrected himself. 'James, he's nineteen . . . lives in New York, that's where my first wife moved after we split up.'

'Do you see much of him?' Rita asked.

'He came out for a couple of weeks this summer and I see him when I go East.'

Gary worked on the new kitchen for two weeks and Rita looked forward to their meetings. She liked him, finding his conversation interesting and witty, and his body appealing. She liked his voice and his looks and his intelligence. On the day the kitchen was finally completed she knew she had to continue seeing him, but every ploy she considered sounded so corny and obvious that she called Sharon and asked her for some advice.

'I want to see him again,' she said.

There was a pause on the other end of the line before Sharon spoke, and there was laughter in her voice when she did. 'So, ask him out.'

'Don't be ridiculous,' Rita replied, 'he'll think I'm a man-eater.'

Sharon hooted with laughter. 'Well, launch the new kitchen with a meal and invite him to partake,' she suggested.

'Isn't that a bit like asking him up to see my etchings?'

'Rita,' she replied firmly, 'you're only feeding him, aren't you?'

Rita paused for a moment. 'Sharon, do you think I'm being stupid?'

'Stupid? What's stupid about inviting a gorgeous man for dinner? Stupid is *not* inviting him!'

'Sharon, I'm not sure what to do.'

'Then don't ask him,' she replied with irritatingly simplistic logic.

'I want to see him.'

'Honey, get into that fabulous new kitchen and ask,' she commanded, 'and don't call me again until you've got a firm date!' She put down the phone.

Rita sat on her bed for a long time, still holding the buzzing receiver in her hand. Finally, she took a deep breath and, fearing the worst, made tracks for the kitchen. Gary was finishing off some grouting around the window sill when she walked in.

'Morning, Rita,' he said, smiling at her and standing back to admire his work. 'I think we've done a pretty good job here, what about you?'

She nodded, looking at the carefully crafted units and surfaces. 'I think you've done a terrific job.'

He faked a little bow. 'Thank you kindly, ma'am.'

'Gary, what about helping me to celebrate the opening?' She heard herself and felt completely out of her depth. 'I'm a good cook and I'd like to prepare a meal for us.' She hardly dared look at him.

'Do you know Laurel Canyon?' he asked.

She nodded, feeling not only embarrassed but confused now. 'Yes, I do.'

'Okay,' he grinned, looking almost conspiratorial, 'and are you allowed out at nights?'

'Yes.'

'Can you come out tonight?'

'Yes.'

'Great, then I'll cook the meal if you bring the wine . . . There's plenty of time for you to inaugurate this place.'

'Right,' she agreed.

180

'Right,' he said, smiling at her before returning to his job.

Gary's house was of low, ranch-type construction, with dark wooden eaves and partially clad on the exterior with the same dark wood. It was hidden away in Laurel Canyon amidst pine trees which overhung the building. The driveway was almost concealed from the road by trees and bushes, and Rita's Ford filled up all the remaining space behind Gary's Jeep.

'Mom's got a date,' William had teased as she came down to wish them good-night.

'I'm having a meal with Gary . . . okay? Do I have your permission for that?'

Steve whistled as she came into the lounge. 'You're really dressed up, Mum,' he said.

'This old thing?' She looked down at herself. 'It's nothing special.' In fact she had spent hours discarding clothes in an attempt to find something suitable until, in the end, Sharon had been called in to assist. They rooted around through the depths of Rita's wardrobe until eventually deciding upon a severely tailored Jean Paul Gaultier suit jacket over a short black dress. Sharon discovered a pair of black high heels, which she insisted Rita try on. The dress was cut quite low at the back and Rita wasn't at all certain of the effect.

'It looks sensational,' Sharon assured her, standing back and giving Rita a critical once-over.

'I feel as if I'm preparing for my first date,' Rita said.

'First dat*ees* don't normally have on their wedding and engagement rings,' Sharon replied with a slightly pained expression.

Rita had looked down at her rings but decided against removing them, and now stood outside Gary's house waiting for him to answer the door. After a few seconds he opened the door and welcomed her inside. The house was constructed on a series of different levels and, from the entrance hall, there were steps into a large living area which opened out on to a small patio. Gary led her across the dark sheen of the varnished floor boards and out through the sliding doors into the small garden. It was absolutely secluded. Beyond the patio there was a swimming pool which took up most of the available space. Large terracotta pots were spaced around, full of trailing lobelia and petunias, marigolds, geraniums, cornflowers and asters. Beyond the pool and the paved terrace at the end of the property, the canyon fell away, giving a panoramic view over Los Angeles.

'On a clear day you can see the beach,' Gary said, pouring them a glass of wine from a bottle on a redwood table. He motioned for her to sit down. 'You're looking very soignée, Rita,' he grinned, handing her a glass.

She wondered if that meant she was rather too formally attired. Rita noted his clean Levi's, flashy Adidas trainers, pure white sports socks and Sergio Tacchini tennis shirt. Even the socks had 'Nike' across the ankle. She shrugged off her jacket and took a sip of the wine. Gary gave the expression 'clean-cut' a new meaning, like so many of the Californian men she had come across. They all had this look, scrubbed and bronzed and worked-out and built like the sides of houses. There was a lot of perfection about them and they obviously took great care to choose the appropriate clothes, the correct tan, the best body for their particular life. She had found Gary's workplace dishevelment somewhat appealing and, although he was still obviously extremely attractive to her, there was something missing. It was a small detail but she thought about it and then let it pass.

'I hope you like crab, Rita,' he said.

'Yes, I do,' she smiled. 'Very much.'

'Great, I've prepared Crab Louis.'

She nodded. 'I've heard of that but never had it.'

He looked pleased. 'Well, there's always a first time for everything, right?'

She nodded encouragingly. 'Yes.' She looked around. 'This is a very beautiful house and such a lovely spot.'

'Thanks, I built this place myself.'

'Oh, really?' She sounded incredulous. She thought that building a house with your own hands showed an almost pioneering spirit. 'You're obviously very good with your hands.' She turned to him and burst out laughing.

He caught her double entendre and laughed too. 'I've had few complaints in the past,' he answered.

Rita smiled. 'Yes, well . . . perhaps, at this point, you should show me round the house?'

He nodded and, standing up, walked across the patio and into the lounge. To their left, and down two wooden steps, as they entered the house, was the kitchen. It was cluttered from much use and seemed full of plant life, climbing ivy and ferns hanging in baskets from the pine ceiling. The windows looked directly over the canyon side, and below were the lights of Hollywood. To their right, and up several steps, was the sleeping area, two large bedrooms and two bathrooms.

The walls were white, the ceilings were all of pine and the floors were varnished oak. There was a central fireplace in the lounge, although as the temperature, even in the 'winter months', remained between the mid-sixties and low seventies, Rita wasn't sure how much use this fixture got. In her first Californian winter she remembered how she had swum every day throughout January! It had been yet one more novelty to write home about. There were two long sofas on either side of the fire, covered with a fabric that seemed to resemble an ethnic Indian design, beautiful colours, muted reds and blues, bright

183

yellows and ochres, and square patterns, some shaped like birds and others like strange mythological beasts.

One wall was covered in photographs. Rita looked at these as Gary went into the kitchen again to complete the preparations for their dinner. Pictures of Gary when he was young, athletic Gary, pensive Gary, sixties Gary with flowing blond locks, Afghan coat and beads, Gary in the midst of 'revolution' at Berkeley. Gary with a fat baby and gaunt-looking blonde, Gary with teenage child. The history of his life across the white wall of his lounge.

'You were very pretty in the sixties,' Rita called to him.

He appeared at the doorway. 'What was that?'

'These photographs of you in the sixties . . . you were very pretty.'

He laughed with a certain amount of embarrassment. 'God, the sixties . . . Don't the fashions seem weird now?'

Rita nodded.

'You must have been a student at the same time,' he said.

'A bit before you . . . I graduated in 1967.'

'I started at Berkeley in that year.'

Rita smiled. 'You must have driven the girls mad with all that blond hair!'

'Jesus,' he replied, hugging his arms around his body, 'I drove one girl wild, obviously, because I was married and a father when I was nineteen.'

She looked at the pictures again. 'Your son looks like you, doesn't he?'

'For better or worse,' Gary nodded. 'You know, the kids today are into the fifties . . . He looks just like one of those fifties movie stars, you know, like Jimmy Dean or something. When he looks at those pictures he just thinks they're gross!'

'I suppose their generation has seen the sixties as a

largely discredited era . . . Everything has been turned on to its head since then. God knows what we are responsible for. I sometimes wonder if they resent us for it.'

'Each generation constructs itself in a way it sees as being fresh and innovative. I'm not sure if things really change that much – apart from fashion.'

'And the fact that the legacy of the sixties, the free love, flower power, let it all hang out ethos has been thrown aside by the eighties generation . . .'

'You mean, by things like AIDS?'

Rita shrugged. 'Not only that, although, God knows, I suppose that has to be part of it . . . No, it's more than that. For example, what are all the student revolutionaries doing today? They're all lawyers and accountants and businessmen and -women . . . I mean, after the initial fling, they dropped from the barricades and rejoined the comfortable middle classes . . .'

'Or moved to Hollywood and built houses,' he grinned.

'I'm sorry,' Rita laughed. 'I'm showing my age, aren't I . . . one of the discredited ones!'

'Not at all,' he replied. 'Come on, let's eat.'

Rita went down the steps into the kitchen, where the large old oak table was set complete with large stubby round candles. It was growing dark outside and the lights of Los Angeles looked magical as they blazed in the distance.

'This is the real McCoy,' he said, bringing the food to the table, 'complete with a salad dressing of mayonnaise, chili and horse-radish . . .'

'Capers too?' Rita asked.

'Capers too,' he laughed. 'That's very good, Rita, that makes you a real connoisseur!'

She chuckled. 'Oh, I always research my foreign dishes when I move abroad.'

'Well, ma'am,' he replied, 'we sure do appreciate that!'

185

'It's my pleasure, of course!'

Gary sat down and looked at her through the candle light. 'I'm glad you came,' he said, raising his glass to her.

'Thank you,' Rita toasted him with her own glass, 'I'm very glad that I came.'

After dinner they sat outside on the patio, which was made up of old house bricks constructed into swirling circular patterns. In front of them the illuminated pool gave a lustrous light which looked slightly eerie in the darkness. The lights of Los Angeles spread out beneath them as far as the eye could see. Gary brought the coffee out and they continued their discussion about Rita's tennis match the following week. Kirk had given her the extra lessons but she still didn't feel very confident.

'I could practise with you this week-end, if you like,' Gary suggested.

'Oh, you don't have to do that,' she replied.

'I know I don't,' he laughed. 'I'd like to, really.'

'Okay,' she agreed. 'You can decide the time. The boys are going to Malibu this week-end to see their father, so whenever you like . . .' She picked up her coffee mug.

'What kind of standard are you?' Gary asked warily.

'I'm not that bad,' she replied, 'I'm just not really up to match play.'

'Okay,' he nodded, 'what are you like first thing in the morning?'

'What do you mean by first thing?'

'Nine-thirty?' he suggested.

'Steve's driving them both to the beach, so that will be fine, I suppose.'

'You mean an earlier time would be better?' he jested.

'Good God, no!'

Gary laughed. 'I'll look forward to it.'

'I wouldn't speak too soon if I were you,' Rita warned him.

'I expect you're good, you have an athletic build.'

Rita wasn't sure how to react, but she took it as a compliment. 'I was sports girl of the year at my junior school for two years running.'

'There you go, then.'

'Hmm . . . that was thirty-odd years ago and my expertise in the three-legged race doesn't seem quite relevant to round robin at the country club, somehow!'

'Oh, I don't know, if you play the doubles with Sharon you could always tie your legs together . . . It would certainly put your opposition team off for a while.'

'They take it all very seriously, that's why I need all the help I can get.'

'What does your coach say?'

'Kirk is enormously encouraging, he works on the basis of the self-fulfilling prophecy . . . if I think I'm good I will be!'

Gary smiled. 'Okay, tomorrow it is, then.'

Rita looked into his eyes and experienced a feeling of enormous desire, so powerful that she found the coffee mug shaking in her hand.

Sharon must have seen her car lights because she called Rita just before midnight. Rita stepped out of her high heels and picked up the phone, lying on the bed as she put it to her ear.

'So, what happened?' Sharon asked, eager for the information.

'He made us dinner,' Rita replied.

'Did he . . . you know . . . try anything?'

'Yes, we had Crab Louis!'

'You know what I mean,' Sharon said. 'Did you get anywhere close to the bedroom area?'

'I saw his bedroom.'

'And?'

'It was white with a pine-clad ceiling.'

'Rita!' Sharon sounded exasperated.

'Nothing happened,' Rita said, laughing.

'Nothing?'

'No.'

'Not even a good-night kiss?'

'Not even that.'

'My God,' Sharon grumbled, 'what's the matter with the man?'

'But I'm seeing him in the morning.'

'Another date, that's very good.'

'He's coming here to play tennis.'

'Good,' Sharon sounded more cheerful, 'very good. He won't be fully dressed, that should make things easier.'

'Sharon,' Rita replied, sounding terribly shocked, 'I am not about to have an affair with Gary.'

There was a pause at the other end. 'Well, are you doing anything else, apart from ogling one another from the other side of a tennis net?'

'I don't know yet, and we will not ogle.'

'And wear something appropriate.'

'What do you suggest, a cocktail dress?'

'Don't be smart, Rita, it doesn't become you,' Sharon giggled. 'No, wear your Lacoste tennis outfit, it's *very* slinky.'

'I'll think about it,' Rita agreed.

'Gary will be impressed,' she assured her.

'He's volunteered to help me out because of you entering us for that stupid tournament.'

'Bullshit, he's helping you out because he's got the hots for you.'

'I'm hanging up now, Sharon,' Rita laughed, 'and I'll call you tomorrow with the latest bulletin.' She replaced the receiver and lay back thinking.

Rita had promised herself that she would spend the

week-end working, in an effort to complete the book. Now she had arranged something else. 'You're just a sucker for a good-looking man, Rita,' she said, sitting up and staring at her tired reflection in the wall-length mirrors, 'you're just a sucker.' She got up and unzipped the little black dress, dropping it on to the floor and walking into the bathroom, where she removed her make-up and scrubbed her teeth. On her return she picked up the dress and draped it across the armchair by the window. By the time she got into bed it was almost one o'clock and she fell immediately asleep.

The week-end seemed to pass quickly. She played tennis with Gary for most of Saturday, with intermittent breaks for liquid refreshment and various snacks throughout the day. He was, as Rita had imagined, an excellent tennis player and, as she had also imagined, turned up in immaculate tennis clothes with the Fila logo attached, black tennis shorts and a cerise shirt. He carried a large tennis bag with a number of rackets inside, and among the various accoutrements she noted Lacoste headbands, sweatbands and towels. For her part she had chosen to wear the baggy khaki shorts and matching T-shirt. She looked down at her scuffed tennis shoes, red and dirty from the court surface. Gary's looked new.

She prepared an evening meal, and he left around eleven-thirty. This time they kissed good-night, nothing too dramatic, Rita considered, but enough to suggest theirs was a relationship that might have the makings of something. Rita certainly felt something more than just friendship for him.

As she undressed that night, Rita realized that, for the first time in two years, she hadn't thought of Nathan once during the course of their day together.

* * *

'Dad's got a girlfriend,' William informed her as they walked through the door on Sunday evening.

'Oh,' Rita replied without batting an eyelid, 'is she nice?'

'We didn't actually see her,' Steve answered her, dropping his bag on to the lounge floor.

'Oh,' Rita said.

'He had a photograph of her on the kitchen notice board,' William said.

'How do you know it's his girlfriend?' she asked.

'Because he said it was a friend from work who we would probably be meeting one week-end when we were down at the beach.' William sat next to her. 'So, it's obvious, isn't it?'

Rita shrugged. They seemed to be accepting the situation for what it was. They were obviously aware that Gary had been around for the last few weeks and that she had gone to his house for dinner. The news of Paul's 'girlfriend' made Rita feel, somehow, less underhand.

'Do you think he'll want to marry her?' William suddenly asked.

Rita smiled. 'I have absolutely no idea . . . I think perhaps it's a wee bit early to be talking about marriage.'

'Or divorce,' Steve said.

'Would you mind?' William asked.

It was obvious that they had been cooking this up on the drive back from Malibu. It was so obvious that Rita couldn't stop herself from grinning. 'Has your father said anything to you on this topic?'

'No,' Steve replied, 'you must be joking!'

'Well, look, I don't know what his plans are either, but let's just take everything one step at a time before you get too excited about impending weddings . . .'

'Or divorces,' Steve reminded her. 'There have to be divorces before you can have weddings.'

'What do you think about your dad and this girlfriend of his?' she asked, looking from one to the other.

William shrugged.

'It doesn't have much to do with us, does it?' Steve replied.

'Well, no, but I would imagine you had some feelings on the subject,' Rita said.

'Maybe it would be good for Dad to have someone, maybe he would stop being so crotchety,' William said.

'Dad's still married to Mum,' Steve reminded him.

'Yes, but they're not living together,' he looked at his mother, 'are you?'

Rita shook her head. 'Obviously not and, from the way things stand at the moment, it looks increasingly unlikely that we ever will.' She decided to be perfectly frank about it. 'But I doubt very much if we are actually going to get divorced in a hurry . . . We haven't even discussed that.'

'What happens to us?' William asked her.

'Nothing happens to you,' she replied.

'What if you do divorce?' William wanted to know.

Rita shrugged. 'Things would remain very much as they have done since the summer.'

'So, you won't go back to London?' Steve asked her.

'It's unlikely.'

'But not impossible?' he persisted.

'Steve, nothing is impossible. It's very unlikely. What do I have to take me back to London?'

The conversation continued for a while in a rather circumspect fashion but the boys seemed happier about the whole topic of her and Paul when they had finished. They went on to discuss their respective week-ends. Steve and William seemed to be more excited about her prospects in the imminent tournament than Rita, who just wanted to get it over and done with as soon as possible.

* * *

191

Rita had arranged to meet Paul at the beach house. It was the last week of school before the Christmas holiday and he was taking a couple of days off and doing some work at home. It was the week after the tennis tournament and Rita, to her amazement, had reached the final – only to lose very badly in straight sets. However, as Gary told her in the car afterwards, it was the playing that counts. Steve and William were full of ebullient praise. Sharon wept and Kirk, who had come to watch without telling her, gave one of his most fabulous smiles and a big hug, which Rita much appreciated. There was a surprise party at home with several bottles of Dom Pérignon and it had been like Christmas arriving two weeks early.

Rita smiled at the thought of it now as she pulled up outside Paul's house. The weather was warm and fine, a perfectly clear day, reminding her of early autumn in England.

Paul had been out running and was relaxed and seemed pleased to see her. He looked tanned and very healthy. His hair was cut short, which made him look younger. Rita had put on some new Levi's and a plaid blouse under a green windcheater for protection against the fresh Pacific breezes. Paul suggested a walk along the sands and she agreed. He congratulated her on the tournament.

'The boys were full of it,' Paul said.

'Never again,' Rita told him, squinting as she looked across the ocean, which was reflecting the strong sunshine. 'I assume that you're not coming to London with us this Christmas,' Rita said, turning to him as they walked along the shore. 'You haven't said anything and we still have your ticket.'

Paul was silent for a few steps. 'I should have made that clear, I'm sorry,' he began. 'No, I think I'll stay on in LA . . . The boys have probably told you that I'm seeing someone.' He turned to her as he said this.

Rita nodded. 'They're very intrigued.'

He smiled. 'She comes to the hospital. They haven't met her yet because she's always been working when they've been here.'

'What's her name?' Rita asked.

'Joanne,' he replied, looking down at his feet. 'She's a gynaecologist . . . in private practice,' he explained. 'She does some teaching days for us.'

Rita stood for a moment to watch a seagull swoop over the surface of the water. 'I see.'

'I understand that you're seeing the man who built the new kitchen?'

'Sort of,' she replied. 'You haven't been up to the house to see it yet . . .'

'Didn't he make us those redwood chairs, and the table?'

Rita was amazed that he should remember. She nodded. 'He's really very talented.'

'I remember Sharon singing his praises once. Isn't he a bit of an actor as well?'

Rita laughed. 'A bit actor, yes.'

'Oh, I see,' Paul smiled.

They walked on for a while without speaking. Rita was the first to break the silence. 'We ought to talk after Christmas, to sort out just what we are going to do.'

Paul nodded. 'I don't know about you, but I'm not really thinking about divorce . . . I mean, I'm not intending to marry anyone else.'

He sounded so reasonable that Rita was completely taken aback. They walked on a bit further, sitting for a while on the sands, looking out over the Pacific swell. Rita felt that there was an enormous gulf between them, in the space of a few weeks really they had become such strangers. It no longer even felt sad to her, just inevitable. She had moved here two years before in order to keep

193

the family together, thinking that, one day, everything would be back the way it once was between them.

She felt a desperate desire to talk about Nathan with Paul, to talk about him with his father. She wanted more than a sounding board or a sympathetic ear, she wanted more than professional advice, what she needed was someone to listen to her who knew Nathan, someone who would understand exactly what it was she had gone through and was still experiencing and, if it wasn't to be Paul, then it couldn't be anybody because he was the only one who could possibly understand. Rita knew that it was hopeless even to mention Nathan to him. Paul's knee-jerk, reflex action was to abandon all rationality; he was incapable of speaking about his son.

And so she was left, despairing of any solution, feeling terribly alone. Dr Allan had told her she was looking for perfection and that she expected too much from the people around her.

Paul had wandered to the water's edge, where he was standing, hands shading his eyes, looking out at a group of racing yachts with billowing sails and puffed-out spin-nakers, bright reds and oranges and yellows against the blue of the sky. Paul had been the perfection she craved in a man, he had meant everything to her. Without Paul she had once doubted if there would be a life for her. Over the years things changed in subtle ways, falling in and out of love are not always necessarily dramatic events. Rita knew at twenty-one that she had never been in love with him in the way he was in love with her. She still craved him but there was always a part of him that seemed dead to her, some emotional response that was lacking, a failure to understand what it was *she* wanted, what it was she needed to sustain her through the difficult times. So, when Dr Allan suggested she expected too much from Paul, she had to disagree. In truth, she had never expected anything and certainly never enough. In truth, she should have expected much, much more.

The last few days in Los Angeles before the trip to London had been spent gathering together bits and pieces of last-minute shopping and organizing the boys.

'What I wouldn't give for a real English Christmas,' Sharon said.

'There's still Paul's ticket,' Rita suggested.

'Don't tempt me.'

Rita laughed. 'You're going to Hawaii, there's nothing to feel envious of.'

'Christmas in London,' Sharon sighed. '*A Christmas Carol* and all of that stuff.'

Rita had assured Sharon that it wouldn't be in the least bit like that. And now she looked down as the aircraft banked, watching the LA urban sprawl beneath them. It looked, somehow, arid and strange in the hazy winter sunshine. She imagined Gary in one of the cars on the freeway far below and Paul at the beach, even though he would be at work by now.

The plane climbed steadily and then the seat-belt signs went off and they were free to roam. The boys were already stretching their legs and going up to the observation lounge.

Rita sat back and closed her eyes. She felt regret at leaving Gary even though she was unsure about what, exactly, was to happen with them. Perhaps by the new year things would be clearer. Paul might know what it was he wanted. If they were to divorce, Rita decided she would prefer it to happen sooner rather than later, not wanting it to drag on and on interminably. However, to be honest, neither of them seemed very anxious to take that step.

She opened her eyes as a steward offered her coffee,

and watched as he poured it and, smiling, handed it across to her. The captain welcomed them all aboard, gave a few details about height and cruising speed, and said he would point out anything of interest as they flew over it. Steve and William returned after a short while and, putting on their Walkmans, sat back to read their magazines.

Rita finished her coffee and looked out at the clouds. There was a certain comfort in flying, she decided, a powerlessness in which one was entirely in the hands of others, every whim catered to, everything brought to your seat, music to lull you into a false sense of security, a film to distract you. It was rather like becoming a child again.

She was looking forward to seeing her family and various friends. Vanessa, a former colleague from London University had kept in touch with Rita since her departure for California and they had arranged to meet once she was safely ensconced at Chalcot Square. They had always been good friends and Rita contemplated this with pleasure.

She smiled at Steve and William, who were tapping away to their favourite pop music, seemingly oblivious of their surroundings. She closed her eyes for a moment and was soon fast asleep, dreaming of the redwood table under the palms where she'd worked for most of the summer. Rita had packed the completed manuscript with care, keeping it with her in the hand luggage, ready for one final read-through before submission. Her head turned slightly to the light, her hands crossed on her lap, Rita was dead to the world.

Chapter 6

William was standing in the kitchen at Chalcot Square with only his pyjama bottoms on. He was rubbing his hands together and had been searching for food.

'You'll catch your death,' Rita told him, heaving her shopping bag on to the table and beginning to unpack the basics of civilized living: tea, coffee, milk, bread, cereal and some rather sad-looking apples.

'Cold, isn't it?' William said.

Rita nodded. 'Go and put some clothes on, then.'

'Are you going to make breakfast?'

'Go and get dressed,' she commanded. 'I'll make us all some tea . . . Is Steve awake yet?' she called after him as he raced up the stairs.

'No,' William yelled back, thundering along the landing.

Rita sighed and returned to the food, hearing signs of life above her as Steve shouted to William through the bathroom door, telling him to hurry up. She smiled and made a pot of tea, inspecting the insides of the brown teapot before using it. She was reading the paper at the table when the boys finally came down, dressed and starving. Rita pointed to the cupboards and told them to help themselves.

'When are we picking the car up?' William asked her, turning to speak just as the milk boiled over in front of him. He removed the little saucepan quickly, blowing hard on top of the frothing liquid.

'William,' Rita complained.

'It's okay, I'll clear it up.' He dragged a rather dubious-looking cleaning cloth from the sink and dabbed tentatively at the stove top. 'What sort of car is it?' he asked.

'I don't know . . . I think it's a Ford Sierra,' she replied, returning to her newspaper.

'Can I drive it?' Steve asked.

'We'll see,' she answered without looking up.

'London can't be any worse than Los Angeles,' Steve ventured.

'I would bet on that,' she said, turning a page.

'When are we going to see Grandma?' William asked, pouring the remains of his hot milk over his breakfast cereal.

Rita had meant to phone her mother earlier, and felt a pang of guilt at delaying the call. 'I'll ring her up in a minute or two.'

'I'll speak to her,' William said, sitting at the table.

Rita looked over the top of her paper at him. 'She'll never understand your accent!'

'Oh, Mum,' William laughed, 'is it that bad?'

'Not bad, just rather different.'

'Is Dad ringing today?' Steve asked.

'I'm not sure,' Rita replied. She had no idea if Paul would call them or not. He had spoken to the boys during the previous evening to wish them a good trip, but Rita hadn't spoken to him on that occasion.

Her mother was out shopping when she at last made the phone call. Instead Rita's grandmother answered and, bright as ever, wanted to know how everyone was and what time they were arriving.

'Dorothy's expecting you for the evening meal,' her grandmother said.

'We'll be there before then, Gran,' Rita replied. She looked up from the breakfast table and grinned at the boys, who were washing up. The wall-phone cord was stretched to its utmost as Rita sat back in the old chair.

'Vi's so excited, she's gone to have her hair done,' her grandmother continued, laughing at the antics of her other daughter. 'How are the boys?'

'They're here,' Rita replied, motioning to William and Steve to come to the phone. 'I'll hand them over to you.' She smiled as she heard her grandmother's surprised voice as first Steve and then William spoke to their great-grandmother in their new accents. They each chatted to her for a while before Rita retrieved the receiver and terminated the conversation. 'We have to go now, Gran.' She handed William her tea cup. 'I've got to pick up a car . . . See you in a while.' Her grandmother said something else, which made Rita laugh before putting the phone down.

'What did she say?' Steve asked.

'She didn't believe you were Steve and William!'

'Didn't she really?' William asked.

'Wait till she sees you!' Rita replied, standing up and returning the receiver to its place on the wall. 'You've both grown several inches and filled out quite a bit in the last year.' She went up to comb her hair and put some make-up on. 'Ten minutes,' Rita ordered. 'I'll be ready to go in ten minutes.'

Her mother's house never changed, yet it felt so strange to Rita to be back. The little house in Walthamstow was exactly the same, like a time capsule full of the same things, the same people and, for Rita, many of the same emotions, which were dredged to the surface each time she went. The drive had been fraught with difficulties, mainly because she kept forgetting about clutch and gears. She lost count of the number of times the car stalled, and realized she should have specified an automatic.

Her mother met them at the gate of the neat little terraced house. Mother and daughter hugged one another for a long moment before making way for Steve and William, who seemed to tower over their grandmother. Rita noticed how brown and healthy they looked, and how big against the frailty of her mother. They moved quickly from the cold of late afternoon into the house. Everything was the same. The brown three-piece suite with its faded art deco pattern, the huge fireplace which dominated the room, the contraption with glazed, red-tiled doors and chromium handles, doors which opened into warming ovens, a large space at the bottom, a smaller one above. The grate was blacked and shining, a bright fire blazing in the hearth, with the old black kettle, steaming, pushed next to the grating which held the coals in place.

The mantel was high and above it hung a bevelled mirror etched with an art deco design. Rita could remember, as a little girl, staring up at the mantel, looking at the treasures sitting along its length. They were still there, arranged exactly as she recalled. From left to right, an orange vase in the shape of a trumpet; a miniature ship's bell hanging inside a tiny ship's wheel complete with a tiny red hammer fitted into the base, with which to strike it; a small clock in a wooden case, which had never worked and always showed half-past two; a comb and brush set with bakelite handles. Then came a framed picture of her grandfather, a silhouette cut out of a black shoe-box top. It had been done in the trenches of the fourteen-eighteen war and dated by the artist. At the opposite end was a fluted vase made from copper, in which her mother kept her hair pins and nets.

Her grandmother came in from the kitchen. She was slightly stooped but moved quickly, giving Rita a hug and smiling delightedly, standing back to look at the boys, who were still waiting just inside the room. 'Come in, come in,' she said, going to them and kissing each in turn. Both boys had to bend low to enable their great-grandmother to reach. 'Sit by the fire,' she commanded. 'It's a cold one today, isn't it?'

Rita noticed how enormous the boys seemed inside the small room. They looked slightly ill at ease, constrained by the lack of space and at a loss as to what, exactly, they should do. Within a short space of time her mother was bringing them all cups of tea and slices of orange sponge cake. Rita and Steve took an armchair each, William sat on the floor between them, her grandmother took her usual chair whilst her mother flitted between the kitchen and the arm of the sofa, where she perched between whiles.

The two older women chatted on about the boys and Rita, how much they had all changed, how different they all looked, their clothes, their accents, their size . . . Rita having reduced, the boys having expanded in every direction! Rita sat back eating the delicious home-made cake and drinking the strong tea whilst listening to the chatter. Catching up on a year away from London, who was 'hatched, matched or dispatched', as her grandmother described it. The clock chimed and her mother got up to take the dirty tea cups out. Rita followed her into the kitchen.

'What can I do?' Rita asked.

'Oh, good Lord, girl, I don't want you to do anything,' her mother replied, filling the sink with hot, soapy water.

'No Paul this time, then?' her mother said, placing cups on the draining board.

Rita turned to her, a drying cloth in her hand. 'We've decided to make our separation permanent,' she admitted.

Her mother nodded and didn't seem at all surprised. 'You mean divorce?' she asked calmly.

Rita had no idea what would happen. 'You knew, didn't you?' she smiled at her mother.

'I knew that something was up . . . I read between the lines. You can't keep secrets, Rita, not from me . . . You never could!'

Rita laughed.

'What do the boys think about it?'

'Since Nathan's death they seem to take everything else in their stride. They've developed this superficial gloss of sophistication, *everything* is such a bore to them!'

It was her mother's turn to laugh, 'You were just the same.'

Rita dried her hands on the clean towel hanging behind the back door and excused herself. 'I need the loo,' she said, leaving the kitchen and finding the boys playing shove-halfpenny with her grandmother. It was quite a change, she considered, from their usual computer games.

In the afternoon Rita took the boys out for a walk to the shops. She felt the need of a little fresh air and a chance to stretch her legs for a while after the cramped living room with its blazing fire. Steve and William walked on either side of her, muffled up against the cold, both towering over Rita. She felt as though she was retracing a pathway, feeling like a waif, a refugee from the future, stepping, stepping, stepping into her own past, an interloper now.

'Everything seems so small and cramped,' Steve said, his breath steaming white as he spoke.

'I went to school over there,' Rita said, pointing across the road towards a red-brick building.

'You tell us that every time we walk down here,' William laughed. 'It was your junior school.'

'We hardly ever come here,' Rita said.

The boys looked at one another and grinned. 'It's not even a school any more,' Steve said looking at the Victorian building, 'it's a Sikh temple.'

'And the hospital I worked in during the holidays is over there,' Rita said, continuing her conducted tour by pointing to an ugly building that was probably constructed in the early part of the century.

'Right,' William replied, sounding totally uninterested. 'What are you going to buy, Mum?'

'Some flowers,' Rita replied, 'and some chocolates for Aunty Vi. I've forgotten to bring her anything.' They approached the long high street of Walthamstow town centre, finding a florist and sweet shop in quick succession. She bought her mother a potted plant, and a box of chocolates with kittens on the front for her aunt. Steve and William bought pop magazines before pushing her into a little American-style burger bar, where they ordered giant-size milk shakes and a sickly looking blueberry pie. Rita had a black coffee. 'Don't you ever stop eating?' she asked hopelessly.

'Sure,' William replied, slurping up his drink through a flexi-straw, 'when we're asleep.'

'Very funny,' she replied.

'So, what's it like to be back, Mum?' Steve asked.

'Cold,' Rita replied, looking at him.

'I meant back at Gran's house.'

'I know what you meant,' Rita said, looking up at the plastic ferns hanging above their heads.

'So?'

'It always feels a little strange to be back,' she admitted. 'I'm always surprised at how small the house is . . . it seems to shrink a bit more each time I return!'

'Gran doesn't change though, does she?' William said.

203

Rita shook her head. 'No, she's always the same,' she laughed. 'They're *all* always the same!'

William finished his drink and turned his attention to the pie. 'Why do they stay in that old house?' he asked, looking up at his mother.

'Convenience, I suppose . . . familiarity?' she suggested. 'You both belong to the throw-away generation, you wouldn't understand . . .'

'You mean they enjoy living like that?' Steve said.

'Like what?' Rita asked bluntly. 'They have everything they want . . . I admit that it's not very fashionable . . .'

'But it's comfortable,' the boys chorused, mimicking their grandmother's words.

'Yes,' Rita smiled. 'Don't be so smart. It may be a bit old-fashioned but it's clean and warm . . .'

'And *cold* upstairs,' Steve interrupted. 'Let's not forget the lack of central heating.'

'Well, dear heart, my grandmother is eighty-nine and these primitive conditions don't seem to have done her much harm!'

'You'll be telling us that we're spoiled brats next,' William laughed.

'You probably are,' Rita grinned.

'I wonder what they make of us,' Steve said.

'I think they're a bit shocked,' Rita admitted. 'I mean you've changed quite a bit in the last year . . . and they still think of you as children when, in reality, you're ugly great brutes!' She laughed at their disapproving expressions. 'Hurry up, if we leave now we should be back just in time for tea.'

William laughed. 'Now you're talking.'

Steve was already getting out of his chair to put his coat on. He winked at his mother and smiled.

* * *

Her mother had to go out for a while at five-thirty to help close up the shop and Rita sat down with the boys. Her grandmother was busy in the kitchen and they were toasting tea cakes on a long toasting fork. In a while Maud came into the room with a tray of clattering tea cups, plates, knives, jam and butter. She placed the tray on the table and put the butter dish into the grate for a while in order to soften the butter a little. Steve held the toasting fork, William began to butter the tea cakes and their great-grandmother dispensed the cups of steaming, strong tea.

'Vi will be in soon,' her grandmother said, almost as a warning. 'She's been in a state of extreme excitement for the last week,' the old woman chuckled.

Rita took her tea cup and saucer and William handed her a tea cake, hot and oozing with butter and home-made jam. It tasted delicious but, Rita considered, she would weigh two hundred pounds by the time this holiday was over. She decided to go out for a jog the next morning. Aunty Vi burst into the house in a state of joy mixed with copious tears of emotion. She kissed and hugged Rita and the boys in turn.

'I've been waiting all week to see you,' Vi said. 'Did Mother tell you?' Her voice was high and breathless. 'I left work early . . . I told everyone that you were coming.'

The clock chimed six times. 'How are you, Aunty?' Rita asked, having just managed to save her cup from her aunt's rather ample embrace.

'I'm fine, dear,' Vi replied, removing her heavy winter coat and putting it in the cupboard under the stairs. 'And you,' she said, smiling at Rita, 'you look so young.'

'Rita is young, Vi,' her mother said.

'And the boys,' Vi continued, ignoring the remark. 'Steve looks more and more like Paul, doesn't he, and you've both grown so big!' she laughed, sitting down heavily in the armchair next to the table. 'And you've all got accents now!'

The boys smiled but it was obviously becoming rather a bore to keep on having this pointed out. William handed his great-aunt a toasted tea cake, which she received gratefully. Munching the cake and drinking her tea, she asked Rita every question under the sun about her life in California, the house, where the boys went to school and the shops. Vi was a great shopper and if she couldn't be out shopping herself she loved to talk about it, comparing the prices and the quality of the goods in the stores. Rita's aunty Vi could, as her grandmother often reminded her, 'talk the hind legs off a donkey!' Vi continued the barrage of questions until her sister returned and all three women began the final preparations for the evening meal, leaving Rita and the boys by the fireside.

'Okay, you two?' Rita asked.

William nodded.

'I think I'm too full-up to eat a meal now,' Steve said.

'Well, just try . . . What about you, William?'

'I'm still hungry.'

'Surprise, surprise,' Rita replied, laughing.

'It seems odd that you used to live here,' Steve said.

'Odd? What's odd about it?' Rita wanted to know, whilst feeling exactly the same. It seemed odd to her now as well.

'Where could you work?'

'In here . . . During the summer I worked in my bedroom if it wasn't too chilly but, in the winter, that was impossible because there was no heating upstairs . . .'

'How could you do it?' William joined in. 'How did you study for your examinations?'

'Mother used to put a cloth over half the table and I would spread out my books and do the best I could . . . It really wasn't that awful.'

'What wasn't?' her mother asked, coming into the living room with place settings.

'I was telling the boys about how I used to study in here.'

'Oh yes,' her mother grinned at the memory, 'we all had to creep about when your mum was at her studies . . . What was it, Rita, six to nine every weekday night?'

'Something like that,' Rita said.

'It used to drive your aunt Marlene mad!' she laughed. 'We didn't have a TV set in those days but we had a wireless and Marlene would sit right up next to it, her ear pressed against the speaker so as not to disturb her sister.'

'Don't, Mum,' Rita protested with a laugh, 'it makes me feel guilty! What a little swot I must have been . . .'

Her mother shrugged. 'You worked hard, Rita, and it was worth it in the long run. After all, without paper qualifications, where are you?' She was speaking to Rita but addressing her comments to the boys as well.

'We work hard, don't we, Steve?' William said earnestly.

Rita smiled, reaching forward to ruffle his hair, 'Gran wasn't getting at you . . . she knows how hard you work because I tell her in my letters.'

'Of course I do, love,' Dorothy said. 'Come on, let's get this table organized so that we can eat something!'

It was freezing as they stepped out of the house at nine o'clock. Rita had forgotten how raw this kind of weather could be. The pavements sparkled with a frosty ice and she had to scrape the car windscreen with a plastic credit card. She had insisted that the women stay indoors but they all donned coats and hats and came out to wave them away. Her grandmother's large woollen hat fell over her eyes so that, with her coat collar turned up, only her nose protruded, making the old lady look a comical sight.

'Safe journey,' Aunty Vi called, as though they were about to cross Antarctica by dog-sled.

Rita hooted the horn and, easing the clutch out with care, slowly pulled the car away. The heater was on full blast, blowing freezing air into the car, and William, in the back, was leaning forward peering out through the greasy windows into the night.

'Do you know which way to go?' Steve asked her.

'Of course I do,' Rita replied, attempting to find second gear.

'Do you want me to drive the car?' Steve asked.

'Shut up,' she commanded, turning right into the high street, the car skidding slightly as she accelerated across the road. The car became warmer and the vision clearer as she headed towards the city. Steve played about with the radio until he found a station he liked. William was sitting with his arms folded now, his eyes heavy with sleep. 'That was all right, wasn't it?' Rita said.

'Fine,' Steve agreed. 'They still pile on the food, don't they?'

Rita laughed, drawing the car up for a red light. 'Can you imagine how fat I used to be as a girl? Still, if you're shoving food in, then you won't get up to any other mischief!'

'And did you?' Steve asked.

'Did I what?' Rita pushed the gear lever into first and they lurched away again.

'Get into any mischief.'

'Me?' She glanced at him. 'How could you suggest such a thing about your own mother?'

Steve grinned. 'Is that why you feed me and William up?'

'I do no such thing . . . In any case, the situation is entirely different, you're growing lads. In California you

208

can run around all year and burn off the calories, when it's cold you don't feel much like it.'

'Anyway, it was great,' Steve said. 'Do you think you'll be as fit as Great-Grandmother Maud when you're her age?'

'I very much doubt it, Steve. She just carries on as though things haven't changed, which they haven't for her. She still looks after her children in exactly the same way she's always done.' Rita pulled out from behind a red double-decker, moving faster than she really felt was sensible and not enjoying the drive at all. 'When I'm her age, God forbid, you'll probably have me in one of Sharon's brother-in-law's happy homes for the geriatric!'

'No, I wouldn't do a thing like that for my old mother . . . you could come and cook for me, if you really wanted.'

'Thanks a lot,' Rita replied, checking her wing mirror before moving to the centre of the road and indicating a right turn. 'I can't honestly say that I've much enjoyed cooking for the last seventeen years.' She found a gap in the oncoming traffic and moved quickly across. 'I think I'll take a rain check on that idea.'

Steve laughed. 'Don't say I didn't ask.'

'I won't, love, but just don't ask again.' They had entered Camden Town by now and Rita gave a silent sigh of relief. A few more minutes and they would be home. She managed to bump the front wheel against the kerb-stone as they parked, which jolted the car and woke William, who had been snoozing on the back seat. She locked the car and then fumbled around in her bag for the house keys. 'You're not going to believe this, boys . . .'

'Come on, Mum,' William called from the house steps, 'it's freezing.'

She had visions of them all bundled up together in the car for the night, then her hand grabbed hold of the leather square which hung from the front-door keyring. 'Okay, panic over,' she told them, running over the slippery pavement and letting them into the house, which felt wonderfully warm and inviting even though there was still a faint smell of damp and mustiness. The boys decided to watch a late film but, feeling tired, Rita went up to bed, where she read for a while before falling asleep.

Rita went out for a jog the following morning, muffled up in a pink and green tracksuit from LA with matching trainers. It was still freezing and she had added a scarf, gloves, extra socks and a thick jumper underneath her running ensemble. It was seven-thirty when she stepped out of the house, turning left out of Chalcot Square and running down through Primrose Hill and into Camden Town, stopping in Camden High Street to buy a morning paper. The roads were busy and the lights bright in the gloomy morning. Rita ran by familiar houses and streets, areas where she had walked and driven year after year, and yet, as the grey dawn began to rise, she realized how old and timeworn everything looked. A certain dilapidation appeared more obvious after her year away. Rita understood that she was experiencing a kind of culture shock, although it felt strange when applied to her own city!

As she ran down Hampstead Road, turning right into Euston Road and then up through Regent's Park on her way back to the house, she thought about her mother and grandmother and Aunty Vi all cooped up together in that tiny house in Walthamstow; she considering it bearable only in small doses. Rita found it all rather claustrophobic and suffocating, much as she loved them all. It made her nervous to think about their lives, three old women, living and breathing one another, hopelessly intertwined and engrossed in the minutiae, the trivial details of one another's existence.

When she returned, the boys were still in bed and the house was quiet and felt warm. Rita took a shower and sat on her bed afterwards, towelling her hair dry and flicking through the morning paper. Eventually she dressed, dragging on a pair of Levi's and a thick, baggy jumper over a white T-shirt. She was going to make herself breakfast but paused at the top of the stairs and, going back along the landing, went to the door of Nathan's room. It was at the rear of the building and had never been used since his death. Despite the estate agent's protestations concerning the loss of rent, Rita had insisted that it be advertised as a four-bedroomed house.

No one could face clearing away Nathan's things and so everything remained very much as he had left it. Various items of furniture had been stacked in one corner and there were some empty packing cases piled up against one wall. Rita hesitated for a moment before stepping inside. His posters were still on the walls and a pin board with family photographs and post-cards from friends abroad sat above his desk. She sat down carefully on the dust-sheeted arm of his comfortable easy chair facing the window. Nathan's bed was to her left against the wall, a pair of his tennis shoes poking out from under the bedside cabinet.

Rita sat there for a long time, going over the events of that morning in her mind. She remembered his laughter and his smiling face at the front door just before he left. For more than two years now she'd repeated his name over and over again until it echoed inside her head, on and on and on like a mantra for her lost child, calling out for him through the darkness of death and despair. Her breath caught in her throat. Rita was so used to tears that she wasn't even aware for a moment that she was crying and, dabbing at her eyes, stood up to look around the room.

Nathan's wardrobe hadn't been touched, his clothes remaining exactly as he had left them. She ran a hand across them, examining each jacket and shirt and coat with care. A crumpled pair of jeans and a muddy football shirt lay at the bottom where he had thrown them. She picked up the green shirt and was startled to discover that his aroma remained on it. Rita pressed the material to her face, breathing him in. It was almost as if he was there, present for her in the room. She couldn't stop crying.

Steve's voice was calling out to William and then she heard them laughing about something. Rita replaced the shirt and shut the wardrobe door. She was trapped, not wanting the boys to see her upset, not wanting to leave Nathan's room. For a moment she felt she couldn't continue, life seemed so hopelessly painful, the point of going on with it escaped her. Perhaps she was finally going over the edge, losing grasp of reason, and she began to panic, terrified that this could be true.

William shouted to Steve and he clattered along the landing and slammed the bathroom door. She gradually began to regain her composure and, by the time the boys were dressed, she had gone downstairs to the kitchen and was in the middle of preparing breakfast. She had dabbed cold water on her face and was busily occupied when they came in. Their normal preoccupation with food meant they weren't paying too much attention, although William did give her a quizzical look until she returned a reassuring smile. He seemed satisfied with that and Rita thought how clever and adept she was at this particular performance.

* * *

Later in the morning William and Steve drove off to see some old school friends whilst Rita, taking her courage into both hands, went to the West End. Vanessa had called the previous day and they'd arranged to meet for lunch in Covent Garden. Rita was also intending to brave the mayhem for a spot of last-minute Christmas shopping. She found Oxford Street intolerable; having fought her way through a rugby scrum and into Marks and Spencer, where she wanted to buy a few extra things for her mother, grandmother and Aunty Vi to supplement the gifts she'd already brought them from LA, she seriously began to wonder if she would ever get out again. Everyone seemed to be writing cheques at her check-out and Rita began to feel hot and irritated and inconsiderate. At last she flung her assortment of knickers and thermal underwear and pretty housecoats on to the counter and, with a sigh of relief, grabbed the various carrier bags and moved slowly through a sea of people towards the exit.

Christmas muzak jingle-jangled above the crush of seething humanity, making her even more annoyed. Refusing to give in, despite the feeling that she was developing agoraphobic tendencies, Rita fought on. She dropped into a few of the clothing chain stores, hoping to pick something up for the boys, perhaps a shirt or pullover, but the deafening pop music which blared out from every direction, the oppressive heat and the crowds inside, made the sleety rain and cold of Oxford Street seem infinitely more appealing.

She paused in front of an electrical goods store, looking at the latest in pop-up toasters, wondering if the old women of Walthamstow would make any use of it. There was a nice portable radio too but, remembering the fate of the microwave oven, Rita decided against anything electrical and moved on. She crossed from Oxford Street making her way down Regent Street finding shirts for the

213

boys in a department store before rushing off towards Covent Garden and lunch.

Vanessa was already at the restaurant when Rita arrived. She had almost thrown herself in front of a cab in order to make one stop but was twenty minutes later than their agreed time. It was an Italian pasta restaurant, with Italian newspapers stuck all over the walls, and red paintwork. Large ceiling fans moved slowly in the hot atmosphere. Covent Garden always amused Rita these days. She remembered when it was still a fruit and vegetable market, when it dealt with the essentials of life. Now it was full of frippery, sanitized and soulless. The structures remained, clean, beautiful and solid, but the spirit was gone.

'Darling,' Vanessa said, standing up and giving Rita a big hug and a kiss. 'What have they done to you?' she asked, stepping back, grasping both of Rita's hands in her own. 'You look absolutely marvellous.'

Rita laughed. 'Californiating Rita, eh?' She sat down, looking over the table at Vanessa. She had worked with her for years and they had been good allies at London University. Vanessa was tall and angular, with rather prominent features which were emphasized by the severe way she always wore her long black hair, scraped away from her face and tied into a ponytail. She had a wide sensuous mouth, which she always painted a pillar-box red, a rather pointed chin, and lustrous black eyes which could be mesmeric. Vanessa was an expert on Chaucer and really quite formidable, with many scholarly articles to her credit. She had also published several books over the years, one of them regarded as a definitive text. Vanessa was married to Gunter, who was a successful architect, and they had two brilliant children, Clara and George, who were around the same age as William and Steve.

214

'So, you're an Angeleno now?' Vanessa asked, smiling. 'You have a bit of an accent, you know.'

'You should hear the boys,' Rita replied, 'they're almost indistinguishable from the real thing!'

Vanessa laughed. 'Are you still busy, still working?'

'I've completed the book, if that's what you mean.'

'Splendid,' Vanessa said, clapping her hands together. 'I can't wait to read it,' she grinned. 'Any new ideas or conclusions?'

'No, not really,' Rita admitted. She didn't know if it really mattered any longer, she didn't know if it was really very important. The idea of writing the book hadn't been hers in the first place. Her head of department had encouraged her and she'd been carried along on the wave of his enthusiasm. He'd told her that she was capable of 'great things'. Nathan's death, however, saved her from that, perhaps. At least, it had made the idea of writing a book full of 'great things', even if one existed within her, virtually pointless. 'I've concentrated upon *Mrs Dalloway* and *To The Lighthouse*, *Jacob's Room*, of course . . .' Rita faltered, her mind suddenly so full of Nathan that he pushed everything else out, every other thought aside.

Vanessa smiled. 'Oh, yes, *Jacob's Room*, her experiments with time and stream of consciousness . . . Are you all right, Rita?'

Rita's mind clicked back. 'What? Oh, yes, I'm fine . . .'

'Are you sure? You're very pale.' Vanessa looked concerned.

'I'm just tired,' Rita explained. 'I'm fine, *really*,' she assured her friend, returning to the topic of their conversation. 'Anyway, it's really just a collection of essays for undergraduates. I tried to bring out Woolf's major themes and ideas.'

'Good,' Vanessa encouraged, 'I'm sure it's absolutely marvellous. I can't wait to read it,' she repeated.

Rita looked doubtful. 'I read it again on the flight over. It seems a bit pedestrian, a bit of a rehash.' She considered her slim typescript, her painstaking research, and felt a little sad, a little disillusioned.

'You're not happy with it?' Vanessa asked.

'*A Room of One's Own* still has so much to say,' Rita sighed, 'it's still so important . . . I mean, women aren't physically locked out of college libraries any longer and they can have careers, but we're still held back.' She paused. 'Virginia Woolf says that we breed and give birth to and wash and teach the entire population of the world, we *are* responsible for our children and it holds us back . . . It's as true now as in 1928!' Rita felt guilty then, as though she was blaming her kids for something, and guilty for Nathan because she had had her career. She'd had the money and the room of her own and still everything had gone wrong.

Turning the conversation away from Virginia Woolf, Vanessa asked, 'So, apart from the book and concentrating upon the body beautiful, what else have you been up to?'

'Oh, and I've split up with Paul,' Rita announced, watching as Vanessa spluttered on the wine she was sipping.

'Good God!' Vanessa picked up the paper serviette and dabbed at her lips. 'Are you serious?'

'Of course,' Rita said.

Vanessa took a deep breath. 'Well, I'm shocked, I can't pretend that I'm not . . . I mean, I knew you had some problems . . . What's going to happen?'

'I don't know but I think it's past the patching-up stage. I think it's quite irredeemable.' Rita was listening to herself and was surprised at just how calm she sounded. Vanessa stared at Rita, her eyes wide. 'It's been traumatic, nevertheless,' Rita continued, 'as you can imagine.'

216

Vanessa nodded. 'Good God,' she almost breathed.

Rita shrugged.

'Is it to do with an *affaire de coeur*?' Vanessa asked in hushed tones.

Rita shook her head. 'No, not at all,' and she went on to explain the situation to her friend. Separated from it all by thousands of miles, Rita found herself able to discuss events in a detached way without feeling at all emotional. It might have been the story of another man and woman, and many of the facts were so well rehearsed by now that she found herself repeating them without much thought, as though by rote. 'Of course,' Rita said towards the end of her explanation, 'this is all from my perspective . . . I have no real idea about Paul's feelings.'

'It's perfectly dreadful,' Vanessa said, 'you've been together for *so* many years.'

Rita suddenly felt exhausted. She really didn't feel much like continuing this particular conversation but, having let the cat out of the bag, it was too late. 'Not so dreadful,' she replied, smiling a little as the waiter brought over their orders. 'Anything is better than the rows and the awful silences.'

Vanessa looked uncertain but nodded all the same.

Rita stared at her lasagne and suddenly felt very hungry.

'I wish everyone would stop making stupid remarks about our accents,' Steve said, slamming the front door behind him and following William into the kitchen. They'd just returned from their visit to old school friends.

'It's only because we don't have anything in common with them any more,' William replied, taking two mugs down from a high cupboard. 'When do you think Mum will be back?'

Steve shrugged. 'I can't imagine ever having anything in common with those jerk-offs!'

'Well, you did,' William assured him, spooning instant coffee into the mugs.

'God,' Steve complained, closing his eyes and leaning back in a chair, 'why did we have to come back here for Christmas?'

William put a bottle of milk on the table and poured boiling water into the mugs, carrying them to the table. 'Don't let Mum hear you saying that,' he warned.

'As if I would,' Steve replied, leaning forward and reaching for his drink.

William sat down. 'I don't mind being home . . . it's all right. The old place could do with a lick of paint, though.'

'This house gives me the bloody creeps,' Steve admitted.

William didn't reply.

'I half expect him to walk in at any moment.' He turned to his brother. 'Don't you feel that too?'

William shook his head, looking pensive and unhappy, 'There are no such things as ghosts.'

'I don't mean that . . . I just feel that Nathan was such a strong influence when we lived here and nothing has changed, it's exactly the same as the day we left . . . and the day that he died.'

'Well, we've changed,' William insisted. 'It's only because you're not used to being here and everything is so different from Los Angeles . . .'

'It's so fuckin' cold, I know that, I'd forgotten just how cold it can get.'

William grinned. 'It was cold in Gran's house, that bathroom was like Siberia!'

'Jesus, her house is medieval,' Steve complained.

'It's funny but I can't think of Mum as coming from there,' William admitted, 'they're all so different . . .'

218

'Mum was really bright,' Steve replied, tapping a finger to his head, 'and she used her brains to get out.' He nodded to himself. 'Yes, she was real smart, went to university and married Dad.'

'You make it sound incredibly calculating.'

'Maybe it was,' Steve shrugged, picking up his coffee and taking a sip. 'She wasn't about to remain in Waltham-stow now, was she?'

'Well, they wouldn't have lasted for twenty-odd years if it had been *that* calculating,' William argued. 'They must have loved one another.'

'Who knows,' Steve sighed. 'It was Nathan who fucked them up . . . it was Nathan who fucked us all up.' Steve's voice had taken on a hard edge. He looked tense, the muscles in his neck standing out slightly, his hand wrapped tightly around the mug.

William began to feel slightly panicky at his brother's attitude and bearing. 'Listen, I don't really want to talk about this right now.' He looked into Steve's dark eyes. 'Okay?'

Steve stared back in a strange way, as though searching William's face for some answers to his own questions. He smiled suddenly, touching his brother's arm. 'Okay . . . Jesus, don't let's get heavy here,' he laughed. 'Come on, what's on TV? There might be a film.' He scraped his chair across the untidy cork tiling and went through to the sitting room to examine the programme guides.

William remained seated for a while longer, feeling ill at ease and perturbed. He was aware that Nathan's influence was still in the house. Everywhere you looked there were signs, from the broken bannister rail on the top landing where they played illegal games of midnight cricket (when their parents were away) and Nathan's back-swing had been a bit too adventurous, to the beer stains on the bathroom ceiling from the brewing kit that went disastrously awry. When Nathan had been around there was never a dull moment. No one knew what to expect next and the place was always full of his friends. William had yet to meet someone as popular as Nathan had been. Everyone had loved Nathan, which made the nature of his death so inexplicable to him. There had never seemed any possible explanation.

Rita returned to Chalcot Square just before the temperature fell to freezing point. It was late afternoon and the sky had cleared for the last hour or so of daylight, with a dipping sun shining out amidst the perfect, fading blue. She had left Vanessa in Mercer Street, promising to ring her before she returned to America. She propped her bags and packages on the hall table before going into the sitting room, where the boys were watching a John Wayne film.

'Hi,' William said, without taking his eyes off the screen.

'You just love watching junk, don't you,' she told them, sitting down next to Steve on the sofa. 'What about a cup of tea for your poor old mother?'

Steve grinned. 'Did you get us anything?'

'I might have . . . Did you take care of that car?'

'Of course, no problem, I'm an expert driver.'

'And cocky with it!'

'What's to eat?' William asked as the adverts flashed on to the screen.

'Didn't you have any lunch?' she asked him.

'They gave us burgers, really measly little burgers . . . I suppose they wanted to make us feel at home.'

'Don't be mean. I suppose you wolfed it all down, anyway.'

'I had to, I was starving.'

'Oh, change the record, *please*,' Rita replied, putting her hands to her ears, 'change the record.'

The film came on again and Rita pulled herself up and went into the kitchen to revive her flagging energy with tea which, she admitted, was her one true addiction. William followed her a little while later, hanging around without any particular purpose. 'Make yourself a sandwich,' she told him, 'we won't eat for a while yet.'

He opened the fridge door as though examining the potential for a snack but shut it again without removing any food. 'Mum,' he said, sitting down at the table.

'What?' Rita replied, pouring water into the teapot to warm it before spooning in the tea.

'Are you going to the cemetery?'

'Yes,' she turned to him, 'yes, I thought I'd go towards the end of this week.'

'I'd like to come as well.'

Rita smiled. 'Okay, fine.' She poured the boiling water into the pot, dropping on the lid and putting the old, dirty cosy over it. 'Perhaps we can all go.'

William shrugged. 'I haven't asked Steve . . . What if he won't?' He sounded very serious.

It seemed an odd way of phrasing it, Rita thought, but carried on with her preparations, taking down cups and saucers and cutting up the cake her grandmother had thrust into the car as they left the previous night. 'No one's going to force Steve. It must be up to him, don't you think?'

William nodded.

'It's not exactly a thing any of us look forward to,' Rita continued.

'You mean it's a duty,' William replied.

'A sort of duty,' she agreed. 'I feel I ought to go, at any rate . . .'

'I guess you think I'm morbid now for asking.'

221

'Don't be silly,' Rita said gently.

'We could go in the morning,' he suggested.

Rita found the tea strainer in the rather dirty-looking sink and washed it out under the tap. 'We're having lunch over at Walthamstow,' she reminded him.

'Oh,' William watched as his mother poured the tea. 'Mum,' he said.

'What?' Rita placed the things on the table.

'It doesn't bother you being back here, does it?'

She stared at him. 'Bother me?'

William looked uncomfortable, a pink flush came to his cheeks. 'Yes, you know . . .'

Rita nodded. 'If we hadn't all moved to California we would probably still be living here. It only seems strange because we're visitors now and our memories of Nathan tend to be centred in this house.' She smiled at William, outwardly calm whilst the screaming sounds were locked up inside her head: *Nathan, Nathan, Nathan* . . . 'In a way it's good. It means we have to face it the way it is, we come back and we don't pretend . . . okay?'

'Okay.' William smiled at last.

'Well, if that brother of yours wants tea, you'd better go and nab him now.'

William nodded. Pausing at the door for a moment, he smiled at her.

Rita drank her tea and nibbled her grandmother's cake without really thinking about the calories. She had been putting off any decision about visiting Nathan's grave although she knew she would have to go at some point during their stay in London. She picked up the cup and sipped the strong liquid. Outside it was almost dark. Rita looked up and smiled as the boys came through the kitchen door.

* * *

They all went to the cemetery on the following Saturday morning. It was very windy and cold and it took them a while to locate Nathan's grave amidst the confusing rows. In the end they came upon it almost by accident.

Steve stood, feet apart, hands deep into his coat pockets, staring down at his brother's headstone. Rita felt a little lost, she wasn't sure what they were supposed to do now. None of the family could be said to be exactly religious, in fact the whole exercise, the idea of placing someone under the ground and covering them with earth, had always rather appalled Rita. However, like so many other things, it had been Paul's decision to bury Nathan, taken when she was too deeply in shock to make any real, coherent sense. Steve bent down to pick some of the undergrowth away from the graveside.

They appeared to be the only people amidst the bleak landscape. The headstones went off in all directions in neatly formed rows. Some were carefully tended with fresh flowers, others were derelict and unkempt. They actually paid to have Nathan's grave cleared and kept tidy but it still looked neglected. Rita had brought some flowers with her, which she stuck into the stone urn in front of the headstone. It was ludicrous, Rita thought, the flowers would be ruined within hours by the freezing temperatures. However, whilst they remained there the blooms did look bright and did give a certain sense of dignity to an otherwise sordid scene. She couldn't bear to think of what was under there and it didn't help her to think of him as being 'at rest' in that freezing place. She would have preferred to have scattered his ashes over the warm earth of California.

Rita pulled her coat collar up against the chill, standing back to look at the flowers. 'Right,' she said at last, 'ready to go?'

Steve looked at her gratefully, following her along the gravel pathway back to the car park.

Rita listened to their feet crunching into the stones and waited at the car, looking back to see William still standing close to the grave. In a moment he turned away, coming up to them.

'What's keeping him?' Steve asked, snapping open the door and hunching himself up inside. He was scowling and tight-lipped, his eyes staring ahead of him.

As soon as William reached the car, Rita got in and started the engine and they drove away in silence. Rita felt numbed by the whole experience. It made her feel neither better nor worse. Knowing that Nathan had been given a proper 'Christian' burial did not serve to lessen her own feelings of guilt. A shower of wet snow began to fall, causing Rita to slow down to a crawl as she located the switch for the windscreen wipers. By the time she had driven back to the house the roads were wet and slushy. The only sound in the car the *slap*, *slap*, *slap* of the wipers. As they got out, a brilliant sun broke from behind the clouds and patches of blue sky appeared.

'What stupid bloody weather,' Steve complained, slamming his door.

'Careful,' she replied, 'this is only a hired car!'

Steve waited for her to lock the car and let them in before expressing his relief at being back again. 'That was awful,' he admitted, throwing himself on to the sofa in the sitting room.

Rita followed him in. William went upstairs. 'Well, it's over with now,' she said, sitting next to him.

'I just don't ever want to go there again.'

She turned to him. He still looked tense and angry. 'Okay, Steve, I think you've made your point. No one was forcing you to come along.'

'I know that,' he replied more reasonably.

224

'It's supposed to help,' she told him, and then shrugged. 'God knows how, but they say it does.'

'Do you feel better for having gone?' he asked.

'I'm glad I did it.'

'Are you?' He seemed surprised. 'We never even go to church . . . I don't know why he was buried like that.'

'Because your father wanted it that way.'

'What about you?'

'Stop it, Steve, let's just accept things the way they stand, okay?'

Steve was about to say something else but, thinking better of it, sat back and picked up a paper at his side.

Rita went up to her room. William was lying on his bed reading, plugged into his Walkman and tapping his feet to the music. He seemed all right and so she didn't bother him. She looked at herself in the wardrobe mirror. The wind and snow had wrecked her hairstyle and she noticed how pale her skin looked. She had worn Levi's and a chunky black sweater under her leather jacket. In California she would probably be sitting out by the pool, watching the boys swimming.

She wondered if, apart from the trip to Nathan's graveside, their enforced enclosure was having an effect upon their emotions. The Chalcot Square house was large but she found it claustrophobic after living in LA and her mother's house seemed little more than a rabbit hutch.

Rita took a deep breath, steeling herself for the next three weeks and for lunch the next day at Walthamstow. She sat down at the dressing table, combing her hair into place, staring at her own reflection.

Chapter 7

Rita sat up in bed, suddenly wide awake from a dream she could no longer remember. It was early and still dark outside. She switched on the bedside lamp, blinking as the light hurt her eyes, and looked at her watch. It was six forty-five and it was Christmas Day. Rita yawned and slipped out of bed and down to the kitchen to make herself a pot of tea. She filled the kettle and wandered into the sitting room, where she pulled open the curtains, cupping her hands to her eyes and peering out into the gloom. The room lights shone on a dusting of fine snow. Embers from the fire they had lit the previous evening were still glowing in the hearth and someone had forgotten to switch the Christmas-tree lights off.

The house felt chilly even though the central heating had been on all night, and Rita took her tea upstairs and returned to bed, where she finished off the crossword from the previous day's *Guardian* and listened to Christmas carols on the BBC until they got too much for her. After a while she snuggled down into the warmth of her bed and dozed off again. The next thing Rita knew, the boys were bounding into her bedroom and it was daylight outside.

'Where are they, then?' William asked, diving on to the bed beside her.

'For God's sake,' Rita protested weakly, poking her head above the covers.

'Come on, let's get opening.' Steve handed her a large, carefully wrapped flat box.

'How do you know I've got you two louts anything?'

Rita joked, sitting up and inspecting her big package with interest. She smiled at them both. 'Open my wardrobe and, as you seek, so you will find.' She laughed as they raced over the carpet, flinging open the wardrobe doors and finding their gifts, which they brought back to the bed.

'Okay, you first,' Steve commanded her.

She picked the present up and shook it. 'Well, it doesn't rattle so I guess it isn't a clock . . . or jewellery,' Rita teased.

'Open it,' William told her.

'It seems such a shame to spoil such lovely wrapping paper.'

'Mum,' William said, exasperated, 'just open it.'

Rita carefully opened the present, raising the lid and exposing, under a layer of green tissue paper, a strawberry-red bathrobe with bottle-green piping on the cuffs and around the collar. She pulled it out and felt the expensive towelling material soft against her cheek. 'It's fabulous, thank you,' she said, reaching to kiss each of them in turn.

'We were sick of seeing you in Dad's tatty old robe,' William explained.

Rita laughed. 'I'm sorry to be such a slut!'

Steve grinned. 'There's something else in there as well.'

'Really.' She delved into the box again like an excited child, her hands feverishly moving through the tissue paper until they came across another, smaller, package. 'Oh, my God, what is this?'

'Open it and see,' Steve suggested.

'Read the card,' William said.

Rita looked at the tag in the shape of a Christmas tree with a yellow star on top. She turned it over and saw that it was from Paul: 'To Rita, love, Paul'. Opening the little box revealed a bottle of Chanel No. 5, which Rita had

227

always loved, regarding it as the height of decadence. As a little girl in Walthamstow, she remembered her mother receiving some as a Christmas gift from her father. The little bottle had been carefully guarded and remained in the top drawer of her mother's old-fashioned dressing table for years. Rita wondered if the old woman still kept it, a treasure from the past, a tiny empty bottle with a life-time of memories. Tears came to her eyes. It didn't take much these days to start her off, but she smiled and thanked them again for the fabulous gift.

'What did you give Dad?' Steve asked.

'Gold cuff-links from Rodeo Drive,' she grinned. 'I had his initials engraved on them.'

The boys started to unwrap their gifts from Rita and Paul. They both had an assortment of clothes, shirts and T-shirts, socks and underwear, expensive Fila tracksuits and then individual presents, a Pentax camera for William and a portable compact-disc player for Steve. They were terribly pleased and very happy with their abundance of presents and Rita couldn't help thinking just how spoiled her children were. However, she didn't really mind, in a way it made up for her own childhood when Christmas meant the chance of a new school uniform or a serviceable dress or pair of shoes. There was little enough money for the essentials in those days and Rita had always craved the extravagant, something that didn't have to be looked after with care, something that was there to enjoy. Something frivolous and silly.

At last she got up. The bedroom seemed to be covered with Christmas wrapping and, kicking a way through the debris, she pulled on the new robe and dabbed Chanel behind her ears just before going down to make breakfast. Paul's parents had sent their gifts by post. They opened them after their cereal and toast, a rather nice fountain pen each for the boys and a printed silk headscarf for Rita

228

with horses' heads on it. Rita made sure the boys rang Hampshire to thank their grandparents for the gifts, before they left later that morning for Walthamstow. Rita had a quick word, promising they would be down to see them before returning to Los Angeles.

'Thank you for the scarf, Mary, it's lovely,' Rita said in a sudden fit of good will, bolstered by a large mid-morning Scotch. They said their goodbyes and wished one another a merry Christmas, then Rita replaced the receiver and reached for the remains of her drink, which she downed in one gulp. 'Jesus Christ!' she said under her breath, dropping the glass into the washing-up bowl before running upstairs to get dressed. 'We're going to be incredibly late.'

Rita had put on Levi's and Western-style boots and a thick tan shirt under a thicker black pullover. The boys were loading her mother's presents into the boot of the car and a freezing blast of icy air was blowing into the hall as she came down. She slid into a brown fake-fur coat and ran out to the car, giving the front door a hearty slam as she left the house. It was extremely cold and, instead of snow, a misty, drizzly rain fell, which made them all feel miserable for the first part of the drive until the car had heated up. They had not yet become used to the difference in temperature and it still seemed odd to dress up in coats and scarves and gloves after a year away; and Rita had never really been warm since she had arrived.

The trip to Walthamstow was the smoothest yet, Rita having mastered the gears at last and become used to using a clutch pedal. Her mother came out to greet them, closely followed by Aunty Vi and her grandmother, who were muffled up against the chill wind. Rita kissed them all and attempted to hurry them back inside the house, but they refused, helping to carry in the things Rita had brought along: several bottles of spirits, Guinness for her grandmother and dry sherry for Aunty Vi. The boys carried in the presents and they were soon squeezed round the roaring fire whilst her mother dispensed drinks to everyone. Steve and William were allowed lager.

The old women loved their thermal underwear and the various knick-knacks that Rita had got in Los Angeles. The boys had insisted upon buying the old women 'Hooray For Hollywood' T-shirts which were extremely garish and in the worst taste possible: a picture of the Hollywood sign overprinted with various badly drawn faces of dead stars – Monroe, Gable, Bogart and the like. Her grandmother was given one with the Marx Brothers, which she immediately put on over her navy-blue two-piece, causing much laughter. William had loaded up his new camera and was already taking pictures.

It was into this rather raucous scene that Marlene and her two daughters suddenly entered. Everyone fell silent as they eased their way into the rather crowded living room. Aunty Vi looked quite shocked, even though the Donald Duck sunglasses she had just been given by William made her look also a trifle lunatic. Marlene must have thought she was walking into bedlam. There was hardly space to breathe. The room was bedecked with paper chains and sprigs of holly, Christmas cards were strung across every available inch of wall space, a huge tree stood in the corner next to the sofa and there were balloons, in various stages of collapse, hanging from the ceiling and light.

'Marlene,' her mother said, standing and greeting her daughter and grandchildren.

Marlene looked at her mother in a pair of Mickey Mouse ears, her grandmother with the Marx Brothers all over her chest and Aunty Vi with miniature Donald Ducks saluting on either side of her jumbo-size dark glasses, and seemed somewhat nonplussed. 'Merry Christmas,' she said to them all.

Rita went over to kiss her sister. She was quite shocked by her appearance. Marlene was careworn, a bit dowdy and down at heel, a raggedy, tired blonde who looked in need of a good meal. The children, Julie and Kim, however, looked just the opposite, beautifully turned out in fashionable new coats, their blonde hair neatly cut and shining. Julie was fourteen and smiled at everyone, kissing her grandmother and then Rita. Kim was twelve and held back, looking ill at ease.

'What a lovely surprise,' her grandmother said. 'Why didn't you tell us that you were all coming?'

Marlene looked embarrassed. 'I hope it's all right, Mum,' she said.

'All right?' her mother laughed. 'What a question! Of course it is . . . The more the merrier!'

'Oh, Aunty Vi!' Marlene laughed, bending to kiss her on the cheek. 'Where did you get those?'

Aunty Vi removed her sunglasses. 'They're a present from William. I shall wear them to work first day back after the holiday.'

Marlene winked at the boys, who had moved away from the fire to make room, and she sat in the armchair next to Rita, the girls sitting on the floor at her feet. Rita looked more closely at her sister as they chatted, catching up on a year apart, not that they were exactly close any longer.

Marlene had recently been divorced and looked considerably older than her thirty-seven years. She was too thin, which gave her a haggard appearance, and Rita noticed that her finger nails were bitten to the quick, the skin around the cuticle chewed and raw. When she was twenty, Marlene had married John, a commercial traveller for a soft drinks company. He was eventually promoted to regional manager, and then left Marlene, after

231

thirteen years together, for his secretary. Rita had always liked John, although she hadn't seen him for years. Everyone chatted happily until lunchtime, when the table extension was eased out and nine places were set. As usual, the meal was huge, an enormous turkey with every conceivable trimming.

'How did you get that in the oven, Mum?' Marlene asked.

'With great difficulty,' she replied, her face red with the effort of carrying it in from the kitchen.

'You want to be careful, you'll do yourself a mischief, Dorothy,' Aunty Vi warned her.

The old women helped to serve the meal and, when everyone was ready to start, Christmas crackers were brought out and they all had to wear the funny hats and read out the awful jokes. Rita, wearing a rather fetching yellow crown cocked slightly in a rakish style, had to read her excruciating joke: 'What did the little light bulb say to its mother?' she asked, looking around the crowded table at the blank faces. 'Okay, the answer is: "I wuv you watts and watts!"'

Everyone groaned as though she had been responsible for it. William told everyone to smile and took a picture of them all grinning like mad and pretending to eat at the same time, the flash blinding them all for a second or two. The meal progressed. After the turkey came the Christmas pudding, which was doused with brandy and set alight, the blue flame flickering and seeming to hover above the brown ball before it expired and the food was dished out.

'Watch out for the coins,' her grandmother warned, and several twenty-pence pieces were regurgitated as the pudding was consumed.

After the Christmas pudding came the mince pies and cups of tea. Rita was groaning towards the end, she had eaten far too much. The boys, of course, had hollow legs and were still munching away quite happily. Finally it ended and Rita was the first to volunteer for the task of washing-up. Marlene said that she would help and, for once, their mother didn't protest. After the Queen's speech, the three old women fell asleep in front of the fire, still wearing their paper hats. The kids seemed quite happy to watch a film, leaving the two sisters to clear everything away.

'What do you want to do,' Marlene asked, 'wash or dry?'

'My God,' Rita laughed, 'that takes me right back to when we were kids . . .'

'We took it in turns,' Marlene recalled.

'Well, I don't mind. I'll wash, if you like.'

Marlene nodded and handed Rita an apron that was hanging over the back of a kitchen chair.

Rita turned on the ancient water heater, hearing the popping noise as the gas was lit and the water steamed out into the sink. She squeezed in the detergent and picked up the little mop, preparing to begin work. 'So,' she began, 'how are things with you?'

Marlene stood by the sink, waiting for the first few plates to drain a little before drying them. 'Oh, you know.'

'No, I don't. I only know what Mum tells me, and that is precious little.'

'She doesn't like to think of me being divorced.'

'That's ridiculous!'

Marlene looked out of the window at the cold afternoon. 'Mum thought the world of John. She hasn't said anything but I always think she feels it was my fault.'

Rita mopped away at a large dinner plate, finding a certain pleasure in the cleansing action. 'How are you managing?'

'I've got a job now.'

'Oh, really,' Rita smiled at her, 'that's good.'

'It isn't anything very spectacular, it's a part-time job on the tills at a local supermarket!'

Rita nodded. 'I guess it fits into the girls' schedule, though.'

Marlene began to pile the dry plates on the table behind them. 'Yes, but it isn't exactly what I'd planned.'

'Mum said you were still living in Harlow.'

Marlene nodded. 'It's a box on an estate . . . that isn't exactly as I'd planned either.' She went into the living room and returned with another pile of washing-up. 'What about you?' She lowered the dishes into the hot water. 'Mum showed me pictures of your house in Los Angeles. Is it as fantastic as it looks?'

Rita nodded. 'It's a rather grand house, yes.' She turned to her sister. 'It's super for the boys, but a house isn't everything.'

'It's a good start, though. Just before John left me we were thinking of moving out into rural Essex, we'd even been to look at some places . . .'

Rita wasn't sure what to say. Marlene obviously felt very aggrieved at her lot in life, she felt thwarted in her ambitions . . . a pleasant house in the country, nice car, a kind husband who would provide for her. Rita felt guilty. It was easy for her, Paul was earning a small fortune and, if the worst came to the worst, she could always maintain a reasonable standard of living for herself, their children had everything imaginable . . . But Marlene couldn't be poverty-stricken. The girls looked healthy and well dressed, so John must be giving her money for them.

She looked at Marlene. Her sister was wearing a cotton summer dress in the middle of an English winter. It was white and flouncy with a décolletage and was entirely wrong. Marlene's sticklike, skinny arms were shown to

234

their full 'advantage' and her breasts seemed to have completely disappeared. Marlene had never been exactly buxom but Rita found it shocking to see her like this.

'You've lost a lot of weight,' Rita said.

'So have you,' Marlene replied. 'You're looking very trim . . . I was always too fat,' she added.

'Have you been on a diet then?' Rita asked.

'No.' Marlene continued to dry the mountains of fresh washing-up. 'I just don't seem to have much of an appetite . . . I ate a bit today, otherwise it would just upset Mum, but I never cook meals like that for myself. It's funny really 'cause I do cook for the girls. Your own cooking never tastes that good, though. Do you find that?'

'I just eat whatever I'm preparing for the boys. I can't say that I really think much about it.'

'How do you keep so thin, then?'

'I exercise.'

'Do you?'

Rita smiled at her sister. 'It's a different approach to life out there.'

'I never thought you would like it,' Marlene said.

'No?'

'You seemed so settled in London . . . both you and Paul.'

'Nathan's death changed everything,' Rita said, tipping the greasy water out of the bowl and starting all over again. Marlene continued to bring in more plates and dishes to wash.

Marlene sighed. 'Well, you seem to have it made now, beautiful home, jet-setting life-style . . .'

Rita was forced to laugh at that. 'Hardly jet-setting, Marlene, we come home once a year . . .' She turned to her. 'Did Mum tell you about me and Paul?'

Marlene nodded. 'Are you going to divorce?' She made it sound so easy.

'I don't know,' Rita admitted.

'How long have you been separated?'

'Since the end of May.'

'Was there anyone else?'

'No.'

'What about now?'

Rita didn't really want to discuss the topic any further. 'No.'

'No?' Marlene sounded surprised.

'Well, I think that Paul has started to see a woman recently.'

'At least he hasn't ditched you for a girl half his age . . . she's not, is she?'

'I haven't met her but I don't think she's half his age, no.'

'Anyway, you're rich,' Marlene stated flatly.

'I'm not sure that has anything to do with it,' Rita replied, a little surprised at her sister's attitude.

'For a start it means that you wouldn't have to end up in a shoe box on an estate!' Marlene sounded very bitter.

'Mum said that you'd had a lot of work done on the house . . . she always says how nice it is.'

'After this dump, Mum thinks that anywhere is a palace!'

'That's hardly fair, Marlene. There are much worse houses than this.'

'You wouldn't live in them though, would you?' she challenged.

Rita didn't quite understand where this conversation was heading and decided to ignore the question and change the subject. Marlene was obviously still upset about John and she certainly looked ill. The dim light and the yellow paint made her sister's skin look sallow. Her face, once rounded and full, had sunk until there were deep hollows where rosy cheeks had been. Rita seriously began to worry that Marlene might be suffering from anorexia nervosa or some horrible wasting disease. The thought of cancer crossed her mind more than once but, surely, her mother would have known if it was something serious, and told her. Rita concentrated on the large saucepan she was scrubbing with the Brillo pad.

'How are Julie and Kim doing?' she asked, 'they look very well.'

'They're all right. Julie seems to be the bright one. I keep telling her that she has to work hard in order to get a good job like her aunty Rita . . . and a good husband.'

'Is she doing well at school?' Rita enquired, anxious to finish off the chores.

'As well as she can . . . our local comprehensive is hardly renowned for its pupils getting university places.'

'Is that what Julie wants, then, to go on to a university?'

Marlene shrugged. 'I expect your kids will go to university, won't they?' Her tone was almost hostile.

Rita spun round. 'Look, Marlene, what is it with you?'

'I don't know what you mean,' Marlene protested.

'I can't help it if your marriage is over and you're feeling hurt. It isn't my fault, so don't take out your bile on me, okay?' Rita had spoken quietly but *very* firmly. 'If you have a problem and you want to discuss it, then fine, let's do that, but for God's sake stop this bloody moaning.'

Marlene glared at her, snatching at the door knob and taking the table cloth outside, where she shook it several times. 'It's easy for you, isn't it? You're rich, what do you know about our problems?'

Rita had gone to the open door, standing on the worn step. 'Well, I appreciate that I don't have financial worries . . .'

'Even if Paul divorces you, you'll still have plenty of

237

money, your kids will still have everything they want, you'll still have a big house . . .'

'Doesn't John have to give you money?' Rita asked quietly.

'It isn't the same,' Marlene snapped back, turning and walking further down the long garden.

It was incredibly cold. Rita folded her arms against herself, following her sister into the gloom of late afternoon. She could hear music and loud laughter coming from the house next door. 'Look,' she began, 'if it's money you need, then perhaps I can help out.' Rita spoke gently.

'I don't want your bloody charity,' Marlene said. 'Coming over here, swanning in like Lady Muck with your la-di-da bloody kids . . .'

'There's nothing wrong with the boys. What do you mean by that?' Rita asked angrily.

'Isn't it always the same, Rita, isn't it always the soddin' same! You get the education, the rich husband, the well-paid job . . . you get everything and I end up with bugger all!'

'What are you talking about?' Rita sounded totally amazed. 'I worked very hard to get to university . . . I've always worked hard.'

'And didn't we always know it, the blue-eyed girl, our Rita the little swot who was going to make it . . .'

'You were never interested in school,' Rita said, suddenly focusing her attention on a row of frozen Brussels sprout stalks.

'I never had the opportunity.'

'You had every opportunity.'

'Everything in that house,' she said, pointing towards the little terrace, 'was for your benefit. "Don't make a noise, Rita's working. Be quiet, Rita's studying for her exams . . ."'

'Marlene,' Rita said, shocked at her sister's diatribe, 'that was all twenty years ago! Why the hell are you bringing it up now?'

'Because I feel like it,' Marlene replied tartly.

Rita's teeth started to chatter and she was anxious to move back inside. 'Come on,' she encouraged, 'it's freezing out here. Let's go in and join the others . . . don't spoil Christmas Day for Mum.'

'Me, spoil it? I wasn't even invited.'

'Oh, really, Marlene,' she said in disbelief, not wishing to hear any more, 'I'm going inside.'

'What's going on?' her mother asked as Rita walked into the kitchen. 'It's freezing with that door wide open . . . Where's Marlene?'

'Sulking down the garden.'

'Sulking? She'll catch her death of cold. What's the matter with the girl?'

Rita shrugged. 'You tell me.'

'Have you been arguing?'

'*I* haven't . . . she's feeling aggrieved about her lot in life.'

'You *have* been arguing.' Her mother sounded furious.

Marlene came into the house, looking blue with cold, throwing the table cloth on top of the kitchen table. 'Talking about me, are you?'

'What's the matter with you, girl?' her mother asked.

'Nothing,' Marlene snapped.

'You must be mad, going out in the garden in that summer frock.'

'It's my only decent dress.'

'Rubbish!'

'I don't have Rita's money to throw around.'

'No, but you threw John's money around with enough abandon until he grew sick of it.'

239

Rita looked at her mother, open-mouthed with surprise.

'It's nothing to do with you,' Marlene replied, her voice raised.

Rita was caught in the middle of the argument. 'Look, can't we just cool it? I mean, it's Christmas, for God's sake!'

'What's the matter with you?' her mother asked Marlene again, ignoring Rita, talking directly across her.

'There's nothing wrong with me,' Marlene replied indignantly.

'Then why can't you behave yourself?'

'I'm not twelve,' Marlene sulked.

'Then don't act like it,' her mother warned.

'Then don't treat me like it,' Marlene replied nastily.

For Rita it was like being transported back in time to when they were children. It was almost, word for word, the same argument. She had forgotten how awful it was. Marlene would be annoyed with Rita for having to be quiet whilst her sister did the never-ending homework and would suddenly explode into anger and frustration. Rita could see them both clearly in her mind's eye . . . Two little girls, two sisters who were so terribly different from one another in looks, temperament and intellect. Rita always liked to read, she had what her teachers called an 'enquiring' mind. Marlene hardly ever read, she wasn't remotely interested in what happened outside her own small world. Everything was opposite. Marlene was obsessed with fashion and hair and make-up and pop music and boys. Rita's interest was only passing, she had to work to achieve her aim and nothing would stand in her way. Marlene never understood why anyone would want to go to a university.

'Why do you want to go to a place where all you do is read books?' Marlene asked.

'It won't be like that,' Rita replied.

Marlene pulled a face. 'All those boring swots and no decent men!'

'How do you know there won't be any decent men? You know nothing about it.'

'They'll be spotty swots with milk-bottle-bottom glasses,' Marlene replied, pulling a length of bubble gum out of her mouth as she leant over Rita's homework, chewing it rather overtly back into her heavily made-up face.

'Oh, shut up,' Rita snapped. 'They can't be any worse than those creeps you hang around with.'

'At least I have fun. You don't do anything but work.'

'Rubbish.'

'It isn't normal, Rita,' Marlene said. 'You could be quite pretty if you tried . . . lots of boys round here would go out with you if you wore a bit of make-up and did something with your hair.'

'I'm not interested in the boys round here,' Rita replied with distaste.

'You'll end up a spinster, on the shelf just like poor old Aunty Vi.'

Rita didn't reply.

'Is that what you want?'

'Of course not.'

'So, why not do something about it?' Marlene asked, picking up a history textbook and flicking absently through the pages.

'Because,' Rita began, snatching the book away from her, 'I'm too busy . . . I want to get out of here and make something of myself. What are you going to do that's so great?'

'At least I won't be a dried-up old spinster, a book-worm, a boring swot!'

'No, you'll end up on a council estate with six screaming brats and you'll be stuck and going nowhere fast.'

Marlene had given a contemptuous laugh. 'You've got to be joking! Whilst you're swotting for your exams I shall be working and going abroad for my holidays and making sure that I have a bloody good time.'

Rita looked at her sister now, remembering the interminable arguments, seeing what had happened to Marlene, who was now in floods of tears, unable to cope, unable to understand quite why life had been so cruel to her. Her mother was telling Marlene to get control of herself, to think about the children, to stop being so silly. Poor Marlene, Rita thought, thirty-seven years old and her life crashing about her in ruinous disarray, just about hanging on by the finger tips, alone and resentful and lashing out at all comers. Her own presence was like a red rag to a bull. Rita, who to all intents and purposes had everything. Rita, who had it made. Rita, who had grown up and out of her past and who stood now as a stranger, recalling, witnessing but no longer being part of it.

They drove back to Chalcot Square after supper, reflecting upon the events of the day. Even the boys were satiated, refusing a second piece of their grandmother's Christmas cake. Marlene left with the girls after tea. She had been very subdued and hardly said a word for the remainder of the time she spent with her family. Rita was having her mother, grandmother and Aunty Vi over for Boxing Day and invited Marlene and the girls, but she declined. John had the girls on Boxing Day and she would stay in by herself.

'I'll be all right,' Marlene said, 'I don't want anybody to worry over me.'

'Come on, Marlene,' Rita encouraged. 'Come with Mum and the others.'

'I'll be all right,' she insisted. 'Don't fuss.'

Rita watched her go, driving away into the darkness in a battered old Mini.

'Well, I don't know,' her mother sighed as the car disappeared into the night.

'Why didn't you tell me?' Rita asked, taking her mother's arm as they walked back to the house across the slippery path.

'Tell you what?'

'That Marlene was behaving so oddly.'

'Oh, Marlene has always acted like that . . . It's the girls I feel sorry for.'

'But, Mum,' Rita protested, 'she looks so ill and she's really let herself go. That dress she was wearing!'

'It's since John left her . . . you should see the house!' her mother said, turning to Rita as they approached the front door. 'It's a real tip.'

'Can't anyone help?'

'We've tried, God knows, your gran and me and Aunty Vi.' They walked into the warm living room. 'I've lost count of the number of times we've gone up there and cleaned through her house, haven't we, Vi?' she said to her sister.

Aunty Vi nodded in agreement. 'Shocking,' she said in dismay, 'I don't know what's got into Marlene, I really don't.'

'Has she seen a doctor?' Rita asked.

'A doctor?' her mother asked. 'Marlene isn't ill, she's just slovenly, can't be bothered.'

'Keeps the girls nice, though,' Aunty Vi insisted.

Her mother had nodded. 'She doesn't seem to care about herself but the girls never go short of anything. And John's really good, he won't let them miss out on anything.'

Rita pulled the car into Chalcot Road. She had no idea what to do about Marlene. It seemed an impossible situation. She could hardly be responsible for herself and certainly didn't feel that she could take Marlene's problems on board as well. Rita parked the car outside the house and they all clambered out with their return load of Christmas presents. She sat down heavily on the sofa, feeling at a loss and terribly distanced from her family. To them she must appear as the proverbial cuckoo in the nest, the interloper who returns for a while and then, literally, flies away again. Perhaps Marlene's behaviour was merely exasperation with her older sister's attitude.

'All right?' William asked, handing her a mug of tea which she hadn't asked for and didn't feel like but accepted with a smile anyway.

'Yes, did you have a good day, boys?'

Steve looked up from the magazine he was reading. 'What's up with Aunt Marlene?'

Rita shrugged. 'Your guess is as good as mine,' she replied.

William sat down next to her. He looked tired and ready for bed. 'She hardly spoke to us.'

'I think her divorce from Uncle John has caused a great deal of upset.' It was hardly an earth-shattering observation.

'She looked weird,' Steve said.

'She looked ill,' William yawned, 'and why was she dressed for summer?'

'God knows.' Rita sipped the black tea and put the mug carefully down by the side of the sofa.

'Does divorce always cause such problems?' Steve asked her.

'I don't know, I shouldn't think so.'

'Why did Uncle John leave her?' he asked bluntly.

'He fell in love with another woman,' Rita replied.

Steve looked at her, ready to ask another question but,

thinking better of it, perhaps, slumped back into the chair, turning over the pages of *The Face*.

'I'm for bed,' William said after a silence.

Rita reached up to kiss him good-night as he left them.

'Are you and Dad going to get a divorce?' Steve asked her after William had long gone to bed.

Rita turned to him. 'Give it a rest, Steve,' she complained.

'Well, you're both seeing other people now.'

'Steve,' Rita began wearily, 'I've told you before . . . don't jump to so many conclusions.'

'Well, what *are* you going to do?'

'It's Christmas, Steve, give me a break!'

'Okay,' he nodded, giving up for a while.

'When there's something to tell you we'll make sure that you both know but, right now, things will go on in pretty much the same way.'

'What about you and Gary?'

'Me and Gary?' she smiled, suddenly missing him a lot. 'There's nothing to report on that front either.'

'Come on, Mum,' Steve laughed.

'It's bedtime,' Rita said, terminating the discussion and getting up. In the morning there would be a mad scramble to complete preparations for her family, who would expect continual food and drink. She wasn't looking forward to it especially and wondered if she should still try to coax Marlene along. 'Don't stay up too late, Steve,' she warned, 'it's almost twelve now.'

'Okay, okay,' he replied without looking up from the magazine.

'And a merry Christmas to you too,' Rita retorted, heading for the stairs.

'It was the usual thing,' Rita was saying to Vanessa over the phone a few days later, 'gigantic meals, my family

245

snoring all afternoon and endless cups of tea . . .' There was a loud knock on the front door, which interrupted their conversation, and Rita opened it to find Marlene standing on her doorstep. Rita showed her sister into the sitting room and quickly finished her conversation with Vanessa, saying she would ring her back later.

Marlene was standing with her back to the room when Rita walked in. She was looking out at the rather forlorn garden.

'Would you like a drink?' Rita enquired. It was another bitterly cold day and Marlene was wearing a thin-looking cardigan over a cotton blouse and cheap denim jeans. On her feet were a very tattered pair of trainers and rather grubby white socks.

Marlene nodded, turning to face Rita.

'Tea, coffee . . . something stronger?' Rita smiled.

'Coffee would be fine,' Marlene answered. She appeared to be tense and uncomfortable.

'Sit down.' Rita motioned to the armchair by the glowing fire. 'The coffee's already percolated, it'll only take a second.'

Marlene was sitting by the fire, rubbing her hands together and then holding them out to the flames. 'This is a lovely house,' she said, taking a mug from Rita, 'you have such nice high ceilings.'

Rita nodded in agreement, sitting on the sofa.

'Our house is so box-like compared to this.'

Rita continued to smile. She didn't know what to say or why Marlene had suddenly descended upon her. She was wary in case Marlene was about to launch into another tirade of abuse. 'So, how are you?' Rita asked.

Marlene looked. 'I'm fine,' she replied rather shrilly, 'couldn't be better . . . I left Julie and Kim with Mum this morning and thought I'd come over to see you. Bloody car almost gave up on me but I made it!'

Rita smiled. 'Steve and William are out at friends',' she said.

Marlene sipped at the hot coffee. 'Sorry about the fuss on Christmas Day, Rita, I wasn't feeling myself.' She glanced rather nervously at her sister.

'Are you really that unhappy?' Rita asked.

'I just told you,' Marlene replied, her voice becoming harder, more belligerent, 'I wasn't myself.'

'What did you do on Boxing Day?' Rita asked.

'I got drunk with the girl from next door.' Marlene laughed at the memory. 'Her old man's walked out on her too.'

'I see.' Rita put down her mug. 'Did the girls have a nice day with John?'

Marlene pulled a sour face. 'He just spoils them rotten,' was all she said.

'Listen,' Rita began, standing up, 'I was planning to take a walk over Hampstead Heath . . . to blow away the cobwebs, you know.' She felt a strong desire to get Marlene out of the house and thought a walk would be as good an excuse as any. Besides, she had considered taking a stroll across Parliament Hill.

Marlene didn't seem especially keen. 'Nah, I can't be bothered, I only called in for a minute. Mum's giving us all lunch.'

'Oh, I see.' Rita sat down again.

'When are you going back to America?' Marlene asked after a long silence.

'I think it's the ninth of January. It's a Saturday, anyway.'

Marlene smiled. 'Got it made, haven't you, jetting back to the sun.'

'We're going to Mum's on Friday. Are you going to be there?'

Marlene thought for a moment. 'New Year's Day?' She

shook her head. 'John's sister's invited us to her house for the afternoon . . . Do you know Kay? She's nice, she is.'

Rita shook her head. She looked at her sister before asking the next question. 'Marlene, have you seen a doctor recently?'

'Me?' Marlene laughed at the idea. 'Whatever for?'

'Well, you don't look very well, you're terribly thin.'

'Fashionable, isn't it? You're not exactly heavy yourself. Besides, I needed to lose some weight.'

'Are you eating properly?' Rita asked.

'I eat enough. I don't have a big appetite, not like when we were youngsters . . . do you remember? I never stopped!'

Rita recalled that, and smiled. 'You know I will help in any way I can.'

'Help?' Marlene sounded suspicious. 'Oh, money, you mean . . . We're not charity cases yet.' She pulled at the sleeve of her old cardigan. 'Oh, I know I look a bleedin' mess, but that's just me, Rita, I'm just not interested any more.'

'You used to be,' Rita replied. 'You used to be the height of fashion!'

Marlene shrugged. 'That was years ago. Things have changed around, haven't they? You were always the frumpy one then.'

'Did you think I was frumpy?' Rita asked, smiling.

'You were fat and you always wore the most terrible things.'

Rita looked into the flames. 'Perhaps we could go to the sales together . . . I could treat you.'

Marlene shook her head. 'I don't want your charity, Rita. I don't want anything from you. I know exactly what I am, a rotten disaster, couldn't even keep John and he never wanted very much . . .' She sighed. 'I don't know why, Rita, but I just don't care any more.'

'What do you mean?'

'I look at myself sometimes and I think, "Christ, what a bleedin' mess, what man is ever going to be attracted to you?" But I've got the girls and they're all right, aren't they?'

'Why, yes, of course,' Rita encouraged.

'I could do a lot more with my life, but what's the point?' She stared at Rita. 'I mean to say, look at you . . . all those years at school and university, and then the disasters you've had: first Nathan, and now Paul leaving you. I mean, Christ, girl, it's not as if we've either of us exactly made a complete success of our lives, is it?'

Rita felt shocked. How could anyone be quite so callous? The problem was, Marlene didn't see how hurtful she was being. There was little point becoming upset or angry with her. 'So, you won't be at Mum's for New Year's Day?' Rita asked again.

Marlene shook her head.

'Perhaps we can arrange to meet before I leave, then,' Rita suggested.

Marlene shrugged. 'If you like.'

'Don't you want to?' Rita asked bluntly, turning to her sister.

'We can if you like,' she replied.

'It's not if *I* like, Marlene,' Rita insisted.

'I'd invite you over to Harlow but it's such a dump . . .'

'Perhaps we could arrange to meet at Mum's house, then.'

'You'll see her before you go back . . . I'll ask her to let me know when.'

Rita felt exasperated. It was like dealing with a mad person who made very little sense. 'All right.'

Marlene stood up and prepared to leave. 'I hate this time of year, Rita,' she admitted, gathering the old cardigan around her scrawny frame. 'I suppose it's the same for you . . . especially being back in this house with all its memories.'

'I think we have to try and be positive,' Rita replied.

'Yes, but it's difficult, isn't it?'

Rita opened the front door and followed her sister out into the cold air. 'Well,' she said as Marlene fumbled with her car keys, 'I hope we'll see you soon after New Year.'

Marlene looked at Rita and then up at the house. 'Did you ever discover why he did it?' she asked.

Rita was confused for a moment. 'What do you mean?'

'Nathan . . . why did he kill himself?'

'No,' Rita shook her head, 'no, there was never any explanation.'

Marlene sighed. 'At least I never had that to cope with. It must be awful.'

Rita watched as she drove away, the ancient Mini spluttering and belching a choking plume of thick exhaust. She closed the heavy front door behind her, feeling panic-stricken and sick. Marlene didn't seem aware of the hurtful things she was saying, and Rita didn't know whether to be angry or sad. She just wanted to get away from it all, her family and this house with its painful memories and the dreary, cold climate which made every-thing seem a hundred times worse. She wondered what Gary was up to in LA and how Paul was getting on with his new woman and, sitting down in front of the fire, she shed a few more tears – this time for herself and the way everything had turned out.

The house was deserted when William and Steve returned in the early afternoon.

'Did Mum say she was going out?' Steve asked.

William shook his head, poking at the fire and placing more coal on the glowing red embers. 'Maybe she's left a note,' he suggested, turning from the fire to the television.

Steve came back with two glasses of lager. 'There's nothing in the kitchen. Do you think she's out shopping?'

William didn't take his eyes off the screen. 'Maybe. Who knows? She's been in an odd mood since Christmas.'

Steve slurped at his drink. 'I shall be glad when this vacation is over.'

William nodded. 'I hope Mum doesn't end up like Aunty Marlene if her and Dad divorce!'

'Marlene is a mess,' Steve replied dismissively.

'They don't have much in common, do they?' William said. 'Mum seems to have inherited the brains and the looks!'

'Lucky for us,' Steve grinned.

'I felt a bit sorry for Julie and Kim,' William admitted.

'Why? They seemed all right to me.'

'Well, would you like to have Marlene for a mother?'

Steve shrugged and was silent for a while before changing the subject. 'What do you miss most about California?' he asked his brother.

William thought for a moment. 'The weather, of course, and the ice cream,' he laughed. 'I don't know . . . I thought I'd enjoy coming back home but there's nothing here for me any more. I don't exactly seem to fit in.'

Steve nodded in agreement. 'You once had doubts about staying in LA.'

'Not any longer,' William admitted. 'I don't think I'd want to come back to school here now.'

'Everything seems so small and claustrophobic, even this house . . . And it's so cold and dark all the time.'

William laughed and then looked more serious. 'I wonder if Nathan would have liked LA.'

'Yes, why wouldn't he?'

'I just remember him as being so English, I guess.'

'We were all the same. It doesn't take very much to change.'

251

'But in different circumstances we might not have liked it so much.'

'If Nathan hadn't died, you mean?'

'I don't know,' William replied. 'He wasn't due to move with us, anyway.'

Steve looked thoughtful but didn't reply. He sat back and watched the television. 'The TV doesn't have enough stations either!' he remarked.

'You never wanted to move to begin with,' William said. 'But once we were there, you seemed to settle in the quickest.'

Steve shrugged. 'It was easier than I thought.'

'Nathan never seemed very interested, did he?'

'He had other things on his mind,' Steve replied quietly.

'I remember when Mum and Dad used to talk about moving to California, he would normally find some excuse to leave the room.'

'I don't remember that . . . He was studying for his exams.'

'No, it was more than that.'

'You're letting your imagination fly away with you,' Steve said. 'After New Year, all Nathan did was work.' He sounded slightly irritable.

'I tried to talk to him about moving,' William insisted, 'and he always turned the conversation away from it.'

'Well,' Steve sighed, 'if it was you, how would you feel about your whole family leaving London, lock, stock and barrel?'

'He could have visited . . . What did he say to you?'

'Nothing,' Steve insisted.

'Oh, come on, you were always with him, he must have said something.'

'What is this,' Steve half laughed at his brother's probing, 'the third-degree?'

'No,' William said, sounding less sure of himself, 'it's

252

just something that I've been thinking about . . . I wondered if that was why he did it.'

Steve was silent for a long time, his eyes intent upon the crazy antics of the cartoon characters flashing across the large screen. 'That isn't the reason,' he replied at last.

William turned to him. 'Do you know what is, then?'

Steve looked back. 'No,' he said finally. 'No one knows.' His voice sounded gruff and strained.

'There must have been *some* reason,' William said softly, almost to himself.

'Why are you bringing this up now?' Steve asked. 'Nathan's dead . . . just leave it at that.'

'It wasn't like him, that's all,' he finished uncertainly.

'People do irrational things sometimes.'

'Wouldn't you like to know why he killed himself?'

'What difference could it possibly make?' Steve said, beginning to sound really annoyed now.

'It would make a difference to me,' William replied.

'What difference?'

William didn't respond for a moment. 'It would help me to understand. It wouldn't bring him back but it would help me to understand.'

Steve nodded but made no reply and, after a short while, got up and went into the kitchen, where he made himself some toast. The house was gloomy in the dull afternoon, the shadows uninviting, almost sinister. He hated this house, he hated to come back and find it haunted with Nathan's memory. Each day he promised himself he would go into his dead brother's room and each day he refused. He hated to visit the graveside and he couldn't stand to see his mother tearing herself apart, a little more of her strength, her resolve ebbing away as the days went by. This wasn't a holiday, it was as though they were paying a penance, each one circling around the others, pretending that it was all right now, that they had got over Nathan. Being brave, smiling in the right places, attempting to deal with it in the best way they knew how and no one admitting the truth. William asked the question *why*? What good would it do to find the answers?

The bread had caught fire under the grill and the kitchen was full of acrid smoke. He picked up the grill pan and tipped the flaming bread into the sink, where he turned the cold-water tap on it.

'What's the matter?' William asked, coming through to see what the noise was about.

'Nothing . . . I burnt the fuckin' toast!' Steve tried to explain.

William looked at his brother strangely. 'You're crying, Steve.'

'No,' Steve insisted, 'it's the smoke,' and he wiped his eyes in an angry motion. 'It's the smoke,' he repeated, looking at William hopelessly before leaving the kitchen and running up the stairs.

Rita had driven to Hampstead Heath, where she walked, striding out across the frozen ground, muffled up against the chill, hardly aware of her progress. At one point she had stood looking through the stripped winter trees towards the skyline of the city, the buildings crisp and sharply defined against the clear, icy sky. All she wanted to do was run away, perhaps to Gary, at least to a degree of security. London no longer felt like home to her. It represented the most awful period of her life and why she had been stupid enough to imagine that Chalcot Square would be anything else other than full of Nathan's ghost she couldn't imagine. Her family, much as she loved them, drove her to distraction. Everything measured in cups of tea and enormous meals. Marlene was insane and made Rita feel her own reason was only a fragile entity that might crumble away into dust at any moment. Her children seemed to be fading into the greyness of an English winter, looking large and at odds with the country of their birth. They were all misfits within their own country, outsiders in a foreign land now. She could hardly believe it.

Rita found herself by Whitestone Pond, where Shelley was supposed to have sailed his paper boats to amuse the children. There was a flagstaff marking the highest point on the Heath. She turned to look about her. They used to bring the boys to the Heath in the winter when there was enough snow for tobogganing. Rita could remember their screams and yells of delight as they were pushed off down a slope, Nathan at the back, attempting to steer the other two as they sped along to a safe landing. She could see them quite clearly, muffled and bobble-hatted, mittened and wellington-booted.

Rita walked slowly back to the car. Marlene had come to her as a warning, she realized. Whatever happened, she would not end up like her sister, there had to be more left than that. Marlene had simply given up, hanging on for the sake of the girls and, perhaps, even resenting them for making her continue. Her father came to mind, a sudden feeling of sadness for him overwhelmed Rita for a moment, making her stop short and take a deep breath. He had been dead for twenty-three years and it was only now, at this moment, that it seemed to affect her. She took out a dirty tissue from her coat pocket and blew her red nose, refusing to cry for him, refusing to give in to her rocky, maudlin emotional state.

All this, she knew, was about Nathan's death and how coming back to London had only served to open up all the old wounds. She reached the car and, sitting inside, her breath steaming white in the freezing interior, she broke down into a series of sobs that seemed to reach down into her very soul, making her fear she could not continue. The sounds that came from her were almost animal in their intensity, they were savage and painful to her, making her gasp for every new breath until, finally, her body shook and tears flooded down her cheeks as she bowed her head against her folded arms on the steering wheel. Eventually the power of her grief subsided and Nathan's name came to her lips.

It snowed heavily the next day, much to the delight of Steve and William, who were becoming increasingly bored with their time in London. They went out immediately after breakfast and built a large snowman in the garden.

Rita received an airmail letter from Gary, telling her about his Christmas in LA and how his son had managed to wreck the Jeep in Mexico, which was presenting him with many problems. He seemed to have spent the entire holiday sorting out the problems associated with bringing both his son and the battered Jeep home. It sounded a rather miserable Christmas although he did mention that the new year perked things up a bit, whatever that meant.

She had confused thoughts about Gary, not knowing what would happen when she got back. She hadn't made any effort to contact him and it would be useless sending a letter now because she would be in LA before he received it. She wondered vaguely if he was taking care of her estate car and then dismissed the thought from her mind.

'Come on, Mum,' William called, poking his head round the kitchen door, 'you can have your picture taken with the snowman.'

Rita looked up. 'That's the best offer I've had all vacation.'

William smiled, his face pink and glowing with health. 'Come on.'

She found her coat and went into the garden, where Steve immediately tossed a snowball at her, hitting her on the shoulder. Rita quickly fashioned herself some ammunition and they were all soon involved in a manic free-for-all, bombarding one another with the fresh snow. The snowman was also included in this fight and, by the time she was posed by its side, it was in rather a sad state, with parts of its body and head missing. Rita's brown fake-fur coat was covered in snow and, with her arm around the snowman's shoulder, Steve squatting in front of them, William took a series of photographs. She managed to scoop up a handful of snow and dump it on Steve's head for the final shot, which caused her and William much hilarity.

After lunch the snow stopped, the skies cleared and a bright sun shone. The boys persuaded her to go shopping with them and they spent the afternoon trailing around the sales. Rita noticed that she was expected to pick up the bill every time they purchased something. They made their way from Oxford Street, down Regent Street and across to Covent Garden, where Steve wanted to visit a candle shop which seemed to be constructed inside an old cellar and was very crowded and cramped. Rita bought a candle in the shape of Big Ben for Gary before they tumbled out into the street and found a warm café for a much-needed cup of tea.

'Good fun shopping with us, eh, Mum?' Steve asked, picking up a sugar lump and popping it into his mouth.

'You're absolute vultures,' she joked, 'I'm cleaned out!' The floor around their table was obliterated by the number of parcels and plastic bags they had obtained. 'I must be insane.'

'It was bargain time,' William told her.

'For you,' she said.

'And for you,' Steve reminded her. 'You got that outfit thing.'

Rita had purchased a black jacket with matching skirt. It had certainly been a fantastic reduction but now she doubted the wisdom of such an impulse buy. She seemed to live in jeans, though perhaps she would smarten herself up a bit. But it was no good, her wardrobe was already bursting with things she never wore and her bargain outfit would probably be relegated to the ranks of her other unseen clothes. 'God knows how we shall get it all back. I bet I'll have to pay excess baggage!'

'Nonsense,' Steve replied. 'We were loaded up with all those Christmas gifts before . . . there'll be tons of space.'

Rita looked rather uncertain about this but decided not to pursue the discussion any further. 'I hope you're both ready for the trip to Hampshire in the morning,' she said.

Steve pulled a face. 'Do we have to stay over?'

Rita nodded. 'Afraid so.'

William groaned. 'Two days in Hampshire.'

'Never mind, we go back at the end of the week.'

'They're such pains, though,' Steve said.

'Well, it's because of you two that we have to go. I'm sure Mary isn't interested in seeing me!'

'What will we do?' William asked.

'What do you normally do?' Rita asked him. 'They have TV, and you'll have lots to eat and, if the weather isn't too bad, you can take a walk in the New Forest.'

'Great,' William said without enthusiasm.

Rita laughed. 'I bet if your dad were here you wouldn't be so reluctant to go.'

'Well, he isn't,' Steve smiled, 'so we can moan.'

'Roll on Saturday,' Rita said with some feeling.

Steve and William glanced at one another and burst into laughter.

* * *

They left early on Wednesday morning, the boys grumpy at being woken up so early, and Rita drove carefully on the icy roads out of London. It did seem a stupid exercise, driving hundreds of miles to visit people who weren't really interested in seeing them and who they were most certainly not interested in seeing. It began to snow again as they left the city and Rita found the going hard.

'What's going to happen when we get back?' William asked as they approached Southampton, removing his Walkman earphones for the first time in over an hour.

'Get back where?' Rita asked, confused, peering through the greasy windscreen for a sign showing her where the A35 had gone to.

'California,' William replied.

Steve was fast asleep on the back seat, and she glanced at his prone body in the rear-view mirror. 'What do you wish would happen?' she asked, pulling up at a busy roundabout and winding down her window in order to see more clearly, allowing the freezing air and rain to enter the car. She found a gap and accelerated away with a jerk.

William shrugged. 'You and Dad to get back together?' he suggested.

'Not that again,' Rita complained, seeing a sign for Bassett and then another with A35 on it. 'Well, that won't happen . . . you know it won't.'

He nodded. 'What if he stops seeing his new woman?'

Rita laughed. She indicated she was going to move into the nearside lane and, finding her chance as there was a gap, swerved across, causing a lorry behind to flash her. 'Bloody fool,' she murmured under her breath before answering William. 'Why should he stop seeing her?' she asked.

William shrugged again.

'I don't know what you're worried about. You see more of your father than you ever did when he was living in the same house with us . . . *and* you complain about it!' she reminded him.

'What are you going to do, then?' he asked after another pause for thought.

'What do you mean?'

'If Dad wants to marry her.'

'He doesn't,' she replied immediately.

William was quiet again for a while. 'You might want to marry someone else.'

'I very much doubt it.'

'You might.'

'And pigs might fly!'

William laughed. 'You could, you're not that old.'

'Thanks.'

'I bet there are lots of men who would marry you.'

'For God's sake, William,' Rita roared with laughter, 'I don't suppose that you have anyone in mind, do you?'

'Gary?' he suggested tentatively.

Rita shook her head. 'Not Gary.'

'No?'

'Nope!'

'Oh . . . I thought you were dating him.'

'You know,' Rita replied, smiling, 'I'm not entirely sure if this is the sort of conversation most fifteen-year-olds have with their mothers!'

'Come on, Mum,' William replied, as though she were the child, 'I could be a father at my age.'

'You're not, are you?' she asked, turning to him for a second. 'I didn't even know you were dating seriously.'

William grinned. 'I was being hypothetical, actually.'

'Oh, were you now, *actually* . . . Listen, don't worry about me or your dad. Whatever happens, you and Steve

260

come first, you know that, so stop being such a little whittler.'

'Kids who come from a broken home become over-anxious . . . they teach us that in community studies.'

'You're not from a broken home,' Rita protested.

'You and Dad live apart.'

Rita sighed. 'Okay, you're right. I give up . . . poor deprived children!'

William flipped open his Walkman, removing one cassette and inserting another. 'I was only joking, Mum.'

'I should bloody well hope so. Your dad would go spare if he ever heard you talking about us like that.'

'It's his fault we're like it,' William said, sounding bitter.

Rita didn't reply. It had begun to rain more heavily and she was having to concentrate on her driving. William had switched on his Walkman again and she could hear a faint buzzing sound from his direction. Steve was still crunched up on the back seat, still dead to the world and looking extremely uncomfortable.

She was remembering a conversation with Sharon concerning the future, more specifically her future after the boys had left home. Sharon's idea was that Rita should begin to plan for this eventuality now. However, whilst understanding Sharon's point, she couldn't actually come to terms with what, exactly, her future should be like. She didn't know if she would teach again, she wasn't sure what she wanted. It seemed a daunting prospect. By the time William was ready to leave for university she would be in her mid-forties. No, Rita decided as the car sped through the rain, it was not a good time to be starting out all over again. Sharon would have told her to go for it, to grasp a new challenge, but Rita wasn't convinced she had the stamina.

Rita had always thought that when the boys left, there

261

would be more time to spend with Paul. They could do all the things they hadn't had space to do over the previous twenty years. It was a pipe-dream, of course, she had always known that. She had assumed that after child-care they, she and Paul, would slip into a graceful middle age together. She had never imagined, not even in her wildest dreams, how terribly their lives would have changed. How in the space of two years both her eldest son and her marriage would have died. It still seemed incredible to Rita, at times almost a fiction, a horror story. But her life hadn't ended, she no longer felt unable to struggle on, William and Steve had, unknowingly, dragged her through all the blinding pain and wretchedness in the aftermath of Nathan's suicide. So, her life hadn't ended but her own sense of purpose, even her own sense of value and worth, had become lost with Nathan.

Rita had never wanted to live through any of her children, she had never wanted to cling to them, but she had a constant feeling of anxiety about William and Steve. Rita tried hard not to show this and, to a great extent, managed to hide it away from them, but whenever they left the house, there was always the question in her mind: Would she see them again? She often wondered how Paul dealt with it, or even if he did. The last two years had been a tremendous struggle for them all and Rita had been at the centre of the family, attempting to pull the whole thing back together again. With Paul, she had lost or he had just given up, but with the boys, she felt that things could have been a lot worse. She hoped that they were through the worst now, although she sometimes doubted or was afraid to acknowledge it, not wishing to tempt providence again.

Steve woke up as they reached Ashurst, sitting up and stretching. 'God, it's cold,' he said, yawning.

'It can't be,' Rita said, 'this heater is on full blast.'

'Well, it doesn't seem to be reaching the back.'

'We're almost there,' Rita told him, noticing a big sign for Lyndhurst flashing by.

'Great,' Steve replied without any enthusiasm.

William took off his earphones and turned to his brother. 'Sleeping Beauty wakes, eh?'

Steve leant forward between the two front seats, staring at the road ahead through the slapping wipers as the rain turned to sleet once more. 'I hope Gran's got us something good to eat.'

'Mary's a good cook,' Rita replied. 'I expect you'll both be able to pig yourselves . . . may I say, as usual!'

'Oh, Mum,' William complained, 'we're growing lads.'

'You're gannets,' Rita said.

'I hope she's in a good mood,' William remarked.

'Mary insisted that we come, it's not as if we were forcing ourselves upon them.'

'Has she always been like this?' Steve asked.

Rita nodded.

'She's never been nice to you?' William asked.

'Mary always hoped that your father would marry into the county set . . . he was always extremely popular with the girls down here.'

'So, why did he marry you, then?' William turned to her with a smirk.

'Because I was fabulously good-looking, clever, vivacious and witty!'

'Why did you marry him, Mum?' Steve asked her.

'What a question,' Rita complained.

'They were in love, weren't you?' William said, laughing at the soppy idea.

Rita nodded. 'Of course we were,' she added.

'Did you only date Dad when you were at university?' Steve asked.

'Yes, I met him straight away . . .'

'It was love at first sight,' William laughed.

'Not exactly,' Rita said, turning into Lyndhurst's high street.

'Lust, then,' William continued.

'Don't be so cheeky,' she told him, smiling all the same.

'You've gone past their turning,' Steve warned her.

'No, I haven't,' Rita insisted.

'You have, we've just gone by it,' Steve said. 'It's a psychological reaction . . . you don't really want to be here at all!'

Rita pulled the car up to the kerb and checked her bearings, realizing that Steve was quite right. 'It looks different in the rain and snow,' she said, winding down her window to inspect the road behind her before performing a U-turn. 'So, Mother made a mistake,' she told them as the boys laughed. 'At least I got you here safely.'

William groaned. 'Big deal.'

They were soon pulling up in front of the large Georgian house, the car crunching over the gravel drive. Mary was already at the doorway, waving a large black umbrella in their direction, coming down the steps to meet them.

'Okay, here goes,' Rita said, switching off the engine. 'Everybody smile!'

Chapter 8

Rita had always rather admired her parents-in-law's house. She didn't covet it, exactly, but had always entertained vague thoughts about Paul's ultimate inheritance. It was a large house, passed down through the generations on his father's side of the family. It was full of splendid furniture, most of it antique, and beautiful ornamentation.

She had always liked the town of Lyndhurst too. It was the administrative centre of the New Forest, the place where the Verderers' Court sat to administer the forest laws. She loved the forest with its oak and beech and birch trees and the thickets of hawthorn and blackthorn. There were deer running wild in the woodlands, along with the donkeys and ponies.

Paul's father knew every inch of the surrounding countryside and she remembered how, in years past, he had taken her out and pointed to different trees, the conifer yew, which he always called 'Hampshire weed' because it flourished all over the county on the chalk soil, and beech 'hangers', so called because they appeared to hang on to the hillsides. At every opportunity she would walk out with him, leaving Paul to his mother.

She had never been that close to her father-in-law but she had been an attentive listener, which was all he required then, someone new to whom he could impart his knowledge. Even if she hadn't found it interesting, Rita would have gone along with him. Anything to avoid Mary's disapproving gaze.

* * *

Mary was putting the breakfast things into the dishwasher when Rita came down into the warm kitchen the following morning.

'We didn't like to disturb you,' Mary explained. 'There's still some coffee and I can do you some toast if you like.'

Rita yawned, peering up at the pendulum clock on the wall. It was just after ten o'clock. 'Where are the boys?' she asked.

'They're watching television.' Mary sounded disapproving. 'Coffee and toast?'

'Just coffee,' Rita replied, sitting at the table and watching as Mary took down a cup and saucer and poured out the steaming black liquid which filled the kitchen with its aroma. 'Where's Dad?' she asked, taking the coffee and drinking it black.

'He's in his study . . . Thursday is his correspondence day, he'll emerge at lunchtime.'

Rita nodded. 'How is he?'

Mary sighed. 'It took him a long time to get over our trip to America.'

It was a pointed remark and, Rita felt, one addressed directly to her. 'Oh,' she replied.

'But he doesn't seem too bad at the moment . . . I mean, what can you expect for a man of his age?'

'Quite,' Rita replied.

'How are things?' Mary asked.

'Okay,' Rita nodded.

'What about you and Paul?'

'We're the same,' she said.

'He never tells us very much . . .'

'Paul's seeing someone else,' Rita told her, 'didn't he tell you?' She looked at the surprised expression on Mary's face.

266

Mary closed the dishwasher and switched it on. 'So, what does this mean?'

Rita shrugged.

Mary sat opposite Rita. She was wearing a thick tweed skirt and a bottle-green cardigan over a checked blouse, her steel-grey hair smartly in place. Mary always looked in place, always correct and dressed for the occasion. At home she presented herself as the expensively, almost carelessly, dressed county woman. The sort of woman she had hoped Paul would marry. 'Is he serious about this new woman?'

Rita was wearing Levi's and an outsize man's jumper. It was thick and plum red and fell almost to her knees. Her bare feet were cold against the flagstones of the kitchen floor. She had no idea if Paul was serious or not. 'He spent Christmas with her,' she admitted.

Mary tut-tutted, shaking her head slightly. 'And what do you propose doing about it, Rita?' she asked, making it sound almost like a challenge.

'Do?' Rita looked confused.

'Yes. How long is this nonsense going on for?'

Rita blinked. 'I'm not sure what you mean.'

'Well, my dear, do you want Paul back or not?' Mary asked bluntly. 'You're both behaving like a couple of spoiled brats.'

'I don't think it's a question of whether I want Paul back or not any longer . . . Paul hasn't any intention of coming back!'

'Are you quite sure?'

'Perfectly,' Rita assured the old woman.

Mary sighed. 'I can't believe that Nathan's death has caused so much havoc.'

'No, you've never really understood it, have you?'

'Well, of course, I realize how difficult it must have been . . .'

267

'Yes, I think I know how you feel about Nathan's suicide,' Rita said, interrupting her mother-in-law and not really wishing to carry on with the present topic of conversation.

'It was bound to be difficult between you both for a time . . .'

'Mary, *please*,' Rita insisted, 'let's not get into this now.'

'But have you ever stopped to consider how Paul must have felt?'

'How Paul must have felt?' Rita's voice took on an edge of amazement. 'What about me?' She pointed at herself. 'No one ever wanted to know how I was feeling . . : It was always Paul and the boys. I was just supposed to recover quickly and cater to everyone else's problems.'

'Oh, Rita, why do you insist upon dramatizing everything?'

Rita looked but didn't respond. Mary had always made her feel about six inches tall. Everything with Paul's mother had to be clear-cut. Somebody dies, you do your grieving, get over it and carry on again. It was all as simple as that. If Rita had been a half-decent wife, she would have accepted Paul's behaviour and kept the marriage together.

'Paul has always been a good husband, hasn't he?' Mary continued. 'He was a good provider, a good father.'

'He was absent for the majority of the time and I did work, Mary,' she reminded her.

'Well, you know what I think about that,' she replied, dismissively.

'We're not living in the Dark Ages, Mary,' Rita responded. 'Women have the vote and everything now, you know.'

Mary had a pained look. 'I'm not criticizing you, dear, but you've always seemed to believe you could have absolutely everything – home, children, career . . . everything your own way.'

'That's nonsense. I know what you're saying,' Rita's voice was becoming hard and angry, 'well, I never neglected my kids . . . that has nothing to do with it.'

Mary sighed. 'Sometimes the truth is very hard to bear.'

'The truth,' Rita laughed, 'what do you know about that?'

'At some point you'll have to face facts, Rita. You will have to realize everything that happens in this life isn't done as a direct insult to you.'

'I never said it was.'

'But look at the way you've behaved . . . Have you ever really thought about the reasons why Paul left you?'

'Many times.'

'You think they all stem from Nathan's death, don't you?'

Rita looked at Mary suspiciously. 'Well, don't they?'

'Your marriage wasn't exactly perfect for a long time before that, was it?'

'Our marriage was fine and it's none of your damn business anyway,' Rita snapped, suddenly afraid Mary might be on to something.

'I can remember coming to your house in London and hearing you arguing violently a year or more before Nathan died.'

Rita bit her lip. 'So, what are you saying?'

'I'm not saying anything, dear, I'm just commenting upon the facts. You seem to think everything was all right up to Nathan killing himself and I'm suggesting your memory is being selective.'

'Everyone argues,' Rita replied. 'Even you and Dad, I would suspect.'

'Never to an audience,' Mary replied smugly.

'How come you're the expert on marriage and children

all of a sudden?' Rita asked nastily. 'You only ever had one and you've spent the rest of your life bemoaning that fact.'

'Why are you being so abrasive?' Mary asked, sounding confused. 'Can't you see that I'm trying to help you?'

Rita laughed. 'Help me?'

Mary nodded. 'I don't want to see you and Paul divorced, dear.'

'Look, Mary, it's very nice of you but I don't really think you quite understand the situation . . .'

'I understand it perfectly,' she corrected Rita.

'Then you're doing a whole lot better than the rest of us,' Rita admitted.

'Do you want him back?' Mary asked.

Rita sighed. 'It's not a question of what *I* want, Paul made the decision to leave.' She looked at the remains of her coffee. 'It's over, there is no chance of us getting back together. Whether we divorce or not remains to be seen.'

'You're a very hard woman, Rita.'

'So you said.'

'What about the boys?'

'The boys are fine,' Rita insisted and, as though on cue, William came into the kitchen on the look-out for food.

Mary decided it was time for coffee and cake for everybody and busied herself around the stove, where she began to heat milk for instant coffee.

Rita left William to help his grandmother and found Steve, who was reading in the lounge. 'Hi,' she said, sitting next to him, 'what's the book?'

Steve turned the cover towards her. 'Steinbeck,' he said.

'*Grapes of Wrath*,' Rita smiled. 'I won that for the school English Literature Prize once . . . I must have it somewhere at home.'

'This is Nathan's, he lent it to me. It's taken me this long to get round to it.'

'Nathan was quite a Steinbeck fan at one stage.' Rita smiled at the memory. 'He must have collected most of his books.'

'Maybe I could look when we get back to London. Will they still be in his room?'

Rita felt her heart lurch. She felt a strange reaction, not wanting anything of Nathan's to be touched but, dismissing her initial response, smiled at Steve. 'Sure, why not? They're only sitting there gathering dust.'

'What are you going to do with his things, Mum?' Steve asked.

Rita hadn't thought about what should happen to them. 'We ought to sort them out, I suppose,' she replied. 'Most of them could go to a charity shop . . . it's crazy just hanging on to them, isn't it?'

Steve nodded. 'We could do it when we return to London,' he suggested.

Rita shrugged. 'I doubt if there will be time this trip. We won't be back until the afternoon tomorrow and my mother is coming for dinner in the evening.' She looked into Steve's serious, dark eyes. 'We're leaving for LA on Saturday.'

'It was just a thought,' he said.

'Is there anything of his that you or William might want?'

Steve shook his head.

'We'll see, then,' Rita told him, standing up and walking through the house, going through the kitchen and out of the back door into the bright, cold morning, the freezing air hitting her and clearing her head after the stuffy warmth of the house.

* * *

After lunch Rita and the boys went out for a walk in the surrounding woodland. Paul's father had gone upstairs for a rest and Mary was sitting in the lounge. Mary always sat in a small tapestry-covered armchair by the window, where she knitted for an hour or so in the afternoon light.

'Wrap up warm,' Mary told the boys.

'Yes, Gran,' William replied, his voice muffled by a thick scarf she had found for him to wear.

'We won't be long,' Rita said.

'A walk will do you all the world of good, get some of that awful Californian smog out of your lungs.'

'Right, then,' Rita said, ushering the boys out ahead of her, 'see you a bit later.'

Mary nodded and returned to her knitting, the needles clicking together quickly and expertly.

'Breathe deeply now,' Rita joked as they walked along.

'I wish they had a dog,' William said. 'We could throw sticks for it to fetch.'

'Poor thing,' Rita teased. 'I could always throw a stick or two for you to fetch, if you like.'

'No, thanks,' William replied as they trudged across the frozen heathland towards the trees.

Rita looked at them, wrapped up in their American multi-coloured ski jackets, bright yellows and reds and blues, virtually fluorescent against the muted and frozen landscape. She wondered if, in later years, they would resent being taken off to California during such formative times in their lives, leaving with an almost indecent haste following the death of their brother, and being transplanted into another culture. For the time being they seemed happy to reject everything English in favour of a rather aggressive, chauvinistic Americanism, and only the future would show the outcome of their move, the decision to leave London. They seemed fully immersed in the teenage Californian free-for-all, the consumer dream where almost everything was available to them. Rita had to admit that, so far, William and Steve had kept a sense of proportion and their choice of friends seemed, on the whole, to be sensible.

However, the shadow of Nathan's death still fell across Rita's thoughts and was a constant reminder that things could still go disastrously awry. Rich American kids took drugs, became drunks, got killed in car wrecks, drowned in surf-boarding accidents . . . she read horrendous statistics concerning teenage suicides and the so-called hidden deaths, children who wiped themselves out in car accidents when drunk, or drowned in the ocean or their parents' swimming pool. William and Steve always seemed too sensible for anything like that to happen, but so had Nathan. And so she watched them, always resisting the strong urge to gather the boys around her and keep them there.

A group of ponies trotted across the bridle path in front of them, breath steaming white from their nostrils. Rita caught up with the boys as they stood watching the animals pass.

'Do they belong to anyone?' William asked.

Rita nodded. 'They're all privately owned.'

'I wouldn't mind a horse,' he mused.

'You can't even cope with that wretched hamster,' Rita insisted. 'A horse would be a little too ambitious, I think!'

'I hope the hamster is okay,' he said.

'Jem said that he was going to pick it up for you and look after it this week,' Rita reminded him, and they began to walk on.

'I bet they'll all have really amazing tans from their trip to Hawaii,' William said.

'Poor hard-done-by child,' Rita teased, 'only a month away in London . . . aren't you deprived!'

'What are we doing in the summer?' William asked.

Rita shrugged. 'I haven't any idea.'

'We didn't do anything last summer,' he complained.

'You went to the beach,' she reminded him.

'That's not like a vacation, though.'

'No? It would have been when I was a child.' She hated these kind of discussions, they always made her feel so ancient.

William had no answer to that.

'Didn't you ever go away?' Steve asked her.

'We sometimes went to the coast for a day,' Rita replied, 'but we didn't have *weeks* away.'

William began to play 'Hearts and Flowers' on an imaginary violin, humming the tune and using his stick as a bow.

'It's all right for you,' Rita told him, unable to prevent herself from smiling, 'you have no idea of what it's like to be hard up.'

'You should be pleased about that,' William told her.

'I am,' Rita insisted, 'of course I am.'

'But you think we're spoiled brats,' William stated.

'Did I use that expression?' Rita asked.

'You implied it,' Steve added.

'All I'm saying is that you've never known anything other than relative affluence . . . okay? That's all, end of discussion.'

The boys looked at one another and laughed. 'Poor old Mum,' Steve said, 'what *are* you going to do with us?'

Rita smiled but didn't answer, leading them on, circling around towards their grandparents' house again. The boys eventually ran ahead of her, kicking pine cones between them, shouting and laughing as they charged along.

Usually Rita's arguments with Mary left her drained but, this time, when she was again criticized for depriving the children of a father, as they prepared dinner that evening, she was not undermined by the old harridan. Mary behaved as though absolutely nothing had happened and they all sat down to dinner and spent the entire meal quizzing Steve and William about their school in Los Angeles and what they intended to do in the future. This was fine as far as Rita was concerned, she had no wish to converse with her mother-in-law. Instead she chatted to the old man about the UCLA Medical Centre, which had impressed him greatly and which, he seemed to imagine, Rita frequented on a regular basis. He droned on throughout the meal whilst she ate like a pig. The tussle in the kitchen with Mary had only served to improve her appetite. Later she sat with the boys, watching a science-fiction film, the old folk having long retired to their beds.

'You and Gran don't get on very well, do you?' Steve asked, his eyes fixed to the screen.

'That is rather an understatement,' Rita replied.

'I don't think she likes us very much either,' William added.

'I'm sure she does,' Rita said, although she had no positive proof of that.

'She's very fussy about everything, isn't she?' Steve said.

'Your gran likes things to be done properly,' Rita agreed.

'But she's always so straight-backed,' Steve continued, 'and she hasn't any sense of humour.'

'She's old,' Rita explained.

'So's Great-Grandma,' William said. 'She's much older than her and she's always laughing.'

'Well, I don't know,' Rita admitted, 'perhaps she just doesn't find us very funny.'

Steve, who had been sitting on the floor at her feet, turned his head around to look up at Rita and laughed. 'Come on, Mother, we're *funny*!'

Rita chuckled. 'Funny peculiar.'

'She never speaks much to Grandpa,' William said. 'I don't think she likes him much either.'

'I just think that your grandma finds us all a little too much to cope with at times . . . You two have changed so much in the last two years and old people don't like change.'

'She keeps correcting my English all of the time,' William complained. 'She said I'd lost my "beautiful" accent!'

'You have,' Rita replied.

'But who cares?' Steve asked.

'Things like that seem important sometimes,' Rita told him. 'You have to see it from her point of view, she feels that your father has left for ever and, I expect, it's rather a daunting prospect when your family is so far away.' The boys had both turned to listen now, forgetting the film they had been so engrossed in.

'Well, I never understand it,' William admitted. 'She never seems exactly pleased to see Dad, and you don't get on with her.'

'I think she's unhappy,' Steve said.

Rita nodded. 'That's probably closer to the truth.'

'Why?' William asked.

'I don't really know, but she's always been the same . . . I suppose we should really feel sorry for her.'

'Do you, then?' Steve asked her.

Rita looked at him but did not reply. She really didn't feel anything for Mary . . . a certain anger sometimes. Paul's mother was a cranky old thing with little regard for the feelings of others, but most of the time Rita just had to accept the situation as it was, not as she would wish it to be. Any sadness she felt was directed at Paul, who always kept emotionally distant from his mother, which removed any real contact between them. Their relationship, devoid of hugs and kisses, of easy physical interaction, of natural and easy-going communication, seemed to have, somehow, blighted him for life.

Paul had once admitted to her that he never understood why his mother drew away from him but he remembered, as a little boy, feeling somewhat lost and mystified at her seeming inability to reach out to him. It made her feel sad to think of Paul as a little boy wanting so much to be loved by his mother and feeling so much rejection. Not that Mary ill-treated him. On the contrary, Paul always had everything that was necessary, was fed, clothed, sheltered and schooled in the traditional sturdy manner of the English middle classes. Pictures of him as a child often showed him with his arms around the neck of his dog, Jenna, a huge, floppy Old English sheepdog. Mary often said that, as a boy, Paul seemed to live for Jenna and treated the animal like a playmate; or a sibling. She was quite obviously not very enamoured of the memory.

It had taken Paul quite a time within their own relationship to understand that touching didn't always mean sex and that everyone needed the touch of another human simply to feel a part of something, a relationship, and to experience the warmth and comfort within an affectionate embrace. For Rita, always a very tactile person, the idea of remaining distant from someone she loved, from her own flesh and blood, from her own children, seemed inconceivable. Therefore, when the boys arrived, she actively encouraged Paul to hold them. However, throughout their marriage there had been periods of withdrawal, inexplicable occasions, even quite early on, when he would almost recoil from her touch and turn in on himself. At these times he would become almost morose and silent, as though deep in thought, nursing some distant wound. Rita understood later that Paul was afraid, perhaps even terrified, of being rejected, that, like the child, he was testing out her love for him. It was then that she began to hate what Mary had done to him but she could never really hate Mary. In the end her sadness for Paul would extend to his mother.

'We all learn to become the people we end up as by such a variety of different things,' she began. 'Some of them are taught to us when we are children and other things we pick up by instinct. For some reason Grandma was unable to show your dad how much she loved him . . . maybe it was something in her own upbringing.' Rita shrugged. 'Whatever it was, your dad and his mum have always existed with this invisible wall between them, unable, or perhaps too afraid, to break through and say how much they loved one another, or to show it by simply holding on or touching.' She smiled at her boys. 'So, you see, you have a lot to thank my crazy family for because, when I was a child, that little house in Walthamstow contained all the love and warmth and security in the world. At least,' she paused again, 'that's my maudlin perception of it.'

'Poor old Dad,' William said, almost in a whisper.

'Not so poor,' Rita replied. 'He has you two.'

Steve looked away at the smouldering logs, their ash white around the remains of the fire, which glowed a comforting red. 'I've sometimes felt that distance with him . . . Nathan and Dad always seemed closer somehow.' He spoke quietly, his voice sounding wistful.

'I'm sure that your dad always loved you all equally, there were never any favourites . . .'

'Except that he was the first-born,' Steve continued. 'Nathan was the one Dad expected to follow on, just as he followed on in his father's footsteps.'

Rita was taken aback at just how much like Paul Steve sounded, it was almost eerie in its similarity to the young

278

Paul she had first known. Of course, she was forgetting his slight American accent was missing now. She had noticed in the last week or so how their accents had faded. It was discernible to her if not to their fascinated (or appalled) friends and relatives. 'Your dad was always pleased that Nathan was going to study medicine but, I'm sure, he wouldn't have minded what he did.'

'That's not how Nathan saw it,' Steve replied, his head still turned away from her.

'No, how did Nathan see it?' Rita asked.

Steve moved towards the fire on his hands and knees, reached for a poker and stabbed at the broken logs, breaking them up and pushing them together in order to create a final blaze before they really died. He didn't answer Rita's question. Instead, he sat back watching the flames licking up around the wood. 'What time are we leaving in the morning?' he asked.

'As early as possible,' Rita replied. 'I want to see *my* mum tomorrow. There's precious little time left before we have to leave.'

William yawned. He had almost been asleep on the sofa for the last few minutes. 'Bed,' he said, suddenly sitting up and looking around him.

Rita laughed at him. 'Come on then, sleepy,' she said, placing her arm around him. 'You can walk me up as well,' Rita told him, 'walk me up the wooden hill to bed.'

Steve turned and smiled. 'God, Mum, I haven't heard that one in a long while.'

'No?' she said, pulling William up after her, an arm around his shoulder, leaning slightly against him. 'Well, the old ones are the best.' She stopped at the door. 'Don't be too late, Steve.'

'No, ma'am,' he replied in a thick American accent.

Rita smiled. 'Good-night then.'

Steve looked at her for a moment . . . it could have

been Paul . . . before bidding them both a good-night and watching the end of the film.

They left after breakfast the following morning. Mary had got up terribly early to prepare it for them, insisting upon a huge cooked meal, which Rita really didn't feel much like eating. Orange juice, followed by porridge, followed by bacon, eggs and sausage, toast, coffee or tea. The boys, of course, were in their element. Whatever the time of day, give them a meal, point them towards a table, and they were content. Mary nibbled a little dry toast, sitting at the end of the kitchen and watching them eat. There was little conversation. Rita felt exhausted. She hated getting up in the darkness and realized just how much she had always loathed English winters.

They went in to see Paul's father before leaving. He was propped up in his bed, a huge breakfast cup at the bedside, the *Daily Telegraph* in front of him. He looked grey and ancient. Rita seriously wondered if they would ever see him alive again. She bent to kiss his cheek, her lips brushing his white stubble, smelling the camphorated spirits on his night clothes. Mary literally sprinkled him with the smelly stuff, which was supposed to ease his congested chest. The boys shook his hand and he told them to be good and to work hard and that he hoped to see them again soon.

Mary saw them off, shaking their hands and thanking Rita for bringing the boys down to see them. She stood, framed by the door, on the top step, dressed in her thick tweed skirt, a bottle-green jumper with an old black cardigan draped across her shoulders. A cold, murky day had emerged from the darkness with an icy rain driven by a strong north wind. Rita was the last to leave, looking into Mary's unsmiling face.

'Safe journey then, Rita,' the old woman said, her steely eyes staring back.

'Thank you for having us,' Rita replied, breaking away and walking briskly towards the car. She hooted the car horn at the end of the drive and, breathing a sigh of relief, pulled away into the gloomy January morning.

Rita's mother listened as her daughter told her about the trip to Hampshire. They had got back to Chalcot Square in the early afternoon and Rita rushed out to shop for the evening meal. She had decided upon a traditional roast beef dinner as a grand finale to their stay in England. Her mother came straight from work by tube, forgetting Rita's instructions to take a cab.

'I haven't seen Paul's mother in years,' she told Rita, helping to lay the kitchen table.

'You're lucky!' Rita replied.

'The last time was at Nathan's funeral but we didn't say much. I always thought *he* was very nice . . . for a doctor.'

Rita smiled. 'The old man is fine, he's very doddery now, though.'

'Shame,' her mother commented.

Rita nodded. 'God knows what she'll do if he dies . . . but that's Paul's problem, I suppose.'

'What will you do when you get back?' her mother asked.

'No idea,' Rita said, picking up a saucepan lid and poking at the boiling potatoes with a fork. She replaced the lid and, reaching up into a top cupboard, produced a half-finished bottle of Johnnie Walker, pouring them both out a drop and handing a glass to her mother. 'I'm going to stay in California, at least until the boys have completed their schooling. I can't uproot them again and their father will be there for a few more years at least.'

Her mother nodded, sipping at the whisky and sitting

281

on an old kitchen chair. She looked up at Rita. 'Well, Rita, I can hardly offer you advice about your marriage,' she said, 'I can only hope that things work out for you both.'

'How did you manage when my father left?' Rita asked.

'Manage?' her mother asked. 'I didn't manage, I never even wanted him to leave, not really.'

'So, why did you make him?'

'You know why . . . he was having an affair, he wanted to marry her.'

'Why didn't you fight for him?'

'For someone with all your education, Rita, you can be extremely dense sometimes.'

'What do you mean?' Rita laughed.

'He lied to me,' she replied. 'It was as simple as that.'

Rita stared at her mother. 'I can't understand him at all.'

'He was in love,' she replied simply, putting down the whisky glass and folding her arms across her chest.

'Don't you ever regret it?'

Her mother nodded slowly. 'Of course I do, I loved the man . . . It's twenty-four years since he died and I've never once forgotten him, not a day goes by when I don't think about him. He was a handsome chap, a little bit of a rough diamond, but he was nice enough.'

Rita smiled. It was an odd way to describe her father. 'What do you think he would have made of us now?'

Her mother sighed. 'He would have given Marlene a jolly good box round the ears for acting so stupid but, as for you, he wouldn't have understood what had happened to you.'

'Wouldn't have understood?'

'No, Bill wouldn't have known what to do with you now, what with your education and everything . . . Let's face it, Rita, you left us all behind years ago.' She waved her hand in a dismissive gesture. 'I even stopped trying to understand what it was you were studying.'

'Nonsense, you understand exactly what it is I did.'

'And now you've done a book . . . I bet we'll never get to read that.'

'It's not that sort of a book.'

'There you are, then.'

'It's really only an academic text, for students . . . if it's ever published.'

Her mother held out the empty glass. 'Let's have another nip then, Rita. Don't be hiding it now.'

Rita poured them both another measure of whisky. Sitting next to her mother at the table, she picked up a fork and scored the prongs across the clean cloth, ploughing a line of straight grooves. 'Do you think that the boys are all right?' she asked, turning towards the old woman.

Her mother nodded. 'Flourishing, I'd say. I think it was the best thing to have happened in the circumstances, a fresh start for them . . . It's just a pity that you and Paul couldn't have found some way to stay together.'

'His mother thinks it's my fault.'

'There's no use blaming anyone, as far as I can see. No one knows about a marriage but the people who are living inside of it.' She took another sip of her drink. 'Are you still friendly with him?'

Rita thought for a moment. 'Sort of. We're still communicating, he seems happier now we've finally decided not to salvage the marriage and he has another woman . . .'

'What about you?' her mother interrupted.

'I don't know,' Rita replied.

'You don't know? What sort of answer is that? I thought California was supposed to be full of film stars!'

'I don't actually get to meet that many film stars, Mum . . .'

'Do you get to meet anyone, though, Rita, stuck out in that big white house of yours?'

'Let me get out of one relationship first, give me a chance,' Rita complained.

'Well, don't wait too long,' her mother advised sagely, 'you have to get on with living this life. There has to be a little bit of fun too, you know.'

'I know,' Rita replied, 'I know that.' She felt tears coming to her eyes. Her mother was telling her to move on a few paces now, move away from the recent past and, whilst not forgetting, put all the pieces of her life back together again. 'I wish you would come out to visit us,' she said, clearing her throat, taking the offered hand and squeezing it hard.

'There's your gran to consider,' she replied.

'Well, Gran could come too . . . and Aunty Vi! Why not?'

'Your gran will be ninety this February, do you really think that she could fly at her age?'

Rita hadn't thought. 'I've always imagined Gran could do anything.'

'Don't be silly,' her mother chided, 'and Vi couldn't cope with Mother for more than five minutes . . . They drive each other mad if I'm not at home keeping the peace.'

'Well, promise me you'll think about it, Mum.'

'I'll think about it,' she assured Rita, 'but what would an old stick like me do in California?' She laughed at the very idea.

'You'd be a great success . . . you'd love the climate.'

'We'll see.'

'Aunty Vi and Gran could manage for a few weeks,' Rita encouraged.

'A few weeks?' Her mother sounded horrified at the

idea but she laughed all the same. 'They wouldn't last together more than a day and a half.'

'Two weeks, then,' Rita suggested.

'We'll see,' she repeated.

Her mother left at half-past ten in the cab that Rita insisted she take back to Walthamstow. The dinner had worked out better than expected and everyone seemed to enjoy it, although she often wondered if William and Steve actually tasted their meals as they seemed to eat everything so quickly.

'Are you two packed?' she asked, coming into the sitting room from the kitchen with a tray of steaming mugs full of cocoa. For once the television was off and they all sat in front of the fire. A strong wind was blasting around the house and whining down the chimney.

'I am,' William said. 'Nearly, anyway.'

'I want everything ready by nine o'clock in the morning. We're going to Walthamstow and then directly to Heathrow.' Rita handed the drinks around. 'There won't be much time to do anything tomorrow.'

'I can't close my case,' Steve said, sipping at his hot cocoa.

'I expect we'll be miles over the weight limit,' Rita replied. 'Maybe we can shift things between the cases.'

'Are you light?' William asked.

Rita shook her head and laughed. 'No.'

'What's the point, then?' William looked at her as though she were feeble-minded.

'Maybe if we sat on it,' she suggested to Steve.

Steve grinned. 'We can sure try.'

'So,' Rita said, sitting down for a moment, 'are you looking forward to leaving, or what?'

'I'm looking forward to going home,' William replied without hesitation.

'What about you, Steve?' she asked.

'I won't be sad to leave here,' he told her. 'I always feel as though Nathan will walk in at any moment.' There was a long silence between them as they all seemed to be considering that. 'What about you?' Steve asked at last.

'Me?' Rita turned to them both. 'I shall be sad to leave Gran and Great-Grandma and Aunty Vi, of course, but I'm looking forward to going back . . . for the warmer weather if nothing else.' She hadn't mentioned Gary even though she was looking forward to seeing him again as well.

Rita helped the boys to complete their packing until everything was stowed away and ready for the next day, their travelling clothes laid out, freshly washed and pressed. She took a bath and then lay awake for a long time brooding over the events of the holiday, the events of her recent history. Rita felt exhausted by the trip to London. She disliked staying in Chalcot Square and was certain that the house had to be sold now. Her family seemed as dotty as ever, whilst her sister Marlene had grown strange and distant. But, what could Rita do? None of them would thank her for interfering, Marlene had already shown that in no uncertain terms. Life went on, that's what everyone told her but, however far she travelled, whoever she met, whatever the future, Nathan would always be there. He would be with her for the remainder of her life, he would be there as a terrible reminder of the way her whole world had changed. When she considered this and when she remembered her dead son everything else felt insignificant. She went on, but the burden of the guilt she felt for his death remained with her and she could see no end to it. The explanation she craved was still a total mystery.

Rita sat with the boys in the departure lounge. They had begun by chatting animatedly to one another but now sat silently. They had spent a final hour with her family at Walthamstow, the panic steadily rising in Rita's stomach as the time to depart drew nearer. She sat in front of the polished range with her tea and cake watching them, the two elderly sisters and the ancient grandmother, realizing they were a fragile grouping, each one in her own way keeping the others going. Her grandmother always seemed as though she would go on for ever but Rita understood, really for the first time, how one day, perhaps not too far distant now, the family would start to fragment. She tried not to imagine it but she faced the reality of the situation and then felt guilty at leaving them again.

The morning was fine and clear and freezing, with a chilling breeze. The old women wrapped themselves up and came out to the car. Rita cried as she said goodbye, going to her mother for a final embrace, almost begging her to come out to California that summer. She had driven away, her eyes red and full of brimming tears, the boys hanging out of the car windows, waving until they turned the corner at the end of the road and the women were gone from sight.

William was tapping his foot as he listened to a tape on his ever-present Walkman, oblivious to the surrounding airport noise. Steve was reading *East of Eden*, his head bent down, engrossed in the book. There was a delay in their departure and Rita had attempted to settle, trying to read the news, flicking through the pages of the various papers but finding little to distract her there. She thought she would feel better once they were airborne, once there was no going back.

On the day of Nathan's funeral – Rita was unable to divorce her mind from this catastrophic event – her mother had held her for a moment, her black gloved hands pressing into Rita's back, her lips brushing against Rita's cheek as she told her daughter never to blame

287

herself. Rita was in too much pain that day to comprehend. Her mother took Rita's hands between her own and squeezed them tightly for a second or two, looking into the bleary red eyes of grief and destruction.

'You're going to have to be strong now, Rita,' she instructed her.

Rita looked back but was unable to reply. Her mouth became dry, her breathing fast, the graveyard seeming to spin for a moment. Paul came to her side and supported Rita. 'He's dead, Mum,' she managed at last. 'He killed himself.'

'But it wasn't your fault, that's what I'm saying.' The old woman turned to Paul. 'You tell her that,' she insisted, releasing Rita and walking back to take care of her own mother. 'Make sure she understands.'

But Paul had never told her. She had often wanted to hear it from his lips, she had wanted him to tell her that there was no blame involved, that *she* wasn't at fault, but he didn't say anything. Instead he offered the solace that perhaps there was no reason. Rita had never accepted any of it, not Nathan's death, not Paul's reaction, his strangeness, his inability to behave with any degree of decency. All she ever wanted from him was a kind of companionship in their mutual grief. She wanted him to hold her, even to protect her from it all, to ease her passage back to normalcy or, at least, to a type of normal behaviour so they might function like the family they once were. Instead there was nothing. She was used as a receptacle for his own grief but there was nothing left of him for her. There had no longer been love involved, even at their most intimate moments. From the moment of Nathan's death Rita had been deserted, forced to cope with everything alone.

* * *

288

She excused herself, telling the boys to save her seat and look after her small travelling case, as she walked away to the toilet.

'Jesus,' Steve said when his mother was out of earshot, 'I shall be glad when this is over.'

William removed his earphones. 'What?' he asked.

'I'll be happy when we've landed back in LA.'

'Mum's upset,' he stated.

Steve nodded. 'You know she went to Nathan's grave first thing this morning, don't you?'

William shook his head.

'That's the trouble with holidays . . . saying goodbye is always horrible,' Steve continued.

'Maybe she's upset because Aunty Marlene didn't show up,' William suggested.

'Marlene is a clown,' Steve answered bluntly. 'She's more likely to have been relieved because of that. Her daffy sister would only have made things worse.'

William sighed. 'I'm not coming back here,' he said.

'Of course you are,' Steve insisted.

'I'm never staying at Chalcot Square again, though,' William replied.

'I wonder what Dad's been up to over the vacation?' Steve asked, stretching out in the uncomfortable plastic seat.

'New York with his new woman,' William mused.

Steve grinned. 'Maybe we'll get to meet her properly when we return.'

'What about Mum and Gary?' William asked.

'What about them?'

'Do you think she'll carry on seeing him?'

'I hope so,' Steve laughed. 'He's still got her car!'

'But, you know, do you think anything will happen?'

'Happen?' Steve replied, ribbing his brother.

'You know, live together or something.'

'Jesus, don't complicate things any further . . . Let's just take one thing at a time.'

'You like Gary, don't you?' William asked a little uncertainly.

'Sure,' Steve nodded, 'Gary's fine.' He watched as his mother came back to join them. Her eyes looked a little red, it was obvious that she had been crying.

'Have they called the flight yet?' Rita asked, sitting down next to them, peering across at the large flight-information board.

'All right?' Steve enquired.

'Yes,' Rita glanced at him, 'are you? I expect you're bored, aren't you?'

'Will Sharon know we're delayed?' William asked her.

'I suppose she'll call the airport before leaving home,' Steve replied.

'It'll be good to see her,' Rita said. 'It seems an absolute age.'

'Sharon will look brown, they'll all look sunburnt and bursting with health,' Steve said.

'Don't start *that* again,' Rita warned him. 'Perhaps you can persuade your father to take you off to the Hawaiian Islands for Easter or something!'

Steve laughed. 'Can you imagine Dad in a grass skirt doing a hula-hula on the sands with a garland of exotic flowers hanging around his neck!'

Rita hooted at the idea as this vision of Paul came to her mind. 'No, quite frankly. It's not your father, is it!'

'What was the best holiday you ever had?' William asked her.

'Not this one, that's for sure,' Rita replied with feeling. 'Those in Greece when you were all younger and times were slightly less fraught.' She recalled an evening in Athens, it seemed a hundred years ago now. They had gone with some friends, who were baby-sitting the boys

290

whilst they attended a concert during the Athens Festival. A performance of Prokofiev's Piano Concerto No. 3 in the Odeion of Herodes Atticus, the Acropolis floodlit above them. A very old woman was the brilliant soloist and Rita remembered the warm air and the strange scents of the great city in the darkness, the sound of crickets and, above all, the powerful performance of the music, and how she was carried away with the excitement of it.

Their flight was suddenly called. Rita stared as the destination and numbers clicked over on the flight-information board. 'Come on then,' she told the boys, standing up and smoothing down the skirt of the smart black suit she had purchased in the January sales.

'There's no rush, Mum,' Steve told her, 'it's only the first call.'

'I don't care,' Rita replied, 'let's just get on board and into a comfortable seat.'

Chapter 9

Paul returned from New York with Joanne, suddenly feeling that his life had clicked back into some kind of order. Joanne was a gynaecologist with an extremely successful practice based at Santa Monica. He obviously had a lot in common with her but, more than that, Paul found her to be highly intelligent, very perceptive, witty and warm and loving. He also found her terribly attractive, stunning rather than classically beautiful, her Swedish ancestry giving her blue eyes and almost white-blonde hair, a fine complexion and strong features. Joanne was tall and athletic, a natural athlete who enjoyed jogging and swimming with him. At forty, she had an enormous zest for life and a forthright and positive attitude to everything.

He had known her for some time, in fact she was one of the first people he'd met when taking up his post at the UCLA Medical Centre, but she had really only entered his life in the late autumn. She encouraged Paul to sort out his life with Rita and make some decisions about his marriage. She thought he should either salvage his marriage or cut his losses and seek a divorce. It was as simple as that to Joanne.

'You have to think about Rita,' she told him, 'she has a life to get on with as well.'

Paul looked into her clear blue eyes and nodded his head, as though it was the first time such an idea had been suggested.

Joanne liked people to be positive and decisive. She hated having to wait around whilst others made up their minds. If Joanne wanted to do something – for example, go to a concert or a film – she might ask Paul along but, if he didn't want to go, or couldn't make up his mind in time, she was just as happy to go by herself. Joanne had always been full of confidence and, in all areas of her life, was *very* independent.

Paul found that the time he spent with Joanne was becoming increasingly important to him until he started to miss her when she wasn't around. She had taken to staying over at the beach house, usually in mid-week when her work days took her to UCLA, although sometimes at week-ends too. She found Paul's feelings towards his wife complex and confused. At times he seemed almost resentful about Rita, at others morose that their marriage seemed irredeemable. Paul and Joanne had an easy-going, friendly relationship which he contrasted with the last difficult years of his marriage. Sometimes this made him feel guilty, as though he were doing Rita a disservice.

The week-end of Rita's return from London, they were both staying at the beach house. Joanne had been jogging along the sands and emerged from the bedroom, rubbing at her long hair with a towel, and walked into the airy lounge where Paul was working.

'I thought you were determined not to do anything today,' Joanne said, standing at the open balcony doors, looking at the Pacific, which shone in the morning sunshine.

'I just wanted to check this over,' he answered.

Joanne turned to him. 'Listen, if you'd prefer me not to be here when your kids arrive . . .'

'No,' Paul said, putting down his papers, 'I want you to meet them.'

'Okay.' She sat down next to him for a moment. 'But I have to leave early this evening, anyway.'

Paul nodded. 'They won't be able to stay for long . . . they both have school in the morning.'

'Steve looks like you, doesn't he?' she said, looking at their photographs on the bookcase opposite. 'Is William like Rita?'

'A bit,' he smiled. 'You'll be able to see them for yourself in another few hours.'

Joanne stood up again. 'In that case, I'd better get dressed.' She had wrapped a bath sheet around her like a Dorothy Lamour sarong.

'I like what you have on,' Paul said, lifting up the edge of the towel with his toe.

'Why didn't you run this morning?' Joanne asked, looking at him dressed in his shorts and running top. 'It's important to keep the exercise programme up, particularly for a man of your age.'

'What's that supposed to mean?' Paul laughed. 'I'm not exactly Methuselah!'

'No, but you'll be forty-three this year and you're a prime candidate for a heart attack.'

'I don't smoke, I don't drink much, I don't eat red meat and I take regular exercise,' he protested.

'Not this morning you didn't.'

'Okay, I'll run in a while.'

Joanne grinned. It made her look particularly attractive. 'Good show,' she said, mimicking an upper-class, English-twit accent, then turning and going into the bedroom to dress.

The boys arrived in the early afternoon. Paul and Joanne were sitting on the balcony reading the Sunday papers. She was browsing through the review pages when they walked in, Steve first, followed by his brother, who was carrying two enormous plastic shopping bags. Paul welcomed them, introducing Joanne, who moved the papers off the chairs and made space for them. Joanne found them both to be bright and engaging adolescents. Steve was remarkably like his father in the physical sense, their voices were similar and even their gestures seemed the same. He was articulate and entered into conversation easily. William presented his father with the bags full of gifts from his mother and father and Rita's family, with sundry other offerings from friends they had seen over the course of their holiday.

Joanne sat back and watched them interacting with their father. She noticed how Paul retained a certain emotional distance from them. There was a hesitant quality to the way he approached them, whilst the boys, obviously used to this, chatted about London, bringing her into the conversation as much as possible. Joanne assumed their social development had come from Rita. Paul was holding up a large and rather lurid jumper from Aunty Vi, vertical stripes of bright blue, grey, yellow and pink with matching bands at the elbows.

'This will frighten the patients to death!' Paul laughed.

'You could wear it for jogging,' William suggested. 'We'll be able to spot you from a long way off then.'

Steve smiled. 'It's the thought that counts, anyway.'

'Absolutely,' Joanne agreed.

Steve turned to her and grinned.

She looked from Steve to Paul, who was still shaking his head and laughing at Aunty Vi's bad taste, and wondered if Steve saw in his father how he would look in twenty years' time. When the gifts were all unwrapped, Paul went in to make coffee. Steve and William weren't staying for a meal and he had bought a large chocolate cake for them to devour. William joined his father in the kitchen, leaving Joanne to talk with Steve.

'Do you know London at all?' Steve asked her.

'I know the main tourist haunts,' she admitted, 'but I haven't been for some time.'

Steve nodded, looking beyond Joanne to the ocean. 'We were all jet-lagged, didn't wake up until almost noon today. Dad says it's all a state of mind.'

'Maybe it is for him,' she replied, 'but for most of us it's pretty disruptive. It always finishes me off for twenty-four hours at least!'

'Dad says you live in Santa Monica,' Steve went on.

'Sure do,' Joanne smiled, 'solid old Santa Monica.'

'Do you live on the beach as well?' he asked.

Joanne nodded. 'I have a small house, not quite as splendid as your dad's, but it's okay and I have my surgery and office in town . . . You must know Santa Monica, though.'

'I think we're closer to it than we are to Malibu,' Steve suggested. 'But we go to Venice more often.'

'Ah yes,' Joanne grinned. 'A bit of a freak festival, it tends to attract more interest.'

'Our neighbours are all crazy about the beach, and we tend to hang out at Topanga or Las Tunas.'

'Have you been further up the coast?' she asked. 'I mean, towards San Francisco. What about the incredible coast of Big Sur?'

'We went there when we first came to Los Angeles,' Steve told her.

'Only once?' Joanne sounded shocked. 'I tend to go there a lot . . . Whenever things get tough, a week-end up around Monterey, with lots of solitary walks along those wild coastlines, is enough to blow the cobwebs away and make everything okay again.'

'Sounds good,' Steve agreed.

'What does?' Paul asked, stepping out on to the balcony

296

carrying a tray of coffee, with William behind him bringing out the chocolate cake.

Joanne told him about their conversation. 'We're planning a trip there in a few weeks,' she admitted.

William resumed his seat and gave his brother a knowing look. 'Dad's brought us each a present from New York.'

'Have you?' Steve asked his father.

Paul began to cut slices of cake for everyone. 'Don't sound so surprised, son. I have been known to treat you both in the past.'

'I know.' Steve looked a little embarrassed. 'But we already had our Christmas presents from you and Mum.'

'Well, this is a little extra.' He turned to Steve. 'Okay?'

'Fine,' Steve replied, taking his cake and eating it.

'So, what did you think?' Steve asked as they drove back to Westwood.

'I thought she was all right,' William said, examining the watch his father had given him. 'What about you?'

'She's okay,' he agreed. 'Bit different to Mum, though.'

'Blonde, you mean?' William said.

'She's a doctor, like Dad . . . They work together some of the time, they have a lot in common.'

'Mum and Dad have a lot in common,' William replied. 'They have us in common.'

'Precisely,' Steve answered. 'But not much else.'

'Mum said they weren't going to divorce,' William insisted.

'Do you seriously think they will get back together again?' Steve asked him.

William was silent for a while. 'They might,' he said, staring out at the traffic on the Santa Monica Boulevard. 'They could.'

'Come on, William, grow up,' Steve told him as they

turned into the canyon road towards their mother's house. 'And if Mum asks us anything about Joanne, just make out she was nothing special, okay?'

William nodded in agreement. 'Shall we tell her about the new watches?'

'Sure, why not?'

William shrugged. 'She might think that Dad's trying to buy our approval.'

'With a watch?' Steve laughed, pulling the Rabbit into the driveway, where they found Rita inspecting the flower beds. She turned to wave as they approached.

'Well?' Paul asked her. 'What do you think about them?'

'I thought they were terrific,' Joanne told him. 'I couldn't get over how much like you Steve is.'

Paul looked at her. 'That's what Rita always says . . . sometimes as an accusation.' He smiled at that.

'Tell me about Nathan,' she said. 'What was he like?'

Paul hesitated for a moment before replying. 'He was like Rita, I suppose. I mean, he had her sense of humour, her temperament . . .' He looked at Joanne. 'He was going to medical school the summer he died.'

'Did you get along with him?'

'Sure. I mean, of course there were the usual difficulties with adolescent males, but generally we got on well.'

'What about William and Steve?'

'They all got on well together.' Paul nodded. 'That's why Nathan's suicide was such a tremendous shock . . .'

'Why did he do it?' Joanne asked gently.

'We never knew,' he admitted, 'we never understood why.'

Joanne took his hand. 'You never talk about him.'

'I find it very difficult . . . I don't like to discuss it . . .'

'Have you ever, with Rita, I mean?'

Paul shook his head.

'You've *never* discussed it?' Joanne sounded incredulous.

'No.'

'Poor Rita,' Joanne concluded.

'My mother always used to say something about "least said, soonest mended",' Paul told her.

'Are you serious?' She looked at him hard.

'There was no reason for Nathan to kill himself, no reason at all. There was nothing to talk about . . .'

'What about Rita, hasn't she wanted to discuss it either?'

'Rita wants to do nothing else but discuss it . . . that's why she sees an analyst.'

'Because you won't talk to her?'

'Because she gains some benefit from it.'

'Is Nathan's death the reason why you don't feel at ease with William and Steve?'

'I feel okay with them,' he assured her.

'Really?' She sounded unconvinced.

'Really,' Paul insisted. 'They're feeling a bit odd at the moment, loyalties being strained between their mother and me . . . that sort of thing, you know.'

'They seemed perfectly at ease, if you ask me. You were the one who was finding it difficult to make conversation.'

'I don't think so. Do you really think that?'

'You haven't seen them for over a month. Why do you have so little to say to them?'

Paul shrugged but didn't answer.

'Perhaps if you tried talking to them like adults rather than children. Steve's going to university in the fall, isn't he?'

'He's hoping to go, yes.'

'So, he's no longer a child, is he?' she said.

'I suppose not.'

299

Joanne stood up. Light was fading across the Pacific and the room was growing dark. 'Listen, I really have to go now.'

'Don't go,' Paul said with a degree of urgency.

'I have a patient to see at nine-thirty . . . I have things to do at home,' Joanne explained. 'I *have* to go, Paul.'

'I don't know what you want me to say,' he told her. 'Why don't I feel at ease with my own kids? I don't know the answer to that . . . you tell me.'

She sat down again, facing him this time. 'You know, this is the conversation you should be having with your wife.'

Paul stared back. 'I can't talk to Rita . . . I've already explained that.'

'Don't be ridiculous, you've been with the woman for over twenty years. She's the only other person you *can* talk to about it . . . I didn't even know Nathan.'

He looked away but did not respond.

'I have to go,' she said again, standing up and walking to the door. 'Are you going to see me out?'

Paul followed her out into the cool evening, kissing her at the door, 'I wish we didn't have to keep living apart,' he told her.

She looked into his eyes. 'We agreed it would be better this way,' she replied.

'Better for whom?' he asked, sounding miserable and hard done by.

'Better for everyone involved,' she said, smiling at him. 'Don't be such a sourpuss. I can't resolve what has happened between you and your kids, you have to work that out for yourself.' She took his hand and walked him over to where her car was parked. 'Look,' she said, reaching up to kiss him again, 'go and see Rita, talk to her, for Christ's sake, and stop this stupid brooding . . . you'll grow a tumour!' Joanne got into the brand new

Saab and pulled away from the sandy driveway, waving once and disappearing in a flurry of sand and dust.

Paul stood on the drive for a moment until her silver car had disappeared, before walking back in a rather disconsolate fashion, hands in pockets and head bowed as though deep in thought. He returned to his work, planning to read through some notes for the next hour, but his thoughts were full of Joanne's words and he couldn't concentrate. He looked at the pages of neat typescript but they were meaningless.

Going over to the framed pictures on the bookcase, he picked up a photograph of himself with all his sons, taken just a few weeks before Nathan died. They were all dressed up and ready for one of the many farewell dinners that were given in his honour. Rita had said something just before taking the picture and they all burst into laughter. Paul's hand shook slightly as he held the frame, and he wondered if Nathan's death would ever seem a distant memory to him or if it would always be at the forefront of everything. Perhaps Joanne was right and he should call Rita and rake up the ashes of Nathan's suicide, but he wasn't sure if he could face that prospect. He had controlled himself for the past two years, he could deal with the fact that his eldest son had died, he could carry out his extremely demanding job and manage to do it well . . . On the surface everything was fine, but Paul knew how, in reality, he was merely hanging on by his finger tips. The pain and ache of grief had never decreased and, at times, especially after seeing Steve and William, it became worse and harder to bear.

After a while he replaced the photograph and went on to the balcony, where he sat in the cool evening air watching over the dark waters.

* * *

Paul sat up, suddenly wide awake, one foot on the floor, as though ready to dart out of bed. It was the middle of the week and Joanne was staying the night. She stirred and was fumbling for the lamp switch at her side.

'What is it?' she asked, touching Paul's broad back.

'I thought someone was in the room with us.' He turned to her. 'I dreamt it was Nathan.'

Joanne moved to his side, putting her arms around him. He was shaking. 'It was only a dream,' she soothed.

'Why the hell would he do such a thing?' Paul asked softly. It was almost a question addressed to himself.

'Do you have *no* ideas?'

He shook his head.

'I thought you said there didn't have to be a reason,' Joanne said to him.

Paul remained silent. After a while he broke away from her and wandered off into the dark reaches of the house.

Joanne lay back and sighed. In a while she heard the balcony door sliding open and she knew he would be sitting out under the stars, listening to the rush of the surf, brooding about the past, looking back and constantly asking himself why. She switched the bedside lamp off and rolled on to her side. At these times Paul was completely unapproachable and there was little point in making the effort to break through his wall of silence. Joanne was soon fast asleep once more.

Steve and William came for the week-end. They walked along Malibu Pier on Saturday afternoon, watching the people fishing, leaning over and looking down into the water as though on board some odd cruise liner going nowhere fast. It was a warm afternoon which reminded Paul of early autumn days in England. There was a fresh feeling to the climate, which he found exhilarating. The boys were chatting to a young fisherman who, by the

302

looks of things, hadn't been having very much luck. Paul was leaning against the pier rail when they walked back to him.

'You've never fished, have you, Dad?' William asked, standing next to his father, shading his eyes against the bright sunlight and peering out across the Pacific to the horizon.

'I used to do a bit of sea fishing. My father kept a little boat at Mudeford, and we used to fish offshore around there . . . But that was when I was about your age. I haven't done much since then.' He smiled at William, who was looking at him again now. 'Why, do you want to start?'

William shrugged. 'I'm not sure.'

'What about you?' Paul asked Steve.

'Don't have the time,' Steve replied. 'I'm not that interested, really.'

'Fair enough,' Paul told them. 'Had enough, then?' he asked. 'Shall we make tracks?'

'Sure,' Steve said.

'Where's Joanne this week-end?' William asked as they walked back to the car.

'She's busy,' Paul replied. 'Besides, I thought it would be good if we spent some time together, just the three of us.'

Steve glanced at his brother, his eyes full of surprise, even suspicion, but he got into the Mercedes without saying anything. Ever since they arrived, Paul had seemed to be going out of his way to please them. Instead of working his way through a briefcaseful of work, he seemed to have put UCLA Medical Centre out of his thoughts for the week-end. Steve was sure that this new approach was Joanne's idea – his father would never have thought it up for himself! He had even allowed Steve to drive the Mercedes all the way to the pier, remaining calm throughout the journey. There was a new air of friendliness about Paul. He was, in the language of southern California, being extremely laid back, something which tended to unnerve Steve. But then, if he considered the way his father's life had changed since the beginning of the previous summer, this new, mellow Paul was the logical result. Steve recalled how seeing his father living in shorts and sweat shirts at week-ends, jogging on the Malibu sands and swimming in the ocean, had contrasted wildly with the rather conservative man of a few months before. At one time Paul would have felt positively undressed if he wasn't wearing a tie, but now he was definitely less fuddy-duddy, less, as Steve would normally express it, of a tight arse.

Paul began to prepare their evening meal when they returned to the beach house, whilst William and Steve watched the Los Angeles Rams playing on TV.

'What's going on?' William asked his brother.

Steve shrugged. 'Beats me . . . maybe he's on something.'

'He's being so extra friendly, it's weird!'

Steve laughed. 'Well, don't knock it, it's better than his usual welcome – you know, glad to see us but doesn't want his week-end disrupted too much. What's happened to his files and reports?'

'It has to be Joanne,' William said.

Steve watched the screen, nodding, 'Let's just hope it lasts . . . wait till Mum gets to hear about this.'

'I don't think we ought to say anything,' William warned.

'Why not?'

'Because if his current mood is to do with Joanne, it will only make her feel worse.'

Steve picked up the large bag of potato chips and took

a handful. 'I don't see why it should,' he said as he crunched the chips. 'After all, she's got Gary.'

'It's not the same, though.'

'Why isn't it?' Steve asked.

'Because Gary isn't living with her,' William replied.

'Bull, how do you know they're not having an affair?'

'How do you know they are?' William looked at his brother. '*Do* you think they are?'

Steve was silent for a moment, seemingly intent upon watching the match. 'Beats me,' he said, reaching down for his Coke bottle. 'Beats me.'

'Mum said she wouldn't divorce Dad,' William said after another pause.

'That's not quite what she said,' Steve corrected. 'She said they weren't *planning* to divorce . . .'

'Do you think they will, then?' William asked, sounding less sure of himself.

'How do I know?' Steve laughed. 'They don't tell me their plans.'

'She told us not to worry about it . . .'

'Then don't,' Steve instructed his brother.

'Don't you mind?' William asked, pursuing the topic.

Steve shrugged. 'What can I do about it?' He turned to his brother.

William looked at him. 'I don't know why they just can't try and get it together again.'

'Yes, you do. Can't you remember what it was like, their awful rows, an atmosphere that you could cut with a knife . . . why do you want all of that again?'

'It needn't be like that,' William protested.

'But it would be,' Steve said frankly, 'it would be.'

'Well, I wish it was like it used to be . . .'

'Before Nathan died, you mean?'

William nodded.

Steve munched another handful of chips. 'It'll never be the same,' he said softly. 'You can't go back.'

William was thoughtful. He looked as though he might burst into tears for a second or two but this moment soon passed. 'I just hope this never happens to me,' he said with feeling.

'What?' Steve asked, sounding bemused. 'You hope that what never happens?'

'That I don't get married for twenty years and then suddenly see it all come to bits!'

'I'm sure Mum and Dad never planned any of this,' Steve told him.

'But don't you think it's kind of ridiculous?'

'It's up to them,' Steve answered in his world-weary way.

'Don't you mind?' he asked Steve again.

'Of course I mind . . .'

'But there's nothing we can do about it,' William interrupted, completing his brother's sentence for him. 'I know that too.'

'So, there you are, then.'

'I just sometimes think this isn't the way Nathan would have wanted us to go.'

'Nathan isn't around to face it though, is he?' Steve said with a degree of rancour evident in his voice.

'No, but even so . . .'

'These things just happen. Marriages break up. We're luckier than most kids. At least our parents aren't trying to murder one another, at least they've stopped the shouting . . . it's ending with a bit of dignity.'

'But I don't want it to end.'

'Grow up, William,' Steve snapped. 'No one wanted any of this to happen.'

William concentrated hard on the television screen, not making much sense of the game, his mind churning with thoughts of his parents and of Nathan and of Steve's apparent hardness. 'Do you think you'll ever get married?' he asked after a while.

'Give me a chance!' Steve replied, laughing at the idea.

'I mean, when you've finished university.'

'I suppose so. It's the normal thing to do, isn't it? Most guys get married unless they become priests or they're queer or something . . .'

William reached for the potato-chip packet. 'Won't all of this put you off?'

'Give it a rest, William,' Steve complained. 'It's not that bad, really it isn't.'

'I think it is,' William said bluntly.

'That's because you're still a kid.'

'I'm only two years younger than you,' William protested.

'It makes a difference,' Steve said. 'I mean, I shall be eighteen this year.'

'Big deal,' William replied, slumping back into his chair. 'That doesn't mean you know everything.'

'I never said I did,' Steve said with irritating calmness.

'You act as though you do, though.'

'Crap!'

'If Nathan were here you wouldn't say that . . .' William got up suddenly, tears beginning to spill down his cheeks, moving swiftly past his brother.

Steve grabbed William's wrist, holding it tightly. 'Whoa there,' he said, resisting William's efforts to get free. 'What's the matter with you?' he asked, looking up into his brother's tear-stained face. 'Come on, tell me,' he insisted gently.

William wiped his eyes with his free hand. 'Nothing. Let me go, please.'

'Okay,' Steve nodded, releasing his grip. 'So, now tell me what's wrong.'

William remained rooted to the spot, his head bowed. A large tear fell on to his training shoes, leaving a dark spot.

'Tell me!' Steve said again. 'Come on, William,' he encouraged.

'I want Nathan,' he replied, running from the room and out through the balcony doors, clattering down the wooden steps to the beach.

'William,' Steve called after him, easing himself out of his seat and walking out on to the balcony. He watched his brother running out across the sands towards the Malibu surf.

'What's going on?' Paul asked, joining Steve on the balcony.

'I don't know,' Steve replied, still watching William as he slowed down towards the water's edge.

'Have you been arguing?' Paul asked, bemused.

'No.'

'What's the matter, then?'

Steve turned to his father. 'You tell me.'

'What?'

'You tell me what's wrong, Dad.'

Paul stared at Steve but made no response.

'William is upset over Nathan. This is something you've not had to deal with,' Steve said. 'He gets like this from time to time . . . He's uneasy about what's going to happen between you and Mum, he thinks you're about to divorce her and marry Joanne.' Steve shrugged. 'Something like that, anyway.'

'Have you told him that?' Paul's voice had an edge to it.

'No,' Steve replied calmly.

'Then who's been saying those things to him?'

'Dad, no one needs to tell William anything about anything . . . He hates all of this.' Steve put out an arm, as though encompassing the entire beach. 'He wants us all to be one big happy family again, Dad. You know, just like we used to be?'

Paul continued to stare at Steve. 'Oh . . . does he?'

Steve turned away to watch William, who was wandering slowly at the tide line, bending down from time to time and skimming flat stones across the surface of the ocean. 'Yes, sir, he does,' Steve replied, nodding to himself.

'Doesn't he understand?' Paul asked, feeling stupid.

'Of course he understands, William's a bright kid.'

'Don't try to be clever,' Paul told him.

'Listen, I don't know why William's upset. I expect he's upset because of Nathan and because of you and Mum, because of this . . .' He felt his voice becoming tight and unsteady. 'Because . . . because we're all fucked up, Dad, we're all fucked up . . .'

Paul blinked, watching Steve's face. More than ever he could see how mature Steve had become, more than ever he could see how distant they were. It had been the same with Nathan. As Nathan had grown so Paul had found it increasingly difficult to cope. Paul had become removed from Nathan just as his father had become removed from him. Boarding school at eleven, a kind of shutting-off process, a closing-down of something, a rite of passage from childhood into a kind of nowhere land, caught up somewhere between innocence and the painful fumblings of adolescence. Paul had repeated the same pattern. What had transpired between him and his father had occurred with his own children. It had not been intentional, Paul had always loved the boys, he had loved them as children and as they grew into young men.

He thought about Nathan, whilst following William's antics at the shoreline, considering how alone and small he looked, standing there against the rolling Pacific swell.

Paul didn't know what it was he wanted to say to Steve, something about feeling love for them both, something about how much they meant . . . that they meant everything, that Nathan had meant everything and how his loss was almost impossible to bear, but instead he stood facing his son, saying nothing. Everything, all his success, his material wealth, his renown, his great skills as a surgeon, it all seemed pointless, as though he had worked towards his goals for nothing, and he was suddenly overwhelmed with exhaustion and depression.

'The last few years haven't been easy,' Paul began, clearing his throat, 'for any of us.' He realized he was sounding like the important surgeon standing at the terminal patient's bedside.

Steve looked at him. 'The reason we're all in this mess,' he began, 'the main reason is your total inability, your refusal to ever discuss Nathan with any of us, with Mum or me or William!'

Paul said nothing, digging his hands deep into the pockets of his faded Levi's and looking down at the sun- and salt-bleached boards beneath his bare feet.

'My brother died,' Steve continued, his voice finally breaking, 'and we never once sat down as a family to discuss anything about it, not the nature of his death, not the way we felt . . . It's like he never even existed.'

'Don't be ridiculous,' Paul replied gruffly.

'It isn't ridiculous, Dad. Did you care that Nathan died?' Steve demanded. 'You never acted as though you did.'

'Of course I cared, how can you ask that?' Paul felt physically sick.

'Then why have you never said a damn thing? You've spent more time and love and energy on your hospital duties than you ever did with any of us.'

310

'That simply isn't the case, Steve,' Paul protested, like the condemned man calling out his innocence.

'His death should have brought us closer together as a family, shouldn't it?' Steve asked, an element of amazement in his voice. 'Why did it drive us apart?'

'It didn't . . . we're still a family, we still see one another . . . You and William stay here all the time, you're down most week-ends.'

'Yes, we arrive on Friday nights or Saturday evenings, that's what passes for normalcy around here. We see our father at week-ends and live with our mother during the week. You're dating another woman, Mum is seeing Gary . . . Jesus!' Steve gave a bitter laugh. 'This has nothing to do with being a family. It would have been better if we had never come here at all. You could still have taken your prestigious job, we could have stayed in London . . .'

'You're talking nonsense. You like it here, you *wanted* to come.'

'I wanted to come because I could see that my family was cracking up. Coming here was supposed to make things better!'

'We can't look into the future, Steve. How can we know what we're going to feel and be and want in another year's time?'

'That's just a cop-out . . .'

'I'm trying to be honest,' Paul replied.

'I don't think you even see us,' Steve said. 'I think we're here in your house but you don't see us. You don't know anything about us.'

'You're my sons, for God's sake.' Paul sounded horrified at Steve's suggestion.

'Then why don't you ever *talk* to us?'

'I talk to you.'

'Sure, you discuss the weather and our school grades,

you ask us what we want for our birthdays and Christmas, you treat us at week-ends, when you're not too busy with work . . . The thing is,' Steve said, looking for a moment at William, who was still prowling along the shore, 'the thing is, Dad, that I want to be with my friends at week-ends and you, obviously, want to be with Joanne.' He let the sense of this sink in before continuing. 'I can't keep coming down to the beach every week-end.'

Paul swallowed hard. He felt very emotional, as though he were losing control. He cleared his throat. 'Okay,' he nodded, 'I can understand that . . . that's no problem.'

Steve scratched at the nape of his neck. 'Okay,' he replied. 'Maybe every other week-end,' he said.

Paul nodded.

'Right.' Steve looked at his father. 'I'd better go down and fetch William back.' He began to walk along the balcony. 'He'll be there for the rest of the day!'

'Steve,' Paul called to him.

He turned at the top of the steps. 'What is it?'

'Don't become a stranger, though, eh?'

Steve paused for a long moment before answering. 'Every other week-end,' he said, before clattering down to the beach below.

Paul watched him jogging across the sands towards his brother. He watched as Steve reached William, putting his arm around his brother's shoulders, guiding him along the beach, deep in conversation, their heads almost touching. He envied their closeness, that kind of sibling relationship he never knew, that sort of love. He continued to watch until they were far in the distance and then sat in the late afternoon sun, resting his head back and closing his eyes.

'Why didn't you tell Steve you loved them?' Joanne asked him the following Wednesday night as they lay in bed together. They had begun to make love but Paul, who had been particularly tense, lost his erection and was unable to consummate the act. Joanne told him not to worry and spent a long time reassuring him that everything would be fine.

They were both very tired and, in reality, she just wanted to sleep anyway. Paul was not a particularly adventurous lover. She had not found his love-making especially exciting or even completely satisfying over the months of their affair, but that was nothing new to her. Over the years she had found that a lot of men weren't aware of what it took to satisfy her completely. This wasn't a criticism of Paul, more an acceptance of the facts of life as she had learnt them. Maybe it was a trifle cynical, she wasn't sure.

She was extremely fond of Paul and enjoyed his company, she even admired him, but that didn't keep her coming back to him. Paul was certainly an attractive man. A lot of women had a thing about him. The problem with Paul was that he was quite a complex man, a man who hid away his emotions, had become used to hiding them, probably ever since he'd been a child, and, consequently, to an extent refused to acknowledge them. The more she got to know him the more she was intrigued and, on occasions, amazed at his monumental self-control. But she had probed and dug and attempted – she hated the phrase – to put him in touch with his emotions. It made her cringe when other people said that but it seemed to express quite clearly what she wanted to do with him. Whatever future existed for them, and there was never any question, as far as she was concerned, of a happy little marriage, she could not cope with him brooding darkly over the past.

Joanne was in the process of persuading him to talk to

his wife about their dead son. It seemed positively ludicrous, if not downright cruel of him, not to allow others to express their grief. However, she wasn't getting too far with this. He was resistant and moody but, without it, without him sitting down with Rita and clearing the air, she couldn't see what future there was. The more she knew him, and since meeting William and Steve it simply confirmed her opinion, the more she could sense the dead boy around their circling conversations. God knows what Rita had gone through in the past two years since Nathan's suicide! She was intrigued to meet Rita, she felt that here was a woman, a sister, with whom she could really get on. It might be difficult in the present circumstances, and Paul would certainly protest, but she would persevere. Joanne rarely gave up.

'Why didn't you express your feelings?' she asked again.

'It wouldn't have felt right,' Paul replied through the darkness of the bedroom.

'Balls!' Joanne said. 'This English reserve really pisses me off, do you know that, Paul?'

'I think you're making it clear, yes,' he said.

They were lying facing one another. 'You're so lucky having those two fabulous kids and you're letting them slip away,' she warned.

'Don't be so dramatic,' Paul said flatly.

'Tell me about Nathan,' she said.

'I've already told you,' he replied.

'You've told me nothing . . . It wasn't the description of a child, more a casual acquaintance!'

'Joanne,' Paul warned, 'that's enough.'

'Tell me,' she repeated.

'There's nothing else to say,' he insisted.

'Nothing you want to tell me, at any rate,' Joanne said quietly.

'This has been a pretty bloody evening so far,' Paul told her. 'I don't feel like discussing Nathan, all right?'

'We don't have to make love every time we hit the sack, you know,' Joanne replied.

Paul didn't respond to that.

'Are you listening to me, Paul?' she asked.

'I'm listening,' he replied grumpily.

'It's only men who bother about it, the great performance trip, up and at 'em, wham bam, another screw successfully over and done with.'

'All right,' Paul said, 'I think I get the message . . . I feel I've let you down.'

'Don't be so stupid. What a lot of crap you men talk. Who teaches you this?' she asked, laughter present in her voice.

'It's never happened before, that's all,' he said, sounding a little pathetic.

'Maybe that's good, then,' she encouraged. 'Maybe it means you were really thinking about something this time!'

'What's that supposed to mean?' he asked, irritated now. 'It doesn't mean anything.'

'Don't fuck me out of a sense of duty, okay?' she said. 'You have nothing to prove.'

'God, but you're a crude woman.'

Joanne laughed. 'Not at all. Anyway, what does it matter? Listen, your life is in such a mess this experience won't hurt any.'

'Why do you say that? My life isn't in a mess.'

'I say it because it's true.'

'Look, William was upset, he's fifteen, it's a difficult time for boys to go through . . .'

'And you're not making it any easier, are you?'

'I'm doing the best I can.'

'By acting like some Victorian paterfamilias?'

315

'Nonsense.'

'You never talk to them.'

'I talk to them all the time.'

'Crap!'

'You don't know them,' he said.

Joanne turned over on to her back. 'How do you get on with your parents?'

'What has that got to do with anything, for God's sake?' Paul asked.

'Just answer the question.'

'No,' Paul replied firmly.

'Why, are you afraid it might incriminate you?'

'How do you get on with your parents?' he asked.

'You know how, we were with them at Christmas. I get on with them just fine.'

'I get on with my parents the same way.'

'Really?' Joanne asked.

'Really,' he said, turning over on to his other side so that his back was towards her now.

'Are you going to speak with Rita?' she asked, after a long silence between them.

'I'm always speaking to Rita,' he replied.

'You know what I'm talking about,' Joanne said.

'Rita's fine. I'm not going to upset her by dredging up the past.'

'Rita is not fine,' Joanne said insistently.

'How do you know? You've never even met her.' He sounded incredulous at Joanne's assertion.

'I know because I'm a woman.'

Paul laughed with disparagement. 'That's absurd.'

'No, it isn't. I know because if it were me I would need to talk.'

'But it isn't you,' Paul replied.

'No, thank God,' Joanne said with feeling.

'Maybe we could arrange for you to live with Rita and

the boys. You seem to spend your time looking out for her interests!'

'Don't be churlish,' she said, turning to poke him in the small of the back. 'I'm trying to take care of your interests too.'

'I wish you'd just leave it alone.'

'I know you do.'

'So, why don't you?' he asked, sounding annoyed.

'Because I care for you?' she suggested.

Paul turned to her, laughing in the darkness and taking Joanne into his arms. 'Then I think you've bitten off more than you can chew,' he told her.

She sighed. 'Christ, the number of times I've done that, it doesn't bear thinking about . . . Stray dogs, stray cats, birds with broken wings, stray men, and none of them standing a hope in hell!'

'Thanks,' Paul said. 'You do a lot for a man's ego. Did you know that?'

Joanne giggled into his chest, her voice muffled when she spoke again. 'Go back to your wife and kids and get the past sorted out between you . . . It's the only route out now. Don't you realize that?'

Paul didn't answer her. His eyes were brimming full of unshed tears for Nathan and now for them all. He was unable to speak. The surf rushing on to the sands sounded loud in the stillness. He released Joanne and, turning away from her again, buried his head into the pillow, wishing he were alone whilst not wanting to let her go. He could not resist her questions as he had Rita's. He felt strangely defenceless with her, sometimes like a child again. She refused to play the usual courtship games and, looking at him with her wise, uncompromising eyes, saw right through the pretence, saw right through him to the pain beneath.

* * *

Paul was pacing his office a few days later, waiting for Steve to arrive for lunch. He had phoned and asked if he would drive across to UCLA after his morning classes. Steve had seemed a bit suspicious. It was not a usual request from his father – Paul was normally far too busy but today was different. Finally Steve had agreed whilst making the point that he would have to miss a 'swim team training session'. Paul offered to have a word with the coach if it presented any problems.

'Do you fancy a drive?' Paul asked almost as soon as Steve arrived.

Steve stood in the doorway looking slightly dishevelled, in a red plaid shirt with the tail hanging out over worn Levi's, well-scuffed training shoes, white socks. He carried a small backpack slung over one shoulder, its straps trailing, weighted by a few books and sundry student rubbish. Steve shrugged, looking at his father in a bemused way. 'Okay,' he said.

Paul gunned the Mercedes' engine, reversing out of his parking space with a roar and, spinning the wheel, pulled the big car away with a jolt that knocked Steve's head back against the restraint.

Steve turned to his father but said nothing. They drove along the Santa Monica Boulevard at express speed, unspeaking, finally pulling into the driveway of a small beach-front house. 'What's this?' Steve asked.

'Joanne's place,' Paul answered, already getting out of the car and fumbling for the front-door key.

'Is Joanne here?' Steve asked, even more confused.

'No, come on,' Paul instructed.

'So, why have you brought me here?'

'What?' Paul frowned. 'Come on in,' he said, opening the door and stepping inside.

Steve paused for a moment before following his father. The hallway was dark but opened out into an airy lounge

318

full of hanging baskets and ornaments. There were lots of photographs around the walls and a couple of contemporary oil paintings. Beyond the wall-length windows were the beach and the ocean. There was a wide patio with easy chairs and some hanging flower baskets. The furniture in the lounge reminded Steve of his grandmother's house in Hampshire. It was old and had loose covers with floral designs, and the sofa and chairs looked slightly out of place in the modern building.

Paul emerged from the kitchen. 'I'll make us a sandwich . . . What do you fancy?'

'What is there?' Steve asked, putting his hands into his pockets.

'I've found some cheese and the remains of a chicken, so far.'

'How old is the chicken?' Steve asked suspiciously.

'A day or two, we had it at the week-end.'

Steve shrugged. 'Okay.'

'Chicken?' Paul asked.

'Chicken,' Steve replied, walking to the windows and staring out over the sands, where an old man was throwing a driftwood stick for an equally ancient-looking Labrador. His father suddenly walked across the patio in front of Steve, placing a tray with sandwiches and coffee down on the sturdy round wooden table. Steve found a door at the right-hand side of the windows, partially covered by the long curtains and, turning the key, stepped outside. 'Well,' Steve began, picking up a sandwich and pushing a piece of the white chicken meat back between the pieces of whole-wheat bread, 'so why all the mystery?'

'There's no mystery,' Paul replied, attempting a smile. 'I just wanted to talk to you.'

Steve nodded. 'I'm seeing you at the week-end. It must be pretty important, to break your schedule, I mean.'

'I thought this would be better than a restaurant or my office.'

Steve followed the progress of a gull as it swooped low overhead until his eyes met his father's rather grim expression again. 'Joanne has a nice house,' he said.

Paul nodded. 'Santa Monica is rather more sedate than Malibu, more solid.'

'These places all seem the same to me,' Steve admitted.

Paul stared at him. 'I thought a neutral location would be better . . .'

'Neutral?'

'I've been thinking about what you said,' Paul began.

'Have you?' Steve felt rather unnerved.

'Yes.' Paul sat back. 'You think I've failed you, I know that.'

Steve stopped eating, placing his sandwich on the plate. 'I never said that.'

'But it's something you obviously feel . . . You said a lot of hard things the other day at the beach.'

'Listen, Dad,' Steve began, to make some kind of explanation, not really wishing to become involved in another fraught conversation with his father.

'No, no,' Paul interrupted, 'that's all right. You weren't saying anything that probably wasn't true. It's just that . . .' He paused for a moment. 'It's just that I've never been especially good at showing my emotions. I don't know why, I suppose it's to do with upbringing, schooling . . . something.' Paul attempted a pathetic little smile, which didn't quite make it and made his face seem inordinately sad.

'Look, Dad, I was out of order, I shouldn't have said anything . . . I was upset over William.'

'No, no, you were right, everything you said was right. I could have done more, probably *should* have done more to keep the family together but . . .' He sighed and bit

320

into his bottom lip. 'When your brother died . . .' He sat up, his hands clenching the arms of his chair. 'When Nathan killed himself I was in such a state of terror I was never able to see much beyond my own sense of grief. The only way I could cope with it was not to speak about it . . . with anyone.'

'What about Mum?' Steve asked.

'Even your mother . . . particularly Rita,' he said quietly. 'My job was to carry on, to pull us all through. I felt I had to do that, it seemed terribly important to, somehow, get us all through those terrible days . . . The only way I could do it was to carry on as normal.'

'But it was hardly a normal situation. I remember how angry you looked at his graveside that day,' Steve said. 'I thought you would never forgive him for what he'd done.'

'Forgive him?' Paul looked appalled at the suggestion.

'Yes.' Steve looked directly into his father's shocked face. 'It's always seemed as though you couldn't forgive Nathan for killing himself, almost like your mother, who can't face it either.'

'Face what?' Paul asked.

'The truth, I guess.'

Paul was confused. 'I was never angry with Nathan.'

'But you never spoke about him, either . . . If anyone even so much as mentioned his name the atmosphere became frozen . . .'

'I've already explained that,' Paul replied defensively.

'But it's too easy just to say you were never any good at showing emotion . . . It doesn't make any sense. The catastrophe of Nathan's suicide was too great to control. And look what's happened as a result.'

Paul frowned. 'One of us had to retain control,' he insisted, sounding annoyed.

'Why?' Steve asked simply.

'Why?' Paul sounded amazed. 'Because . . . because it

would have served no purpose whatsoever if we'd all cracked up.'

Steve wasn't convinced. 'When I tried to speak to you, when William wanted so much to reach you, where were you? You were never there.'

'I had my duties to fulfil at the hospital, I had my patients . . . sick children can't just be put on hold, you know.'

'You could have made provision for that.'

'It was my responsibility,' Paul was adamant.

'Mum was left to deal with it all,' Steve replied.

'Your mother could cope.'

'You almost killed her too,' he said, becoming more excited, increasingly angry.

'Just what the hell is that supposed to mean?'

Steve, realizing what he had just said, looked away. 'Nothing,' he said. 'It means nothing.'

'Whatever has happened between me and your mother has absolutely nothing to do with your brother's death.'

'No?' Steve turned to his father. 'Do you expect me to believe that? I've watched you together . . .'

'I brought you here in order to give you some kind of an explanation which I thought you were man enough to understand. You have to realize, Steve, that people aren't automatons, and when we don't conform to your idea of what constitutes "normalcy" it doesn't mean that you are necessarily right all the time . . . Don't be so bloody cocky.'

'You brought me here to excuse your own conscience,' Steve snapped back. 'You constantly talk about your responsibility . . . Where's your fucking responsibility where Nathan's concerned?'

'What are you talking about?' Paul was extremely angry now. 'You kids, we give you everything and all you want is to nail us on the cross . . .'

322

'You do,' Steve agreed. 'You give us everything, you're very generous with your hard-earned money, but why have you always found it so impossible to treat William and me as though you actually loved us?'

Paul's mouth fell open. 'Jesus,' he said softly. 'Do you think I don't?' He raised a hand to his head.

Steve looked back into Paul's startled face but made no reply. 'Why *did* you bring me here?' he asked again. His voice sounded emotionless and cold.

Paul was shaking his head slowly from side to side. He blinked, staring at Steve, uncomprehending. 'Jesus, how can you even think such a thing?' It was almost addressed to himself. He covered his eyes with his hand just for a second or two before thinking clearly again. 'I don't know, son,' he replied to Steve's question, standing up abruptly and starting to gather together the lunch things, which were largely untouched, 'I don't know.'

'It's not easy, is it?' Steve said.

'What?' Paul stopped what he was doing.

'Letting go,' Steve continued, 'allowing your emotions to take control of you.'

'It's a recipe for disaster,' Paul replied.

'Is that what happened to Nathan, do you think?'

'I don't know. You tell me, you seem to have all the answers.' Paul flicked a fly away from the uneaten food.

Steve didn't reply. Instead, he got up and walked across the patio and on to the sand, wandering to the water's edge, where he sat down, staring blindly out to sea.

Paul brooded over the lunch-time confrontation with Steve, sitting back in his office chair long after it was time to leave. He closed his eyes, swinging the large high-backed leather seat from side to side. Joanne had been proved right, he couldn't deal with his own children.

323

What had begun as an attempt to explain his own feelings concerning Nathan had gone completely awry.

He still didn't consider any of his actions had been particularly wrong; just because he wasn't prone to bouts of public emotion didn't really prove anything. He assumed the boys had taken Rita's side. It was, after all, quite natural in the circumstances; they felt protective towards her. Paul didn't like being thought of as some kind of ogre but, without him, the family would have been stuck firmly in the mire of grief for ever. He felt his responsibility was to carry on as normal, to bring them with him, dragging them kicking and screaming if it had to be that way, moving them on from their immediate emotional response to Nathan's suicide and facing up to everyday existence again. At this level of understanding Paul could see nothing wrong in the way he'd behaved. Of course he had grieved for Nathan, but that had been done alone.

As for Rita, his feelings were still confused although since meeting Joanne he knew there was really no going back. Rita's picture still sat on his desk and, if people commented about it, he would simply refer to her as though they were still living together. However, he no longer wanted a future with her. Joanne provided everything he needed, she could give him everything that Rita, apparently, no longer could. Paul felt a great sense of gratitude towards Rita but he couldn't really honestly say that he felt any love for her other than that born out of a long friendship, for example. The passion he once felt for her had faltered after Nathan's death and finally died.

Paul had cried himself out, he had felt exhausted with his grief and couldn't cope with Rita's constant demands for discussion and blow-by-blow accounts about the suicide. Finding Nathan's body had, somehow, made him feel completely differently towards Rita, a sneaking, nasty feeling that she might just have been responsible. It was totally irrational, of course, but Paul was never able to console her and, by holding back for just a moment too long, he had, in all probability, ruined them for one another. Rita had always appeared to be such an incredibly strong woman too, he was shaken by her almost total breakdown, the ferocity of her grief. The debilitating atmosphere this created between them made all rational communication impossible.

He tried to reach her. They made love following Nathan's suicide but it no longer had anything to do with desire, it seemed to be about a power struggle between them. He felt all along during this hateful period of their lives that Rita was trying to pull him down with her, as though until he had broken up under the colossal strain she couldn't justify anything of their life together. When they feigned love in their possessive intercourse it was really just a battle of wills. And it was then, at such intimate times, that their love turned almost to hate. Paul would be appalled at his overpowering desire to dominate her, as though by physically taking Rita he would be able to make her see reason. It was a ludicrous and destructive notion and one that he quickly rejected but, afterwards, when the release of his pent-up anger and grief and frustration was complete, he could no longer face her. He began to turn from her sexually because of the empty chasm that loomed for him afterwards, a frightening emptiness in which he was left to flounder as Rita rolled from under him, a blackness in which Paul felt he would almost certainly drown. The pain of this realization was almost too much to bear and so their estrangement began. Perhaps Steve had been right, perhaps it was Nathan he blamed, Nathan who could no longer answer but who had created their total grief and disenchantment.

They had lived on together but in name only. As Rita's

initial grief subsided she would sometimes welcome his advances but, by then, there was nothing left for Paul to give. He resorted to masturbation but without any accompanying fantasy. Paul realized then why it was referred to as self-abuse. He derived little actual relief from it and it seemed, on reflection, to have been practised almost as an act of abasement.

Paul turned to his work. Steve had been right again – when all else failed it provided a way out, a justification of his life and, when at work, he was able to forget the rest. The life of his patients and the development of his students' talents and abilities became paramount.

He had known after Nathan's death that the marriage was faltering. Things had probably not been very good between them for a year or so prior to the suicide, but they had gone on, busy people not always noticing how far things had altered between them and, if they had, not really commenting on it. Paul left Rita when living with her became totally impossible for him. He felt that she was draining him of every resource, that she was sucking him dry. Paul acted quickly then. Already knowing about the Malibu house through the grapevine, he rented it with an option to buy at a later date.

Not wishing to upset Rita any more than was necessary, Paul had thought this might suggest to her that all was not lost. Later he realized how cruel this particular deception had been.

Joanne called in to see him on her way back to Santa Monica that evening. 'Why aren't you at home?' she asked, leaning against the door jamb.

'Why aren't you?'

'Work,' she replied.

Paul nodded.

'How was lunch?' she asked. 'Did you see him?'

'Sure,' Paul said.

'And?'

'And it was bloody awful.'

Joanne sighed, folding her arms. 'What happened?' she asked in a tone suggesting that it was his fault.

'God knows.' He sounded weary.

'Aren't you ever going to work this thing out between you?'

'I'm trying,' Paul insisted.

'Not hard enough, or so it would appear.'

'Joanne, I need *someone* to be on my side,' he told her. 'Not everything is my fault.'

'It's not a question of sides,' she replied, 'it's a question of you relating to a seventeen-year-old son.'

Paul stared at her. 'What are you doing tonight?'

'I'm going out with Dolores and Tess.'

'Oh.' He thought for a moment. 'Can't you put it off?'

'No,' Joanne replied without any hesitation. 'I'll see you tomorrow,' she grinned, 'just like we planned, okay?'

Paul nodded, the flicker of a smile at the corners of his mouth. 'Jesus, but you're a bloody hard woman.'

'I don't jump every time you click your fingers, if that's what you mean!'

'I just need you sometimes, that's all.'

'You don't *need* me, Paul, you need someone to pat you on the head and to stroke your feverish brow and tell you that everything is all right.'

'What's wrong with that?' he protested.

'Nothing, but you'll survive one more night alone,' she smiled. 'Okay?'

He watched her leaving. 'At least ring me later,' he called.

'I'll see,' she replied without turning back.

* * *

Steve's car was parked outside as he arrived at the beach house. Paul found him sitting out on the balcony. The sun was setting across the dark waters and the horizon was glowing with hot oranges and reds as the sky reflected the dying sunlight. Paul dropped his briefcase on the sofa and walked on to the balcony. 'Steve,' he said. 'All right, son?'

Steve turned to him. 'I called in on the off chance, I wasn't sure if you'd be coming back tonight . . .'

Paul nodded. 'Does your mother know you're here?'

Steve watched as the sun gradually slipped away. 'Sure, I told her I'd drop in after swim practice.'

Paul noticed Steve's damp hair and the black tracksuit complete with swimming badges and the logo of his school on the right-hand thigh. He remembered Steve just a few years ago, as a boy in maroon blazer and grey trousers, the archetypical English school child, and now he was American youth personified. 'Have you eaten?'

'Mum's keeping supper for me, I can't stay long. Don't let me hold you up, though . . .'

'No, no, that's fine,' Paul replied, sitting down opposite his son, watching him across the round table in the bright house light. The horizon had darkened until just a thin band of gorgeous red remained, and that soon faded away into the gathering blackness. 'How goes the swimming? I never seem to get to any of your meetings.'

'Okay,' Steve said without much enthusiasm.

'Good,' Paul replied.

'Dad,' Steve began, fidgeting nervously with his car keys, which he moved from hand to hand, twisting and turning them around on their ring, which had a tab with the Volkswagen logo printed on it. 'I'm sorry about what I said at lunchtime.'

'There's no need to be,' Paul said.

'I always seem to be apologizing to you just recently.'

'We all say things in the heat of the moment, Steve,' Paul told him. 'It doesn't really mean anything.'

'I still don't understand, though,' he admitted. 'I mean, I don't understand you at all . . .'

'Really?' Paul was forced to smile a little. 'I thought that was the province of parents, not to understand their children!'

'Didn't your parents understand you, then?' Steve questioned.

'I doubt it,' Paul replied.

'What didn't they understand?'

'Oh . . .' Paul thought for a moment. 'They didn't really ever understand, or entirely approve, of my choice of career. They would have preferred it if I had continued the family practice in Lyndhurst, I suppose.'

'But you've achieved much more than that,' Steve insisted. 'Aren't they proud of you?'

Paul shrugged. He'd never really thought much about it. 'I don't know.' He shook his head. 'They've never said one way or the other . . . it's just a feeling I get. You may have noticed I don't exactly have the closest relationship with my parents!'

Steve grinned for the first time that evening. 'It's noticeable.'

'Well, that's the reason why I don't want the same thing to happen between me and my kids.'

'And do you think it has?' Steve looked directly at his father. There was a discernible air of tension between them. 'Do we have that type of relationship?'

Paul cleared his throat. 'You tell me, son.'

'We've always known you were something special. Nathan was always very aware of it, he was trying hard to emulate it.' He paused. His father's face looked full of pain and stress, he looked, somehow, exhausted and old all of a sudden. 'You seemed to be a distant figure as we

329

grew up, you were always at the hospital . . . I'm not knocking that, just making the point.'

Paul nodded but didn't say anything. He shifted his position in the chair, putting one foot up on the opposite thigh, holding on to the ankle with his hands.

'I suppose, in the end, we just came to accept that your work was the main thing in your life, that you were away a lot, travelling abroad a lot, because you were this famous doctor and, because of that, we enjoyed the benefits of your success . . . good schools, nice house, foreign holidays . . .'

'Steady on,' Paul said, 'I was a bit more than a meal ticket, wasn't I?'

'Sure, but you became distant. You still are. Nathan spent his whole life asking Mum when you were coming in . . . I think he seemed to need you the most. William and I have always just muddled along.'

'I always tried to be there for you all.' Paul sighed, feeling extremely uncomfortable. 'Success has its own demons, Steve. It's great and it's wicked and you never know exactly where it'll take you next. I suppose the only real solution is not to get involved with anyone, not get married, not have children . . . If I'd known what was going to happen, then I would have thrown it all up – anything to have Nathan back and to have us all as a family again – but we can't do that, we can never go back and, therefore, we simply have to face the past and do whatever we can to make up for it or redeem ourselves because of it.' He watched Steve carefully. 'The thing to remember is that you were all conceived out of love and you were all children who were desperately wanted. Throughout all of these terrible times for this family I have never lost sight of that truth. In fact, it's something I've hung on to tenaciously . . . In the end it's the one thing that's brought me through when I wondered if *I* could carry on.'

'But you always appeared so self-contained. It's as though Nathan's death hardly touched you.'

'Oh, but it did, Steve, by God it did!'

'We seem to have lost everything,' Steve remarked.

'Not everything,' Paul said firmly. 'We're all still here. You and William and your mum are together. I'm still just down the road for you all. It's not perfect but it is real.'

'Nathan was . . .' He looked away over the dark ocean.

'Yes?' Paul encouraged.

'Nothing,' Steve replied at last. 'Listen, I'll have to get going. Mum will be expecting me home.'

'Right,' Paul replied, standing up to show him out, walking to the car with him. He'd noticed a yellowing love-bite on Steve's neck, partially hidden by the turned-up collar of his tracksuit top. 'You ought to be a little careful of those,' he told Steve as they stood in the porch light, moving the collar down and giving the mark a cursory glance.

'Come on, Dad,' Steve complained, laughing it off in an embarrassed way.

'It's a dangerous world these days,' Paul replied, but smiled all the same, making it a kind of joke yet something of a warning too. 'You know, safe sex and all of that?'

Steve nodded. 'Sure, sure, sure.' He laughed again. 'Don't worry.'

Paul shrugged, tapping the top of the Volkswagen as Steve got in. 'Car running all right?' he enquired.

'Great.' Steve started the engine, slamming the door and winding the window down. 'See you in a few days, then.'

'Fine . . . love to William.'

'Regards to Mum?' Steve smiled.

'Love to your mum as well,' Paul insisted, watching Steve driving away, waving once as the red tail lights disappeared into the darkness. He walked slowly back into the house, his feet crunching across the sandy driveway, the sound of surf in the distance.

Joanne crept into his bed in the early hours.

'What's this?' Paul asked sleepily.

'I got home, went to bed and then missed you,' she explained, wrapping herself around him. 'Do you mind?'

'How was your evening with Loretta and Bess?'

'Dolores and Tess,' she reminded him.

'Ah, how was it?'

'Fine, what about you?'

'Fine, Steve turned up.'

'Oh.' She sounded suspicious.

'It was all right.'

She breathed a sigh of relief. 'That's good . . . tell me about it in the morning,' she said, yawning.

Paul listened to her steady breathing as she fell asleep again. He felt better for his talk with Steve but couldn't help feeling that his son was holding something back. Quite what this was Paul wasn't sure but he felt there was something.

When he woke up the following morning Joanne had already showered and was wandering around the beach house in his towelling robe, smoking her one and only cigarette of the day and carrying a large glass of freshly squeezed orange juice.

'If you only smoke a little, why not give it up completely?' Paul asked, dragging himself out of bed and padding, naked, into the bathroom.

'You're such a grouch in the morning . . . I'll go outside if it bothers you that much,' Joanne replied, shaking out

332

the jacket of her suit, which had been left crumpled up on an armchair all night.

'It's tantamount to being unethical. How can you face your patients, reeking of tobacco smoke?' he asked, switching on the shower.

Joanne walked into the bathroom, pulled back the shower curtain and blew smoke at him. 'I don't *reek*!' she complained, sitting on the closed lid of the toilet seat. 'It's my one little vice.'

'Ha!' Paul snorted as he began to soap himself under the powerful jet of water.

'Okay,' she said above the drumming of the shower, 'I'll quit smoking if you go and speak to Rita.'

Paul didn't respond for a moment but, poking his soapy head out of the shower, squinted across at Joanne. 'You smoke if you want . . . Just don't moan at me when you come down with some ghastly respiratory disease!'

'One cigarette a day?' she laughed in amazement. 'Listen, my grandmother smoked fifty cigarettes a day and lived to be ninety-seven!'

'Fluke,' Paul replied, ducking back under the shower and finishing off his morning ablutions.

They left the house together, laughing at something Joanne had just said. Paul kissed her goodbye and saw her off before getting into the silver Mercedes and driving to UCLA. He felt better this morning, better than for a long time. Perhaps he could change the way things were, regain his children's confidence and even maintain a reasonable relationship with Rita.

He wondered if there was still a chance for him to reach out to his own parents, to attempt a meaningful relationship with them before it was too late. Paul made a mental note to write that evening with a view to visiting them in the spring. There was a conference in Paris about AIDS he was thinking of attending. It would be easy to go from there to England and spend a few days with his parents. He wondered if Joanne would be able to go as well and decided to suggest it to her. God knew how his mother would react to Joanne's presence but, if the trip was kept short, the old woman might not be too difficult. In her last letter his mother had moaned about the decrepitude of his father and how exhausted she was becoming taking care of him. It was only to be expected, the old man was an octogenarian and in poor health.

He pulled into his parking space and went directly to his office, where the morning always began as he went through the voluminous mail. Within a short space of time Paul was engrossed in his work and all other thoughts were lost.

Chapter 10

Los Angeles felt very strange to Rita after her weeks in England. The space and light of her house and the January temperature, which was normally in the sixties, made her feel so much better. No longer would she have to sit cooped up in front of a fire in order to keep warm, and even getting up in the mornings became almost a pleasure compared to the chilly ordeal she had faced at Chalcot Square. On the first week-end after their return the boys went to visit their father and she invited Gary to stay with her. They had spoken on the phone but this was their first meeting since before Christmas, and Rita was nervous.

'He's just a man,' Sharon told her, looking rather spectacular with her deeper than usual tan from their trip to Hawaii, and her blonde hair worn long.

'You know what I mean,' Rita replied. 'Anyway, he isn't *just* another man, is he?'

'Isn't he?' Sharon asked, smirking.

'No,' Rita admitted, 'I think I really like him.'

'*Like?*' Sharon sounded disappointed.

'Well, you know,' Rita replied.

'No, do tell.'

'I mean, I think I like him in *that* way.'

'Oh,' Sharon said, her voice low and conspiratorial. 'And what way might that be?'

Rita grinned. 'Stop it!'

'Stop what?' Sharon protested her innocence.

'You know exactly what I mean.'

'Is he staying the whole week-end?' Sharon asked.

'I'm not sure.' Rita looked at her friend. 'I suppose he will.'

'Don't you want him to?'

'What do you think?' Rita asked.

'Well, honey, I suppose you do,' she laughed, getting up and preparing to leave. She gave Rita a stern look. 'Just be careful,' she said.

'Careful?' Rita was confused.

'He's a very attractive man, Rita, but if you're not sure . . .'

'Okay, thanks for the advice, but if you say anything else I'll probably chicken out.'

'Right, then give me a ring and let me know all the details,' Sharon said, leaving, as usual, through the patio doors and heading across the grass towards her own house.

Rita waved her away, wondering quite what she was letting herself in for now.

Rita had prepared a traditional roast beef dinner for them. It seemed an appropriate answer to the West Coast delicacy he had given her. A sort of hands-across-the-sea exercise in respect of their different nationalities and cultures.

At Sharon's suggestion she had visited the hairdresser and returned her hair to its former, shorter style. In fact, it was even shorter than usual but it felt better and, Rita thought, made her look a little less ancient. As the evening was informal and, in any case, Gary had worked in the house and seen her in shorts, bathing costume and a variety of other 'recreational' clothes, she decided to wear her favourite Levi's, grabbing one of Steve's sweat shirts at the last minute when she couldn't decide what top she should put on.

Gary turned up a little after seven-thirty with a gift for

her and looking even more attractive than usual. He was wearing blue jeans and training shoes with a pastel green T-shirt under a smart suit jacket. He seemed very blond and tanned and healthy.

'Hi, Rita,' he said, kissing her and then looking hard, scrutinizing every detail. 'You're looking rather fantastic.'

Rita laughed, taking his hand and leading him into the lounge, where she had lit the gas fire with the fake logs for a cosy effect. It wasn't a particularly chilly evening but Rita considered this a nice touch. She had a vision of them sitting in front of it with brandy and coffee after dinner. It was an awful cliché, she knew, but one she wasn't averse to using.

'Here you go,' Gary said, handing her the carefully wrapped gift.

'You shouldn't have,' Rita told him.

'It's a small thank-you for loaning me your car.'

'Oh, for God's sake,' Rita laughed, pulling off the wrapping and discovering a large bottle of Chanel. 'My absolute favourite . . . how did you know?' she asked, kissing him on the cheek.

'Sharon told me,' he admitted.

'I'm not exactly dressed for Chanel,' she grinned, 'but what the hell.' She opened the bottle and dabbed perfume at either side of her neck just underneath her ears and rubbed a little on her wrists. 'I brought you something too,' she confessed, reaching forward to the low table in front of them and picking up a rather hurriedly packaged gift, which she placed into his large hands. 'I hope you like it.'

Gary laughed as he undid it, finding the candle of Big Ben and giving a whoop of delight as he held it up. 'This is great,' he told her.

'All the way from Covent Garden. I was terrified it would break on the trip back.'

'It's great,' he repeated, grinning all over his face, like a child.

'Right,' Rita sighed, 'and now the food.' She got up. 'I thought we'd eat in the dining room. It's so rarely used these days, it's got candelabra and everything . . .'

'Lead on, then,' Gary told her. 'I'm starved.'

'Did you know I was going to ask you to stay?' Rita asked him, sitting up in bed and brushing a hand through his short hair.

Gary looked up at her. 'I hoped you would.'

'But you weren't sure?'

'I noticed you'd removed your rings . . . I thought you would.'

'Oh, a private eye in my midst!'

'Not at all, not at all.'

Instead of the log fire they had taken their brandy up to bed with them. Rita had opened a bottle of wine with the meal and then decided on champagne to go with their dessert. Champagne always had a marvellous effect upon her, she could drink it by the bottle and would never get hung over. Now she felt perfectly sober but her memory of how, exactly, she got Gary into bed was a bit fogged. She just hoped she hadn't dragged him immediately from the dinner table but, somehow, she thought this might have been the case.

She remembered how seeing him naked had been a bit of a shock to her. Gary was really *extremely* muscular. Not quite in the same league as Arnold Schwarzenegger, but powerfully built all the same. She wanted him inside her almost immediately but he waited a while, lingering over her body, telling her how wonderful she was, and Rita seemed to drift along in a warm, erotic dream, a part of the act and yet also distant from it. Gary was tender and thoughtful, hitting base on all the right erogenous zones, until, finally, his forefinger began to caress her clitoris and she thought she would burn up with excitement and desire for him. She pulled him on to her, spreading her legs wide and reaching down to guide his erect penis inside her. She remembered her head moving from side to side, calling out his name as he started to thrust, moving first terribly slowly and then faster and faster until she climaxed, pushing against him, never, ever wanting it to end. Gary came with a great bellow which seemed to rise up from the depths of him, thrusting at her with a greater ferocity than before. 'Rita, oh Jesus, oh Jesus God . . .'

They had slid apart, Gary falling at her side, gasping for air, whilst she had just wanted it to go on and on and on.

'How did you sleep?' Rita asked, waking up with Gary wrapped around her.

'Are you okay?' he asked, stirring from underneath the bed clothes, yawning as he spoke.

Rita turned to face him. 'I feel relieved.'

'Relieved?' He blinked into the light.

'Hmm,' Rita grinned at him. 'I mean I was so tense before . . . the first time with anyone is always a bit fraught.'

Gary stretched and then sat up, scratching his head. 'I felt a bit fraught too,' he admitted.

'Were you?' Rita sounded a bit surprised, watching as he left the bed and walked over to the windows, where he partially drew back the curtains. He was then framed in the golden glow of morning sunlight, which shone through the downy blond hair on his legs and arms, giving a kind of halo effect around his nude body.

He turned to her for a moment and smiled. 'Sure I was nervous.' He looked out at the pool, opening the balcony door. 'Would I be offending local propriety if I was to go skinny-dipping before breakfast?'

Rita sat up at last, placing a pillow behind her head. 'No, we're very broad-minded around these parts, but you'd better take a towel down with you.'

Gary nodded. 'Okay.' He pointed towards the bath-room door. 'In there?'

'In the cupboard next to the basin.'

'Closet,' he said. 'Speak American!'

Rita laughed, getting out of bed and pulling on her robe. She went out on to the balcony, leant over the rails and looked down to the terrace below, before closing her eyes and turning her face towards the warm sun. Gary came up behind her, putting his arms around her waist. 'Oh, Jesus!' She turned to him, laughing. 'You scared me.'

He bent to kiss her. 'Good morning,' he said.

She looked into his eyes. 'So what do you think?' she asked.

'Think?' He seemed confused.

'About this . . . situation,' she continued.

'Situation?'

'Yes,' she smiled.

'I think that this situation is just great,' he replied, kissing her again. 'Just amazing.'

'You're not just saying that,' she joked.

'Would I?' he said with fake shock, standing back and placing a hand across his heart.

'Probably.'

Gary hitched up the bath sheet around his waist and went off for his swim. Rita watched as he appeared from the house beneath her, running across the dewy grass, leaving a track of his footprints across the beautifully tended lawn. The wet grass meant that Gary made dark prints across the white concrete pool surround. He paused at the diving board, looking up to make sure she was still watching, dropped the dark green bath sheet to the ground and, climbing up to the board, paused for a moment, jumped on to the springy end and dived perfectly into the still blue water. The white skin of his buttocks flashed in the morning light as though some strange fish were leaping through the pool.

Rita watched for a little longer, saw him surface and wave to her. As he began to swim strongly from end to end, she went back into her bedroom to shower and consider breakfast. Men were just enormous children, she thought, showing off and wanting, needing, the approbation of those around them. Wanting to exhibit themselves and display their ability and finesse to whoever was fool enough to look and admire. It was generally done for the benefit of other men, however, whatever the particular arena – work, play, even sex . . . Rita thought about that. Maybe it was a little harsh! She stepped under the needle spray of her shower and picked up the bar of fragrant soap. She didn't really care at that moment why they behaved as they did, for all she wanted then was Gary . . . and the rest, their future, could wait a while.

She made a salad for their lunch, using up the remainder of the cold beef from dinner the previous evening.

'Do you think I was a bit obvious last night?' she asked him, crunching into a celery stick.

'Obvious?' He laughed, showing off his very white, straight American teeth. 'Listen, just relax, don't worry . . .' He leant forward and spoke in hushed, conspiratorial tones. 'You weren't obvious, Rita!'

'Well.' She looked at him, feeling dangerously out of control with the situation. 'Sex has become an increasingly rare commodity for me these days.'

'It shouldn't ever be a commodity,' he replied.

'You know what I mean,' she said. 'What about you?'

'Oh, me? Well, let's see now, I've tended to stop sleeping around these days . . . you know, cruising the chicks on the Strip!'

Rita grinned. As she grew older, her desire after twenty years with Paul, and one minor indiscretion with Marco, Gary was the second potentially serious involvement in her life. It made her feel incredibly unsophisticated, after all it was her generation who were supposed to have been responsible for sexual liberation among the masses! She was amused at her own 'innocence', the fact that her carnal knowledge had been reduced to so few encounters.

'What is it?' Gary asked. 'You still have that dirty grin across your face.'

'I do not,' Rita protested.

'I noticed it last night, just before we hit the sack.'

'You did not!'

'Okay,' Gary told her, giving in. 'Listen, I have a great idea for this afternoon.'

'Yes?' She looked at him with a degree of suspicion.

'You're grinning again,' he warned her. 'Let's go to Watts, have you been there?'

'I thought it was a ghetto, didn't they riot there in the sixties?'

'The Watts Towers,' Gary continued, 'let's go see the Watts Towers.'

'I've heard of them,' Rita replied.

'But you've never been to take a look?'

She shook her head. 'We never got around to it, no.'

'Do you want to, then?'

'Sure, why not?'

'Good, we can go on to the beach and have an evening meal . . . it'll be great.'

'Okay,' she replied, smiling at him.

'Right,' he reached for her hand, 'all right.'

* * *

342

Gary pulled off the Harbor Freeway, parking the car a little way from the towers, which stood over a hundred feet into the blue Los Angeles sky. Rita shaded her eyes with a hand, peering up at the three towers built out of concrete and chicken wire, steel rods and broken tile, glass and sea shells. She laughed at the audacity of them. They tapered into the air, one something like an oil derrick, another spiralling upwards, a series of pointed crown-like shapes at its base. Mosaic walls, like crazy tombstones, surrounded the towers.

'See what you've been missing,' Gary told her. 'Forget about historic old London town, this beats the lot. What do you say?'

'I think they're absolutely bloody marvellous,' Rita chuckled.

'A man called Simon Rodia built them . . . took him thirty-three years!'

'You're kidding.' Rita turned to him in surprise.

Gary shook his head. 'He finished them in 1954 when he was seventy-five and then he left, never to be seen again.'

'But why?' Rita asked.

'Why?' Gary said, looking at the structures. 'Why not?'

Rita laughed again. 'Why did he leave them after spending so much time building them?'

'Because he'd finished his work.' Gary came over, took her hand and walked her slowly round the towers. 'The City Building Department tried to tear them down in 1959, claimed they weren't safe . . . but here they are, still standing.'

'God, I must bring the boys here, they'd love it.' Rita was examining a design of pebbles and pottery pushed into the cement at the base of the towers. 'They'd absolutely love it.'

Gary took her into his arms and kissed her. 'They have mythical sexual power as well. Didn't you know that?'

'Don't be ridiculous,' she laughed.

'It's *true*!'

'Stop it.' Rita pushed him away. Taking up her camera, she shot him as he stood next to a mosaic wall then, moving back, took a picture of him with the towers framed against the almost perfect sky.

'Good old Simon, eh?' Gary grinned back.

'He certainly left his mark,' Rita agreed.

'Of course, they're ridiculous,' Gary continued, 'but aren't they marvellous too, something about the indomitable nature of man-, and woman-, kind.'

'You're not contemplating a project like this, by any chance, are you?' Rita enquired.

'No, garden furniture, the odd house now and again, that's about my limit.'

They walked slowly to the car, Rita turning once more to stare at the towers. 'I wonder whatever happened to Simon Rodia,' she mused.

'Beats me. Maybe went off somewhere else and started another project, probably just went off and died quietly . . .'

'It's a bit sad really, isn't it?'

'Nope,' Gary replied, unlocking the car doors, 'it's very uplifting and it always gives me hope when I look at them. If one old man can do that with his bare hands for absolutely no reason, then just think what we can achieve when we have an aim and some resolution . . .'

'You sound very Californian,' Rita admitted.

'A bullshitter, you mean,' he replied, getting into the passenger seat of her car and handing the keys across to Rita.

'No, not at all,' Rita said, starting the engine and driving slowly away, 'not at all.'

* * *

344

They walked on the beach for a while, ate at a seafood restaurant down from Venice and returned to Rita's house just before nine o'clock.

'Okay, what do you want to do?' he asked.

'Are you kidding?' Rita asked.

'I've got kind of a headache tonight, Rita,' he play-acted, placing a hand to his brow.

'Come on,' she commanded, grabbing his hand and leading them upstairs to her bed, 'I'll find you an aspirin!'

'God, but you're a hard woman. This is what it must be like to be a gigolo.'

Rita laughed. 'Gigolos are very young and terribly . . .' She paused. 'How shall I say? Energetic?'

He kissed her on the mouth at the top of the stairs. 'You have direct experience of these people?'

'No, but I saw that film with Richard Gere.'

'Jesus,' he said in disbelief, 'you're not turning this into a sexual fantasy, by any chance, are you?'

'No, of course I'm not.'

'Okay,' he looked her straight in the eye, 'as long as I'm not just an object of your lust, then.'

Rita giggled. 'Come on,' she instructed once more, pulling him along the landing towards her bedroom. They undressed quickly, dropping their clothes where they stood and diving headlong on to the huge bed. Gary leant across to her, kissing her for a long moment, moving his body against her own, his hand stroking her skin as it slid down from shoulder to thigh. Rita felt his muscles tense hard as she reached down, taking his erect penis into her hand and running her fingers slowly up and down until he pulled away from her.

'Jesus,' he breathed, 'don't make me come yet . . .'

She grinned up at him, pushing him on to his back and moving down the bed, rolling over and taking his penis into her mouth, where she played her tongue around the

345

swollen glans, feeling the tense muscles of his thighs underneath her hands. Finally she raised her head. Moving astride Gary, she lowered herself until he was inside her and she could sit still for glorious moments, feeling him filling her. Rita moved slowly, her hands planted firmly on Gary's hard chest, watching him twisting about underneath her, climaxing violently just as he came, everything straining and hard, as if his flesh had become steel for those seconds, before collapsing on him and feeling his penis sliding out. His eyes were tightly shut, his teeth bared with the delicious release of orgasm. Their bodies were wet as they touched, and she kissed him with a greater urgency, never wanting any of it to end, feeling that she could go on for ever now.

Later she watched him sleeping, lying in a tangle of sheets, looking for all the world like some marbled creation, the smooth curves of his buttocks and thighs perfectly formed as though out of the imagination of the sculptor. She thought him the most beautiful thing then, somehow beyond the real world, as though he might disappear if she were to blink or if daylight filled the room. If it wasn't for the fact that she could hear his steady breathing, it might have been a dream. At that moment all Rita wanted was to be with Gary, her heart thudding violently in her chest as she realized what was happening, as she suddenly understood that she was in love with him.

This was a truly frightening revelation for Rita because it meant a break with her past. There would be no going back, no hope they would ever be a complete family again. No Paul, no husband, no marriage. Gary groaned in his sleep and turned on to his back, arms spread out across the bed. She had no idea what he thought of her, he obviously liked her, but more than that it was impossible to tell. Rita smiled at herself. She was a forty-two-year-old woman with a teenage crush, except it was long past that stage and she didn't feel there was enough time left for silly games, for ritualized courtship, for things left unsaid. Rita was determined to go across and wake him up and demand an answer. Did he love her and, if so, just what did he propose doing about it? But she remained stuck to the chair, leaning forward, looking at him, staring hard at parts of him, an arm, his chin, the rounded muscles on his chest, the heavy thighs, wanting to possess every part of him and feeling completely beyond help now.

The past few years seemed almost impossibly distant as she sat there. That vile period in their lives, in her life, could now be relegated to history . . . Because it seemed possible to her, and because she wasn't sure how Gary felt towards her, she found herself crying silently in the strange silvered light which filled the room from the bright moon, frustrated and angry with herself for needing someone so badly.

Finally Rita took a deep breath and went back to bed. Gary turned on to his side, his back towards her, as she slipped in next to him. She closed her eyes, falling, almost immediately, into an exhausted sleep. She dreamt of Nathan. Rita was walking down the stairs at Chalcot Square and he was at the front door, turning and smiling as he closed it behind him, shutting her out for ever.

Gary woke her late the following morning with a breakfast tray – orange juice, coffee, toast and the pot of honey she had brought back from Hampshire. He kissed her as she opened her eyes, and Rita sat up feeling unsettled and not really understanding why. He went in to shower whilst she read the *LA Times*. Rita imagined Paul and the boys at the beach, Paul and his woman. She had irrational feelings concerning him and Joanne, she had never quite come to terms with him walking out. She had discussed it with Sharon, who obviously found her attitude strange.

'So, if you'd walked out on Paul, that would have been all right?' Sharon asked.

'I wouldn't have walked out on him,' Rita insisted.

'You don't know that.'

'I just hate being rejected,' Rita said.

'Who doesn't?' Sharon asked wearily.

Rita had shrugged. She felt she'd been the 'good wife' and still harboured the feeling that they could have made it if Paul hadn't just given up. At least he hadn't left her for another woman, at least there was that, and it gave her some solace.

Gary came out from the bathroom, smelling steamy and soapy, a towel wrapped around his waist. He smiled at her. Rita smiled back. Despite her doubts, she still found him absolutely irresistible.

'What shall we do today?' he asked.

'I don't mind,' Rita shrugged.

'Are you okay?' he asked, looking at her carefully. 'You seem a bit down.'

'I'm fine,' she replied a little too brightly.

'Fancy the beach?' he asked.

'Which beach?' she laughed.

'*Any* beach!' he grinned, dropping the towel and pulling on a pair of boxer shorts.

'No, not really,' Rita decided. 'We don't have to do anything, do we?'

'No, ma'am,' he shook his head.

Rita smiled. 'Good.'

'Okay,' he said, as though they had just made an earth-shattering decision, 'that's cool.'

She lay back watching him dress, wondering if there really was a chance for them.

'So,' Sharon said later that evening, 'what's going on in that head of yours?'

They were sitting in Rita's kitchen drinking wine. The boys had returned from Malibu and were wandering around with sandwiches in their hands, supposed to be getting things together for school the next day. As the two women spoke their conversation was interrupted from time to time with a variety of requests. William had just been through to ask where his favourite jeans were. Rita poured herself some more of the dry white wine, sitting back in her chair. 'What did your last slave die of?' she asked as he left the kitchen.

She attempted to explain her feelings about Gary. 'I mean he's fantastic, of course, but what's going to happen ultimately?'

'For God's sake,' Sharon complained, reaching for the wine bottle, 'does anything have to happen *ultimately*? Why can't you just enjoy what's happening now?'

Steve came in, going to the fridge and, taking out a quart of milk, then wandered out again, smiling at them both as he did so. 'Bloody gannets!' Rita complained. 'Do your lot eat and drink twenty-four hours a day?'

Sharon laughed. 'They're growing boys . . . When are you seeing Gary again?'

'Wednesday evening,' Rita said, grinning like an idiot. 'He's coming over for supper.'

'Well, honey, I think it's all going to be fine. Gary's a really nice man.'

Rita agreed. 'He's exceptionally nice but I'm still not sure if I'm ready for all of this.'

'Don't be such a sourpuss, of course you're ready . . . just see what happens,' Sharon encouraged.

'You mean wait for him to grow tired and then walk out on me too.'

'Rita,' Sharon warned her friend, 'you're being just a little depressive here. Maybe you should think about seeing Dr Allan soon.'

'I am,' Rita replied, swigging back the last drop of wine from her glass. 'I have an appointment with him on Wednesday too, usual time, usual place . . . usual thing, I suppose.'

'You know, honey, if this is what you're like when you're supposed to be on top of the world . . .'

'I'm sorry,' Rita said, sitting up and pouring out the last of the wine. 'You're right, I'm being stupid.'

'Dumb,' Sharon corrected, 'we say *dumb*!'

Rita laughed. 'Okay, I'll stop it at once, I promise.'

'I'll drink to that,' Sharon replied, holding up her glass.

'To stopping it at once,' Rita proposed rather drunkenly, slopping wine over herself.

'Jesus, Rita, be a drunk by all means but keep it in the glass!'

'To Wednesday, then,' Rita said.

Sharon nodded. 'To you and Gary.'

Rita continued to see Dr Allan just as she continued to see Gary. As the weeks progressed, Gary began to stay the night sometimes during the week. This had worried Rita to begin with, she wasn't sure how William and Steve would react to the actual fact of them sleeping together. However, as usual, the boys took it in their calm, 'mature' way, accepting Gary's presence without any fuss. Gary was interesting enough to break through to them, he looked young, he was sporty and athletic, he smiled easily and always had time for them. In short they liked him and he was probably itinerant enough to warrant their attention. She had worried about tense atmospheres and associated problems. There were none.

350

Peace reigned at home, the memories of Christmas at her mother's faded and Rita settled back into Los Angeles life. She had vague thoughts about another book but, as yet, hadn't started anything. Instead she picked up her classes with Sharon and continued to jog around the canyon roads most mornings. The one thing she was most determined about since coming back from London was her desire not to slip into a comfortable middle age. Rita wasn't exactly fighting age, just trying to remain ambulatory. She might end up an old crone in expensive jogging shoes but that didn't seem to matter any more, at least she would be trying.

Her life with Gary fell into an easy pattern spent between his house in Laurel Canyon, mainly at weekends, and her place during the week. Rita's guilt pangs still occurred but they were less frequent than previously. As they emerged into the southern Californian spring, their lives, she thought, were in a reasonable state of repair. The boys thrived, she felt happier and Paul seemed to have calmed down of late, although they were actually spending less time with one another than before. Since Steve drove to Malibu with William now, even that meeting point was lost to them. More often than not they communicated over the phone. Conversation seemed to focus upon the progress of the boys and what Steve was going to study when he went to university the following autumn. Paul had taken to calling it the fall but she always found the American words uncomfortable if she used them. Sharon was always picking her up on things like petrol and curtains and pavement.

'You'll only confuse people,' Sharon warned with a grin.

'I feel silly using different words,' Rita replied, 'it sounds false.'

351

'You'd speak French in France, wouldn't you?' Sharon reasoned.

'That's not the same, though,' Rita said.

'Of course it's the same . . . you want the natives to understand you, don't you?'

'They do!'

Sharon looked sceptical. 'Listen, honey, I've been with you in a restaurant when you've asked for the bill and everyone's looked totally confused.'

'That's just one example,' Rita protested.

'It proves my point.'

'I haven't even developed an accent.'

'That's what you think, honey.'

'Do you think I have?' Rita wasn't sure whether she should be pleased or not.

'Sure, of course you have . . . it's kind of refined but it's an accent of some sort.'

Rita laughed. 'Okay, I'll attempt to speak your language.'

Sharon nodded with satisfaction. 'We'll make you an Angeleno yet.'

Rita smiled at her friend. She was never entirely certain if that was what she wanted.

Dr Allan was resting back in his chair, hands clasped together against his chest. 'Why does your happiness with Gary result in you feeling guilty about Nathan?'

Rita looked out through the tinted glass windows at the familiar white houses clinging to the canyon sides. She sometimes felt as though they had been sitting facing each other for years. 'I feel fine for most of the while . . . I feel great and then something clouds it all . . . and I don't feel comfortable with these emotions, it's as though Nathan's always there.'

'So, what are you saying, Rita, that Nathan wouldn't have wanted you to be happy?'

'I'm not sure what I'm saying.' She gave up, feeling dispirited again. 'I'm not even sure if I deserve to be happy.'

Dr Allan stared at her hard. 'Why should your happiness be conditional?'

Rita shrugged but made no effort to reply.

'Do you intend to spend the remainder of your life in this state of guilt for Nathan?'

Rita bit her bottom lip. 'I don't enjoy it, if that's what you mean.'

'You have strong feelings for Gary?' he asked.

She nodded. 'I'm not sure where it will lead.'

'And then you begin to have guilt pangs?'

'I can't help feeling that there must have been something . . . something else that I could have done, something to save Nathan. It never goes away, it's with me every single day.'

'Do you accept, rationally, that there was nothing you could have done?'

'I just keep asking why,' Rita admitted, 'why me?'

'Do you ever feel anger?'

She nodded, reaching down into her jacket pocket for a tissue, which she retrieved and dabbed at her eyes with. Rita felt she could sit in her chair in Dr Allan's office for ever and still not find the strength to deal with her loss. 'You mean with Nathan?'

He nodded. Sitting forward and picking up a pencil from his desk top, he scribbled a note on the carefully placed pad in front of him.

'I sometimes feel anger, yes.'

'With him, with Nathan?' he persisted.

'Yes,' she answered curtly.

The doctor nodded as though to encourage her, as though that was a good sign.

Rita blew her nose. 'The tears I've shed in your office,' she suddenly said, attempting to compose herself.

'You do very well, Rita,' he said almost warmly.

She smiled.

'Whatever the pain, and it will possibly always be there, you now have to accept what has happened and move on . . . Perhaps Gary may be one of the answers,' he suggested.

'I wouldn't want Gary to feel that he was being used in that way.'

'We all use one another precisely in that way,' he told her. 'You move on with the help of others. You mustn't view it in a negative way.'

'I don't want to go on alone,' she told him.

'When will you stop feeling guilty about Nathan?' he asked.

Rita almost winced at the question. 'I don't suppose I ever will.'

'Do you want to stop?'

She considered that cruel and didn't respond immediately. 'I want to know why, that's all, why he should do such a terrible thing.'

'And what if you never know?' the doctor asked her.

'Then I suppose I'll always think about it . . .'

'But what if you could know and it *was* your fault, what then?'

'At least I would know, even understand . . .'

'Do you think it's your fault, Rita?'

'Sometimes.'

'I see many victims of suicide,' he began, 'the parents and siblings of children who have taken their own lives, perfectly ordinary men and women whose lives have been devastated, and do you know something?' He leant forward across his desk top, his eyes firmly fixed on her. 'More often than not they all feel exactly the same as you and I tell them, "*don't.*"' He sat back again, still watching Rita. 'And that's my message to you.'

Rita blinked and remained silent.

'What did you do that was so awful, Rita? What did you do to him? Have you been telling me lies for the past months?'

'No,' she shook her head, 'I don't feel I ever did anything . . .'

'Then why the guilt?'

'Because he was my baby,' she said, breaking down completely. 'I should have known,' she insisted through the tears.

'What if he was sick, I mean momentarily deranged, how could you have known about it? How could you have helped? You were at the other end of London.'

She had no answers. 'Okay, you're right, rationally you're right but emotionally . . . in here,' she thumped at her breast, 'those kind of answers have no meaning.'

'Would Nathan have wanted this?' he asked directly. 'All of this horrible aftermath?'

'He's not here to experience any of it,' she replied sullenly. 'He wasn't there to see those faces at his funeral . . . our friends who looked at us with a mixture of pain and doubt, wondering just what Paul and Rita were doing to their children, just what we'd done for Nathan to kill himself . . .' Rita stopped, realizing what she'd just said. For a moment she had been furious with Nathan. She cleared her throat. 'Listen to me,' she said with embarrassment, 'listen to me,' her voice almost lost in a whisper.

Rita threw her car keys on to the coffee table between the sofas in the lounge and stepped out on to the patio, where she stood for a while, taking in the carefully tended grounds, her mind whirring over her session with Dr Allan. Something felt as though it had broken inside her. She had experienced a rage for what Nathan had done, anger which had surfaced and which remained with her. Suddenly she felt terribly hard done by, that Nathan had let her down or, perhaps, that she hadn't had the courage to do what he'd done.

She turned into the house, taking off her smart, businesslike suit and replacing it with jeans and T-shirt. She was sure she wasn't fooling Dr Allan by her immaculate appearance. He could spot a disorderly mind at twenty paces. Rita began to wonder what he must think of her. They discussed the most intimate details of her life and yet he always remained passive and self-contained, nodding away to encourage her, leaning back with his arms folded to listen, leaning forward, hands clenched on the desk in front of him to make a point. His little office had become a microcosm of her own life. Sometimes she even started to wonder if her life existed outside the white paint and chromium steel office with its garish oil paintings and tinted windows. At least, it seemed to Rita that Dr Allan's office was the only place left for her to be honest, to say what she wanted without alternatively upsetting or boring people.

Since the family Christmas at home, the trauma of her sister, the fear of her mother and grandmother's age creeping up on them, Rita had attempted to be more positive, to look forward and, whilst not forgetting the past, to put it in a more realistic framework. Gary was partially responsible for this new mood of optimism because in him, perhaps, she could see her future whilst accepting the past for all its horror.

She wandered out to the palm trees and sat at the redwood table, closing her eyes and trying to picture

Nathan's face but, as hard as she concentrated, nothing came.

In the spring Gary took Rita and the boys backpacking to Yosemite, where they pitched two tents under the pines on the dusty, ash-like earth. Gary explained the basics to them, things like the importance of keeping a clean camp site and hanging anything edible up in the high branches.

'And why is that?' Rita asked innocently.

'Bears,' Gary replied, standing back to admire his work, having just finished putting their tent up.

'You're joking!' Rita replied.

Gary shook his head. 'Look around you if you don't believe me.'

She turned a full three hundred and sixty degrees, looking up at the bags of food hanging down like peculiar pine fruits above the camp sites nearby. 'Bears?' she asked again with disbelief.

'Sure, they've been known to come down into the camps and they don't wait to be asked in before crashing through your tent!'

'My God,' Rita replied.

'The rangers keep a sharp eye out. They'll wake people at any hour if they find a dirty site . . . You just can't be too careful, Rita.'

'Did you hear that, boys?' Rita called across to Steve and William, who were still having problems with their own tent, which was pitched close to the round ring of stones where the camp fire could be lit as darkness fell.

'Sure,' Steve replied, pulling at a guy rope, 'we've to hang everything from the trees.'

'Have you brought a gun?' William asked Gary seriously.

'You've got nothing to worry about, honest,' Gary

357

assured them all. 'Just a few simple rules, obey them and everything will be fine.'

'Maybe tents weren't such a good idea,' Rita said. 'We might still be able to rent a lodge.'

'It'll be fine . . . do us all the world of good,' Gary insisted.

'Were you a Boy Scout?' William asked him.

'Nope,' Gary smiled, folding his arms across his chest.

'We don't have to light a camp fire and sing songs around it, then,' William continued.

Gary laughed. 'Listen, by the time we've hiked a few miles, you won't feel much like anything but hitting the sack!'

'That sounds like a threat,' Steve grinned, hammering in another tent peg.

Rita poked her head out of the tent, looking up at Gary and then across towards the boys, and wondered quite what she'd let herself in for.

Gary woke everyone early the next morning and cooked them all a breakfast of eggs and bacon and beans. Mist was hanging between the trees and there were sounds of other early risers in the distance. A group of men with London accents were gathering together mountains of climbing equipment on a nearby site. Steve and William crawled out from their sleeping bags like wriggling pupae. Gary poured them each a mug of hot black coffee and soon everyone was squatting around balancing breakfast on their knees.

'What part of Yosemite is this?' Rita asked.

'We're in the heart of Yosemite in the valley of the Merced River,' Gary explained, 'and in a while, when you city slickers are quite ready, we're going to take a gentle hike up through the pines towards Glacier Point.'

'Sounds miles,' William remarked.

'A few,' Gary agreed.

'Sounds ominous,' Rita yawned.

'Nonsense,' Gary chided them. 'What are you, boys – men or mice?'

Steve looked up. 'Give us a lump of cheese and I'll show you!'

Gary roared with laughter, standing up and beginning to clean their camp. 'Come on, come on, we don't want to waste this fabulous morning, all this clean air and not a trace of smog!'

Rita stood up, stretching and feeling about a hundred and twenty. Despite the best will in the world she couldn't really admit to enjoying life under what Gary euphemistically called canvas. However, she liked to think of herself as being a good sport and she was sure the fresh air would be good for them all. At last they put on their small backpacks with their 'rations' for the hike and set off.

Over the next few days Gary led them on several expeditions. From Glacier Point to Mirror Lake, which they admired at sunset with Mount Watkins in the distance. From Yosemite Falls to the base of Half Dome. She felt permanently ravenous and the boys, true to form, never stopped eating from morning to night. Even with all her athletic endeavour, her tennis and aerobics and jogging, Rita still felt the strain of the hikes Gary took them on but she did feel a sense of achievement at completing them. She enjoyed the outdoor life despite the somewhat primitive conditions and she loved Yosemite. Gary had taken her at dusk to see Half Dome reflected in the Merced River, the falling sun making the rough granite walls red and orange, with its clear image caught in the still, dark waters. They had left the boys at the camp site whilst they stood, hand in hand, looking at the beautiful sunset, the crisp outline of the tall pines set against the fading sky.

Gary put his arm around Rita. 'This is okay, isn't it?' he said.

She smiled. 'It's fabulous,' she replied.

'One more day to go.' He watched as the last rays of sun disappeared and darkness descended.

'We can come back in the summer,' Rita suggested, 'take a lodge or something.'

Gary chuckled. 'You mean, you'll forsake the tent?'

Rita laughed. 'Absolutely.'

He took her hand again and they walked back to the camp, finding that the boys had already gone to sleep.

Gary and Rita whispered together in the silence, undressing together in the confined space of their tent, bumping and touching each other, giggling and attempting to stifle their laughter as they tried to establish some space for themselves. When Gary had stripped to his underpants and Rita was in T-shirt and briefs, he rolled across, leaning over her, kissing her, his hands roving across her body.

'Have you ever done it in a tent?' he asked, laughter in his voice.

'You're too noisy for a tent,' she replied, 'we'd wake everyone up!'

Gary laughed, kissing her once more before breaking apart and wriggling into their sleeping bag. 'Come on, Rita, get your bod in here and keep me warm.'

Rita grumbled something and finished undressing, dragging a brush through her hair before climbing into the sack with him. She wrapped herself around Gary's body, falling asleep almost immediately.

They spent their last afternoon swimming and sunbathing by the Merced River. Steve was dozing in the afternoon

360

sunshine whilst Rita and Gary were engrossed in conversation, their legs dangling in the water. William was swimming, and watching some youths diving into the river from a fallen tree.

Rita was laughing at something Gary had just said when she turned and saw William standing on the thick trunk. He stumbled, seemed to have regained his balance and then suddenly crashed forwards, falling headlong into the river. Rita smiled at his prank, telling Gary to look at the antics of her youngest son. She continued to smile until people on the opposite bank began standing and pointing at the spot where William had gone under.

'My God!' Rita said, her voice almost a whisper. She stood up as Gary dashed by her, dived into the river and swam across to William, dragging him out and pulling him on to the bank.

Rita stared in horror, frozen to the spot, looking at the blood dribbling from a gaping wound on William's head. Gary immediately began the kiss of life. Steve was crouched nearby, his face drawn and white. A group of onlookers had gathered at a discreet distance to watch. Rita waited and waited for William to start breathing again. Gary took another deep breath before putting his mouth over William's and starting the process once more.

She listened to the rasp of Gary's breath, watching William's chest rising as his lungs were gently filled. Everything seemed quite unreal to her, it was as though the nightmare was beginning all over again, only this time she had witnessed it. Gary was raising his head again. Everything seemed to be happening in slow motion. She was certain that William was dead. Gary bent over. Steve was crying, rubbing at his eyes. Rita looked down at the back of Gary's head as he breathed into William again. There was a sudden clicking sound and a bubbling, choking noise. William's head jerked back and turned to the side and Gary sat up as the boy's eyes flickered open, uncomprehending for a moment.

Rita and Steve moved close, kneeling at William's side. They were both crying and laughing, crying and laughing, crying and laughing.

They drove back to LA, racing at break-neck speed in Gary's new jeep through Fresno and Bakersfield and on to the city. A local doctor had patched William up, putting some stitches in the open wound on his head and attending to some other cuts and grazes on his body.

William was immediately admitted to hospital, where he was examined carefully and admitted into a private room overnight. Apart from a headache, he seemed in good shape. They all took turns sitting with him. He watched TV and dozed, the lights of LA bright in the blackness beyond his high window.

Rita called Paul, leaving a message on his answering machine, and he duly arrived late that evening, still in evening clothes from a dinner he had been attending. Rita explained exactly what had happened, feeling shaky and sick at the memory.

'Where the hell were you?' Paul asked her.

'We were on the opposite bank,' Rita replied, looking him directly in the eye, as though not quite believing the question or the way he had asked it.

'How long was he under for?' Paul demanded to know.

'Seconds,' Gary replied, standing close to Rita. 'It was a matter of seconds by the time I'd got him out.'

Paul nodded at him before turning his attention to Rita. 'I can't believe you would let this happen,' he told her angrily.

'Me?' She sounded appalled at his suggestion. 'I didn't do anything . . .'

'You were supposed to be in charge of him.'

'It was an accident, Paul,' Gary interrupted calmly.

Paul stared at him but made no reply before brushing past them both and walking into William's room. He examined his son, who, by this time, was feeling a good deal brighter.

'Did you hit a rock or something?' Paul asked William.

'They said it was a rock . . . I slipped off the tree trunk and couldn't control my dive.'

Paul nodded. Holding a forefinger up in front of William's face, he moved it towards the bridge of the boy's nose, watching the reactions carefully. 'You'll probably have a headache for a few days,' he told William at last.

William nodded. 'That's what the other doctors said. Why do I have to stay in here? I feel okay.'

'It's a precaution. You can go home in the morning.'

'I feel fine,' William protested.

'Did you know that Gary saved your life?' Paul asked matter-of-factly.

'Sure.' William looked serious.

'You've been extremely lucky, William,' Paul told him. 'You gave your mum a nasty shock.'

'I didn't mean to, it was a mistake.'

'Hmm, a mistake that nearly cost you your life.'

'Oh, Dad,' William complained.

'If Gary hadn't been so quick-witted, the outcome could have been disastrous but . . .' he sat on the edge of the bed for a moment, taking William's hand, 'let's thank God you're fine now.'

William sank back on to the pillows, closing his eyes. 'I feel sick,' he said.

Paul smiled. 'You will, it's perfectly normal.' He squeezed his son's hand again before standing up to leave. 'You're a very lucky chap . . . I'll call in tomorrow, then.'

William attempted a grin. 'Thanks for coming, Dad.'

Paul smiled again. 'Try and get some rest now,' he ordered, walking away.

'All right?' Rita said, standing up as Paul emerged from the room.

'Fine,' he nodded. 'You both look shattered . . . He's fine, you've really no need to stay here now.'

'I'm going to stay,' Rita replied. 'Gary will take Steve back in a while.'

Paul put out his hand and shook Gary's. 'We were lucky you were able to deal with it,' he said. 'Thank you.'

Gary smiled. 'It was pure instinct . . . I learnt resuscitation years ago. I never thought I'd ever have to practise it for real and I hope to Christ I'm never in that situation again!'

'Well, William has you to thank for his life.' Paul looked at Rita. 'Are you okay?'

She nodded.

'You look bloody awful . . . Go home and get some sleep,' he instructed her.

'I'm okay,' she replied. 'Just a bit shocked, that's all.'

'Take a sleeping pill and go home to bed,' he told her, turning to Gary for support. 'Can't you make her see some sense?'

'I think we'll stay for a while, all the same, Paul,' he replied. 'It's been quite a day for us all and we're a bit beyond sleep at the moment.'

'I'll call you later then,' Paul said to Rita, turning to leave. 'How's Steve?' he asked, pausing for a moment.

'Upset,' Rita said. 'We sent him down to get some coffee.'

Paul nodded. 'I'll call, then,' he repeated, and was gone.

'Jesus,' Rita breathed, turning into Gary's arms. 'I *knew* he'd blame me.'

'He was upset,' Gary comforted her.

'I'd hate to be one of his students, he's so bloody imperious,' she complained.

'Maybe he was right, maybe we should go home . . . What's the point of sitting around here all night?' Gary asked.

'You go,' Rita said wearily. 'You and Steve go.'

'I'm not going,' Steve said over her shoulder, 'no way. You two go, I'll stay.'

Rita broke away from Gary and turned to Steve. 'Where's the coffee?'

'The machine's out of order.'

'Right.' Rita took a deep breath and counted up to ten. 'I'm going in to sit with William for a while. Maybe you two could rustle up something hot to drink,' she said, leaving them standing together in the corridor.

William was sleeping, the light still on over his bed. Rita leant across, gently brushing his hair away from his forehead, examining the row of stitches which ran in a neat line across his left temple. There would be a scar but it wouldn't be too noticeable.

Rita switched off the light and sat down heavily in the bedside chair. With a moment to consider what had happened, with a chance to sit and think for a while, she knew just how close they had come to disaster. Her hands were shaking uncontrollably and she began to sob in the shadowy room, now lit only by a small lamp, with a blue shade, sitting on a cabinet in the far corner. She had relaxed for a moment, she had allowed herself the luxury of believing everything was fine, and this had happened. She could see William falling and remembered laughing at him, thinking it a stunt of some sort, and the awful realization, that sweet sickness rising in her stomach as the truth hit her.

William called out some nonsense in his sleep and moved about for a moment before settling down again.

She said a private prayer to a deity she had no belief in: 'Please God, no more . . . no more . . .' she repeated over and over again.

William returned home early the next afternoon, with instructions to take it easy for a few days. He sat out by the pool, watching Steve and Jem swim, whilst Rita took a belated tennis lesson with Kirk.

Kirk was looking his normal immaculate self and Rita was looking and feeling thoroughly dishevelled after not having slept the previous night, and she was still feeling the strain of what had happened in Yosemite. Kirk fed her forehand returns and Rita swung the racket head back, hitting through the ball, making crisp responses, each return harder than the last until Kirk was dancing all over the court. She began to find some relief in the concentration and the physical effort. The lesson progressed smoothly for the next hour. She did everything well, even passing him down the line on her backhand returns. Her serve was accurate and, at the end, Kirk came round the net to congratulate her as she leant over her tennis racket, breathing hard.

'You're getting better,' he smiled.

Rita looked up into his handsome face. She laughed for the first time in what seemed an age. 'I've a good teacher,' she replied.

'Your service action is still a bit out, though,' he said, standing behind her, making her stand up and pulling her racket arm through the motion of a swing. 'Do you see?' he asked, repeating the motion.

She could feel the warmth of his body through the dampness of her tennis clothes, the baggy khaki shorts and a blue T-shirt. He moved to her side as Rita practised the action again. 'I'm not strong enough to get much power behind it,' she said.

'You don't need that much power, it's just a question of weight distribution . . . putting your weight behind the shot.' He picked up a tennis ball. 'Watch,' he told her, tossing the ball up high and hitting it across the net with tremendous speed and weight of shot. It was like having an animated textbook on court. 'Do you see?' he asked, smiling and turning to her.

'Yes, I suppose so.'

'Okay,' he grinned, 'lesson over.'

'Phew!' Rita breathed out. 'That was a tough one.'

Kirk nodded. 'Steve told me what happened . . . I wasn't sure if you'd want the lesson,' he said as they left the court.

'Listen, dear heart,' Rita said, placing a hand on his forearm for a moment, 'you're a real life-saver. This is very therapeutic, almost better than seeing my shrink.'

He looked at her. 'Well, if there's ever anything I can do to help . . .'

This seemed to be rather outside his usual frame of reference but Rita felt quite touched at his concern. 'Just keep on batting those balls at me!' she laughed, realizing how ludicrous it was. 'Come on, have you got time for a Coke?'

Paul came over after work. He had dropped in on William early that morning and had phoned later to see how he was. Rita invited him to come and see for himself, and he stayed on for supper. Steve was at Sharon's for his evening meal, and William had gone up to his room and was fast asleep by nine o'clock.

'How are you feeling now?' Paul asked her.

'Fine. A bit tired but okay.'

'It must have been quite a shock.'

Rita nodded. 'It was, I just don't know what would

have happened if Gary hadn't been there. I mean, he could have been off hiking . . . anything!'

Paul nodded. 'Anyway, William seems fine now. Steve looks in worse shape!' he said.

'Steve's overtired. He's hardly left William's side . . . I virtually had to push him out of the door this evening.'

'He's scared, quite obviously.'

'History repeating itself.' Rita felt unnerved at the idea. 'This time it was an accident, though.'

'Just when you think everything is somewhere back to normal . . .' He looked at her. 'I thought we were getting over Nathan a bit.' He shrugged.

'Jesus, that's taken you many a long year to say, hasn't it?' She sounded surprised. 'You've never said his name without some prompting from me before.'

'Then perhaps the healing process has begun at last,' he replied calmly.

'I don't think you ever get over it, you just learn how to survive it, to carry on with a semblance of normality.'

'I think you've done terribly well, Rita,' he admitted, pouring more wine from the bottle he had brought along.

'You always behaved as though I was the guilty party.'

'No.' He pointed his fork at her. 'You've always borne all the guilt, you took it all on board.'

'Well, that hasn't changed,' Rita admitted.

'You have no reason to feel guilty over Nathan,' he insisted, shaking his head. 'You've always been a wonderful mother to our kids . . .' His voice suddenly caught with emotion and he had to stop speaking. Tears sparkled in his eyes.

Rita was completely taken aback. Part of her thought it very touching. Part of her felt as though they were playing out a scene from some schmaltzy film or play. She knew just how 'wonderful' she'd been, and she didn't really need Paul to tell her that now at this late stage in the proceedings. 'You've *really* changed, do you know that?'

Paul blinked. 'Changed?'

'I think it must be the influence of Joanne . . . she's obviously bringing you out a bit.' There wasn't a hint of rancour in her voice. Rita actually felt pleased for him, thinking how awful it would be for him to spend the rest of his life locked up inside some paternalistic, macho-British-stiff-upper-lip nightmare. Perhaps the Paul of twenty years ago was beginning to emerge once more. 'Tell me about her,' she said.

'Joanne?' Paul sipped his wine. 'Oh, Joanne is just . . .' he shrugged, and then laughed. 'Joanne!' But he did tell her, outlining her background and her successful career, attempting to describe her and what she was like. Revealing just how much he loved her.

It was a complete revelation to Rita to see him so animated and so happy. The understanding of just how unhappy they had been over a number of years was only now becoming clear to her. Joanne had turned something on inside Paul and it was almost rejuvenating in its impact. Rita had given up ever expecting him to discuss Nathan with her, and yet, here he was introducing their dead son into the conversation. She felt an unexpected warmth for Joanne that was entirely genuine and heartfelt. In an odd way Joanne was keeping her family together, which, again, was an extraordinary turn of events.

'So, you're happy, then?' she said. She also grinned so that it didn't become an accusation.

'Are *you*, Rita?'

'I asked first,' she replied.

Paul smiled. 'I suppose I am, yes.'

'Don't be so grudging about it, then,' she said.

'I'm not grudging.'

'You spoke about Nathan before,' Rita said to him.

'Yes.'

'Do *you* think we will ever get over it?'

'I doubt it, like you. The next best thing is to get on with the next stage in our lives.'

It sounded like the sort of practical advice Dr Allan might give her.

'Do you think he hated us?' she asked suddenly.

'Hated us?' Paul sounded shocked. 'Nathan?' He looked at her, perplexed at such a suggestion. 'No, of course he didn't hate us.'

'Me, then,' Rita said.

'No,' Paul replied firmly.

'Then why did he do it?' It was the constant question inside her head, the one she asked herself a hundred times each day.

'You know there isn't an answer to that,' he said calmly.

'I can't help thinking there must be one.'

'There doesn't have to be.'

'I wouldn't even mind if it was my fault . . . if only I knew.'

'We both have to deal with our guilt, we have to learn how to do that.'

'I've read case histories about this sort of thing,' Rita continued. 'Sometimes, years and years afterwards, when everything seems all right again, the mother of a suicide kills herself . . .'

'Oh, Rita, for God's sake, what are you saying this for?'

'Because I'm scared rotten, I suppose, and because I'm falling in love with Gary and I'm not sure if it's very fair. I don't want him caught up in all of my troubles.'

'Gary's the best thing that could have possibly happened,' Paul insisted. 'He's a good man.'

Rita smiled. It was almost like his mother talking about

people as 'good sorts'. 'He's fantastic but do I deserve him?'

'Of course. I should have thought that question ought to be reversed – does he deserve you?'

'How gallant! You know, it's like being with you when you were eighteen.'

'You didn't know me when I was eighteen,' he reminded her.

'Well, whatever . . . God knows what happened to us.'

'Nothing happened to us.'

'Nathan died,' she said quietly.

'He did, but that's no reason for you to suspend the remainder of your life. We go on, Rita. As people, we just endure and carry on . . . It's all we can do now, and Nathan wouldn't have wanted it to be any different.'

She thought about Paul's words. 'You left me when the pain of staying became too much for you to bear. I think you did the right thing,' she nodded in agreement with herself, even smiling a little at the memories now. 'If we'd remained together I suppose one of us would have been destroyed by it all.'

'I think it's all going to work out,' he admitted.

'There's some good old Californian optimism for you!' Rita laughed. 'God, you've changed.'

Paul looked at her but made no response. For a second there appeared to be a great sadness in his eyes.

'We have some good memories,' Rita suggested.

'Of course we do. We were a good team, and an extremely happy family . . .'

'"*Nous avons changé tout cela*,"' she said without really thinking, quoting Molière.

'Situations changed us,' Paul said, 'Nathan's death was the final straw.'

'And, yet, it could have brought us closer together.'

'There were things going wrong with our marriage a long time before that,' he replied gently.

'Yes.' She placed her knife and fork on the half-empty plate and finished her wine. 'But, anyway,' she said more brightly, 'at least we're still together in a kind of way . . . I hope we can remain friends in the years ahead.'

'Of course,' he answered, reaching across the table and taking her hand for a moment. 'For God's sake, we're still married!'

Rita laughed. 'God knows what we're going to do about that.'

'Why, are you planning to marry again?' he asked with interest.

'No!' Rita was surprised at his question. 'Are you?'

Paul shook his head.

'Once bitten, eh?'

'Not at all . . . I just don't want another wife.'

Rita wasn't quite sure but she took that as being a compliment and, raising her glass, albeit empty now, made them a toast. 'To the next twenty years, then.'

Paul smiled and raised his glass to hers. 'To the next twenty years.'

Steve arrived home a little after his father had left. Rita was in her room, lying on top of the bed, wrapped up in her robe, the one the boys had given her for Christmas, when he came in to see her. She was reading another best-seller, one that Sharon had suggested, an enormous volume full of torrid sex and exotic surroundings with heroines who always had shattering orgasms with men who always serviced them to perfection.

'Okay?' Steve asked, flopping down opposite her in the armchair by the window.

'Yes, your dad stayed for supper.'

'Oh, yes . . . how's William?'

'Fine, he's been asleep for most of the evening but that's okay, your dad says it's a good sign.'

'Right.'

'Did you have a good time over at Sharon's?'

'Sure.'

'Good, what did you do?'

'Watched TV and went over some school work with Jem.'

'You're going back to school in a week, your final term before university.' She closed the book. 'Are you looking forward to it?'

'Sure.'

'You don't sound very enthused.'

'It's a long way off, I'll get more interested when it's nearer the time.'

Rita nodded. 'Are you pleased that you and Jem will be joining the Law Faculty together?'

'It should be a help, yes.'

'But you would've preferred to be going somewhere other than UCLA?' she said.

'It's not that.'

'Then what?' Rita asked.

'It's still having to live at home as well.'

'I thought that's what you wanted.'

'Jem and I were talking about getting an apartment . . .'

'I suppose it's a possibility,' Rita replied.

'It needn't be straight away,' he said.

'I agree,' Rita told him. 'I'm sure we can sort something out.'

'Really?' Steve smiled at last.

'I'll speak to your father and Sharon and Bill, of course, see what they all think.'

Steve got up and walked to the door. 'I'll check on William before bed,' he told her.

'Okay, if he's awake he might want a drink or something.'

'I'll see to it, then,' Steve assured her, closing her bedroom door quietly behind him.

William was awake when Steve went into his bedroom.

'Okay?' Steve enquired.

'I've got a stinking headache . . . Dad left some pain-killers over there.' He pointed to the top of his cluttered work surface, where his school books were spread out with work he was doing before their trip to Yosemite.

Steve picked up the small white plastic tub of pills and read the instructions. Emptying two out into his palm, he handed them to William with a fresh glass of water which he fetched from the bathroom. He watched as his brother swallowed them down. 'That must have been some knock on the head.'

William grinned, touched the row of stitches and then lay back again. 'I haven't really thanked Gary yet.'

'He'll probably be here tomorrow. He called earlier to see how you were . . . you were sleeping!'

William nodded. 'Dad said that I can go swimming tomorrow.'

'That's good,' Steve replied, smiling.

'Yes.'

'You know we thought you'd drowned, don't you?' Steve said.

'I don't remember anything after hitting the water,' William admitted.

'I thought you were dead,' Steve told him.

William looked at his brother's worried face. 'I'm fine now,' he insisted, 'everything back to normal. I probably won't do much diving for a while but, apart from that, it'll all be pretty much business as usual.'

'I've never felt so frightened,' Steve said. 'It was even

374

worse than Nathan in a way because I was there and felt absolutely useless. Gary had dragged you out before I even fully understood what was happening . . . I wouldn't have known what to do, anyway.'

'Sure you would,' William encouraged. 'We did life-saving classes in London, don't you remember? We had to save one another from drowning and practise swimming lengths in our pyjamas.' He smiled at the memory.

'I missed the mouth-to-mouth bit, though,' Steve said. 'I bunked off and went to the pictures with Nathan.'

'Did you?' William laughed. 'I don't remember . . . Well, it's a good job Gary got to me first then, I guess!'

Steve didn't smile. 'You're all right, then?'

'Yes, I'm okay. Go to bed, you look knackered!'

'Give me a call if you want anything.'

William nodded. 'I will,' he assured Steve.

'Okay,' Steve said, leaving him, ''night.'

'See you.'

Steve paused for a few seconds at the door before going to his own room, where he lay down on top of his bed and stared up at the ceiling, his mind turning over the events of the last forty-eight hours. After William had been admitted to the hospital and the doctors were checking him over, Steve had found a toilet, where he had been ferociously sick. Afterwards he had crumpled down on the floor of the cubicle, shaking and feeling icy cold. He felt that he was in some way to blame. After all, William had asked him to stay in the water for a while longer, hoping that Steve would watch him dive, but Steve felt bored and cold by then and wanted to sit in the sun for a while. When he returned to the opposite bank Gary and his mother were fooling around and they joked with him. Steve spread out a towel and lay down to dry off and improve his tan. He must have dozed off within a minute or so because the next thing he became conscious of was the sound of his mother's voice rising in growing hysteria as she pointed across the water. Gary was in the process of swimming out to where William had gone under by the fallen tree. He watched William's prone body breaking the surface as Gary pulled him out, William's head thrown back, his skin white with a tinge of blueness about his lips. Steve could hardly believe the scene as it unfolded before him. Certain now that William was dead he wished that Gary would stop the pantomime of resuscitation. It all seemed futile and only prolonged the inevitable truth. Steve was stricken with panic and paralysed by fear. He had done nothing to save Nathan and merely sat by as his youngest brother died in front of his eyes.

Now, of course, it was all right, William had been brought back, he was alive and recovering. But still the doubt remained with Steve; if only he'd stayed close by, none of it would have occurred.

He turned his face to the pillow and sobbed, feeling full of guilt, alone and afraid in the depth of such grief, crying for both Nathan and William as well as himself.

Chapter 11

As the summer term began, Rita sighed a breath of relief. She watched Steve and William leaving for school together on the first morning and went to the redwood table. Here she sat with the revision notes she had been sitting on since Easter, suggesting the changes she might make to the Woolf book. She worked for most of the morning, engrossed in the technical nature of her task, until Sharon dropped round for lunch.

'Your boys get off okay this morning?' Sharon asked.

Rita nodded. 'I think they were relieved to be back after the Easter we've had!'

Sharon looked serious. 'How's Steve?'

Rita pondered her friend's question for a while. 'I don't know,' she admitted. 'He's become very unsettled since the accident, veering between extremes of mood . . . Why, have you noticed anything?'

'He just seems a little manic, as though he's on a perpetual high. He never seems to stop moving. Jem's no slouch when it comes to sports but Steve's desire to just play on and on wears even him out!'

'I think William's accident has upset him much more than he's let on. You know, he's *always* with William and, if he's out anywhere, Steve asks where he is and how long he will be and why he's gone.'

'What does Paul say?'

'Paul thinks I'm overreacting. He says Steve is having to deal with a lot of different things at the same time and that, naturally, he's under pressure.' Rita sounded unconvinced. 'You mention Steve's manic behaviour, but he stayed in bed virtually all day on Saturday, which is unheard of!'

'I guess it's just a reaction to events,' Sharon replied. 'I'm sure that once he settles into the term, things will get back to normal.'

'God, I hope so!' Rita smiled. 'I can't take much more.'

'We have to begin apartment-hunting for them,' Sharon said. 'I hope you're prepared for a hard slog.'

Rita grinned. 'I think it could be fun.'

'Fun?' Sharon laughed at her friend's suggestion. 'Say that after we've been at it a few days . . . it'll be hell!'

'They want something at the beach,' Rita told her.

'They'll accept what we can get in the price range we can afford. I think we can safely assume that the beach is out.'

'Well, we can but try.'

Sharon agreed. 'I hope we're doing the right thing.'

'In letting them leave home?'

'No,' Sharon grinned, 'in being foolish enough to volunteer to help find them alternative accommodation.'

'It *will* be fun!' Rita insisted.

'You British have a *very* weird sense of humour!'

Rita laughed at that, tossing the salad for their lunch.

Gary had just landed a small speaking part in a big film that was being produced at Warner Brothers. He took her out that evening to celebrate with a dinner party at a friend's house in Nichols Canyon.

This was the other side of Gary's life, members of the film community, writers and production people rather than actors. She wore her black suit from the London January sales, and looked businesslike and efficient. Everyone else was very casual which made her want to turn and flee when she realized how terribly formal her dress was. It was also not a dinner party, as she had been told by Gary, but a kind of running buffet which extended from the main lounge out along the patio to the pool. The house seemed very similar to Gary's and she wasn't the slightest bit surprised to learn that he had, indeed, been responsible for building it.

Their host was called George and he was huge and hairy with a Karl Marx-type beard and thick blue-framed glasses. George was a writer, a script-writer who had several 'projects' in 'development'. Rita spent most of the evening talking to George's wife Sally, who was blonde and incredibly vivacious and who told her all about everyone in the house. Most of them were between jobs and most of them seemed to be regular beneficiaries of George's largesse.

'Gary's told us a lot about you,' Sally confided, 'he likes you a lot.' She smiled, munching into a thick chicken leg.

Rita smiled back. 'I'm pleased to hear it.'

'No, really, I've never seen him so serious over anyone before.'

Rita laughed. 'Have you known him long?'

'Oh, Jesus, yes, years and years. We're just sorry he never acts . . . the parts he's turned down are nobody's business!'

'Why is that?'

'He won't play their games,' Sally replied confidentially.

'What sort of games?' Rita asked.

'Oh, you know, I scratch your back, you scratch mine.'

Rita shook her head. 'No, not really.'

'He prefers to build things than do crap films,' Sally said. 'God alone knows what kind of money he's given up for the sake of his "art"!'

'Well, that seems entirely honourable to me,' Rita said.

'Sure it's honourable, but when it comes time to pay the rent we can't all turn our hand to building someone a

379

house or turning out expensive garden furniture and poolside tables for Beverly Hills.'

'He's probably too old to make it in films now, anyway,' Rita said.

Sally nodded, waving at somebody across the illuminated pool. 'But he's still incredibly sexy, isn't he?'

Rita laughed. 'He's very nice, yes.'

'You're married, aren't you?' Sally asked, turning her full attention towards Rita again.

'Yes.'

'Your old man's the world-famous authority on something?'

'My husband's a surgeon,' Rita replied.

'But you're separated?'

'Yes.'

'Gary's crazy about you,' Sally said, her words slurring a little as she reached for another drink. 'You're *so* lucky . . . most of the women here would give anything to have Gary.'

Rita laughed.

'It's the truth, really, believe me.'

'Do you work in the film business too?' Rita asked, anxious to change the subject.

'Sure, I'm an out-of-work film editor.'

'Oh . . . I see.'

'Sure you do, dear,' Sally said, patting Rita's arm as she got up rather unsteadily, wandered across to a group of people standing by the pool and flung her arms around an extremely young man, laughing loudly.

'Hi,' Gary said, slipping into the seat beside her.

Rita turned to face him. 'Hello.'

'Having a good time?'

'George's wife was just giving me the lowdown on their guests. It would seem that every female here has the hots for you!'

380

Gary laughed. 'Oh, that's just Sally, don't take any notice of her, she likes to shock.'

'She succeeds!' Rita replied.

'No,' Gary shook his head, 'come on.' He took her hand, pulling her to her feet. 'I'll show you around the place.'

'The house that Gary built,' Rita said, staring at him. When they reached the guest bedroom, at the far end of the building away from the throng of guests, he closed the door behind them and turned the key. 'Are you crazy?' she asked.

He was already removing his jacket. 'Absolutely. Let's be a little crazy.'

'But what will your friends think?'

'That lot?' He gestured behind him. 'They're already out of their heads . . . Hollywood party, coke and dope and God alone knows what.'

'You're kidding!' Rita sounded shocked.

'What difference does it make?'

'I don't want to end up in prison.'

'Relax,' he soothed, moving to her and kissing her gently.

'Look,' Rita said, breaking away from his embrace, 'if you want to make love, why can't we just go back to your house . . . if it's that important to you right now?'

'It's always that important,' he told her.

'Let's go, then,' she said.

He looked at her. 'Really?'

'Yes.'

They stood in silence, the sounds from the party drifting in to them, permeating the dark room, detached and strange. 'Okay,' he replied.

'Won't your friends mind?'

'They won't know . . . we'll just leave.'

'Can we do that? Won't anyone notice?'

'No.' He moved across the room to the window, pulling open the curtains to reveal sliding glass doors which opened on to the pathway at the side of the house. He closed the door carefully behind them and walked ahead of Rita, leading her to the driveway and his jeep, which he had parked strategically at the bottom for a quick getaway.

'They'll think us so ill-mannered,' Rita told him as they drove away.

'George won't think anything,' he insisted.

'He's used to this?' Rita wondered.

'Not exactly,' Gary replied. 'I'll call him later and explain, or we could even go back again.'

'I think you're enjoying this little game of yours just a bit too much, creeping away to have a little junga with your woman.'

'A little what?' Gary laughed at her expression.

'Junga,' she repeated.

'What is junga?'

'A polite word, a euphemism for fuck!'

'Jesus!' Gary roared with laughter, 'let's get to it then, let's get to that junga-junga . . .'

Gary had come very soon after entering Rita and he left her quickly, falling into an exhausted sleep at her side. She'd stroked his shoulder and kissed his cheek and dressed quickly, leaving his house quietly and driving home.

A dark shadow in William's room made Rita's heart stop for a second before she realized it was Steve. He was sitting by his brother's bedside, watching.

'What's the matter?' Rita whispered.

Steve didn't answer at first.

'Steve,' she said a little more sharply.

At last he turned to her. 'I should have done something . . . I could have saved him.' Steve looked strange in the half-light from the hallway.

'Gary was there, he did everything you could have done,' she replied, comforting his obvious distress.

'No, no, no, I don't mean that, I mean Nathan!'

'Nathan?' Rita was confused. She felt her heart beating faster and faster. 'What do you mean, Steve?'

'I knew that something was up,' he continued, suddenly moving from the bedside and brushing past her, almost running down the hallway and into his own room.

Rita followed, finding him face down on the bed, his head buried in a pillow. 'What the hell do you mean?' she demanded, feeling angry and frightened to death at the same time. She wished that Paul was there to cope with this as well.

'He told me,' Steve said, his voice muffled, turning over. 'Nathan told me.' He was breathing very quickly, his words tumbling out as fractured sobs. 'He told me what he was going to do . . . Nathan told me . . .' Steve's face contorted as he started to cry, tears streaming down his cheeks. 'And I could have stopped him.'

'What?' Rita asked, beginning to panic, fear starting to rise up inside her.

'I could have stopped Nathan,' Steve insisted, looking wild-eyed, almost mad.

'No, no, you couldn't,' Rita argued, desperately trying to stay calm herself. 'No one knew.'

'I did,' Steve said, raising his voice in order to make her see, to make her understand.

'Steve . . .'

'Nathan told me he was going to kill himself.' He was almost shouting at Rita now, angry with her for being so dense, angry with himself.

383

'He *told* you?' Rita was astounded. 'When?' she asked, her voice hard.

'A few days, a week, maybe, before he did it . . . He said he didn't want to read medicine at university, he couldn't follow in Dad's footsteps – he was scared of failing . . .'

'But that's ridiculous, Steve, we never made him do anything, there was never any pressure.'

'That had nothing to do with it,' Steve said, sitting up, swinging his legs over the bedside and placing his head into his hands. 'Just being a member of this bloody family was pressure enough.'

Rita gasped. 'Why didn't he talk to us about it?'

'He was scared, can't you understand?' he asked angrily. 'Nathan was always bloody scared, he knew that he would never be a doctor . . .'

'Your father never told him to do any such thing,' Rita said. 'He never showed any signs of being distressed. The day before he died he told me how much he was looking forward to going to university.'

'He was terrified.'

'Terrified?' Rita mouthed like an idiot. 'What of?' Her voice was rising as hysteria grew within her. 'I don't understand what you're talking about.'

'You don't understand,' Steve replied darkly, 'because you've never wanted to understand.'

'That's not true,' Rita said, sitting down on the bed next to him. 'It isn't true.'

'Nathan couldn't tell you,' Steve continued.

'People don't kill themselves over not wanting to attend university,' she replied.

'Life was too much for him, Mum, why don't you listen?' Steve blew his nose and wiped his eyes. 'He never had any intention of going to university.'

'Then why did he appear so keen?' she asked.

'To please you and Dad.'

'But it made no difference to me what he did.'

'All Dad ever talked about was what Nathan would do when he qualified . . . following generations of eldest sons into the profession.' Steve sounded disgusted.

'When did he tell you?' Rita asked, her mind racing over Steve's outburst. 'What exactly did he say?'

Steve began to cry again. 'He said that if he weren't such a coward, killing himself would be the easy way out. He told me he'd got the solution to all of his problems . . .'

'And what did that mean?' she asked.

'The tablets, I guess.'

'Did you believe him?' Rita's voice was calmer now.

Steve shook his head. His eyes were closed tight, the tears squeezed from beneath the eyelids.

'Did William know?'

He took a shuddering breath. 'No.'

'Did you believe him?' she asked again.

'No – I don't know, he was drunk, rambling . . . confused.'

'Why didn't you say anything?' Rita asked, grabbing Steve's arm.

'He told me not to tell anyone. It's my fault, isn't it?' he said, turning to her, his eyes full of fear.

Rita walked from the bed to the window and sat on the padded window seat, looking hard at Steve. 'It's not your fault, Steve, don't be foolish.'

'I could have stopped it from happening,' he moaned.

'How?' she asked sharply. 'How could you?'

'I could have searched his room,' Steve suggested.

'Look, this is getting nowhere . . . It wasn't your fault. What Nathan did, whatever the reasons, was nothing to do with you and he shouldn't have said anything.'

'I loved him, Mum,' Steve told her, sounding for all the

world like a little boy again. 'I did.' He lay down, pulling his body up into the foetal position, sobbing for all he was worth.

Rita sat with him, attempting to soothe away his grief whilst holding her own feelings in. She had been astounded by Steve's revelation but she attempted to deal with his distress before anything else. After an hour or so – it might have been longer – all sense of time had been lost to her, Steve fell into an exhausted, fractured sleep. Still she stayed, waiting until he seemed calmer. She remained with him until first light broke at the window and she was able to make sense of the dark shapes of furniture in Steve's bedroom. She must have dozed off in the chair close to his bed, waking at every murmured sound or sudden movement.

Finally Rita crept along to her own room, from where she called Paul at the beach. He arrived as the sun was rising, the slam of his car door loud through the still morning air. Rita sat with him in the kitchen, pouring them black coffee and explaining what had happened.

'Do you think it's true?' he asked.

She nodded. 'Afraid so. You wouldn't have to ask that if you'd been with him . . . Jesus.' She pushed a hand through her short hair. 'I don't know what to do,' she admitted, shaking her head, starting to cry. 'I don't know . . . when will it all end, Paul?' she demanded.

'Obviously we have to get him some help,' Paul stated.

'Do you think we did push Nathan too far?' she asked, staring at him.

'No,' he replied. 'Don't even think that.'

Rita felt relief at his certainty but she was still unsure. 'I never remember him being upset, never.'

'Whatever Steve says Nathan told him, whatever Steve thinks, *we* have to be sure that there was no undue

386

pressure on Nathan to do anything he didn't want.' He looked at Rita. 'I'm absolutely sure there wasn't.'

'So, what was it, then? Was Nathan mad?'

'God knows, Rita, we can't speculate about it now, it's too late . . . We're not so stupid that we wouldn't have realized something so catastrophic was building up. No,' he shook his head, 'whatever Nathan's reasons, I just don't believe that it was planned in the way Steve suggests.'

'He must have saved the sleeping pills from some-where,' she challenged.

'He could have got them on the same day.'

Rita paced the kitchen floor. 'Then why tell Steve it was all too much? Why tell him he didn't want to go to university, that the pressure was too much to cope with?'

'I don't know,' Paul admitted. 'Did he ever say anything of the sort to you?'

'No, he always seemed keen to go.'

'Do you think I put pressure on him to study medicine?'

Rita shook her head. 'Although I think it was an assumption we made. Maybe that was pressure enough.'

'I can't believe that. Nathan was an intelligent, articulate adolescent, there was nothing abnormal in our relationship with him.'

'There must have been something, Paul,' she said suddenly. 'He's dead!' The word seemed to hang in the air between them.

Paul looked down into his half-empty mug but said nothing.

There was a sudden noise from upstairs, a dull thud followed by the sound of glass breaking. Rita looked up. 'Steve,' she said, rushing from the kitchen, followed by Paul, racing up the staircase and along the corridor into his room. The bathroom door was ajar, light from it streaming into the bedroom. Rita pushed the door open and then stepped back, recoiling in horror. Steve was sitting on the floor, almost under the wash basin, blood seeping from wounds on his wrists, a broken razor blade by one hand that was lying, palm up, at his side. His eyes were closed, his head resting against the white pedestal as though he were asleep.

Paul was kneeling at his son's side, looking up at Rita, mouthing words that she didn't hear straight away. 'Call the hospital . . . now!'

She had no recollection of moving but the next moment she was sitting on her bed, the buzzing telephone receiver in her hand, trying to stop the noise of her banging heart for a second before blindly tapping out the numbers and calling an ambulance.

Rita sat staring at Steve's face in the back of the swaying ambulance. Paul was following in the car. He had assured her that Steve's wounds were not serious, that he would be fine, but her shock was such that Paul's words meant little. She had rushed from the house, the flashing lights cutting a swathe through the pink and blue dawn. Sharon had come over, a white trenchcoat over her long night gown, her running shoes with the laces undone in her haste to be there. Rita couldn't remember what they had said, she was already diving into the back of the low vehicle, but she was aware that Sharon would stay at the house until she got back.

Then they were together, Rita and Paul, sitting in the bright hospital, waiting for the doctors to finish patching Steve up. She rested her head on the cold, white wall, turning to Paul.

'Three down,' she said, beginning to laugh, 'three down and one to go.' She pointed to herself as her hysteria grew, tears pouring down her face as she laughed and laughed and laughed . . . 'One to go,' she repeated, barely able to speak the words.

Rita woke up in darkness. For a moment she was disorientated, sitting up in her bed and not having any recollection of how she got there. The house was still and she moved across the large bed to switch a bedside lamp on, blinking into the brightness. She eased her legs over the edge of the mattress. She had a faint headache and felt groggy going into the bathroom, where she stared at her face in the mirror above the basin. It reminded her of a white mask, drawn and tired, with dark circles underneath her eyes. She turned on the cold water and bent down to splash handfuls of it on to her puffy features, reaching for a towel and dabbing at her skin. Pulling on her robe, she went downstairs, where she found Sharon in the lounge with William and Jem watching TV.

'Hi,' Rita said, entering the room and sitting heavily on the sofa next to Sharon.

'How are you feeling?' Sharon asked, smiling.

'I'm not sure,' Rita replied, scratching her head. 'How long have I been asleep?'

'Since lunchtime . . . about nine hours.' She looked at her watch. 'It's just nine-thirty now. Paul gave you a sleeping tablet when you returned from the hospital.'

Rita nodded, beginning to remember. 'Are you sure he didn't hit me over the head with something?'

Sharon grinned. 'Want something to eat . . . drink?' she asked, standing up. 'I know that Jem and William will.'

'All right, William?' Rita asked him, following Sharon out of the lounge and into the kitchen.

William nodded and smiled, turning back to the screen and the football game.

'So,' Rita began, sitting at the table, head in hands, 'what the hell's going on?'

'Calm down,' Sharon instructed, placing a mug of coffee in front of her. 'Steve's okay, Paul said the wounds were not as serious as they looked.'

'Where's Paul?' She looked up at the kitchen clock.

'He said for you to call when you felt like it.'

Rita yawned. 'Jesus, I feel as though I'd been whacked on the head.'

'You were close to collapse when Paul brought you home.'

'Have you been here since this morning?'

Sharon nodded. 'It's no trouble, Rita.'

'Jesus.'

'William slept through it all, he didn't know that anything was wrong until he came down this morning and found me in the house.'

'Was he upset?'

'Concerned,' Sharon replied. 'He seemed to take it reasonably well . . . Naturally he *is* upset, though.'

'God knows, he's been through enough, maybe he just accepts everything as being par for the course!'

'Paul told him what happened,' Sharon explained. 'I guess it was for the best.'

'What about Steve?' She hardly dared ask.

'Steve's fine.' Sharon placed a triple-decker salmon and salad sandwich in front of Rita. 'Here, eat this, you'll feel better.'

'If only it were that easy,' Rita smiled, 'food as the universal panacea.'

'You've got to eat,' Sharon replied, sounding full of good sense. 'Oh, and Gary's been calling . . . said for you to phone . . .'

'Gary,' Rita said absently, regarding her huge sandwich

390

with a certain degree of trepidation. 'Would you be offended if I left this for the time being?'

'Eat,' Sharon commanded, standing over Rita at the table, arms folded.

Rita shrugged. 'What's going to happen with Steve?' she asked, cutting off a corner of the bread and tasting the delicious mayonnaise.

'Paul didn't say,' Sharon fenced.

'Is he coming straight home, then?' Rita looked at her friend.

'I'm not sure . . .'

'You're an awful fibber,' Rita grinned. 'Come on, tell me, what did Paul say?'

Sharon sat down at the table. 'That Steve's being admitted to a private clinic.'

Rita nodded, taking another bite of the sandwich, feeling increasingly hungry. 'You mean, a psychiatric clinic?'

'For a short while,' Sharon replied gently.

'For a short while,' Rita repeated. 'Okay, well, I suppose it's what is required.'

'I'm sure it's for the best,' Sharon said.

'You look beat,' Rita told her. 'Go home, I'm fine now, really.'

'I don't like to leave you,' Sharon admitted.

'Why ever not?' Rita laughed. 'I'm not about to off myself!'

'I know that,' Sharon said softly, reaching out for Rita's hand. 'I don't want to leave *you*.'

'I'm fine,' Rita said. She stood up and walked Sharon through to the lounge, where she picked up her coat. 'Jem, take your mum home,' she said, smiling at him, 'she's awfully tired.' Rita kissed Sharon good-night, hugging her close and then pushing her gently away. 'Call me tomorrow?' she asked.

391

William had come to the door and they stood together, waving their friends away. 'Are you going to call Dad?' he asked, turning to her.

'In a minute,' she replied. 'Come in and tell me how you are first.' They went back inside, sitting together in the dim lounge, their reflections clear in the dark windows, their heads almost touching as they discussed the events of the last twenty-four hours.

When Rita walked into the room, Steve was sitting with his back to her and looking out of the window. The window was open and the sounds of kids playing could be heard in the distance. 'Steve,' she said softly, taking a step towards him.

'Hi,' he said, turning, smiling a little, pleased to see her. 'Come and sit down.' He got up and moved to the bed, where he sat on the edge.

She bent to kiss his cheek. 'Nice room,' she grinned, sitting down and looking at him. 'You have a TV and everything, I see.'

'Sure, it's just like the Hilton except there are no locks on any of the doors!'

Rita laughed. He was wearing jeans and a T-shirt, no socks or shoes, his wrists covered with neatly wrapped bandages. She looked around her again. 'They have open access . . . we can visit when we like.'

'Sure, they don't put us in straitjackets or padded cells any more.'

'Steve,' she said, gently chastising him, 'this is a highly respected clinic not an asylum!'

'I know, I know, I'm sorry.'

'So, how are you finding it?'

'Fine. A few weeks, that's all they say I'm in here for . . . maybe a little time off for good behaviour, eh?' he smiled.

'The grounds are beautiful.'

'I'm not sure why I did it, Mum,' he began. 'There was no reason, I guess.'

'That was some secret you were carrying around with you,' Rita told him, 'it would have been strange if there had been no reaction.'

'Do you think it was true?' he asked her.

'About Nathan? I don't think we'll ever know for sure . . . He told you one thing, he must have thought it was the truth. For my part,' she shrugged, 'I begin to wonder if your father might be nearer the answer.'

'That there doesn't have to be any explanation, you mean?'

Rita nodded, although she was still reluctant to believe it. 'Whatever the truth, perhaps it doesn't really matter, after all . . . The fact that Nathan took his own life will never be something we can exactly accept and overcome.'

'You think he lied to me, then?'

'I don't know, Steve. He shouldn't have said those things to you . . . It was wrong. What were you supposed to do?'

Steve was watching her and listening intently. 'What happened to William at Easter seemed to bring it all back, just as though it were happening all over again.'

Rita nodded. She knew exactly what he meant but something else seemed to have happened now. Perhaps it was something to do with catharsis. They had certainly been through the most dramatic and terrible of times but now she really believed they were through the worst. It wouldn't be an easy journey back, there would never be complete ease or peace within any of them, but somehow she could now look forward again. There was no need to rely upon anyone else, she didn't require assistance, the future was just *there* and, whatever it held, Rita felt more prepared to deal with it.

She left Steve after more than an hour, smiling to herself as she drove away. Steve would be well, Rita thought, and so would she.

Gary was lying on her bed looking across at her. William was at the beach with Paul and they were alone together. He had just arrived from the studio, where his part had been increased to two whole pages of dialogue and three scenes. Rita had spent the afternoon working on a new idea for a book, the heroines of Thomas Hardy. She felt enthused and ready to start something else even though her work on the Woolf book wasn't yet complete. Just before Gary arrived she'd been speaking on the phone to Steve for an hour.

'Do you think he's okay now?' Gary asked.

'I think he's getting to be okay,' she answered, watching his muscles flex as he put his hands behind his head. He was wearing nothing but a ghastly pair of boxer shorts covered in huge yellow bananas and delicious red cherries. Rita hadn't seen him for over a week. She had kept him at arm's length, not wanting to confuse any more issues. Now she simply wanted him.

'Are you going to be long?' he asked.

'I'm going to have a bath,' Rita told him.

'Do it later,' he said.

'I'm sweaty.'

'I love sweaty!'

Rita laughed, going into the bathroom and filling the tub, taking off her clothes and slipping into the robe. She poured in some perfumed oil and took a large fluffy bath sheet from the linen cupboard. Rita was sitting running a hand through the water when Gary came in.

'Want to take a bath?' he smiled at her.

'I intend to.'

'Shall we toss for the plug end?' he smirked.

'Go back to bed,' she said.

'Have you ever done it in a tub?'

Rita sighed, dropping the robe and getting into the water. 'You can leave me now if you like,' she said, lying back and closing her eyes for a second, then opening them again as he stepped in too.

'Move your feet,' he instructed, sitting down facing her. The water was rising up to Rita's neck.

It was a larger than usual bath but still not really entirely suitable for her to entertain a person as big as Gary. Rita felt his legs against her, his feet tickling the tops of her thighs. 'This is ridiculous,' she complained, laughing all the same.

'A family that bathes together stays together,' Gary said. 'Didn't you know that?' He had an infectious grin across his handsome face. 'Didn't they teach you anything in England?'

'You're nutty,' she replied.

'Nutty? Is that an English term of endearment?'

Rita put a finger to her temple and made a screwing gesture. 'That's what it means.'

'Hmm,' Gary began, draping an arm over the bath, 'so, you're having a bath with an idiot, that's surely something to tell your grandchildren about!'

She laughed. 'Pass me the soap, do something useful.'

Gary sat forwards and, reaching behind him, pulled the plug, watching as the water receded to expose Rita's breasts before halting the flow again. He started to soap her, taking each breast in his hands as he worked, manipulating each nipple between thumb and forefinger until they grew hard. 'Stand up,' he told her.

Rita stood, placing her hands on his strong shoulders, her fingers biting into the muscle as he put a soapy hand between her legs, pushing his forefinger into her, moving it slowly, in and out, in and out, in and out, his other hand moving up over her buttocks until he was gently massaging her anus. 'Oh, Jesus,' she groaned, rocking against him, her eyes tightly closed, concentrating upon the pleasure and the pain. Gradually he sat her down in the warm water and sponged off the soapy bubbles. 'Why do you have this effect upon me?' she asked, shaking her head slowly.

Gary had taken the tablet of expensive sweet-smelling soap to his own body, ducking under the water to wash it away as Rita climbed out. He surfaced as she was drying herself, wrapping the bath sheet around her pink body. 'We have an effect upon each other,' Gary replied, standing up in the water, his tumescent penis making this statement perfectly obvious.

'Come to bed,' Rita smiled, throwing him a fresh towel, 'come to bed.' She left him standing there with a foolish grimace and wanton eyes.

Gary loved everything to do with sex and he would do anything she wanted, but Rita was often afraid to ask. However, it didn't seem to matter because there was a certain honesty between them, an openness she hadn't experienced before. Sex had never been a duty exactly, although Rita had never felt so much a part of it before.

'If only I'd met you before,' Gary said sleepily, breathing out and nuzzling her, his arms, which had been holding her firmly, suddenly feeling less protective as he fell asleep. In a while he turned away.

They had fallen into bed, carried along on a huge wave of lust, Rita feeling hot and flushed, her heart pounding, everything straining to become a part of him, but he was taking his time, driving her crazy, suckling her breasts, moving over her, his tongue leading him on as though it had an independent life of its own. He parted her legs and moved his head slowly down bringing her to a

396

powerful climax, with Rita gasping and feeling a little shocked at the guttural noises she was making. She closed her legs against him, wanting him to keep up this deliciously liquid contact which enabled her to float along, the concerns of her daily existence obliterated for those golden seconds when her conscious mind gave her up to the fleshly delights of rampant carnality.

Gary entered her soon afterwards and took her with a ferocity she hadn't thought possible. He seemed to fuck her for ever and she climaxed again, hanging on to him in a tangle of wet limbs as he continued to thrust himself into her, coming with a cry of her name and a sobbing breath until he withdrew his penis and held her, neither of them speaking, too exhausted to continue.

She drove to the clinic the following Sunday morning, leaving Gary cooking a chicken for lunch. She noticed Paul's silver Mercedes in the car park as she pulled up but thought nothing of it until she met him coming out of Steve's room with a striking blonde woman.

'Rita,' he said with surprise.

She smiled. 'Hello.'

He turned to Joanne and introduced the two women. The tall woman took Rita's hand in a firm handshake. 'Hello,' she smiled.

She looked almost beautiful, Rita considered, when she smiled like that. 'I'm pleased to meet you,' she heard herself saying but, in the end, she knew that she meant it.

Paul saw Steve's doctor at the end of the corridor and went off to speak with her, leaving Rita and Joanne together.

'Didn't William want to come?' Rita asked.

'I don't think so.' Joanne touched Rita's arm. 'He met a girl on the beach and went swimming instead. Paul's dropping in again later with him on the way home.'

Rita grinned. 'Is this a first fling, I wonder?'

'I don't think so, somehow,' Joanne replied. 'She's more interested in Paul, I think!'

Rita laughed at that. 'Poor William.' She decided she liked Joanne. They were very different. Joanne looked immaculate, she was wearing tan slacks with a tweedy man's jacket over her shoulders and a matching tan shirt. All very smart and crisp. She wore her natural blonde hair long, even though, Rita calculated, she must be in her early forties. However, Joanne was very well preserved, she thought, and seemed terribly self-assured and unflappable. Rita noticed her wonderful blue eyes, clear and intelligent, and her high forehead. Joanne was really extremely attractive. 'Well,' she said, as Paul returned, 'I'd better go in and see Steve.'

'It was really nice to meet you,' Joanne said, smiling broadly.

'Thanks, you too,' Rita replied, responding with a grin to Joanne's wonderful smile.

'See you later,' Paul told her as they left.

Rita nodded, watching them go before entering Steve's room. 'Hi there,' she said, 'and how are you?'

'Fine,' he replied. Steve was sitting on his bed in black shorts and a T-shirt with his Christian name printed across the front in black lettering.

'What's this?' Rita asked, pointing to his name. 'Identity crisis?'

Steve grinned, looking exactly like Paul. 'No, come on, Mother, things aren't that bad!'

'Okay,' she agreed, sitting next to him. 'What's been happening, then?'

'There was a tennis competition for the inmates . . . I thought that I might as well join in.'

'And what happened?'

'I lost in the first round,' he admitted.

'Oh, Steve,' she rebuked with mock seriousness.

'The guy who won was a great player.'

'Right,' she said, nodding, 'of course.'

'He was,' Steve insisted, laughing.

'*Right*, I believe you . . . You're looking better,' she told him.

'I feel good,' he replied.

'So, what are they doing with you?'

'Group therapy, individual counselling, you know . . . I think I might be out in another week or two.'

Rita nodded. 'Good.'

'Yes,' Steve agreed, 'I feel much calmer now.'

She took his hand. 'I think we're through the worst part now . . . What about your school work?'

'William keeps bringing stuff in and I'm free most afternoons, so I can keep up.'

'Good,' she nodded. 'I had a letter from your grandmother in Walthamstow yesterday. She's not going to make it over for a vacation with us this summer . . . again!'

'That's too bad,' he replied.

'Your great-grandmother is too old to be left. At least, that's what my mum says. I don't suppose she can be bothered with all the fuss of travelling out here. Who can blame her?'

Steve nodded and they were silent for a while until he turned to Rita and asked about her meeting with Joanne. 'What did you think of her?'

'She seems fine,' Rita replied. 'I only just met her for a moment out there in the corridor.'

'She is all right, Mum,' he told her, looking serious and a little concerned.

'She's attractive,' Rita said, laughing at herself. 'I suppose it's a bit of a shock to see who your dad is living with . . . I didn't expect anyone quite so glossy.'

399

'They're not living together,' Steve corrected, 'just seeing one another.'

'I see,' Rita grinned. 'You mean, like Gary and me?'

'I guess,' Steve nodded. 'Mum?' he asked.

'What, you're not going to ask me about whether we're going to divorce or not, are you?'

'No.'

'What then?'

'I've been thinking about Nathan.'

'Right,' she nodded, feeling herself growing tense.

'I've been thinking about why he would kill himself.'

'I see.' Rita prepared herself for another indictment of her motherhood.

Steve paused, turning to watch a group of people slowly wandering across the lawns in front of his window. 'Do you think it's possible to hate life so much that you can't continue? That it's too painful to go on any more?'

Rita recognized feeling those things herself over the course of the last years since Nathan died but, somehow, she had always managed to get through the dark times, to hang on. She nodded. 'I think it's possible to feel those things, but to actually kill yourself . . .' She stopped at the memory, forcing herself to continue. 'I don't think Nathan meant to die,' she told Steve. It was something she had considered and had wanted to believe. For a moment she actually thought it might be true.

Steve looked at her. 'I think he did,' he replied softly. 'I didn't believe it when he told me but I think he was serious.' He seemed perfectly calm as he spoke, his voice was even, his eyes concentrating upon his mother's reaction. 'I know now that there was nothing I could've done . . . The strange thing was we never spoke of it. In the days afterwards I often wondered if I could have imagined it, dreamt about it. Nathan seemed back to his normal self, whatever that's supposed to mean.' He very nearly smiled at the memory of his brother. 'It was only when he actually did it that I realized . . .'

Rita watched him carefully. She too felt calm, but that almost served to upset her. At last she sighed. 'Your brother was obviously desperate, but the reasons he gave you can't have been the only ones.' Rita stood and walked to the window, turning to face Steve. 'In a sense those reasons don't matter any more.' She listened to the sound of a jet liner overhead as it made its descent towards the international airport. 'The point is that, whatever has happened to this family because of Nathan's death, we have to move on now, not to forget, exactly . . .' She looked away once more. 'Never to do that, but to continue with our own lives as much as possible.'

Steve was studying her face intently. Rita understood just how much of a toll the years following Nathan's suicide had taken. Parts of her were still raw with the experience, she still found it difficult to trust Paul, to forgive him for the way he behaved, but now even her marriage was a thing of the past. Time was accelerating away and Rita had to consider her own life, living with the pain of Nathan's suicide rather than buckling under the weight of her own grief because of it. 'Does that make any sense?' she smiled at last.

'You mean, we have to stop feeling so guilty?' Steve asked.

'I suppose that might be part of it,' Rita replied, whilst considering how impossible it was to expunge her own guilt about Nathan. 'Dr Allan keeps asking me if Nathan would have wanted us all to have gone on feeling like this, would he have wanted *me* to have felt so terrible?' Rita frowned. 'I'm not sure if I have an answer for that yet . . .'

'He didn't do it to hurt anyone else,' Steve insisted.

Rita considered that. Shrugging at last, she stood up

from the window ledge where she had been leaning. 'I have to run, Gary's preparing lunch!'

Steve laughed. 'What is it?'

'Chicken.' She bent to kiss him. 'What are you up to this afternoon?'

'After lunch we have a group therapy session and then the rest of the day's free . . . William is coming in later.'

'Okay,' she grinned, 'see you tomorrow, then.'

Rita waved as she left the room, walking briskly to the car and driving home to the sounds of the Beach Boys blasting out of her car stereo system. She looked out at the bright day and felt suddenly extremely elated. Gary met her at the door and Rita kissed him passionately.

'What was that for?' he asked, looking surprised.

'That was for nothing,' she laughed, walking ahead of him into the house. 'Come on now, where's that chicken? I'm absolutely bloody starving!'

Gary smiled, closing the front door and following Rita inside.

Dr Allan clasped his hands together on the desk in front of him. He smiled at Rita. 'You seem to have come to a lot of conclusions,' he said.

Rita bit into her bottom lip. She wondered if they were the wrong conclusions about her life. 'You asked me if Nathan would have wanted me to have been so unhappy . . . Well, I'm not sure what he would have wanted, or even why he killed himself, but I suddenly feel as though it is something in the past, not as painful as before, not quite as destructive.' She looked nervously into the doctor's face.

'I see.' He picked up a sharp pencil and wrote a word or two in his notebook. 'And this new feeling has emerged since the events of Easter?'

'Don't misunderstand me,' Rita began, 'it's not as

though everything is suddenly all right again . . . No,' she shook her head, 'it's not like that at all. It's more like an acceptance of what has happened.'

The doctor nodded. 'I understand.' He sat back in the big chair behind the shining desk top. 'Do you mean acceptance, Rita?' he asked carefully.

She thought about that but didn't respond to his question, merely looked doubtfully in his direction.

'It seems to me as though you have come to something of an understanding of what Nathan did.' He let that idea sink in before continuing. 'In all our discussions before, you have seemed blinded by your own feelings of guilt.'

'That much hasn't altered,' she admitted. 'I realize it's possible for someone not to want a life, not to want to go on living . . . I know that because I've felt it myself.'

'How does Steve's story help you to understand that in Nathan?' he asked.

'Because I know how I felt?' She sounded unsure.

'Does that make you *accept*, though?'

Rita looked doubtful again. 'I can never really accept that Nathan was so miserable he had reason to take his own life, no,' she admitted, feeling scared that she might have been lulling herself into a false sense of her own happiness, or what might pass for happiness. 'But I feel better,' she blurted out.

'You were never unwell, Rita.'

'I felt as though I was going crazy!'

He smiled patiently. 'You were never that,' he replied as though not wishing to disappoint her. 'You came to see me because you were confused and obviously miserable, devastated by what had happened to upset your comfortable life.' He stopped speaking, as though waiting for her to make a germane comment concerning her own 'condition'. When she didn't say anything he continued. 'What you talk of as being acceptance doesn't mean that you think Nathan's suicide was okay, it means that you can face it, face up to it.' He let the sense of that sink in.

'So, I'm not really happier?' She looked confused.

The doctor smiled. 'Of course, if that's how you feel, then that's what you are!' His smile broke into a gentle laugh. 'Rita, you don't need me to tell you whether you are happy or not.'

'I'd thought we might be coming to the end of something . . . that I might not need this so much.' Rita sounded disappointed.

'And I'm sure we are,' he encouraged. 'We began all those months ago with the idea that you wanted control. Well,' he looked at her, 'you seem to have achieved that goal, you've just come through a period of enormous emotional upheaval, you're starting a new relationship and what has happened?' He stared at her.

Rita shrugged. 'Nothing, I've got through it – I'm getting through it,' she corrected herself.

'So, what does that tell you?'

'That I'm able to cope?' she asked tentatively.

'More than that, surely,' he smiled, leaning forward again, encouraging her.

'I've dealt with it, after a fashion,' she told him.

'Okay, so you weren't perfect, but you soon got over the initial shock, first William, then Steve. I don't think you understand what huge steps you've been taking.'

Rita felt rather pleased with herself, like a little girl being praised. Soon, however, she stopped grinning and looked more serious again. 'I have to come back, then?' she said.

The doctor opened his hands. 'No one's going to force you at gunpoint!'

She laughed. 'I didn't mean it like that,' she assured him.

'I think we're nearly there, Rita,' Dr Allan told her, sounding almost ebullient.

'Okay,' she nodded, 'that's fine.'

And when she left his office Rita was still smiling. She celebrated by having lunch at the vegetarian restaurant, sitting at the same table in the courtyard with the hanging ferns and the shaded tables under their pastel umbrellas. Rita thought of Marco and of the card he'd so carelessly sent, which she still had somewhere. She was grateful to Marco because he had been kind and brought her out of her shell and proved that there was still a sexual life for her. He'd shown her that all was not lost, and now she realized that had been very important. A turning point, almost.

Rita picked up her white wine, looking across at the empty table next to her, and wondered what Marco was up to now.

She spent the remainder of the week completing the work she'd begun on the Woolf book, sitting out at the redwood table, working away under the swaying palms.

On Thursday afternoon Rosa had waved to her from the house, miming the action of a telephone at her ear. Rita walked across the grass and took the call on the patio. It was Joanne, wondering if Rita could meet her in an hour at the Hollywood Roosevelt Hotel, on Hollywood Boulevard. Rita said she would and then started to panic because, as usual, she hadn't any idea what to wear. In desperation she phoned Sharon, who, Rita thanked God, was in.

'Why does she want to see you?' Sharon asked.

Rita threw another dress on to the bed, holding yet another up against her and looking at the effect in one of the mirrors. 'I don't know.'

'Why are you going, then?'

'Because I want to find out,' Rita said, unzipping a skirt and letting it drop to the floor and stepping into another. 'What's the Roosevelt Hotel like?' she asked.

'It's opposite the Chinese Theater,' Sharon replied, eyeing the latest skirt with a certain doubt. 'You know, where the footprints of the stars are!'

'Very appropriate,' Rita said, turning sideways and holding in an already flat stomach.

'What's she doing there?' Sharon asked, passing over a frilly blouse that Rita inspected and then rejected.

'God knows.' Rita took off the skirt. 'Look, we're going to make a decision,' she said, diving into the cupboard and emerging with a navy blue Conran suit in one hand and a plum-coloured wool blazer in the other, with white stripes and a spotted handkerchief sticking from its top pocket. 'Which?' she demanded.

'Halve it,' Sharon replied. 'Take the Conran bottom and wear the blazer with a white shirt.'

Rita dressed quickly, pulled on a pair of dark tights and black high heels and rushed out of the house, Sharon running behind. 'Jesus,' she groaned, rummaging through her bag for the car keys, 'I look a bloody wreck.'

'You look great,' Sharon replied, waving her off. 'Call me when you get back.'

Rita drove swiftly away, attempting to look at her face in the rear-view mirror, touching at her hair and wondering what the hell she must look like. It was Marlene's fault, of course. Rita would never have become this obsessed with clothes if it hadn't been for her sister giving her a complex all those centuries ago, back in the sixties. Now she had cupboards bursting with clothes which she hardly ever wore. Sharon had suggested a garage sale but Rita couldn't bear to part with them. Each garment had a history and a memory of its own and now she could just about trace her life through the past twenty years by what was hanging in her walk-in wardrobes!

She turned out of the canyon road and headed for Hollywood Boulevard.

She found Joanne at the back of the hotel, sitting by a large swimming pool close to a bar. Joanne waved to attract her attention and Rita walked across the very green, very fake grass to meet her. There was a low-level complex of apartments built around the pool area, shining glass in deep recesses behind which tourists moved to and fro, emerging from time to time for a swim or a drink at the bar.

'David Hockney painted this pool,' Joanne told her.

'David Hockney?' Rita was confused.

'He covered it with those fabulous swirling, curving strokes . . . just like in his paintings,' she smiled. 'You know, "Peter climbing out of Nick's pool"?'

'Right,' Rita said, vaguely aware of what Joanne was talking about.

'Thank you for coming,' Joanne said.

'I was intrigued,' Rita admitted.

A waiter came over at Joanne's request and she ordered them a drink. Rita settled for a Coke whilst Joanne had a Perrier. Joanne was looking splendid in a beautiful white suit. It fitted perfectly and had wide shoulders and a rather short skirt which showed off her slender legs. Underneath the jacket she was wearing a high-necked white silk blouse. It made her look rather like a character out of a movie, the idea of how a career woman might dress. 'Cheers,' Joanne said, as their drinks arrived and she took a sip of her sparkling water. 'No one can accuse us of being a couple of old soaks, anyway,' she joked.

Rita slipped off her blazer, pushing up the sleeves of her shirt in the warm afternoon sun. She watched as a young man jumped into the pool, almost landing on top of his shrieking girlfriend. 'It's nice here,' she said.

'I thought we ought to meet,' Joanne said. 'It seems ridiculous that we haven't before . . . Not properly, I mean.'

Rita nodded. 'I've heard a lot about you, though, from the boys,' she explained. 'I imagine you've heard all about me!'

'Sure,' Joanne smiled, 'but it's my experience that people only ever tell you the bits they want you to hear from their past lives. I've spent the last six months getting Paul to say *something* about his feelings towards Nathan.' She took another sip of her drink. 'It's been very hard-going, like pulling teeth.'

Rita shrugged. 'Have you got anywhere?'

'I'm not sure,' she mused, 'I'm not even sure if I'm exactly the right person for him.'

Rita was shocked at her candour. 'Really? I should have thought you were both quite suited . . . I mean, your medical background, for one thing.'

'Oh, yes, there's that, of course, but Paul can be a real tight ass sometimes.'

Rita laughed at Joanne's description. 'Don't I know it!'

'Anyway, we shall see, we shall see,' Joanne nodded to herself. 'So, you're seeing someone else now. The boys tell me about Gary, he sounds fabulous.'

'Gary's fine,' Rita admitted. She was fascinated by Joanne and had only positive feelings towards the woman who was sleeping with her husband. They continued to chat for the next hour, covering their lives and what they had done and what they still wanted to achieve. They seemed to have a lot in common, more than just a strong interest in the same man. They had a similar sense of humour and laughed a lot through the course of their conversation. Joanne obviously liked her children but

Rita didn't perceive this as a threat and she made it quite clear that she had no intention of seeking a reconciliation.

'It's over,' Rita said. 'I haven't really spoken to Paul about what he wants to do. We've said we weren't interested in divorce but . . .'

Joanne laughed, interrupting Rita, guessing what she was about to ask and making it easier for her. 'I don't want to marry Paul,' she said, finding the idea amusing. 'My life is too settled. I have a career that I adore and a comfortable routine . . . Marriage is the last thing I'd ever consider now.'

'What does Paul think about this?' Rita asked.

'Oh, you know Paul,' Joanne replied without thinking, looking at Rita as both women burst into laughter at her comment. 'I don't think he wants it either, although he might like me, or someone, to be around a bit more of the time.' She reached across to touch Rita's arm. 'What about you and Gary?'

'God knows, I'm almost scared to think about it.'

'You like him a lot, though,' Joanne encouraged.

'It's a bit more than like,' Rita smiled. 'I don't really know how he feels, exactly.'

Joanne nodded. 'Things are going along just fine and you don't want to rock the boat.'

'Something like that,' Rita admitted. 'I'm worried about how the boys might react to something more permanent, especially Steve.'

'Steve can handle it,' Joanne assured her. 'He can handle it, for God's sake, he's very fond of Gary and, besides, he saved William's life, didn't he?'

Rita acknowledged that fact. 'Yes, but I don't think the boys are really quite ready for the next step.'

'What does Gary think?'

'I don't know,' Rita confessed, feeling a little foolish.

'We just seem to muddle along without anything specific being said.'

'Jesus.' Joanne put a hand to her head. 'Men are so dumb, aren't they! Doesn't he understand how you feel?'

'Do any men ever understand how women feel?' Rita asked gloomily.

'There's a question now,' Joanne replied, shaking her head. 'Let's have a real drink to ponder it.' She motioned to the waiter, who came across, grinning from ear to ear. She ordered them each a Bacardi Collins. 'I hope that's okay,' she said, after the waiter had left.

'Yes, but I'm not absolutely sure what it is,' Rita told her.

'Oh, you'll like it,' Joanne assured her. 'It's rum and sugar, lemon, ice, soda and a cherry!'

Rita laughed. 'I usually only drink wine.'

'Live a little,' Joanne advised, treating her like a fellow conspirator. 'Okay?'

'Okay,' Rita answered, not entirely sure that rum was the answer to her problems but giving in to Joanne's idea anyway.

'So,' Joanne said, smiling at the waiter, who looked a bit like the young Tony Curtis, 'where does that leave us? I mean, if men don't understand us?'

Rita picked up her drink and sipped at it, finding that she liked it. 'We try to change them?' she suggested.

'I think it's all in the learning process myself,' Joanne told her. 'How often do you hear of boys having to be "made" into men?' She looked at Rita. 'Girls are never made into women, are they?'

Rita wondered if she had tried to make her boys into men; she was sure there had never been any conscious effort. 'Maybe it's something to do with men not being wholly male . . . I mean, the X and Y chromosomes, they're always terrified at being demonstrative or showing emotion.' She said this with a degree of feeling, thinking of Paul.

'But they have all the power,' Joanne said darkly.

Rita took another sip. She knew all these arguments, her mind had once spun with them, all the ideas and aspirations of liberation, the violence of some men, the potential violence of all men. 'Do you think Paul is like that?' she asked suddenly.

'Oh, God, yes,' Joanne said. 'I know you always had your separate careers and he isn't exactly a male chauvinist . . .' She paused to reflect upon that. 'But, on the other hand,' she smiled, 'well, maybe he's more attuned than some men, but he still likes to rule the roost . . . I mean, how much of the child-rearing did he do? How many times did his career take second place to yours?'

Rita blinked. 'Never.' It was wonderful to hear someone else supporting her, even though that person was Paul's new woman. 'But his career was rather exceptional, even for a man!'

Joanne didn't look too sure about that. 'Paul's clever, I'm not denying that for one moment, but he's not *that* clever. He got into his field quickly and then took the main chance, he worked hard, developed his expertise and got a lot of stuff published . . .'

For a moment Rita felt quite defensive towards Paul. She was sure he did possess a major talent and, despite everything that had passed between them, she still had a certain pride in what he had achieved. 'I've always admired Paul for his dedication to his work,' Rita admitted.

Joanne put her drink down. 'But didn't you ever feel resentful?' she asked. 'You had to do two jobs to his one!'

'Sometimes, but lecturing never involved issues of life and death.' She was sure that was an argument Paul had

411

offered her over the years. 'I think you just fall into a pattern of living which seems to work.'

'You mean, he was hopeless at child-care!'

Rita laughed. 'He wasn't very good.'

'They never are. It's funny how men learn ineptitude in certain areas, isn't it?' she mused.

'Well, we're a long way from those days now . . . You certainly seem to have his number, though.'

'I was married once before,' Joanne said. 'I've also had various relationships . . . Jesus,' she smiled, 'I sound like a man-hater but I'm not. It's just that we have to be aware. I'm not saying they're even to blame – children aren't responsible for the way they are brought up, the way they're conditioned and socialized. It's the old nature/nurture debate in a way, I suppose.'

'God, I wonder what you must think of Steve and William!'

'They're fine,' Joanne replied. 'I see a lot of you in the way they relate and behave, especially William.'

'That means Steve is like his dad.'

'No,' Joanne disagreed. 'He may look like Paul but he isn't the same . . . Who was Nathan like?'

'Everyone said he was like me, but I'm not so sure. I wonder sometimes if he was more like Paul.'

'They're fine kids,' Joanne repeated.

Rita smiled, picking up her glass and draining the remains of her drink, feeling slightly intoxicated.

Rita left Joanne at the poolside, never discovering why she had suggested they meet there, or what she was there for herself. She stood outside, looking across at the Chinese Theater. It seemed such an anachronism, the grey-green stone work and the building like something out of a film itself, dwarfed by the hotels towering behind its odd pointed structures.

She ran across the boulevard, stepping across the evenly spaced stars on the dark pavement and on to the hallowed ground where a myriad of Hollywood legends had immortalized themselves, setting their foot- and handprints, in concrete. Rita wandered around the concrete blocks, looking down at the imprints for a while before returning to her car and driving home. She smiled at the idea of a pagoda for a cinema and thought the whole thing just a little sad, the idea of finding immortality in a lump of concrete a trifle weird.

Rita thought about Gary. The encouragement Joanne had given her made her feel that, perhaps, their relationship did stand an even chance. Rita was now determined to discover just what Gary felt about her, to find out what his 'intentions' were. She had a feeling of relief, a new sense of freedom.

'I'd like for us to keep in touch,' Joanne had said as Rita was leaving.

'I'd like that,' Rita'd agreed, putting her hands into her blazer pockets.

'Good,' Joanne had said firmly.

William spent the following week-end with Paul at the beach. Joanne had gone to New York to see her family and Rita was planning a dinner for Gary with lots of champagne. She felt a bit like a spider spinning webs in order to catch its prey. Her intention was to make everything as easy as possible for herself. Hence the champagne, to provide the necessary lubrication for her vocal cords. Not to be loose-tongued exactly but to free an otherwise hesitant voice. She wanted to make everything clear.

'Jesus!' Sharon said, walking into the kitchen unannounced. 'What are you doing with all this champagne?' She picked up a bottle. 'Launching a ship?'

Rita turned away from preparing the sauce for their prawn cocktails. 'I need it,' she said.

'Four bottles?' Sharon was still inspecting the labels. 'Have you done something stupid?' She looked up at Rita. 'You haven't committed bigamy, have you?' she asked suspiciously.

'Don't be ridiculous,' Rita told her, laughing at the suggestion. 'I got it cheaper at the off-licence this way.'

'The what?' Sharon grinned.

'Liquor store, then,' Rita amended. 'I don't intend to drink them *all*!'

'Okay, so what are you giving him?'

'Roast lamb.'

'Hmm, lucky boy.'

'You always seem surprised that I can cook!'

'Not at all, honey,' Sharon laughed. 'The way to a man's heart, after all, is through his stomach!'

'Oh, rot!' Rita began to add salt, pepper and paprika to the egg yolks, mixing them together in a basin. 'He cooks for me too.'

Sharon opened the bottle of wine she had brought and poured them both a glass. 'Here,' she said, handing Rita her drink, 'have a break and come and talk to me.'

Rita finished making the mayonnaise before joining Sharon, who was sitting out on the patio in the hazy warmth of early evening. They chatted for a while about Gary. 'I don't want to get into something that will confuse an already fraught situation,' Rita admitted.

'Do you love him?' Sharon asked simply.

'Yes,' Rita replied without hesitation.

'So, that's all there is to say, surely.'

'But I don't know if he loves me,' Rita said.

'Do you want to marry him?' Sharon asked.

'No.'

'Live with him?'

'Not necessarily.'

'So?' Sharon asked, looking just a little confused.

'It would be nice to have a few words of encouragement from him . . . I'd like to know where I stand with him.'

Sharon nodded. 'Well, I hope it works out for you.'

'You don't sound very sure,' Rita replied.

'I think it'll be fine . . . of course he loves you,' Sharon encouraged. 'But don't invest everything in him. Gary's just a man, he can't make up for everything that's happened, he can't wipe Paul away.'

Rita knew that. 'I just want someone for me,' she replied softly, 'a man who's actually *there* and who cares.'

'No one's perfect,' Sharon warned.

'God, you sound like my mother-in-law!' Rita laughed.

'Well, they're not,' Sharon insisted. 'Don't invest everything in one person, that's all I'm saying.'

'I know, I know,' Rita said quietly, leaning forward and looking down at the roses. 'I know that.'

Halfway through the carefully prepared dinner, Rita looked across the table at Gary and asked him if he loved her.

Gary blinked and then stared at her in surprise, a forkful of food held just in front of his mouth. He put the fork down and grinned. 'Is that what this is all about?' he asked. 'I wondered why you seemed so tense.'

'Do you?' She repeated the question, looking serious and feeling nervous and uncontrolled. 'Just tell me,' she said.

'What the hell do you think?' he asked in amazement.

'Just tell me,' she insisted.

'Yes, I mean, of course, how can you even ask that question?' He began to laugh.

Rita smiled, tears rolling down her cheeks. 'Then why have you never said it before?'

'Haven't I?' He sounded surprised at that.

'No,' she shook her head, 'you know you haven't.'

'I guess I was afraid.'

'Afraid?' It was Rita's turn to sound shocked.

'I felt that you had enough things to deal with, enough problems . . . I didn't want to burden you with any more.'

'How can love be a burden?' Rita asked softly.

'It can sometimes . . . I was also afraid that you'd reject the idea.' He looked serious. 'I was afraid that this was just a fling.'

'A fling?' Rita sounded horrified. 'A fling?'

Gary laughed. 'Stop repeating everything.'

'So, you do love me?' she asked.

'Yes. Don't you believe me?' He sat back in his chair and looked at her with an expression of disbelief.

'I believe you. Jesus,' she breathed, 'this has been just the worst twenty-four hours!'

'I'm not an ogre, Rita.'

'But you never said anything.'

'I thought it was pretty obvious!' he replied, tucking into his main course again.

'How can you eat?' she asked.

'I'm hungry. Film-making is a tough business, all that standing around.'

'For such a small part this film is certainly taking up a great deal of your time.'

'Oh, well now, here's something else I didn't tell you. I now have another whole page of dialogue . . . How's that now?'

'Great,' Rita enthused. 'You'll be the star, if this goes on.'

'Not quite, let's not get too excited here.'

'Do you get more money as well?'

'I'm not sure, I'll have to speak with my agent, I guess.'

'You'll get a screen credit too,' she began, laughter in

her voice. 'Is this the sort of film that one could take one's children to without becoming embarrassed?'

'Absolutely.' He looked at her. 'You could take your mother to it!'

'You'll be famous,' she joked.

'Sure, if three pages of dialogue is fame, then you've got it here in your dining room.'

'I'd rather have it up there in my bed,' she replied, a lascivious smile forming.

'Get right to the point, don't we,' he said. 'I thought you said we had fruit crumble for dessert.'

'Are you joking?' She reached for her wine glass. Three bottles of champagne were standing unopened in the kitchen. 'You *are* joking.'

'I have to keep my strength up,' he replied innocently.

'You're joking,' she said again, dissolving into fits of laughter. 'I'm offering you nights of passion and all you're concerned about is fruit crumble!'

Gary's face took on the innocent expression of a choir boy, his eyes wide and questioning. 'Did I say something to amuse you?'

Rita got up early on Sunday morning, stepping out into the sunshine and sitting down on the patio, where she made the final changes to her book about Virginia Woolf, a copy of *Mrs Dalloway* open on the table in front of her. She had left Gary still fast asleep, not expecting to see him again until lunchtime, when they were going over to Sharon and Bill's house. The morning was quite clear, everything in the garden standing out in sharp relief against the beautiful lawns and the blue sky. The pool looked mirror-clean in the still atmosphere, just an occasional ripple over its smooth surface as a gentle breeze caught at the water. Rita worked steadily through the morning, finishing her revisions just before noon. She

turned the last page over and sat back, hands behind her
head, her eyes closed, feeling as though doors were
shutting on everything to do with the past. London and
teaching and Chalcot Square seemed, suddenly, a million
years ago now. The patio door slid open and she turned
towards Gary, who was wearing his swimming costume
and carrying a large blue towel.

'Are you working?' He sounded disapproving.

'I've just finished,' she said.

'Swim?' he suggested.

'No, I'm going to pack this up and get it ready for the
mail.' The pages of *Mrs Dalloway* flipped over in a sudden
breath of wind. The ghost of Virginia, Rita mused,
gathering her papers together. 'We're going next door for
lunch,' she called after Gary, watching him as he waved
and ran to the pool.

They spent the afternoon with Sharon and Bill. The men
went on to the tennis court, Bill's rather tubby build
belying his agility around the court. The kids had gone to
the beach, leaving Sharon and Rita to clear away after the
barbecue and then sit out by Sharon's circular pool in the
hot afternoon. Rita attempted to explain her feelings
about men, and Gary in particular.

'I guess I've been real lucky with Bill and there was
never any contest between us . . . I mean, I was never
really that interested in a career and he did as much as I
wanted him to.' She removed her sunglasses and started
to clean the lenses. 'Didn't Paul help out?'

'Are you kidding?' Rita laughed at the idea.

'Oh, well, Gary cooks you meals, he can't be that
chauvinistic!'

'Yes,' Rita nodded in agreement, 'but I'm not talking
about domestic chores or child-care. Most men do something, however meagre, to help out. No, it's the wider
condition I'm interested in.'

418

'This Joanne has really got to you, hasn't she?' Sharon said, replacing her glasses. 'Why are you so concerned about this now? Gary's fine, don't analyse everything out of the ball park.'

'It's just that I don't *know* him that well.'

Sharon laughed. 'How much more is there to know?'

Rita shrugged.

'Listen, honey, you've already said that you're not contemplating marriage, you're not even living together at the moment. Just see what happens. Okay, so men can be shitheads, they control everything, they have all the power . . . it's not perfect,' she finished, as though that were enough.

'You're just telling me not to make waves,' Rita replied grumpily.

'No,' Sharon disagreed, 'I'm not, but it's possible for men to feel afraid as well, you know. That's all.'

'Afraid of what?' Rita asked, sounding unconvinced.

'Of what they are. They have a tender side, a feminine side, it's just they can't always show it . . . I think that's true,' Sharon added a little defensively.

'You seem to be saying that nothing can change,' Rita replied.

'Things change,' Sharon insisted. 'My father would have died rather than be seen pushing a baby buggy. Bill was always taking the kids out, changing their diapers, washing them, taking care of them.'

'It's still an unequal relationship,' Rita maintained.

'Okay,' Sharon said. 'Listen, honey, I *agree* with you – and it's too hot for arguments.'

Rita laughed. 'I'm sorry, I don't mean to argue. I feel that everything is suddenly different,' she sighed. 'My kids are growing up fast, my marriage is over . . . It's just a time for reflection, I suppose.'

Sharon nodded. 'And talking to Joanne, finding that

419

she's so marvellous, has made you realize that there's no going back, ever!'

'I expect we'll divorce eventually. After the recent shocks, I wouldn't think that Steve or William would bat an eyelid at the idea now.'

'You're at the beginning of something, then,' Sharon said.

'Do you think so?' Rita asked.

'Of course. Don't be such a dullard, of course you are!'

'God knows what I'm going to do. I can't expect Paul to keep me in that huge house, especially when the boys are both away.'

'What would you like to do?' Sharon challenged.

'I'm only qualified for one thing. Perhaps I could work out here,' she mused. 'I think I *need* to support myself.'

'Then do it,' Sharon told her. 'And as soon as we've found Steve and Jem somewhere to live, we can look out for a suitable place for you.'

'You make everything sound easy,' Rita said.

'It is,' Sharon replied. 'Get him to build you a house,' she suggested, pointing to the tennis court where the two men were still engaged in their match. 'He'd probably offer you special rates,' Sharon giggled.

'That would be taking advantage,' Rita responded.

'So what?'

Rita laughed but didn't say anything.

'Take it all one step at a time, honey,' Sharon advised. 'One step at a time.'

Rita lay back, closing her eyes and listening to the whack of the tennis ball as the game progressed. She fell asleep and had a dream about Nathan. 'It was for you,' he kept telling her, but she didn't understand. As usual she woke up with a start at the point where he smiled and closed the front door of their house at Chalcot Square.

Sharon was in the pool by then and Gary was towelling

420

himself down at the courtside. Bill was sitting in the shade, drink in hand. She stretched and smiled at Gary as he crossed the grass towards her. It was the last time she ever had the dream about Nathan.

William was still swimming when Rita arrived at the beach house later that evening. Gary had left her in the late afternoon, going back to Laurel Canyon to prepare for his last few days on the film. Paul was sitting on the breezy balcony, working through a pile of academic papers.

'Do you mind me having a key for this place?' she asked, sitting down next to him and looking out across the sands, trying to spot William.

'No, of course not, don't be ridiculous, I've a key for the big house.'

She nodded. 'I've just dropped in on Steve. He was due for a session with his doctor so I couldn't stay. He thinks he'll be out in another week.'

Paul closed a folder and put a book on top of it to prevent the papers from blowing away. 'Next week-end, I think,' he told her.

'He seems okay,' Rita said.

'He'll be fine,' Paul assured her.

'Thank God,' Rita replied. 'We'll have to arrange some kind of celebration, nothing too big, but a welcome home at least.'

'Right,' Paul agreed, 'that'll be good.'

'I met Joanne,' she told him after another pause. 'I expect she told you.'

'Yes.' He was watching her carefully, wondering what she was about to say.

'I like her,' she admitted, 'very much . . . I think you're well suited.'

'Thank you,' he replied with genuine warmth. 'She thinks you're great!'

Rita grinned. 'So, you're happy at last?'

He shrugged. 'We were happy, Rita.'

'Yes, but this is different, isn't it?'

'Not so different. Times change, people change . . . We're not the same people we were twenty years ago.'

'Thank God, eh?' Rita joked.

'Not necessarily. The world has a habit of corrupting us all.'

'I know,' she said.

'What about you and Gary?' he asked. 'You're looking as good as I've seen you in a long time.'

She smiled at his compliment. 'We're fine. It's the only other really important relationship I've had, so it had better be good!'

Paul laughed at that. 'Anyway, we've had a good week-end, I think. William has spent most of the time in the ocean.'

'He's the one who seems to have come through this whole business without too many scars, emotional or otherwise,' Rita said.

'William's all right,' Paul replied. 'He's a lot like you, in many ways.'

Rita was about to respond to this accolade when William came clattering up the steps and on to the balcony.

'Hi,' he said to her, looking brown and bursting with health. 'I'm nearly ready.'

'That's okay, there's no rush,' she said, smiling at him.

William nodded and went inside to sort his things out.

'Why don't you bring Joanne to Steve's party next week-end?' Rita suggested as they left.

Paul shrugged. 'Okay, I'll ask her. Her flight's in later tonight . . . I'm meeting her.'

'Good,' Rita said, pulling the big Ford away. 'Give me a ring, then.'

'Will do,' Paul replied, watching them leave.

'You two are very friendly,' William remarked as they drove back.

'You should be pleased.'

'I'm confused,' he admitted.

'And why is that?' she asked.

'You're getting on better with one another since you've been dating other people!'

'Because we're happy people now,' Rita replied without thinking, and then felt pleased with herself.

'I think anyone over twenty is weird,' he announced.

'I'll remind you of that remark in a few years,' she promised.

'How's Gary's film?' he asked her, changing the subject abruptly.

Rita began to tell him about Gary's extra page of dialogue, turning off the coastal road and on to Sunset Boulevard and towards Westwood.

Chapter 12

Rita was talking to Dr Allan about herself. How she felt about her life, her children, her relationship with Gary. 'I still feel better about things,' she told him.

'That's good,' he smiled at her from across his desk, 'that's very good.'

'Yes,' Rita agreed.

'You feel that your relationship with Gary is progressing?'

'I think it's important, yes.'

'And Steve's returning home in a few days?'

'At the week-end,' she nodded.

'So, everything is fine, Rita, no problems?'

'There are *always* problems,' she replied, grinning at the tricks he was trying to play. 'Whenever I'm having a good time with Gary I start to feel guilty about Nathan.' She looked at him.

'Okay.' He was wearing a green and white striped shirt today. It was bold and distracting. 'And how are you going to deal with that?'

'By trying to understand about those feelings?'

He looked at her. 'Is Gary aware of these guilty feelings?'

'I don't discuss them with him.'

'But he knows about Nathan?'

'Yes.'

'And what does he have to say about it?'

'He hasn't ever said very much . . . I try not to bring it up in general conversation.' She sounded slightly annoyed.

'Do you deliberately repress a desire to talk about the subject?'

'No . . . he's aware of it.'

'What about after William's accident? Was it discussed then?'

'No, I didn't see Gary on many occasions between William's accident and Steve's – ' She paused.

'Steve's suicide attempt,' the doctor said quietly.

She felt the familiar kick in the stomach, the nervous ache, the dark, twisting panic beginning to rise. 'Gary's been busy on a film,' she finished lamely.

'Were you avoiding him?' he enquired, as though expertly slipping the switchblade between her ribs.

'I had to deal with those things by myself . . . I wasn't really feeling much like seeing anyone.'

'Were you concerned about how Gary would react?'

'No, I wasn't happy about him being involved. I didn't see it as his problem, anyway.'

'I see,' he smiled, and sat back in his seat.

'I wasn't as sure about my relationship with Gary as I am now.'

'You mean, things have altered between you?'

'Yes.'

'In what way?'

'I wasn't sure if he loved me before.'

'Good,' the doctor said quietly. 'But now you do know that?'

'Yes.'

'And does that make you feel better about the relationship?'

'Well, yes, of course.'

'So, you'd feel more confident about discussing things with him? I mean, about the way you feel, the guilt over Nathan, for example.'

'If it ever arose,' she replied.

'But you said before that it often does arise, that you have feelings of guilt about Nathan when you're with Gary.'

'Yes,' Rita agreed. She pursed her lips and looked at him. 'You think I'm deliberately avoiding the subject with Gary, don't you?'

'What do you think?' he asked, throwing the question straight back.

'I suppose . . .' she sighed, 'I suppose that in establishing a new relationship, when I'm with Gary I haven't wanted to swamp him with a blow-by-blow account of how I feel about my dead son . . . You're saying that I should talk to him, aren't you?'

'How do you feel about that?' he asked blankly.

'How do I feel?' she replied. 'I *feel* that Gary should probably be made aware of what's going on . . . That's what I feel.'

'So?' The doctor opened his hands, giving her the opportunity to tell him what she intended to do about it.

'I can hardly stop in the middle of making love and express my feelings of guilt. I can't tell Gary that my love for him is resulting in a conflict of loyalties!'

'Is that what it's doing?' He sounded surprised.

'Not exactly . . . God, why is this so difficult?'

Dr Allan smiled. 'Because it's painful. Feelings are always difficult, you know that.'

'Okay, okay,' she nodded, 'I need to be more open with Gary.' She looked into the doctor's eyes.

'I think that might be good,' he said encouragingly.

'But I want to move on now,' she insisted.

'You are moving on, Rita.'

'Going over the events of the past with Gary won't help that process, though,' she said, sounding a trifle petulant.

'Disregarding it, or attempting to forget about it, won't help the process either,' he told her gently.

426

She looked at one of the revolting oil paintings. One day she would ask him why he'd chosen such awful things; she didn't really find them conducive to clear thought. 'Right, I know that,' she agreed at last, 'but I can't help feeling so guilty. Nothing seems to make it any easier . . . it never goes away, I just feel it here,' she pressed at her stomach, 'gnawing at me as though it had some physical presence.' She stared at Dr Allan. 'Maybe it's an ulcer,' she suggested, and then burst into laughter at her absurd ideas.

'If I didn't know better, Rita, I'd say that you were now feeling guilty about feeling guilty!' He sat forward. 'Or feeling guilty at trying to get rid of those awkward emotions, especially when you're with Gary.'

'Jesus.' She put a hand on to the top of her head. 'All I feel these days is, "why me?" That's the truth.'

'But that's just falling into the trap of being victim.'

'Okay, so what if I am the victim?'

'We have already established that you're not, though,' he responded.

'Okay.' She thought again. 'I don't want to lose Gary,' she admitted. 'He's experienced enough with the remains of my family and I don't want him to feel that he has a burden to carry as well.'

'Why do you use those expressions, Rita?' he enquired.

'What expressions?' She was confused.

'"The remains" of your family. William and Steve are hardly "remains".'

'I'm sorry,' she said contritely, feeling embarrassed, 'it wasn't intentional.'

'You're putting tremendous pressure upon yourself by this current strategy. You seem to have gone from one extreme to the other. I don't think Nathan ought to dominate your life, but fighting against him isn't going to help either.' He looked at her, searching her face. 'Do you understand what I'm saying, Rita?'

She felt tired. 'You're saying that I should involve those closest to me . . . I don't want to bore people to death!'

He ignored her remark. 'If you feel Gary should know, if you want to tell him something, then do so.'

Rita looked through the tinted glass at the familiar pattern of houses. 'I have some good days and some bad,' she said. 'Since Easter, when William almost drowned, and after Steve's attempt at killing himself, things have improved.' She smiled to herself. 'They could hardly get worse, I suppose . . . I tread very lightly, doctor. I don't want to upset this trend and I don't feel that going on and on about Nathan to people who weren't around will help any more.'

'Don't bottle things up, that's all I'm saying.'

'I thought one of the reasons for being here was to lessen the risk of that,' she replied, thinking of the thousands of dollars that had already passed between them.

He nodded. 'But, hopefully, you learn from what we discuss and practise the things we talk about.'

'I feel better about myself,' she admitted, 'although that doesn't ever change the basis of these consultations.'

'The fact that you're embarking upon a new relationship proves something, does it not?'

'Yes,' she laughed a little, 'that I'm probably a masochist!'

The doctor smiled too, looking at the tiny clock on his desk. 'Have a think about what we've said today . . . Talk to Gary as well.'

Rita stood up, straightening her skirt and picking up her bag. 'Okay,' she nodded. 'Same time next week.' She drove home feeling that her session with Dr Allan hadn't achieved as much as she'd hoped. But that was probably inevitable. He'd warned her there would be times of progress and times of standing still. However, there was an underlying feeling now that, perhaps, she'd gone as far as she could with him. He had brought her through a difficult period but he was another crutch she could now consider dispensing with. It might not be next week, or even next month, but quite soon now.

She spent some time after lunch under the palm trees, working on her new idea for a book at the redwood table. Sharon came over to her, carrying a tray with clinking glasses and a jug of fresh orange.

'Hi,' Sharon smiled, placing the tray down in front of them. 'And how are you?'

'Brain-damaged,' Rita joked. 'Dr Allan makes my head spin sometimes.'

'Tough times, eh?' Sharon asked, pouring out the orange.

Rita shrugged. 'I'm trying to put down some ideas for a new book, but they're not coming too easily.'

'Here,' Sharon passed a glass to her friend, 'drink this.'

'Will it make my brain work?'

'Sure, anything you like,' Sharon laughed.

Rita took a sip. 'Listen, did you "fix" my first meeting with Gary?' she smiled. 'I mean, were you doing your matchmaker bit?'

'Is that what you spend your time talking about with Dr Allan?'

'No,' Rita smiled. 'Did you, though?'

'Absolutely not,' Sharon insisted, although she grinned enough to make it still seem a bit suspect.

'Hmm.'

'You want me to take a lie-detector test or anything?' Sharon laughed.

'No.'

'Sure?'

'Quite sure.'

'What made you ask that, anyway?' Sharon queried.

'It was just something I've wondered about . . . It doesn't matter if you did, I was just thinking about how everything has changed and how things have worked out just recently.'

Sharon nodded. 'You're still having a good time, aren't you?'

'Of course,' Rita insisted. 'I've never felt like this about anyone.'

'Not even Paul?' Sharon was surprised.

'No, not really. Does that sound wicked?'

'No.' Sharon took another drink. 'It sounds perfectly normal to me!'

'You were shocked just a moment ago.'

'Well, just a bit,' Sharon admitted. 'I guess that one's ardour does diminish a bit after twenty years.'

'After the first twenty weeks!' Rita giggled.

'I'm not sure if I still find Bill exciting,' Sharon mused. 'I find him *very* comfortable and we still have a sex life of sorts.'

'Oh, Sharon, you make it sound as though you're both geriatric,' Rita replied with a guffaw.

'You know what I mean . . . Weren't you and Paul the same?'

'I suppose so,' Rita replied. 'Certainly it was different from what I'm experiencing now with Gary . . . I'm out of control with him at the moment!' she admitted.

'Sounds marvellous,' Sharon grinned.

'I don't think Dr Allan quite understands. I've been seeing him in order to gain some control over my life and now this . . .'

'There can be such a thing as too much control, Rita,' Sharon warned her.

430

'Maybe in Los Angeles but not where I come from.'

'Well,' her friend shrugged, 'Walthamstow' – Sharon said the word deliberately, pronouncing it 'Wal*tham*stow' – 'wherever that goddamn place may be, might not always have given you the correct answers.'

Rita looked at her, the fan-shaped palm leaves casting zig-zag shadows over them as the breeze caught the high branches. 'I can tell you one thing, my mother thinks I'm insane, giving up a world-famous authority in paediatric medicine for a part-time actor.'

'And a fabulous builder,' Sharon reminded her.

'And a great lay!' Rita giggled crudely.

Sharon raised her orange juice. 'Well, don't knock it, honey. Here's to that which money just cannot buy.'

Rita burst into raucous laughter.

Sharon began to cackle. 'You see, being out of control is great, isn't it?'

But Rita was laughing too hard to reply.

Rita picked Steve up from the clinic on Friday evening, just as the shadows were growing long and the sky was passing from clear blue to the hazy pinks and mauves as the sun slowly descended. The fine spray from lawn sprinklers caught the dying sunlight, producing faint rainbows as she drove slowly by. Steve was sitting on his bed, his bag at his side. He looked as if he had been waiting for hours but told her he hadn't. Rita had seen his doctor, who assured her that everything was fine.

'I hope so,' Rita replied with feeling.

'Steve was crying out for help,' the doctor replied kindly. 'His injuries were all inside . . . I'm sure that he'll be great from now on.'

Rita nodded and went along to his room. Steve hesitated for a moment, standing at the doorway, bag in hand, before following his mother out to the car.

431

'Do you mind if we don't go straight home?' he asked as they drove away.

'What do you want to do? Have a meal? Go to a film?'

'Could we drive to the beach for a while?'

'If that's what you want,' Rita responded. 'Anywhere in particular take your fancy?'

Steve laughed. 'No, the first one we reach.'

'Fine.' She headed for the Santa Monica Freeway, stopping on the coast between Santa Monica and Venice. They walked across the white sands as the Pacific turned golden in the sunset, watching the surf rolling up on to the deserted beach.

He stood at the water's edge, taking big breaths of ozone and staring out to the horizon. A large yacht was passing across their line of vision, its huge red spinnaker billowing out, running before the wind. 'Jesus, look at that, Mum,' he said, pointing to the beautiful boat.

'Rich folk,' Rita commented, shading her eyes. 'Don't tell me you want to learn to sail now.'

Steve turned to her, grinning. 'No, I just wanted to walk a beach for a while . . . to blow away the cobwebs, you know.'

Rita nodded.

'Dad's lucky, he has this all of the time.'

'I expect he's mostly too busy to enjoy it, though,' Rita replied.

'He was lucky to have you,' Steve said suddenly.

Rita looked surprised. 'Yes, well, things change, times change . . .'

'Don't worry, Mum, I'm not about to ask you when you're divorcing him and marrying Gary!'

'Good,' Rita said, beginning to walk up the wet sand as the water rushed towards them.

'But while we're on the subject . . .'

'We're not on the subject,' Rita insisted.

'Only kidding,' Steve laughed.

She noticed the marks on his wrists. They looked red and angry, but the doctors had assured them that any scarring would be minimal. Seeing them suddenly shocked her; for a while she had almost forgotten the reasons behind Steve's stay in the clinic. She thought she would break down but she quickly regained her composure, turning out to sea to watch the progress of the big yacht. 'Can we go home after this hike?' she enquired.

'Sure,' he chuckled, 'don't you think this is great?'

'It's fine, yes, but aren't you hungry? William will wonder where we are.'

'Okay, okay,' he said, turning to her, 'we can go back in a little while . . . Listen, I wanted to say something, to apologize, I guess, for everything I put you all through.'

'Don't be ridiculous,' she said with feeling.

'No, no, I really mean it. I know now that I should have told you everything before, but you know how it is . . . I kept putting it off until I just couldn't say anything.'

'You'd promised Nathan,' she reminded him.

'Yes, well, he's not likely to know about that now.'

'Look, you have no need to say anything, Steve, I'm just thankful – we're all just so thankful that it's behind us now and that you're all right.'

Steve put his arm around her shoulders. 'Thanks.' He bent to kiss her cheek.

'Don't *thank* me, for God's sake.' She sounded almost appalled.

'Come on,' he said, reverting to an extremely plummy English accent, 'home, James, and don't spare the horses!'

'Bloody cheek,' Rita replied, whacking his behind.

Steve chased off ahead of her towards the car. 'Last one back's a jerk-off!'

Rita started to run after him, watching him sprinting

433

away from her, his heels kicking up the sand in his wake. Halfway across the beach she slowed down. The race was already lost. Steve was out of reach.

Gary arrived when the boys were upstairs talking and watching TV in Steve's room. He looked tired and she put a hand to his forehead, brushing his blond hair back as she tested for signs of a temperature. He kissed her on the lips and they walked into the lounge with their arms around each other and sat on the sofa. 'Tough day?' she asked, after he'd kissed her again.

Gary threw his head back on to the soft cushions and closed his eyes for a moment. 'What is it you say? Knackering? I'm absolutely bloody knackered.'

'Take a bath,' she suggested, holding his hand. 'A hot tub will revive you.'

He nodded. 'In a minute . . . Are you okay?' he asked her.

'Yes,' Rita smiled.

'Steve get home?'

She nodded.

'Will he mind me staying over tonight?'

'No, why should he?' Rita asked.

'It's his first night back and all.'

'He'll be pleased to see you. How was your last day on the set?'

'Fine . . . I'm an out-of-work actor again now.'

'Are you sad?'

Gary shook his head. 'No, not really. My agent dropped in to see me today, wants me to test for this TV cops show thing.'

'Are you?'

Gary shook his head. 'It's out of the question.'

'Why?' she asked gently.

He opened his eyes to look at her. 'Because in the

434

unlikely event of me getting it they would probably want me to sign some kind of long-term contract . . . It's like selling yourself into slavery!'

'Bad as that, huh?' Rita smiled a little.

'And where's the integrity in that anyway, some crappy TV show . . .'

'They're not all awful,' she said.

'I'm not even going to think about it.' He closed his eyes again, opening them after a moment and squeezing her hand. 'Do you want me to do it?'

Rita was taken off guard. It was the first time he'd asked her to comment about his life and what he did with it. 'No, I don't want you to be sold into slavery!'

Gary laughed. 'So, it's back to honest toil from Monday.'

'You're such a snob when it comes to the work ethic,' Rita told him. 'Why isn't creative or artistic endeavour work?'

'Did I say that?'

'Not in so many words.'

'There you go, then.'

'But you're always putting your acting down, you belittle that part of your life as though you were almost ashamed to do it.'

'Maybe I am,' Gary responded. 'I've never really thought of acting as a particularly noble thing to do.'

'Then why pursue it?' she asked.

'A quirk of personality, a wayward gene?' he yawned as he spoke.

'What's that supposed to mean?'

'Listen, my old man always told me that all actors were faggots.' He turned to her. 'When I told him I was going to be an actor he just about burst a few blood vessels. He never forgave me. Even when I was married and had a kid he still didn't believe that I was entirely straight.'

Gary shrugged. 'I don't think he ever really recovered from that decision. Two days before he died I went to see him in the hospital and he took hold of my hand and asked me if I was still doing that fuckin' fag acting!'

'Were you close to your father?' she asked.

'Not really.'

'What did he do?'

'He was a car mechanic . . . ran his own business for years in Stockton.'

'Stockton?' Rita sounded perplexed, 'I thought you came from San Francisco.'

Gary nodded. 'I did, I lived with my mom in North Beach.'

'Is your mother dead too?' she asked.

He nodded again. 'She died in 1980.' He smiled. 'I'm an orphan of the storm, Rita, an orphan of the storm!'

She poked him in the ribs. 'Don't joke about it,' Rita told him. 'Didn't you love them?'

'Sure, my mom was usually three sheets to the wind, drunk as a skunk. My old man allowed me one visit a year and usually beat up on me.' He gave a bitter laugh. 'Boy, that was some family! As soon as I could I got out and away.'

'If you hated your father, why does it matter to you what he felt about acting?'

'Because he was my dad, I guess . . . Jesus, I don't know, why do we care about people?' Gary stood up and went over to the fireplace, then turned to face Rita. 'I cried my heart out when both my parents died. I guess it was as much for me as for them.'

'But you weren't alone, you have your son.'

He nodded. 'Yes, but you can't rely upon your kids to pull you through . . . you have to let them go. With parents it's always different. Love 'em or hate 'em, you're always a part of them. I loved them both in the end, despite everything. My mom didn't even recognize me when she was dying, I could have been anybody. My dad told me to give up my career.' He smiled to himself. 'Jesus, what brought all of this on? Why am I telling you all of this?'

'Don't you think I should know?'

'I don't want to frighten you away,' he admitted.

'Me?' She began to laugh.

'What did I say?' he asked, watching her. 'What's so funny?'

'Oh, nothing.' Rita gasped for breath. '*I've* been scared that you would grow tired of my recent history, all the things that have been happening around here.'

'Are you serious?' He went back to her, taking her into his arms. 'What a pair of idiots,' he said. 'What a stupid pair.'

Rita returned to their conversation later that night as they lay in bed. 'Why did your father hit you?' she asked, turning to him in the darkness.

Gary was silent for a long time before answering her. 'He was a bit screwy, I guess,' he sighed. 'Both my parents drank like fishes, they had hollow legs. He'd get tanked up and take his anger and unhappiness out on me . . . said I reminded him of my mom.'

'How old were you then?'

'My folks divorced when I was nine. It went on from then until I grew too big and too strong for him to risk it any longer.'

'But you still loved him?' she asked, her voice soft in the still room.

'Sure. Kids have this enormous reservoir of love. In any case he wasn't always violent.'

'So, it was drink that made him that way?'

'I guess,' Gary replied.

'Didn't your mother know?'

'I didn't tell her and he sure as hell wasn't about to say anything!'

'How could he have done it?' Rita asked, sounding disgusted.

'I was probably being equally obnoxious . . . I was a real tearaway as a kid. Jesus, I was left pretty much to my own devices from the time my folks divorced.'

'That's no excuse for his actions,' she responded, almost angry now.

'He had his own problems to deal with,' was all Gary would say.

'So, that makes it okay?'

'It was a long time ago, Rita.' He put his arms round her, pulling her close to him. 'Don't start getting uptight about it, or I'll wish I'd never begun this story. Listen, it wasn't like that for most of the time.'

'I know so little about you,' she told him then.

'You know everything there is to know about me,' Gary said earnestly. 'You know everything that's important.'

'I can't bear to think about it,' she said, tears already falling.

'Come on, Rita,' he encouraged. 'It really isn't as bad as I made it sound. It's past history, really.'

'But what it must have done to you,' she complained.

'What, you mean I'm like him? No way, I'm terrified of violence.'

'Jesus, what we do to our kids,' she sobbed.

'Come on,' Gary said gently. 'It sounds much worse than it was.'

'How can you say that?' she asked.

'Because it's the truth. He was always sorry afterwards. For most of the time he was okay.'

Rita took a shaky breath and stopped crying. 'People are sent to prison for less.'

438

'I was a tough kid,' he joked.

'These things take their toll.'

'Yes.' He squeezed her tightly. 'I became an actor!'

'You became a sort of actor,' she answered.

'What's that supposed to mean?' he laughed.

'Well, you've always seemed to keep it at a healthy distance.'

'I grew tired of it and I could always make more money from building and woodwork. That's the truth,' he added.

'I thought acting was supposed to be in the blood,' Rita remarked.

'So, I practise my craft from time to time.'

'I think it's a result of your upbringing,' Rita said.

'Listen,' he yawned, '*everything* is a result of our upbringing.'

Rita didn't answer. In a while Gary fell asleep but she lay thinking about him for a long time, going over what he'd told her. She knew very little about him. He had a whole life of which she really knew nothing. Gary, to her, was as he was, as he stood before her; the influences that had shaped him had, until now, been a mystery. The comments about his childhood seemed to make things worse. Rita imagined him as a solitary child, emotionally and physically battered by disturbed parents. However, his childhood could explain his early marriage and father-ing his own son when he was nineteen. Gary's ambiva-lence towards his acting career seemed to reflect a feeling that it wasn't quite appropriate, not a job for a real man. He apparently took much more pride in his carpentry or the houses he had built in the canyons around Los Angeles. She thought of his large, work-roughened hands with their long, thick fingers. He played the role of artisan, he was built for manual labour and seemed to revel in its sweat and hardship. It was the part he appeared most comfortable in, the one in which he was able to exist and, through it, become the man he desired. Gary always seemed to be the same, it was almost like describing some idealized or fictional character, open and friendly, honest and witty, charming and handsome and sexy . . . the list seemed endless and almost ridiculous to her. There had to be another side, if only to make him more interesting. But then, at the moment Rita was overwhelmed with him, and time, she knew, would be the test. In six months or a year they might not even still be together!

Rita turned over and reflected upon their relationship until sleep caught up with her.

Steve went into William's room the next morning dressed in a pair of green shorts. He was looking for a pair of tennis socks, searching his brother's cluttered drawers and wardrobes. William sat up, yawning and stretching as he woke.

'What's up?' William asked, focusing on Steve.

Steve found the socks and held them up. 'I need to borrow these,' he explained, sitting on the end of the bed and pulling them on. 'Jem's coming round in about five minutes.'

William looked at his watch. 'It's nine o'clock! Are you crazy? Waking me at nine o'clock on a Saturday morning!'

Steve laughed. 'I promised Jem that as soon as I got home we'd play tennis.'

William lay back again. 'Are Mum and Gary up yet?'

'Gary's already had his swim,' Steve replied.

'Jesus, why doesn't anyone lie in around here?'

'Come on,' Steve encouraged, tapping William's leg, 'you should be out there as well. I'll play you this afternoon.'

'It's your welcome-home party this afternoon.'

'Oh, right,' Steve said.

'You don't sound very enthusiastic.' He propped himself up again. 'It should be okay . . . Dad and Joanne are dropping in.'

Steve groaned. 'Gary and Rita and Joanne and Paul and all of them being ever so friendly . . .'

'You'd prefer them all to be at one another's throats, I suppose,' William said, easing himself up into a sitting position, his feet on the floor as he pondered whether to stand up or not.

'Do you think they are all so happy?' Steve asked, turning to his brother.

'Beats me,' William replied, standing up and walking into the bathroom, where he urinated then turned on the shower before emerging again. 'Don't say anything to Mum, she's really looking forward to it,' he warned.

'As if I would.' Steve was playing with William's racket now, holding the head close to his ear and bashing the strings with the palm of his hand. 'I'll enjoy it too,' he decided, putting the racket on the rumpled bedding. 'Do you think they've got me anything?'

William shrugged. 'I doubt it. Was there anything you particularly wanted?'

Steve shook his head. 'Just to be home, I guess.'

William went back into the bathroom and got into the shower. When he trailed back through, wrapped in a large white towel, Steve was still in his room, sitting on the window seat, looking out across the garden. 'You still here?' he grinned.

Steve turned back. 'Sure am.'

'What is it, Steve?' he asked, combing back his wet hair.

'We haven't really spoken since I did this.' He held his wrists up. The marks were slightly raised and a pinkish colour.

441

'Okay,' William nodded, going over and sitting next to him.

'I feel that I owe some sort of explanation.' Steve sounded uncertain for the first time.

'I know what happened. I mean, I know why you did it,' William said, feeling very protective all of a sudden. 'You don't *owe* anyone an explanation . . . Can't we just forget about it now?'

Steve looked at the droplets of water on William's shoulders and back. His brother's skin was smooth and tanned, there were freckles across his shoulder blades and at the nape of his neck. 'I always thought that I could have stopped Nathan, should have stopped him,' Steve began, 'and then . . .' He paused, staring at his hands, picking at the nail of his left thumb. 'And then, after Nathan was dead, I started to feel angry with him, because I couldn't understand how, if he loved me, he could have done such a thing.' Steve looked at William. 'Nathan was much more than a brother, in some ways. He was everything I wanted to be and I was always sort of in his shadow.' Steve spoke in a calm, almost detached way, as though relating a story about two completely different people. 'Anyway, after he died and I'd got over the initial shock, I was left with all of this anger. For a while I think I actually hated him. He told me what he was intending to do, and then he did it and left me!' He still sounded amazed as he related it to William, his voice rising for the first time. 'I'd thought that once we moved here everything would be all right again but, instead, things just went from bad to worse. Mum and Dad were going crazy, then Dad left. Jesus,' he sighed, 'it was a nightmare . . . Didn't you think so?'

William nodded.

'When you almost drowned at Yosemite it was like the whole horrible business beginning over again. I felt that I

442

should have been there to grab you. I would've been if I'd have stayed in the river for a few more minutes . . . I hardly remember anything between Gary dragging you out of the Merced and me lying in hospital with blood everywhere feeling totally confused.'

'And what about Nathan?' William asked.

'Nathan?'

'Did you ever forgive him?'

'Sure.' Steve put his hand on William's bare shoulder. 'I still don't understand why he did it, though,' he admitted.

'You don't think he was under too much pressure, then?'

'Do you?' Steve asked.

'I can't really remember now.'

'There don't have to be any reasons . . . Maybe he was just too unhappy for any of it to make sense.'

'Going to university is hardly a life-or-death decision,' William replied.

'Maybe he was a little crazy, then. Who knows, and does it really matter now?'

William shrugged. He walked to his built-in wardrobes, where he took out fresh clothes. Dropping the towel, he began to dress. 'Perhaps it's us who need the reason,' he suggested. 'Imagine how Mum and Dad must feel.'

'There has to be a time when it becomes less central to your life,' Steve said. 'I don't mean forget, but when Nathan isn't *there* all of the time.'

William pulled on a pair of clean blue jeans. 'Getting over it is one thing, forgetting is something else,' he said quietly.

Steve saw Jem coming across the grounds towards the house. 'Listen, I have to go . . . Are you coming down to watch?'

'See you get beaten?' William joked. 'No, thanks.'

443

'Some hope,' Steve said as he left the bedroom.

William sat on the window seat for a time, watching his brother and Jem walking down to the court. They were talking together and suddenly laughed. Jem paused to pick up some tennis balls that had dropped from the bucketful he was carrying. Steve took one and began to bat it up and down on his racket head as they continued walking.

William wiped his eyes, his vision blurred now, clouded by his tears for Nathan.

The homecoming party for Steve was informal – just Sharon and Bill, their kids, a few of Steve's friends and Paul and Joanne. Sharon helped prepare the giant salads and beat the steaks ready for the barbecue griddle. Gary and Bill were sent out to buy the drink.

'I still have the champagne,' Rita remembered. 'We could have that later.'

'Aren't you supposed to start with the good stuff?' Sharon asked.

Rita thought for a moment. 'We could start and end with it . . . I do have *three* whole bottles left!'

Sharon laughed. 'It'll be like a wedding reception!'

'That's okay. As long as it's a celebration, that's all I'm concerned about.'

The party began in the late afternoon when the boys were in the pool with Sharon's kids, a few other friends, and Gary, of course. Rita and Sharon had been in the kitchen for an hour or so already, chopping and slicing and blending and grating the salad vegetables and preparing the various dressings. Rita had opened one of the champagne bottles, which now stood, almost empty, on the work surface in front of them.

'What's this?' Gary joked, walking in with Bill to fetch the meat.

Rita was giggling with Sharon, waving a carrot in the air as she spoke. Sharon was bent almost double over a chair, chortling away.

'Are you two drunk already?' Bill asked, opening the refrigerator door and passing out a tray of steaks to Gary.

'No,' Sharon said, standing up and attempting to keep a straight face, which made Rita laugh even harder, 'we were just having a little drink . . .'

'A little drink?' Bill smiled, following Gary out to the barbecue.

'Why do men always get to do the cooking part of this?' Sharon asked.

'Because they have to light a fire and use all those sharp implements,' Rita replied. 'Isn't that what they call "man's work"?' she said disparagingly.

'You'd think they'd actually captured the meat, from the way they behave.'

Rita laughed. 'Well, didn't the cavemen hunt the wild beasts while their women picked berries and kept cave!'

'You're not telling me it's inherent within them, are you?'

'Has Bill tried pulling you into the house by the hair recently?' Rita asked.

'Not recently . . . Actually, I think it's something to do with the sight of all that bloody red meat. Maybe you're right, cooking steaks outside calls up some weird remembrance of their ancestry.'

'You mean, like in *The Flintstones*,' Rita added.

Sharon smiled and started to sing *The Flintstones*' theme song. Rita joined in, and they were in the middle of this refrain when Steve and William walked in from the garden. Jem followed them and the three boys looked at their respective mothers with a mixture of confusion and amusement.

'Dad sent us in to help,' Jem announced.

'Ah, the junior warriors,' Rita said, breaking off from her song. 'Well, it's all yours, boys.' She pointed to the salad bowls. 'Come on,' she said to Sharon, grabbing her friend's hand, 'it's time for a drink with the hunters!'

'What's up with them?' William laughed.

'This,' Jem said, swigging champagne from the bottle and passing it round to the others. 'They're pissed, that's all.'

William wiped his mouth and handed the remains of the drink to Steve. He caught his brother's eye and they both grinned knowingly.

Paul and Joanne arrived just as the food was being dished out. It was the first time the two families had been together for almost a year and Rita, feeling less drunk now but still merry, realized there could be a slight tenseness between them. She had, however, forgotten about Joanne, who had a kind of magnetic personality, a smile to melt the hardest of hearts, an ability to fit in anywhere. Within minutes of arriving she had left Paul's side and was helping Bill finish off the steaks at the barbecue. Sharon took Gary off to help her serve the salads, leaving Rita and Paul standing together on the patio. The boys brought their food over and they sat down as a family at the nearest table to eat their meal. When Rita looked up, Gary was sitting next to Joanne and they were deep in conversation whilst Bill and Sharon were sitting around with various kids and their friends.

'Are you enjoying your party?' Paul asked Steve.

'Sure,' Steve nodded through a mouthful of lettuce and tomato. 'Just like old times, eh?'

He missed the look in Rita's eyes as she reached for a glass of iced water. She hoped Steve wasn't getting the wrong idea and, turning to see Gary and Joanne still talking and laughing together, she felt cross and

446

irrationally jealous. William had asked her a question and was waiting for her reply. 'What?' She turned to him. 'I'm sorry, William, what is it?'

'I was asking what you missed most about London. I mean, apart from your folks.'

Rita thought for a moment. 'I suppose I miss not living in a proper city and the fact that you have to drive absolutely everywhere here.'

'What about you, Dad?' Steve asked his father.

'I suppose I agree with your mum. It's taken me a long while to come to terms with the scale of everything here. A lot of it is also incredibly ugly. I still like the beach, however!' Paul smiled. 'Why did you want to know?'

William shrugged. 'It was just something we'd never discussed.'

'What about you?' Rita asked. 'Do you miss anything about London?'

'Just being able to nip out along the road, to the shops or whatever, I guess.'

'Nothing else?'

'Sometimes I miss the rain.' He laughed at that idea.

'They can keep that,' Rita responded with feeling, 'they can keep the rain and the snow and the ice.'

Paul nodded. 'I like the climate here. I don't miss any of the horrors of the English winter.'

'What's happening to the house in Chalcot Square?' Steve asked suddenly.

'We're thinking of selling it once the current tenants move out in the autumn,' Paul told him.

'So, we won't have anywhere in London?' Steve asked.

'I hadn't really thought, I suppose it might be an idea to keep a flat there or something . . .'

'Are you going to stay out here for ever?' Steve asked his father.

Paul glanced at Rita. 'I don't know, son, perhaps not for ever.'

'What about you?' Steve asked his mother.

'Who knows?' Rita asked him. 'Why, are you thinking of going back?'

'No.' He looked at his steak, cutting off a chunk and chewing it for a while.

'Get your education sorted out first,' Paul advised him. 'You can always do a transfer year at an English university if you want.'

Steve nodded but didn't answer or even look up from his food.

'I don't know what I'm going to do,' William told them, 'but I like it here okay.'

'Thank God for that,' Rita said. 'One satisfied customer, anyway!' She looked at Steve, wondering why he was being so contentious. She supposed it was something to do with them sitting there together as a family when, in fact, they were nothing of the sort. Steve seemed to be working towards getting one of them actually to admit it was all over, even though it was obvious. He had always questioned her about divorce and what was going to happen, he had always desired clarity when there often wasn't any.

The truth had, quite literally, come home to them all that evening. What had, perhaps, seemed a bit of a game, a bit of a lark in the past, was now the reality which their children had to face. Sitting as a family only made their split more obvious. Both Steve and William now completely understood that their parents weren't going to get back together at the last minute, and the prospect of divorce sometime in the future was clear to them all. So, Steve was pushing them to a final answer, not about homes in London or what he wanted to do, but about themselves and where they were all going.

* * *

As darkness fell, the Chinese lanterns, which they had strung across the patio and along the pergola, were lit up and glowing brightly in the warm atmosphere. There was loud pop music drifting up from the pool, where the boys and their friends danced and played in and out of the illuminated water. The 'grown-ups' cleared away after the meal and then sat out chatting and laughing.

Gary was talking about the film he'd just made. Rita was surprised to hear him talking openly about his acting and she wondered if he was doing it to prove something to her. Joanne appeared to be fascinated, asking countless questions.

'But why don't you concentrate upon one thing?' Joanne asked him. 'Why not just be an actor?'

'Too hard,' Gary replied with a grin.

'And building houses isn't hard?' She laughed. 'What do you think, Rita?'

Rita shrugged. 'It's a conundrum that I don't bother to work out any more.' She touched Gary's arm. 'I just can't wait to see this film . . . it'll be the first time I've ever seen him act!'

'Will it?' Sharon sounded surprised. 'We saw him in a film on TV the other night . . . a murder mystery thing. You looked very young,' she laughed, turning to Gary.

'Was he good?' Rita asked.

'Sure,' Sharon nodded. 'I think Gary was the mystery killer, or something. He was introduced at the end and exposed.' She chuckled. 'It was terribly dramatic!'

'Jesus,' Gary said, 'can we get off the subject of my ancient film parts?' He turned to Rita. 'I feel like a swim . . . Anyone interested?'

Sharon said she'd make coffee and Paul went in to help her, leaving Bill and Joanne, who declined Gary's offer. Rita walked down to the pool with him, stopping in the weirdly lit pergola, taking his hand and then kissing him. Gary put his arms round her.

'How do you think it's going?' she asked.

'I'll be glad when everyone's gone home,' he said, kissing her again and pushing himself against her, 'if you know what I mean.'

'You'd better get into that water,' she told him.

'Okay,' he agreed, breaking apart from Rita. 'We'd better not shock the children!'

She took his hand and led the way again, walking out of the darkness and into the bright light of the poolside area. Quite a lot of people had left by now. Jem was in the water with two blonde girls, whilst Steve and William were sitting at the edge.

'Are you swimming?' Steve asked her.

She knelt down between them, putting her arms round their damp shoulders. 'Okay, you two?' she asked.

'Fine,' William said.

'Great party, Mum,' Steve replied.

'Did your friends enjoy themselves?' she enquired.

'Yes,' William nodded.

'There aren't many left,' Rita commented.

'There's another party over at La Brea,' Steve told her.

'Did you want to go?'

'No way,' Steve laughed. He seemed surprised at her question. 'Of course not.'

Rita was feeling comfortably drunk. She hugged the boys to her. 'Look at him,' she said, pointing to Gary, who had emerged from the pool house in his red swimming briefs. He stood at the edge for a moment before diving in. 'He's such a show-off!'

'He's good,' Steve said knowledgeably, watching as Gary swam steady lengths of the pool.

'He's a big kid,' Rita said. The blonde girls had climbed out by now and were drying themselves. Jem had also

450

hauled himself out of the water and was sitting at the opposite end watching Gary too. William moved away from Rita, dropping into the pool and swimming over to Jem.

'What's going to happen then, Mum?' Steve asked after a while.

'What do you mean?'

'Well, you obviously like Gary a lot!'

Rita laughed, shaking her head and moving to sit on a sun lounger a few feet away from the pool edge. She sat down, resting her head against the padded back. 'You like Gary as well,' she said to him from the partial darkness.

'Come on, Mum, you can do better than that,' Steve encouraged her.

'I love him,' she replied.

'More than you loved Dad?'

'I can't answer that, I can't quantify who I love the most,' she said.

Steve walked to the lounger and sat on the edge, legs apart, forearms resting on his thighs, playing with a sweet-wrapper he'd picked up. 'I don't know why you and Dad couldn't ever work things out.'

'Yes, you do,' Rita insisted, moving to him and putting her arms around his neck and rocking him gently. 'You never miss a trick, do you?'

'What's that supposed to mean?' he asked, laughter in his voice as he turned to look at her.

'It means that you have to keep picking away at things. Your Dad's with Joanne . . .'

'He won't marry her, though,' Steve said. 'They don't even live together – '

'Not yet,' Rita interrupted, 'not yet!'

'You ought to settle down,' Steve said, sounding as though he were now her father.

Rita laughed. 'Oh, and is that your considered opinion?'

'Sure.'

'And what if I don't want to "settle down"?'

'Everyone wants to settle down,' Steve insisted.

'I've had that,' Rita reminded him.

'What about Gary?' he asked.

'What about him?'

'Wouldn't you like to marry him?'

'Not really,' Rita told him.

'Why not?' Steve sounded disappointed.

'I'm still married, for one thing!'

'But what if you weren't?'

'No,' she shook her head, 'I still wouldn't.'

'Oh.' Steve shrugged. He seemed a bit deflated.

'I wish you'd stop trying to sort my life out,' Rita continued, an amused lilt to her voice.

'Okay,' he agreed, smiling as he got up. 'But don't say I didn't try.'

'You mean, when I'm an ancient crone reliving past glories?'

'Maybe.' He ran to the water and dived in.

Rita remained where she was, listening to Gary and the boys shouting and laughing with one another in the pool. Sometimes she felt that everything was all right again, sometimes she felt safer and more secure but, usually, there was panic rising and a strange feeling of impermanence or transience as though her more recent happiness wasn't meant to last. She got up and walked around the pool, looking down into the water, laughing as Gary headed a ball towards Jem and feigned concussion, slipping slowly under the water, hands above his head.

Eventually everyone drifted back to the house, where Sharon was serving coffee and hot chocolate drink. Bill was taking photographs of everyone. The boys came and sat next to Rita on the swing seat and they had their grinning faces photographed too.

'It was a lovely party, Rita,' Joanne said, coming over to say good-night.

Rita, coffee cup in hand, eased herself off the precarious seat and walked Joanne and Paul to their car. Gary met them as he came down the stairs from changing after his swim. He saw them out as well. It felt extremely odd to Rita, saying farewell to her husband and his woman whilst she remained there with her man.

'All right?' Gary asked as they waved them off.

Rita nodded, turning towards the house. 'I think they enjoyed themselves, don't you?'

'Sure, it was all very civilized,' Gary replied.

She closed the front door. 'What was Joanne having to say for herself?'

'Oh, you know,' he turned to face her, 'this and that.'

'She's an extremely attractive woman, don't you think?'

'Sure, if you like that sort of thing.'

'What sort of thing?' Rita laughed.

'Oh, you know, career-orientated woman, clever and rich and independent.'

'So, what's wrong with that?' Rita asked, walking on through the house.

'Nothing.'

'You don't sound very sure.'

'I'm sure,' Gary insisted, stepping out on to the terrace behind her. 'Really,' he said, looking at her, '*really*.'

Soon there was only Rita and Gary left. William had been the first to retire, soon followed by Steve, and Jem, who was staying over.

'It was fabulous,' Sharon told Rita, kissing her on the cheek.

'You and Bill did most of the work,' Rita smiled.

'He loves being the jolly chef, don't you?' Sharon said, taking Bill's arm.

Bill smiled. He looked very weary. ''Night, folks.' He bent to kiss Rita. 'Tell that son of ours to behave, or else!'

They stood together at the door, watching Sharon and Bill leave, before going up to bed. It was late and the house was very quiet and still.

'Steve asked me if I'd like to marry you,' Rita told him as they undressed.

'What did you tell him?' Gary asked, throwing his T-shirt on to a chair where his slacks already lay crumpled in a heap.

Rita turned to look him in the eye. 'I said I didn't want to get married.'

'Oh,' he replied, slipping into bed, where he picked up his pillow and bashed it into shape before resting his head on it.

'What did you think I'd say?' Rita enquired, pulling off her 'Stop Acid Rain' T-shirt and getting in beside him.

Gary shrugged. 'That's what I thought you'd say.'

Rita lay still for a while, her hands folded against her chest, staring up at the ceiling. 'What was it about Joanne that you didn't like?' she asked at last, turning her head towards Gary.

'I knew it,' he laughed. 'I knew that's what you'd say!'

'You spent enough time talking to her . . . she must have said something to put you off.'

'She didn't say anything.'

'Come on now,' Rita insisted.

Gary sighed.

'Tell me.' She reached across and poked him in the ribs.

'She's just like a lot of other women I've come across.'

'Which means?' She pulled herself up, propping her head on her elbow and looking down at him.

Gary stared straight up into her eyes. 'She's a woman in love with her career,' he answered.

'So?'

'So, nothing. That's all I thought.'

'I had a career before I moved to California. Would it bother you if I had one now . . . or in the future?'

Gary shook his head. 'Of course not.'

'That's easy to say, when you know I haven't.'

'Rita,' he complained, 'give it a rest. I'm tired.'

'I'm not exactly a hausfrau, Gary.'

'I never said you were.' He sounded sleepy.

'But neither do I intend to stay careerless for the remainder of my days.'

'Great,' he said, rolling on to his side and yawning.

'No,' Rita continued, speaking to herself now, 'that I don't intend.' She bent over him for any signs of life but Gary was fast asleep.

Rita got out of the bed and walked across the room and out on to the balcony. She tried to weigh up Gary's response to Joanne. Rita knew that she wasn't anything like Paul's woman but she did have a separate life. Like Joanne, she did have work she could pursue, an alternative to staying at home and catering to the kids. A wave of guilt rolled over her as she considered her former life and the death of Nathan. That fact never left her. Then she wondered just what her sacrifice had been and what would have happened if she had stayed at home. It was the old destructive side of her coming to life for a short while, the part that told her Nathan would still be alive if she'd been a decent mother, a woman who cared about her kids and looked after them properly.

Some of the things Gary had said unnerved Rita. She wasn't sure if he entirely approved of career women, of so-called liberated women, of women who could take care of themselves. For a while she had thought that things would work themselves out but now she wasn't so certain. There was a lot still to learn and it terrified her to think that perhaps Gary was not the one, after all. Not the man to save her, never that, but a person to move her on for a while, to enable her to live with the past.

She leant against the balcony rail, staring out at the city lights in the distance. Rita had drifted through the evening almost as though in a dream, helped by her consumption of alcohol. At times she had looked at Paul and wondered about him. He'd seemed very relaxed, Joanne was obviously good for him and Rita wasn't sure how she felt about this. She found it strange that he should be with someone else. After twenty years it was hard not to feel guilty and jealous. Everything became more and more muddled. The more she thought about it the more confused she became. There were times during the last months when Rita had considered there might still be a chance for them, that she might even still be in love with him. It was a fantasy, of course, irrational and stupid. Paul seemed happy at last, contented with Joanne, whilst she had fallen in love with Gary. But there was always Paul and, she supposed, there always would be. He was too big a part of her life simply to forget, that would be impossible.

Steve's coming-home party had proved a trial to her, one step closer to the inevitable. The outcome clear in their minds. When they sat together that evening, to eat as a family, the split had become even more obvious. For the moment they would go on as before, but the time would come, and it was really very close, when one of them would want freedom from the other, when they would eventually divorce, and then she would see just how strong she'd become.

A car raced up the canyon road, its strong headlights illuminating the sage and manzanita shrub which grew over the steep sides on either side of the twisting route. Rita turned and returned to bed. There was something comforting in having someone there beside her. Sometimes it seemed justification enough for everything else that had gone before.

The boys went to the beach on Sunday, leaving Gary and Rita to their own devices. They had their breakfast on the terrace, the smell of the roses and honeysuckle strong in the warm air.

'I've been thinking about what you said,' Gary told her.

'Yes?' She looked at him over the rim of her coffee cup. 'What did I say?'

'You think I'm a bit of a male chauvinist pig, don't you?'

Rita blinked. 'I never said any such thing.'

'I didn't mean to suggest that women shouldn't have careers,' he continued.

'You were critical of Joanne for her career.'

'Because she has nothing else,' he explained.

'She has Paul,' Rita replied.

'Yes,' he agreed, 'she does now.'

'And she had a husband once . . . Joanne has made her decisions,' Rita said simply.

'Well,' Gary shrugged, 'whatever, but I didn't mean it to sound as though you shouldn't have a career.'

'Many thanks,' she replied icily.

'Rita.' He looked uncomfortable. 'You know what I mean. Stop making it worse!'

'I don't need your approbation for what I do.'

He put up his hands. 'Okay,' Gary nodded, 'I know that. Receiving you loud and clear.'

'You realize,' Rita said, beginning to spoon honey on to her toast, 'we still don't know each other very well, do we?'

'I guess I'm learning fast about you,' he replied wryly.

She looked across the garden at a Himalayan cedar, thinking how attractive everything was. 'What do you want out of the rest of your life, Gary?' she asked him.

He thought for a while before answering. 'I'd like to build a few more things. Maybe do a bit of acting, a movie that my kid could watch and feel proud of . . . Those sort of things.' He poured them some more coffee. 'What about you?'

'I think I'd like to do another book and I'd like to pick up my career again somewhere along the line.'

Gary nodded. 'Sounds good.'

'You wouldn't mind, then?'

'No, ma'am.'

'Sure?'

'I'm sure,' Gary laughed. 'I'm sure.'

Rita relaxed and lounged back in her chair. 'What do you think we'll do, then?'

'Do?'

'Hmm.' She examined his handsome features. 'What will happen to us?'

'What do you want to happen?' he asked.

Rita didn't answer.

'You don't want to marry,' he stated. 'I'm not even sure if you want us to live together.'

'Why does it have to be what I want? What about you?'

'I never really considered getting married again.'

'Having too good a time, eh?' she grinned.

'Listen, I think you've got the wrong idea about me.'

'Really?'

'Really,' he insisted.

Rita was silent for a while. 'Do you think we could live together?'

'Sure,' he replied without hesitation.

'You do?' Rita was surprised.

He shrugged. 'Sure, why not?'

'Where would we live?'

'Where do you want to live?' he asked.

Rita hadn't any idea. 'I can't stay here for ever, it's far too big and expensive . . . The boys will be away soon and, anyway, why should Paul continue to pay for its upkeep?'

'My place, then,' Gary said.

'Do you think it would work?'

'I don't know. It might be a disaster. How do we know anything until we try it?'

Rita agreed, but the next logical step seemed awfully big. 'Your house, then,' she repeated.

'Or I could build us another one . . . Whatever you want. If you're intent on working again, you can support us while I build it!'

It seemed almost a challenge to Rita. 'Put my money where my mouth is, you mean!'

'I guess we'll have to make some sort of real commitment to one another. I'd like us to, I think that would be kind of exciting.'

'You do?'

Gary laughed. 'Stop being so surprised all of the while. Okay, you've had a lousy few years, Rita, but maybe it's time to take a few risks.'

She nodded and then smiled. 'I feel *so* nervous all of a sudden.'

'Good, that means you're alive!'

'We'll do it, then,' she confirmed.

'Okay.'

'When?' she asked.

'Whenever you're ready. Make it soon,' he encouraged.

'What about the boys?' she asked, as though only just remembering about them.

'This is gonna come as a surprise to you, Rita, but I

really like your boys.' He stared across the cluttered breakfast table at her, picking up the *LA Times* and starting to read.

Rita smiled but didn't say anything then. Perhaps it was possible, she did love him, and what were her alternatives? She certainly didn't relish the idea of being alone once the boys had left home. Steve would be gone soon and William not long afterwards. The years flew by now, time didn't hang heavily as when she was young. They were babies one minute and the next they were men, and then they wouldn't really need her any more. The courage to go on was all to do with hanging on to what, or who, was already there. She wouldn't survive by looking for what might be ahead, hoping for some myth that might exist in the future. Rita would be forty-two in a while. This was it, she decided, watching Gary behind his paper. He would have to be trusted and she would have to stop being so damned cautious. 'How soon could you build us a house?' she asked.

'How soon do you want it?'

'I don't know,' she laughed, a slight hysteria, a certain loss of control evident in her voice making her feel edgy.

'We could cut down the cedar after lunch, if you want!' he suggested, looking deadly serious.

'What?' And then she understood that this was his idea of wit, or sarcasm. 'I'm serious,' she complained.

'We have to find a suitable plot first.'

'Right,' she agreed.

'So we're living together, right? Just so I don't misunderstand this . . .'

'Yes,' she said firmly, grinning all over her face.

'Sure you're sure?'

'No.'

'Taking a flyer, huh?' he smiled too. 'I'm impressed.'

'I don't want you to regret anything,' she began.

460

'Shh.' Gary put his finger to his lips, standing and walking round to her side of the table, then taking her hand and leading her inside. 'Come on, let's seal this profound decision in the only way I know how . . .'

'We've just had breakfast!' Rita sounded shocked, as though they were about to offend all the rules of propriety.

'Boy,' Gary whistled, 'you're just a stuffy little English gal at heart, aren't you?' He laughed, putting his arm around her and bending to kiss her on the lips.

'Not at all,' she told him, breaking apart, and smiling. 'Have you always been like this?'

Gary let out a hearty laugh. He hugged her, still chuckling. 'Well, yes, ma'am, I sure as hell have.'

'Right,' Rita said, grabbing his hand and taking the lead, 'let's get up those stairs!'

'You're sure now?' he asked, stopping her in the hallway. 'I mean, there's still time to change your mind!'

Rita surveyed the rather obvious bulge in his shorts. 'Come on,' she said, running up the stairs ahead of him.

She lay with him afterwards, her head resting on his chest, listening to the solid beat of his heart. There seemed nothing else for her but him and, at that moment, in all the world this was where she most wanted to be.

Chapter 13

'I've been thinking,' Rita said. 'Thinking about Nathan . . .'

'Yes?' Dr Allan encouraged.

'We spoke a long time ago about whether or not we had pushed him too hard.'

The doctor nodded. 'I remember.'

'Well, I suppose I was being incredibly defensive then.' She paused to smile. 'It seems such a long time ago now.'

'It was natural to be defensive,' he told her kindly.

'I still don't think we did put pressure on Nathan, not directly, anyway.' Rita sighed. These reflections and memories were still extremely painful to her. 'I suppose,' she began again, 'what I'm trying to say is that by the nature of his home, and who *we* were, academic success was often taken for granted.'

'And Nathan wasn't really up to it?' the doctor questioned her carefully.

'He had to work twice, three times, as hard as anyone else to achieve his results . . . Paul's reputation couldn't have done him any good either.' She looked away.

'So, Rita, what are you saying?'

She looked at him again. He was leaning forward, an earnest expression on his face. 'Looking back, I'm not convinced in my own mind that Nathan would have completed his course of study . . . I don't think he'd have become a doctor.'

Dr Allan clenched his hands together on the desk top. 'And you think Nathan was aware of that prospect?'

'Yes,' Rita replied, feeling strangely calm now, almost

removed from the situation. 'Of course he'd have been completely aware.'

'So,' the doctor began, sitting back into his chair, 'where does that take us now?'

Rita shrugged. She adjusted the cuff of her white cotton shirt, pulling it out beneath the sleeve of the fitted grey pin-striped jacket she was wearing. Another of her businesswoman-of-the-year suits, together with matching bag and shoes.

'If you see this as a reason for Nathan's suicide, then it follows that you accept what Nathan told Steve.'

There was a long silence in the room whilst Rita considered her answer to that. She could hear the *tick*, *tick*, *tick* of the clock on the desk in front of him. 'I can see there might be a connection.'

'You don't sound very convinced,' he replied.

'I suppose it's a case of not wanting to believe.'

Dr Allan smiled a little, scratching his nose and then dropping his hands into his lap. 'How does it feel?' he asked.

'Strange,' she admitted. 'I feel calm and yet I'm virtually saying that I'm indictable.'

'Do you feel responsible, Rita?'

'Of course, yes,' she replied softly, without any hesitation.

'And guilty?'

'Yes.'

'And *are* you responsible?' he asked bluntly.

Tears came to her eyes but didn't fall. She swallowed hard before answering. 'Ultimately, I suppose I must be.' She sounded resigned and virtually defeated.

'No,' he shook his head, 'no, no, that wasn't what I asked. Are you responsible?'

She stared at him but didn't answer.

'Are you responsible for Nathan's death, Rita? It's a

463

simple enough question . . . nothing to do with what you suppose or what ultimately happened – yes or no.'

'I had no idea what he was intending to do.'

'Yes or no,' he demanded again, watching her, his body seeming tense, his voice firm.

'No.' Rita found she was trembling uncontrollably, the poise from a moment ago completely deserting her. 'But that doesn't stop the guilt, it doesn't make it all right . . .'

'And, maybe, it never will feel all right,' he continued, 'but we can learn to deal with that too!' He sounded extremely sure of that fact.

Rita looked unconvinced, all the same. 'I feel terrible,' she admitted, resting her head in her hands.

Dr Allan reached to his left and poured Rita a glass of iced water, which he came round the desk to hand her. 'Here,' he instructed, pushing it towards Rita and leaning against the desk, his arms folded, watching her drink. 'Any better?'

Rita nodded, looking up at him. It was the first time she could remember in any of their sessions together that he had actually come from behind the desk, except when he was showing her out or welcoming her. 'I'm sorry,' she began, handing the glass to him.

'Finish it,' he said.

Rita did as she was told, the chilling water seeming to have a calming effect, making her feel less sick.

'It's always hard, isn't it?'

'Hard?' Rita was confused.

'Coming to these difficult conclusions. It's *very* hard.' Dr Allan nodded in agreement with himself.

'It's easy to absolve ourselves . . . to say no,' Rita replied miserably.

'It's hard, Rita, terribly hard,' he contradicted immediately, 'but maybe it's another step . . . What do you think?'

464

Rita didn't know what to think. 'It just seems to get harder and harder. Sometimes, when I'm feeling happy, I wonder if I'm starting to emerge from this . . . from these awful feelings and emotions, but then I become immersed in such guilt.' She looked into the empty glass still clasped firmly in her right hand. 'It's like having some terminal illness and trying to fool oneself that it will simply go away one day.'

'Okay.' He took the glass from her. 'It's tough, I know that, but try not to despair too much. These things take time.'

Rita watched his face. 'I know, I know,' she said softly, 'and life *is* a terminal illness.' She managed to smile a little at the recollection of that old cliché. 'And things aren't always this bleak.'

'That's right. Just don't be afraid to go with your emotions . . . Are you speaking to Gary more concerning these feelings?' he asked.

'Not really,' Rita admitted, thinking of Gary, who had flown to New York to spend a week with his son and ex-wife.

'Why not?' Dr Allan enquired.

'There just doesn't seem to have been an appropriate moment.'

'I see.' But it was said as though he didn't entirely believe her. 'Well,' he continued, turning to look quickly at his clock, 'what are you feeling now?'

'What am I feeling?' she repeated to herself. 'I'm feeling a little bit like a child who hasn't done her homework.'

The doctor laughed. 'Why is that?' he asked, still smiling.

'Because I never seem to get it quite right.'

'We're providing different strategic plans here, we're discussing what *might* work . . . You're not a machine,

465

you can't expect everything always to pan out!' Dr Allan smiled as he walked Rita out of his office. 'I think you're making progress,' he said, opening the door for her, 'and I'll see you same time next week.'

Rita left him, feeling as though she'd been patted on the head and as though she'd just betrayed Nathan. She returned to her car and drove home, not really remembering any of the journey, so consumed were her thoughts with what she'd just done. Dr Allan was nice enough and he had a good reputation and she did feel as though the sessions with him were of some benefit, even if the professional/client relationship was a trifle paternalistic. Rita tended to succumb to his professionalism and gloss. She fell quite readily into the role of 'patient' and, worse still, almost expected Dr Allan to provide every answer.

'Maybe you're ready to dispense with his services,' Sharon suggested as she listened to Rita's thoughts concerning her analysis.

'I don't know,' Rita replied.

'He's very good,' Sharon said.

'I know,' Rita nodded. 'Also very expensive . . . not that Paul's ever complained,' she added quickly, not wishing to betray Paul any more than she already had done.

'What are you working on?' Sharon asked, changing the subject abruptly and looking at Rita's voluminous notes.

Rita smiled, scribbling out a line and inserting something fresh before turning to her friend. She'd hoped for a free afternoon working at the redwood table but Sharon had come across the lawns for a chat and, whilst pleased to see her, Rita sometimes wished for a little peace and quiet. 'That thing on Thomas Hardy's heroines I told you about.'

Sharon nodded. 'Do you fancy going somewhere this afternoon . . . shopping, for example? The Westside Pavilion?'

Rita thought about the immense shopping mall with its glass dome and luxurious interior. Sharon seemed to spend more and more time shopping these days, or perhaps she just hadn't noticed it before. 'I don't think so, I *really* have to get down to this,' she said, tapping at her notes.

'You loved it the last time we went,' Sharon encouraged.

'Kirk's coming to give me a tennis lesson at four-thirty,' Rita explained.

'We've got hours, then,' Sharon said, smiling across the redwood table. 'It's only one-fifteen.'

Rita had no desire to go shopping. The shopping malls were all like miniature Disneylands, each one more mind-boggling than the last, and Sharon would buy absolutely anything, the most useless frippery . . . battery-operated garden flowers which lit up and smelt 'just like real!'

'No, I have to work,' Rita said firmly, but making it a sort of joke all the same.

Sharon sighed and then smiled. 'Okay, well, I'm still going . . . I'll give you a call later, okay?' She gave Rita a strange, almost pained look which was still evident despite her wide smile.

'Fine,' Rita replied. 'Come and show me what you've bought.'

Sharon agreed, waving as she walked away, stepping out of the shade and into the bright sunlight. 'Don't work too hard, now.'

Rita waved back, watching until her friend had disappeared from view. The boys were down by the pool. William was reading and Steve appeared to be asleep on one of the sun loungers. Rosa was hanging out washing –

467

Rosa was *always* hanging out washing, looking immaculate in her smart grey uniform and crisply starched white apron. Rita felt guilty about letting Sharon down, even though it was only over a stupid shopping trip. Guilt seemed to have become her mainstay, sometimes it seemed to be almost a way of life. Rita turned to her work, concentrating upon the critical notes and essays she'd collected, becoming lost and intrigued in the words. She was reading about Tess's meeting with Alec when Kirk arrived, striding across the grass towards her.

Rita looked at her watch. 'My God, I'm sorry, Kirk,' she apologized. 'Go on down and I'll meet you on the court in a minute.'

Kirk smiled. 'Okay, no problem . . . don't rush.'

Rita closed up her books and carried everything into the house, running upstairs to change for her tennis lesson, the picture of Alec d'Urberville, swarthy and full-lipped, with roving eyes and a touch of the barbarian, still in her mind's eye.

Rita always felt better after a tough session with Kirk. She wondered if it might be more beneficial to stop seeing Dr Allan and spend more time on court with her tennis coach!

'How are the house plans going?' Kirk asked as they walked off court.

'There's a possibility of two sites,' Rita told him, 'Coldwater Canyon or Zuma Beach.'

'What about a tennis court?' Kirk joked.

Rita hadn't given that any consideration. 'Damn, I'll have to book you down at the club . . . Anyway, it won't be for a while yet.'

'I'll miss coming here,' Kirk admitted.

'Will you?' She seemed surprised.

'Sure.'

468

'Well, perhaps Gary will build a court too. Everything is a bit up in the air, as you can imagine.'

'That backhand still needs some attention,' he told her as they walked up from the shaded court, using his racket to imitate the stroke.

'I know,' Rita acknowledged. 'I wasn't concentrating hard enough.'

'It should be second nature to you now,' Kirk laughed.

'I'm not getting enough practice,' Rita admitted as they walked into the afternoon sun, stepping on to the paved surround of the swimming pool. The boys had gone, leaving towels draped over lounger chairs and various empty glasses and mugs.

'Looks tempting,' Kirk said, standing at the edge and staring into the clear blue water.

'Be my guest,' Rita replied.

'I'd love to.' He turned to her. 'But duty calls. I have to be over in Glendale in an hour.'

She walked him to his car. To Rita, Kirk was some kind of untouchable fantasy figure. He was everything a tennis coach should be and he was so handsome that it was almost a joke to her.

'That was good, thanks a lot,' she said, watching his tight little behind, encased in his rather short white shorts, as he walked round to climb into his car. Rita waved him away before racing upstairs and taking a long shower.

She was, Rita realized, annoyed at Gary, irrational and silly as it was, for going to New York. He had simply decided it on the spur of the moment. His son was going to be around and, therefore, it was a good time to go. He'd booked the flight and then told her about it twenty-four hours before he was due to leave. Rita had even driven him to LA International Airport, acting as though this happened to her all of the time. She thought she'd

469

been *very* cool indeed, kissing Gary lightly on the cheek and wishing him a good trip.

Rita stepped out of the shower and quickly dried herself, pulling on a pair of red cotton trousers and a white T-shirt, her hair combed back, her face pink and with a healthy glow. She paused in front of a full-length wardrobe mirror for a moment, wondering what people must think of her, before running downstairs to sort out an evening meal.

Paul was sitting in the lounge with the boys when she walked through the house. He had turned up without any warning on his way home from work. They were sitting around talking about something as she entered the room. It struck her that the whole scene had a particular alien quality about it. She had never seen Paul sitting with his children and making conversation with them!

'Hello,' she said, putting a hand to her slick wet hair and feeling a sight.

'Hi,' Paul smiled. 'I just dropped in on the off chance . . . I hope that's all right.'

'Of course.' Rita looked at him before she smiled. 'Do you want a drink or something?'

'That would be good,' he said.

'Right,' she nodded, looking at the boys in turn. 'Before I start,' she began, 'are you both in for a meal or what?'

'We're in,' Steve informed her.

'Okay.'

'What are we eating?' William asked.

'God knows,' Rita replied, turning and moving swiftly towards the kitchen, where she dug about in the refrigerator for a can of beer. Retrieving one, she turned to find Paul behind her. 'I was going to bring it through,' she said.

He took the can from her. 'I'll see to it,' he said. 'Aren't you having anything?'

'No,' Rita replied, finding a pack of lean mince and deciding upon spaghetti.

'How are things?' Paul asked, sitting at the table and drinking the beer from the can.

'All right,' she told him.

'Gary all right?'

'Yes,' she nodded. 'Joanne?'

'She's fine.'

'Good,' Rita said, beginning to prepare the meal, slightly unnerved at his presence and rather wary. Paul had never been in the habit of just dropping in 'on the off chance'. 'Busy day?' she asked.

'Hell of a day,' Paul sighed, tipping the Schlitz can to his lips. 'What about you?'

'Oh, you know, another typical day – my analyst, my tennis coach . . . What is it, Paul?' she asked. 'What are you doing here?'

'I dropped in,' he explained again.

'You *never* do that. There must be something going on.' Rita was busy chopping onions, dabbing at her eyes every now and again with the clean tea-towel at her side. 'We've been separated all this time and you've never once just called in to see us.'

'We weren't exactly on the best of terms to begin with.'

'Yes, well, when one's spouse walks out on you it doesn't exactly lead to close relations . . .'

'I can see you're not in the best of moods,' he said.

'I'm fine,' she said, relenting a little, starting to feel guilty now about hurting Paul's feelings.

Rita hurried along with the meal, browning the meat and eventually dumping everything into a large saucepan and stirring in a can of chopped tomatoes, and mixed herbs, garlic, red wine and tomato purée. 'Come on,' she

471

said, banging the lid on to the saucepan, 'it's too hot in here to think.' Rita poured the remains of the red wine into a glass and wandered on to the terrace. Paul followed her out. Steve and William were in the pool by now, where William, instructed by his brother, was practising diving from the board.

'They seem okay,' Paul said, sitting down at the table and watching them across the garden.

'It doesn't take much to upset their equilibrium, though,' she replied.

Paul nodded. 'They're so big now, aren't they? I find it hard to believe sometimes, it doesn't seem five minutes since they were toddlers.'

'They're still children,' Rita replied. 'They've a lot of growing up to do yet . . . I only hope that the past few years haven't traumatized them too much.'

Paul didn't say anything in reply to that. 'I'm glad we're still communicating, though.'

'I never stopped,' she advised him.

'No,' he said seriously, 'I know that.'

'It's difficult to maintain good communications when your husband walks out on you.' Rita said this without rancour.

'I didn't think it would work out this way,' Paul admitted.

'No?' Rita challenged. 'Did you really think that we would get back together, that we'd somehow pick up the pieces again and carry on?'

'I don't know what I thought . . . There didn't seem any other way.'

'That's most unlike you, Paul. I thought you always weighed everything up with the greatest care.'

'Come on now, Rita, we were driving each other insane.'

'Well, I don't want to get into all those old arguments,' Rita said, sounding distinctly weary.

'So,' he began after another long silence in which the sounds from the pool seemed very clear, 'you and Gary are building a house.'

'Not exactly,' Rita said. 'We haven't even got ourselves a plot yet, and he's the one who does all the dirty work.'

'Actually, I was hoping to see Gary. I'm thinking of having some alterations made at the beach house.'

'He's away, gone to New York to visit his son.' She smiled at Paul. 'You're going to buy your house, then?'

Paul shrugged. 'I might as well.'

'You could always move back in here once we've gone.'

'No,' Paul shook his head, 'it's too big for a single chap.'

Rita laughed. 'You're not single . . . yet!'

'You know what I mean,' Paul grinned. 'You don't have to leave here, you know that.'

'The boys will be away soon. God knows what I'd do with myself, rattling around this great barn.' Rita finished her drink. 'I want to work again too. I'm not sure if I've really enjoyed being a kept woman.'

'Whatever happens, we'll split it all down the middle. There's still the sale of Chalcot Square to settle . . .'

'Dismantling the marriage, eh?' she asked, half as a joke.

'We can keep the house, if you want,' Paul replied.

'No, what's the point?' It all sounded very final to Rita, not that she hadn't expected this but, now it was becoming a reality, she felt sad, seeing it all as an awful failure. 'I think we must accept the inevitable,' she told Paul. 'I don't find it terribly easy, though . . . I suppose we should think about divorce too.' Having actually said the words, she found them quite shocking.

'Do you want that?' He seemed a little surprised.

Rita looked away. 'Don't you?'

'I don't think it's absolutely necessary . . . I mean, we don't have to consider it now, do we?' He sounded uncertain, as though her idea had thrown him completely. 'I don't want to marry again,' he continued. 'Do you?'

'No.'

'So?'

'That isn't the point. Who knows what we'll want to do in another year's time, or where we'll be, or what we'll be doing?'

'What about the boys?'

'We have to sit down and talk to them about it,' she said calmly. 'Not now but in a while. They know that we're not about to live together again.'

'If it's the legal things you're worried about, the house and the cars, your allowance . . .'

Rita stopped him, smiling as she spoke. 'I'm not worried, but what's the point of dragging things out for ever more?' She looked into Paul's sad eyes. 'You may want to marry Joanne one day!' she remarked.

'Joanne?' He laughed at that idea. 'Do you seriously think that Joanne would marry anyone?'

'People change,' she said. 'A few years ago you'd never have imagined this as a possibility. Once we're divorced, you'll look back and wonder how we could ever have been married!'

'Never,' he insisted.

'Well, I don't want to divorce you tomorrow, but I don't want to be married any more. Does that make any sense?'

Paul looked a little crestfallen but he nodded all the same. 'Okay,' he said gently. 'When do you think the time will be right to tell them?'

'There probably isn't going to be a right time. I'll try to break it to them gently.'

'And then we'll sit down and discuss it as a family?' Paul asked.

Rita hadn't really thought about that. 'I suppose we could.'

'You don't think it's a good idea?' He seemed confused now, a bit unsure.

'We can if you like . . . it seems to be dragging out the agony, though.'

'We'll see, then,' was all Paul replied. 'We'll see.'

'Right.' She smiled, feeling satisfied that they had come this far without any particular nastiness or major argument. Each one on their best behaviour. It felt extremely odd to her.

Paul declined her invitation to eat with them. He was seeing Joanne later and had a pile of work to get through before then. Rita said she understood and, with some relief, watched as he went down to the pool, where he chatted to the boys for a while, squatting down on his haunches and giving them some advice. Paul was making diving motions with his hands, dipping them up and down to simulate some dive or other. After a while he stood up and waved them goodbye.

They sat in the kitchen, big plates of spaghetti alla bolognese, or at least Rita's version of it, in front of them. No one paid the meal much attention. The boys were watching baseball on TV, Rita was reading *Tess of the d'Urbervilles*.

'Why did Dad come over?' Steve asked, pushing his empty plate away and reaching for his glass of Coke. William was at the fridge dishing out giant scoops of ice cream.

'I'm not really sure,' Rita replied, looking up from her book, 'there didn't seem to be any reason.'

'You were talking for long enough,' Steve commented.

Rita nodded, returning to Thomas Hardy.

'Was it about anything interesting?' he asked.

She looked up once more. William had returned to the table with their dessert and was watching her intently. 'We talked about divorce,' she said, taking a spoonful of ice cream. 'Okay?'

'Divorce?' William said.

Rita nodded. 'Divorce.'

'When?' Steve asked.

'I don't know . . . Why are you looking at me like that?' She closed the book. 'It can hardly come as a surprise around these parts that your father and I are no longer exactly the happy folks we once were. We've been apart for long enough, surely.'

'Why does he want to divorce you?' William asked, sounding affronted. 'In order to marry his woman?'

Rita smiled. '*I'm* the culprit, if you must know. It's my fault. I want a divorce.'

'Why?' Steve asked.

'Why not?' Rita replied, wishing she'd never started this in the first place.

'Come on, Ma,' he insisted.

'Because I think it's stupid to stay married. We're never going to live together again. You know what the score is!' There was a defiant glint in her eyes.

'Are you and Gary getting married, then?' Steve asked.

'No.'

'So, why all the rush to get divorced from Dad?' William asked.

'There's no rush,' she said calmly. 'It isn't going to happen next week, next month, not even next year . . .'

'Then why bring it up now?' he challenged her, sounding annoyed.

'Because I don't want you getting any funny ideas about me and your father.'

476

'Such as?' William asked.

'Such as us getting back together again. Isn't that what all this is about?'

'Stranger things have happened,' Steve replied.

'There isn't a snowball's chance in hell of us getting it back together, Steve,' Rita said clearly. 'Understood?'

He nodded his reply, averting his eyes down to his ice cream, moving his spoon around in the mushy mess without eating any of it. 'Is Dad going to marry Joanne?' he asked at last.

'He says not.'

'What do you think?'

'I should think not.'

'Jesus,' Steve breathed, 'isn't anything ever going to go right in this family?' He glared at her then.

'Everything is just fine,' Rita said calmly, 'and don't blaspheme at the dinner table.'

'Why not? You blaspheme all over the place,' he accused.

'I'm the grown-up,' she replied, suddenly realizing how ludicrous that sounded and bursting into laughter at her own pomposity.

Steve started to laugh as well.

William looked at them as though they were totally insane. 'I don't see what's so funny, you two.'

Rita wiped her eyes. 'No, you're right,' she said, tears of mirth rolling over her cheeks. 'But what the hell? Don't look so serious,' she told him.

'Divorce isn't serious?' William replied, sounding stern and moralistic.

'Yes, it's serious, of course it is.' Rita stopped laughing and looked across the table at him. 'But you have to accept some things, William, you just have to accept them without too much fuss.'

'Aren't you sad?' he asked her.

Rita shrugged. 'I was sad when your father left, and now I'm resigned to what has happened . . . I'm trying to be honest with you both, we've been through so much since Nathan died, we've struggled through it somehow. Your dad's just down the road. If we moved to Zuma we'd be next-door neighbours – well, almost!' she smiled. 'What will divorce change?'

'It's the end of something,' William worried. 'An end to our family.'

'How? How is it that?' Rita wanted to know.

''Cause you and Dad won't be married any more,' he replied hopelessly, pushing his chair away from the table and moving swiftly out of the kitchen.

'Now what have I done?' Rita asked, starting to get up, intending to follow him.

'Leave him, Mum,' Steve said, putting a hand on her arm. 'He's better left for a while . . . I'll go and see him in a minute.'

'Did he seriously think we were going to get back together?' She sounded amazed. 'I suppose he must have,' she said, answering her own question.

Steve shook his head. 'No, it's not that.'

'Then what is it?'

'William is still scared that once you're divorced we'll split up . . . that maybe you'll go back to England or somewhere with Gary. He's just a bit mixed up about things but he'll be okay in a while,' Steve assured her.

Rita felt as though she hardly knew her own children then. Steve was acting just like his father all of a sudden, composed and mature and in control. William, who usually appeared to be so full of stoicism, was really brittle and scared under the surface. She knew all this, hadn't she just finished telling Paul that they were still children, for all their adult pretensions and bravery?

'William understands, Mum,' Steve continued. 'He's probably just tired.'

'You'd better go up to him,' Rita advised. 'Go and see if he's all right.'

'He's fine.'

'Go and see,' she said.

Steve smiled. 'Okay, but all he needs is a little time alone, that's all.'

Rita nodded, staring at her half-finished ice cream, not wanting any more of it. She busied herself with the clearing-up, fitting plates carefully into the dishwasher, all neatly stacked and stowed inside. She put everything away and wiped down the work surfaces and the cooking hob before picking up her book and taking it into the cool lounge, where she attempted to concentrate upon Hardy's prose.

It proved to be a useless exercise, however. Her thoughts spun around inside her head. Perhaps she should have made more of an effort to salvage her marriage. Perhaps she'd been unreasonable, perhaps there was even still the glimmer of a hope . . . perhaps, perhaps, perhaps. But she knew it was useless, a lost cause. There was no marriage to speak of. She had maintained an uneasy friendship with Paul for the sake of their children but there had never been any question of a reconciliation since the moment he left the house and moved to Malibu – a bolt-hole that had been secured by stealth some time before his departure.

Rita had always considered Paul to be something of a coward but at least he'd made the break. There was, after all, a certain bravery in what he had done. He hadn't prolonged the agony and, for all of her distrust, that had taken a certain courage. But what was she to do? Take the boys back to London? Go through more upheaval and trauma? It was too late for Rita to do anything other than stay. And so they grasped at straws like drowning men, Paul with Joanne, and Rita with Gary. Her past behind her, her future uncertain, she attempted to reconcile herself to it all, Nathan's death and all of the rest, but it was often a hard and painful road.

She was surprised at how easily the new relationships were accepted . . . it seemed terribly un-British, somehow – Rita smiled at this particular reflection. However, it was true. When she was at work she had always been mildly shocked at the interdepartmental affairs, but here she was virtually living with another man whilst still married to Paul, who was virtually living with another woman. It wasn't really anything to do with morality or decorum, no, it was just such an unexpected thing to have done. The Sunday tabloids at home would have made a great fuss about it: 'FAMOUS SURGEON AND WIFE IN PARTNER SWOP SENSATION!' Here it didn't seem anything at all . . . Or perhaps Nathan's suicide just made nothing else seem so important any more. This streak of Victorian prudery served to make Rita feel uncomfortable. She had no idea where it came from, certainly not her own mother, certainly not her own family background. Perhaps the years of indoctrination from Paul's mother, Mary, had finally sunk in. Mary was a great one for inculcating guilt, and now Rita had more than enough to spread around.

The boys came in after a while. William sat down next to her on the sofa whilst Steve sat opposite them in one of the leather armchairs.

'I'm sorry,' William said contritely.

'Don't be silly,' she said, putting an arm round him. 'Are you all right now?'

He nodded.

'Good,' she said brightly.

'Mum?' William asked, looking serious.

480

'Yes.' She turned to him, wondering what was going to be asked of her now.

'Think I'll have some more ice cream or something.'

'Oh, William,' Rita said, starting to laugh, 'don't you ever stop eating?'

'I'm a growing youth,' he said, a bemused smile growing over his face as his mother dissolved into another fit of laughter.

'You're a gannet!' Rita said at last. 'A gannet!' She watched as he went off to the kitchen, then turned to Steve. 'What did you say to him?' she enquired.

'Nothing,' Steve shrugged. '*He* told me that he'd been stupid . . . I think he realizes now that nothing earth-shattering is about to happen and that we'll all be in the same area for a while yet.'

Rita nodded. 'What do you think about it all?' she asked. 'You didn't seem too pleased about the prospect of us divorcing either.'

'Am I supposed to be happy?' Steve asked, looking at his mother.

'No, but do you understand?'

'Sure,' he nodded, looking away towards the large sliding glass doors which reflected their images against the darkness outside. 'It's not exactly unexpected.'

'What about Gary and me?' she pressed on.

'What about it?' He seemed confused, watching her again.

'What do you think?'

'Come on, Mother.' He looked embarrassed. 'What you and Gary do is your business.'

'Agreed, but you must have some sort of opinion.'

'Gary's great!' was all he would say.

'So, you don't mind, then?'

'No. Would it make any difference if I did?'

'Of course it would,' Rita replied.

'If I objected, you'd dump Gary?'

'Stop playing games,' Rita instructed him. 'I would like to think that everything was going to work out reasonably well from now on.' She reached forward to touch the edge of the coffee table.

Steve nodded. 'I know. It'll be fine.' He smiled at last, looking into her uncertain face. 'Really.'

William came back in a few minutes with his plate piled high with sandwiches and cookies, carrying a glass of milk. 'Time for the game,' he told Steve.

'Are you sure that's enough?' Rita asked. 'I mean, there's stuff in the freezer if it isn't.'

'It's fine, thank you,' William said, sitting down in front of the television screen.

'We might send out for pizzas later,' Steve told her.

'You'll do no such thing,' she instructed.

They nudged one another and sniggered as the game began.

Rita picked up a cushion and tossed it over to them, hitting William squarely on the back of his head. 'Gannets!' she said, leaving them to their sport. 'And don't be up all night.' She went up to her room, where she once again began to read her novel, falling asleep some time after eleven-thirty, the open book resting on her chest and the bedside lamp on.

'God knows what I shall do when you leave,' Sharon grinned as they sat out having breakfast on the terrace after their morning jog.

'We haven't even got a house to live in yet . . . it could be another year at this rate!' Rita responded.

'I hope so,' Sharon said with feeling.

'We'll only be down the road a bit. Don't get maudlin now,' she laughed. 'Anyway, you'll soon be best of friends with the new owners . . . Look at the way you just sauntered into my life.'

'Oh, God, yes.' Sharon clamped her hand to her mouth. 'Did you think I was being a pushy broad?'

'Well, Bill and Paul sort of knew one another, so it wasn't such a surprise!' She smiled at the memory. 'What a mess I was in then . . . the house was in a state, *I* was in an even worse state.'

'And now look at you,' Sharon said.

'Yes.' Rita sounded doubtful. 'Now look at me, about to embark on yet another trip into the unknown.'

'Rubbish, Gary's fine. Don't be so pessimistic, everything is going to work out fine from now on.' She looked at Rita. 'Okay?'

'Don't tempt fate,' was all she replied.

Sharon groaned. 'God, you English, you're so exasperating at times. I had thought that we were on the way to making you a good Californian.'

'I embody most of the traits associated with this place now. I mean, I'm fighting to preserve my youth! I have my analyst, my tennis coach, my maid . . .' Rita chuckled at the thought of all this. '. . . I'm separated, I have a younger man . . .'

'Not much younger,' Sharon added. 'If you wanted to be *really* tacky you'd be with someone of Kirk's age!'

'Anyway, I feel like a character out of one of those great sex-shocker books you keep giving me to read!'

'Ah, now that's where the indoctrination comes in. It was all meant to happen, you see,' Sharon explained, sounding conspiratorial but spoiling the effect by laughing like a drain.

Rosa came back in a little while to remove their used breakfast things and replenish the coffee. They were both cackling together like harpies over a story Sharon had just told concerning an aunt of hers who, being terribly myopic and too vain to wear glasses, had once wiped down the kitchen table with the cat. Rosa smiled rather indulgently over her two charges and moved quietly away once more along the broad terrace.

'I don't believe a word of it,' Rita said, gasping for air and dabbing at her eyes with a napkin.

'It's the truth,' Sharon insisted. 'My aunt Ginger, she was renowned for her eccentricity!'

'It seems as though her niece has taken after her,' Rita replied.

Sharon grinned. She was in a happy mood, having persuaded Rita to go with her to a new beauty salon that had opened up in Westwood Village. 'Shall we have lunch out?'

'I don't know.' Rita sounded doubtful, 'I wanted to get some work done.'

'Oh, come on,' Sharon encouraged as usual. 'We'll have a pleasant lunch somewhere, go to the beauty shop and come out looking like a million dollars, and then go out on the town!'

'You're kidding!' Rita sounded appalled. 'You *are* kidding, aren't you?'

'Sure, but let's have lunch out, at least.'

Rita surrendered at last, giving in to Sharon's pleadings, and arranged to pick her up in a couple of hours.

'Wear something sexy,' Sharon instructed as she left.

'I'll do no such thing,' Rita replied.

'Suit yourself, but the guy who runs this place is supposed to be absolutely fabulous!'

'Sharon,' Rita said firmly, 'I'm going to have my hair cut, all right?'

'Right,' Sharon replied, picking up her running shoes and stepping out over the grass in her bare feet, waving to the gardener as he rattled by on his ancient mowing machine. 'See you soon,' she called to Rita, before starting to run towards her own house.

Rita picked up her coffee cup and felt the warmth of the sun against her bare legs and arms and on her face. She wondered what would have happened without Sharon. From the moment she walked into Rita's lounge things had never been quite the same. She'd encouraged and cajoled and sometimes forced Rita to attempt things she otherwise might have ignored. Certainly the idea of enjoying a morning jog or a game of tennis or a swim would have seemed absurd to Rita before. Sharon had always appeared to be everything that Rita wasn't – supercharged, always ready to go, seemingly unafraid of anything and always there when it really mattered.

Sharon and Bill had in a real sense become family, connected and concerned and always responsive to what was important. Rita loved them dearly, but now felt the need to move away from under their all-protective wings. She wasn't escaping them, exactly. It was just that she felt able to survive in this strange land by herself.

Rosa came back again to clear away the rest of the breakfast things, and Rita went off to shower and change and get down to some work at the redwood table under the palms. The afternoon would be lost to Sharon and the new beauty shop, the evening taken up with the boys and the never-ending attempts to satisfy their hunger pangs. Sitting under the shady palms, looking out over the lush garden, Rita turned back to Hardy and rejoined Tess in the bleak winter landscape, grubbing out the turnips at Flintcomb-Ash. She read, undisturbed, for the next hour, lost and enthralled.

Rita picked Gary up again on his return from New York. He kissed her and took her hand as they walked to the car.

'Miss me?' Gary asked.

'You're so egocentric,' Rita smiled.

'No, no, it was just a general enquiry. I missed you.'

Rita ignored the prompt. 'How was New York?'

'New York was sticky and uncomfortable,' Gary replied, waiting for her to unlock the car doors and then getting into the large Ford.

'What about your lad?' she asked, slamming her door and starting the engine.

'Okay,' Gary nodded.

'And your ex-wife?'

'She's okay too,' Gary replied, smiling across at her. 'Got a new man in her life, another actor.' He sounded very dismissive. 'He's appearing in an off-off-Broadway thing about AIDS . . .'

'What's wrong with that?' she asked.

'Jesus,' he sighed, 'actors with a social conscience!'

'Did you go to see it?'

'Of course, it was almost obligatory.'

'And?'

'It was all right, I guess.'

'What else did you get up to?' Rita asked, turning out of the airport.

'Looked up a few old buddies, wandered around a bit, you know, a bit of a tourist trip, really.'

'I've never been,' she said.

'What's New York?' he asked. 'It's just a big, smelly city . . . We can go sometime if you like.'

'Thanks,' she replied drily.

'No,' he insisted, 'we can go.'

Rita looked at the rushing traffic and smiled to herself.

When they were settled into Rita's house Gary handed her a gift from New York. He had just come out of the shower and had a towel wrapped around his waist. He

486

found Rita in the kitchen, where she was making tea. She undid the small package and produced a pottery representation of the Empire State building with a tiny King Kong clambering up its side.

Rita laughed, setting it down in front of her and turning to kiss him. 'It's lovely,' she said.

'Miss me?' he asked gruffly, holding her, his large hand underneath the thin material of her T-shirt caressing the skin of her back and then her breasts.

She put her arms around his neck, reaching up to him and kissing his mouth again. 'What do you think?' she asked.

'I think we should retire to the boudoir,' he smiled. 'What do you think?'

'I think you're a randy old sod!' But Rita was already retracing their steps to her bedroom, where she quickly stripped off her shorts and T-shirt and briefs. Gary rolled on top of her, kissing her for a long time.

'Jesus, Rita,' he said breathlessly, 'I've missed this.' His finger was already stroking her clitoris as his tongue moved over her nipples and she rose up under him, feeling herself becoming increasingly wet, biting into him as she shifted her position, forcing his hand out of the way and guiding his hard penis towards her, feeling it entering her and filling her up. Rita held him tightly, her smooth skin against the hardness of his muscles, the dangerous quality of his blatant masculinity all around her as she clung on, moving in a deliciously meticulous rhythm as Gary went in and out of her, completely absorbed as everything else became subordinated to achieving that one aim, the rubbing, sweating, grunting absolute climax of their act. Rita began to gasp, that strange voice which she never recognized catching in her throat and emitting odd grating cries as she reached orgasm quickly and then again and again until she felt unable to hang on much longer. He thrust at her a few more times and then collapsed with her, their limbs interlocking and tangled amidst the crumpled bedding, everything hot and damp and relaxed and as one.

Rita kissed him gently and then held him tightly, moving against him, wanting everything now.

They swam in the warm afternoon sun, sometimes circling around one another, unspeaking, their eyes watching and understanding something almost primeval between them. They kissed and splashed and embraced and touched, sometimes under the water, sometimes above, until, exhausted, they lay and dozed together in the sunshine. Later they raided the fridge and took a picnic into the lounge, where they lay on the floor and watched the mindless TV shows, laughing and talking through them until, eventually, they consummated another act of carnality and desire in front of the fake-log gas fire, rolling on the rug and grinning afterwards at the rampant sex and the thrilling stupidity of it all.

'If I thought about it I'd never do it,' Rita admitted.

'Don't *ever* think about it,' he laughed.

Rita drifted away into her thoughts. She concentrated on the flames as they licked over the fake logs which never burnt. Rita remembered the first man she'd ever slept with. He was an older man. Rita was sixteen and he was probably in his middle thirties. She hadn't thought about him for years. He was married and had three sons and she'd met him in the hospital where she worked during the holidays. He was a porter. Sometimes she was asked to take food for the patients on special diets down to the ward, and she would meet him in the rabbit-warren hospital, clattering along the echoing corridors. Sometimes he would come up to the old kitchens on the third floor and pass the time of day. He was friendly and gregarious, quite handsome, with watery blue eyes and sandy-coloured hair. She really couldn't recall now how it had happened but that summer proved a revelation to her. He had a look she'd compared to Paul Newman – there were, she reflected now, passing similarities.

Her Paul Newman lookalike took her back to his house at lunchtimes and he would undress her and introduce her to the many varied and delicious ways of sexual intercourse. He wasn't a particularly bright man but, where sex was concerned, he was a Nobel Prize winner! At least, that's what Rita thought. Afterwards they would hardly ever speak . . . they would have absolutely nothing to say to one another. It wasn't, after all, a love affair, they weren't even friends. He might make a comment about the weather, but generally they dressed in silence, Rita with her back to him, pulling everything on as quickly as possible, anxious to leave and be on her way. It was illicit, certainly, and exciting, but also frightening to her. Rita would consider her loss of control to him, the surrender of her virginity, the strength of her desire with a mixture of fear and relief. She would leave quickly, and, after work, would sit in the bath, soaking and scrubbing away, washing him off her. Marlene would bang on the door and demand to be let in but Rita would tell her to go away, and lie back in the warm, soapy water, alive with new experiences and expectations.

For the next few years, until she went to university and met Paul, Rita continued to see her married man. He told her that you could never stop experimenting with sex and he taught her that it was a reciprocal thing, not just something that men did to women, and she, a willing student, learnt her lesson well. So well, in fact, that, when bedding Paul, Rita found herself expecting so much more. Paul's teenage fumblings were in stark contrast to what had gone before, but she had grown tired of sex without love and was prepared to forgo expert coupling for a more pedestrian but meaningful relationship. Rita never saw her married man again, she never looked into those watery blue eyes or listened to his breathless encouragement as he brought her to yet another climax. It was over and done with, relegated to past history, and never regretted, never even thought about until now.

'What are these?' Gary asked, picking up a folder of photographs at her bedside.

'Some pictures of Steve's welcome-home party. The boys brought them back from Paul's house.'

He flipped through them, stopping every now and then to examine one or smile a little. 'This is good,' he said, handing one to Rita.

She looked at the photograph of Steve and William sitting on the grass with Paul. 'They look so happy,' she remarked, 'you wouldn't think anything bad had ever happened.'

Gary passed another picture to her. 'Here, this one's of us.'

She laughed. 'God, you look so drunk . . . and why do you always wander about in a perpetual state of undress?'

'I'd been in the pool,' he answered defensively.

'I think you're an exhibitionist!' she replied, dropping the pictures on to the table and walking out on to the balcony, where she leant against the rail and looked out at the crisp silhouette of the palm trees against the brightness of a beautiful full moon. When she first arrived in Los Angeles, Rita had stood here and surveyed the garden, drawn to the palm trees, always thinking how strange it was to have them in her back garden. In truth she had no real idea of how permanent her life in California was, in truth the future, her future, still seemed uncertain despite Gary and what she felt for him. One year or two, five or ten, fifteen, the rest of her life? Rita had no idea how long this sojourn would be.

Gary came up to her, putting his arms around her, drawing her to him. Rita looked into his eyes, almost overwhelmed with love for him.

'Are you happy with me?' he asked, sounding uncertain and even a little afraid.

'Yes,' Rita answered without hesitation. 'Yes, I am.'

And in the darkness Rita thought about her children and then about herself. What did she want out of the rest of her life? After Nathan's suicide there had seemed nothing, no future, no particular reason even to live. For a while she had been driven close to the edge of insanity, with only Steve and William to hold her back. She had accepted that there would be no recovery from Nathan's death. Perhaps she could live with it, and some days were certainly better than others, but the pain existed and the terrible emptiness remained. Still, her feelings of responsibility and guilt had certainly lessened. Now she had a new man, work, of a sort, and the idea that she might return to teaching.

She loved Gary, there was no question about that, but she could not subordinate herself to his needs and she wondered if he would be able to deal with her own. Ultimately, perhaps, none of this mattered. Rita had come a long way in the years since Nathan's death. She had little idea of what her future would be but she couldn't hold back from it any longer.

She turned to Gary and put her arms round him, placing her head against his chest and feeling the beat of his heart and the warmth of his body, and she knew then that her comfort lay here. She would go on and she would love him and she would endure.